Never Breathe a Word

Never Breathe a Word

The Collected Stories of Caroline Blackwood

COUNTERPOINT
BERKELEY

The publisher would like to acknowledge the magazines and books in which the following pieces originally appeared: "The Interview," "How You Love Our Lady," "The Baby Nurse," "Who Needs It?" "Please Baby Don't Cry," *London Magazine*. "Taft's Wife" as "The Lunch," *The Observer,* August 13, 1978. "Memories of Ulster" (1972), "Women's Theatre" (1971), *Listener*. "Portraits of the Beatnik," *Encounter,* 1964. "Marigold's Christmas," *Firebird 4: New Writing from Britain and Ireland* (Penguin, 1985). "Matron," "Addy," "Angelica," *Good Night Sweet Ladies* (William Heinemann Ltd, 1983). "Never Breathe a Word," "Betty," "Piggy," "Burns Unit," *For All That I Found There* (Gerald Duckworth & Co Ltd, 1973).

Library of Congress Cataloging-in-Publication Data

Blackwood, Caroline.
Never breathe a word : the collected stories of Caroline Blackwood / by Caroline Blackwood.
p. cm.
ISBN: 978-1-58243-707-1
I. Title.

PR6052.L3423A6 2010
823'.914—dc22

2009038105

Printed in the United States of America

COUNTERPOINT
2560 Ninth Street, Suite 318 · Berkeley, CA 94710
www.counterpointpress.com

Contents

FICTION

FACT

Never Breathe a Word

FICTION

The Interview

"You ask me if I liked the film we have just seen. No . . . No . . . I couldn't really say that I did."

The painter's widow sat facing the journalist in the bar of a hotel. She was much taller than he was. The bones of her elbows were so sharp they looked like weapons. Her black clothes were crumpled and out of style as though they had just been dragged out of some children's dressing-up trunk which had been lying around for years in an attic.

"This film based on your late husband's life . . . Could you give me any reasons why you disliked it?"

"Did I ever say that I disliked the film? I do hope that you won't get too tricky and start misquoting me. Journalists can be so very ruthless. Can I ask you to be a little kind to me this evening? I have to tell you that I am feeling rather peculiar—that I am feeling almost faint. It was so very hot in that projection room—so airless. No . . . it seemed much worse than that—it seemed quite suffocating to me. When you invited me to come to this bar I didn't know that I would have to give an interview. Why did you never tell me that? I have nothing to say which could interest you. But you seem to be a very charming young man. Could we just drink and talk for a while and forget about the interview? It's a treat for me suddenly to be alone with a charming young man. I never go out you know. I don't think that you could imagine how rarely I ever go out."

"I was wondering if you could give me a few of your reasons for disliking the film."

"Disliking? Oh, that most inadequate word again! All the time they were showing me that film it never once occurred to me to try to judge it as though it was a Western. I was really only thinking how fortunate they were in the old days for they never had to go through anything like that. I was thinking this was a new kind of torture."

"Could you expand on that? Could you expand?"

"Well, in the old days at least they allowed you to lose your dead, to lose them so successfully you no longer felt them to be much of a loss. I'm sure that was very much better. But why are you looking so alarmed? Am I making no sense? Am I being too rhetorical and affected? I'm afraid it's because I so rarely go out. If you are always alone you start to lose the knack of talking normally to other people. But I'm afraid that I can't really blame it all on loneliness. My husband often used to say that whenever I felt anything very strongly, I always became flowery, and embarrassing, and tended to overstate. He said that was why I would never be able to paint. He was right of course, and I knew it. I gave up painting as you may know, although I had quite a little reputation in my day."

"May I quote you as saying that your husband forced you to give up painting?"

"You are becoming tediously tricky again. He was certainly never frightened of my competition, if that's what you are getting at. It was something a little more intricate than that. Can you just tell me how two people can expect to live together for more than a week if both of them want to paint? Maybe you can have a couple both doing the same thing in other arts. Two musicians might possibly be a little noisy. But all the paraphernalia of painting. Oh dear! And then two separate studios—his and hers. Surely that becomes more than faintly ridiculous. And can you imagine two sets of crippling bills from the framer and a couple squabbling because both of them want to grab the north light?"

"Could you talk a little more about the film?"

"Oh, I was so afraid that you would want me to do that! I have been rambling. I can see by your face that already you are starting to find me impossibly tiresome. But it's curious that while I was watching that film I was wondering if my tiresomeness was not one of the qualities that my late husband most valued in me. It made it possible for him to use me as a lightning conductor for the dislike that he tended to arouse so easily in so many people. If I was present he could always trust me to deflect all the zigzags of their hate away from himself."

"That sounds interesting. Will you please go on?"

"Why do you keep on speaking to me with such exaggerated politeness, young man? I find your professional soft-spokenness very disturbing. It makes me feel that I must be nearer to the end than I care to face. It's as though you were laying down straw to muffle the sound of carriage wheels outside my house. You don't need to use so much courtesy to extract a lot of indiscreet prattle for your copy. Can't you just drop all your dreary deference and get me another drink?"

The journalist watched uneasily as her spiky arm reached out and sucked her new whisky under the curtain of black fishnet veiling which draped down from her enormous hat. The journalist had never seen such a hat.

"You want me to get back to that obnoxious film . . . Well, all the time I was sitting there in the dark I was thinking that tapes and reel can sometimes be rather a violation—particularly tapes. It was hearing his voice that I found worst. Oh I do think that they were lucky in the old days! There were portraits and drawings then, of course, but they can have none of that awful mirage liveliness."

"Are you trying to say that this film distressed you because it reminded you of your husband?"

"I never once tried to say that it reminded me of my husband. Oh, I'm so sorry! Oh, please excuse me! I didn't mean to snap at you. It's just that although you may find me a befuddled old woman, you may notice that I tend to be rather careful when it comes to using words. To be reminded of someone—surely they have to be absent. Then, of course, any trivia can be a reminder, a photograph, an ashtray or a sock. But he wasn't absent this afternoon. It was precisely that which I found so unsettling. There he was . . . He was speaking—he was moving—he was smiling. He was present. But I don't think that I ever felt before that he was quite so absent. Why do you think I am sitting here with you in this odious bar? You have your wonderful white teeth and your shy grin. You have very strong hands—

I always notice hands. You have eyes as cold as tiny frozen French peas. But one forgets that as soon as you give your corrupt little disarming grin. And then you have that nice tufty hair. But do you really think that I like you so much? Do you think that I long to give an interview? Tonight I just don't feel that I want to be alone. He looked so healthy and he looked so lively, and even when I was staring at the great polished studs on his coffin, I don't think that I ever felt that he was quite so dead."

"Is there anything I can do? Would you like to move nearer to a window? Would you feel better if you had more air?"

"I must apologize for my seizure of swaying and shaking. I assume that you find all my black veiling absurd. I wonder if you are glad now that it makes it difficult for you to tell if I am laughing or crying? But why do you make me feel that I am wasting your time? You are so anxious to continue—you are so relentless . . . And yet you are really very kind to me. My little breakdown has made you so nervous that I see you have suddenly ordered me a full bottle of whisky. You don't need to charge it up on your expense account you know. I can pay for my own drinks. I can't do much anymore. Maybe that's why I so like to pay."

"Are you sure that you feel well enough to go on? . . . Would you say that this film will give the public a fair picture of your husband?"

"A fair picture! You must excuse me for laughing! What a jackass they made him seem. But somehow that didn't really surprise me."

"A jackass?"

"Oh, yes. How very awful they made him seem—so sort of fatuous, and famous."

"Was there anything in the way that your husband was presented which you found specifically objectionable?"

"Why are you staring so suspiciously at my fingers? Do you find it intriguing that they tinkle like tambourines when I move them, they are wearing so many rings? But to get back . . . Oh I suppose that I was bound to be most depressed by all that frightful smiling. Now I concede that he must have smiled occasionally. How else could they have got hold of so much film of him grinning like some cartoon cat? But I must say that one can sometimes be quite grateful that one's memory is so feeble. For although I may remember various unsavory things about him I still thank God that despite this film, I will never, ever, remember him as a man who was always smiling. This afternoon on the screen, it was really amazing! If he primed a canvas in his studio—there he was beaming. Even if he took a walk alone by the sea he still seemed to be chortling. Oh, it was really horrifying to see him! Whether he was chatting with some celebrity, or receiving some honor, or just cracking his egg for breakfast, it was like an affliction the way that he seemed so unable to ever stop smiling. You know sometimes I felt like shouting at him from my seat, but I thought it might be a little disturbing for the director and all those distributors."

"Could you tell me what you would like to have shouted?"

"Oh, I don't know. Just something silly, like children shout. What's so funny, Mr. Bunny?"

"Apart from his smiling, was there anything else that troubled you in the film?"

"Oh, yes. I was quite troubled by the way that he seemed to have learnt so little."

"Could you make yourself a little clearer?"

"If someone comes back to pay you an afternoon visit from the dead somehow one expects that they will have learnt something—

maybe even have been a little changed by their experiences. But he seemed to know rather less than the last time that I saw him. It was as though he was too pleased with himself, and too busy smiling to have taken in anything at all. Maybe it was because they kept showing so much film of him as a young man. All the same, I couldn't help finding him a rather disappointing Lazarus."

"I think you will agree that your late husband was considered to be a notoriously egocentric and difficult character. As his wife, no doubt you suffered more than anyone from what might politely be called his 'artistic temperament.' Is it possible that you disliked the film, not for any of the reasons you have given me, but because you resented the fact that it presents what might seem to you to be such a whitewashed, half-picture of the man?"

"He was incontinent at the end. Did you know that?"

"What has that to do with my question?"

"I was just wondering if you would now like to suggest that I disliked the film because it gave no close-ups of his incontinence."

If she had won a round there was no one listening to keep her score.

"It has sometimes been said that in your relationship to your late husband, you were always more of a mother to him than a wife. Would you say that was true?"

"Oh, I know that people always like to say a lot of boring simplistic things like that. No, I would almost certainly never say that I was ever his mother for the very obvious reason that he always had a mother. Admittedly she was a disapproving old prune of a woman and it always upset and embarrassed him whenever she came to see him. But there she was. And she outlived him, and the fact is that he always had her. If he had any mother apart from his real one, I would say that in his last years it was most probably only alcohol. Certainly that was the only thing which could get him up and dressed in the morning and help him to go toddling and tottering from A to B. It was the only thing which could soothe away a few of his aches and anxieties and get him to sleep at night . . . What more can you expect from any mother?"

"Did your husband continue to paint when he was under the influence of what you call this 'mother'?"

"Oh, yes. He always went on painting spasmodically. It didn't matter. I never let him release any of the work that he did in that last period. Whenever he finished a canvas, I usually went into his studio a little later and ripped it to pieces with a razor. There's always a certain pleasure in getting rid of rubbish. I suppose that's why housewives enjoy spring cleaning."

"Was your husband grateful for your solicitude—your spring cleaning?"

"Oh, it would make him snarl and smash things, of course, and sometimes it would make him cry, but I never worried about that too much."

"I'm quite sure you didn't!"

"You are so shocked, my pure young man! But your piety is so platitudinous—the piety of the Press. Now can you imagine a man who has had his hands cut off? How would you hope for him to be treated by anyone close to him? Surely in so far as possible they should try to be his lost hands. Well, if a man loses his judgement . . ."

"When you took it upon yourself to judge your husband's work did it ever occur to you that the other critics might consider your destruction of these paintings to be an act of criminal irresponsibility?"

"Naturally I knew I was destroying work which certain people would consider valuable. Oh, I could have let the dealers into his studio of course. They would have only too quickly pronged up all his litter like gardeners cleaning up a public park. But you must remember that even when he became very little more than one big hiccup of a man, he still went on being that curious insect-like creature, the paranoid. He could walk blind, but his antennae were out in front, always quivering and ever-ready to detect the insult. Do you think that he wouldn't have sensed that they were all stripping him, although they found it time-wasting even to look at his work? Who bothers to examine the designs on pieces of paper if those pieces come from the mint? Under such circumstances, what use would a few more soulless sales have been to someone who was already rather like a steaming punch-bowl of mixed alcohol, all the fuss of his own fame had made him feel so fraudulent?"

"Your protective concern for your late husband's feelings all sounds immensely touching, but is it true that you now own the world's largest private collection of his paintings?"

"Maybe I do. How would I know? I think that people are often shocked on the rare occasions that they come to my home, because I have never bothered to hang a single canvas. They are all lying about unframed and dusty, just stacked against the walls, exactly as they used to be when they were in his studio. My husband always said that he found it repulsive for a painter to hang his own work. He always had a horror of imposing on his guests and friends—of forcing them to comment—worst of all to praise. He said there were few things as depressing as a house which makes you feel that some seedy gallery was having a one-man show."

"But your husband disliked the idea of displaying his own work. May I ask you why you take this peculiar pride in refusing to hang work which is not your work?"

"His work is my work."

"Your collection has now become immensely valuable?"

"Very possibly. I've certainly never troubled to have it valued. I've kept all his clothes, you know. I never look at them—I never display them. I found most of them pretty shabby when he was alive. I certainly don't like them any better now. But somehow I don't get rid of them. It's exactly the same with the paintings."

"Naturally. Naturally. I know that you pretend to be completely disinterested in the value of your collection, but you have admitted to me that you destroyed a lot of your husband's work—work which for all anyone knows may have included many masterpieces. Could it be that you were simply frightened that he might overflood his market? Were you really only protecting your own future investments?"

"Masterpieces! Masterpieces! Oh, how you love the patter of your own mindless jargon, my little journalist! What on earth can the very word 'masterpiece' mean to you? Anything that's one big fat masterpiece of money. Now allow me to ask you a question. Why are you sitting there writing down my whisky-soaked words? You have no possible interest in me—and just as little in him. To you we are both simply like the cardboard wrappers on some best-selling soapflake. Your only concern with us is in our closeness to a successful commercial product?"

"May I compliment you? You are very quick to avoid answering the awkward question."

"Oh, yes . . . My husband always used to say that I was like the punchballs that boxers use for practice. They look as though they are pinioned there just waiting to take a slam, but they turn out to have just that little bit more mobility than you think and sometimes they can dodge and spin on their springs and can leave you punching at air."

"You are all dressed up in your black. It is obvious that you like to meet the world as the bereaved widow. Yet whenever you mention your husband's name your tone is always curiously malicious and scathing. Will I meet with your famous evasiveness if I ask you if you can claim that during his lifetime you and he were ever very close?"

"How odd it is to be sitting here in this unpleasant hotel with the Muzak soothing me like a lullaby, while I allow a stranger to pester me with painful and impertinent questions. Oh, we were close all right . . . but only in the sense that the criminal is close to his accomplice. I think that it was always a relief to him to have someone with whom he felt he could share his guilt. But then there was an uglier side. There was also so much distrust. Today when I saw him again on the screen I was wondering if it was really always only fear which made him feel that he had to stay close to me—if it was as though I knew too much, and he was convinced that he had to pay me off, for unless I was perpetually placated he might find himself exposed. You couldn't possibly understand a guilt like his, it was like a perforated ulcer leaking blood into his intestines. You would find his crime so pathetically unimportant. And yet in a sense he died to atone for the act that at its best, his work was so deeply second-rate . . ."

Like someone whose eyes have become accustomed to the dark the journalist found that he was starting to be able to see through the murky clouds of her veiling. He could make out eyes so sunken and black they looked like craters, corrugated cheeks which were flaked and mealy with face-powder, a collapsed mouth which was scarlet, greasy, and painted.

"And yet he was always so frightened of death. It's funny, I really never have been."

The journalist nodded, for as he stared at her it seemed to him that death had already made some gigantic attack on her and failed. Now he saw it as very unlikely that it would find the energy quickly to try again. All the flesh and fluids of her body appeared to have been already carried off. It was as though there was nothing left to her which could ever become dried up or destroyed. As she sat there, he felt she was embalmed, safely pickled and preserved for eternity inside her crusty parchment skin. When she repeated that she had never had any fear of death he grunted quite sympathetically, as though for the first time he felt that what she said was true.

"You seem to be a very forceful and ambitious woman. As a failed painter yourself, it cannot have been very easy for you to live in the shadow of your husband's success. Would you admit that some old feeling of rivalry may be operating when you get so much obvious pleasure from denigrating his achievement?"

"What can you possibly know of his achievement? Oh, how I wish you would stop using all those vacuous newspaper words! I very much doubt that you had even heard his name before you were sent out today on your assignment. And now I find it really rather comical—if I say that his work was second-rate you give a jump! And what makes you dare to assume that I say it disparagingly? Does it never occur to you that, as a failed painter myself, I might consider that in the scale of things, the second-rate painter ranks really rather high?"

"Your open admiration for his second-rateness must have always been a great comfort and encouragement to your husband in his lifetime!"

"Oh, yes . . . But you don't need to give your sarcastic little laugh. In some perverse way I most certainly think it was. You see, when he became so fashionable, it was as though he felt publicly branded with some kind of total worthlessness. He was oddly honorable, though that side of him never came through in the film. He was also intelligent, though often his intelligence could only act as an irritant to plague him. He always feared that fashion was like those modern garbage disposal units which can gobble up anything—or rather anything that's small enough—potato peelings, mushy tea-leaves, any old rotten bones. I always tried to make him remember that the same machine can also suck down small flowers. But I'm afraid that all he cared was that once it had pulverized and reduced everything to the same swilly consistency—it usually sank it deep in the ground."

"Now your husband may have been as troubled by his success as you like to claim, but I find it hard to believe that you yourself found it all that disagreeable. This is impertinent—but from the way that you speak of him—I wonder why you stayed with him. It's as though all you ever felt for him was some kind of lofty contempt and hate."

"Hate? Hate? . . . Oh I certainly tried to make him die, if that's what you mean. I smuggled him so many bottles of whisky into the hospital, and when his doctors discovered they treated me exactly as though I was a murderess. He was just one big tissue of needles and plastic tubes at that point—and more than all the pain, I knew that he minded the indignity. His great doctors squeezed him out about four extra months by taking so much cosseting care of his liver which was a sinking ship of an organ if ever there was one. But maybe they were right. I often think about that. When I visited him just towards the end, he told me that once you knew that that was it . . . then it wasn't quite so bad. He said that your whole time-sense changed and that the most trivial experience seemed valuable and in some new and magical way, total. He claimed that he could just lie and watch a fly buzzing across his room and get as much out of it as he once had from visiting a new country. Of course, I never believed him for one second—he was much too cowardly for there to be any chance that what he was saying was true. He was always someone who made you feel that if you were to cut open his brain, you would find it all pitted and eaten up with some sort of dreadful dry rot of morbid fears. Under the circumstances, how could one believe that someone like that could get all that much comfort from watching the buzzing of some dismal fly? But still—he claimed that he could—so one assumes that he was trying to spare someone. He was never in the very slightest bit unselfish—so one feels it was unlikely that he was trying to spare me . . . Did you know that the ancient Turks had a favorite torture? They used to leave their prisoners lying all day tied to planks which were nailed so that they jutted out over the sides of precipices. In the evening, the planks would be sawn away, but meanwhile, the victims were given a lot of time to examine every needle-point of rock that lay down below in the ravine where they knew they would soon be hurtling. His great doctors kept him on a very similar plank in that hospital, I think. But that's old stuff and nothing can be done about it now. I can see that you are looking quite glazed with boredom. You feel that you can't use a word of this for your interview. Ask me more questions, young man. It amuses me to see you taking such a professional pride in all your provocative questions. I really rather love your ludicrous little idea that an experienced approach is needed to draw me out. If only you knew . . . After seeing that film today, I'm afraid that no very expert handling is needed to make me talk. I can promise you, my dear young man, that if I was at home alone tonight, I would be talking to the mirror . . . I wonder if you know anything about budgerigars. They are such very silly birds. They start to pine if they find themselves alone in a cage, but if you give them a mirror, they perch themselves in front of it and start to preen themselves and chirp. You see, when they see their own reflection, they think they have a mate. Now I don't know if you've realized—I'm sure you think that you are very sophisticated, and to me you seem quite naïve—but all the time you've been questioning me I've been wondering whether I should take you back with me to my house when it gets late. I was thinking that if I was to go on talking, and talking to you all night—just using you as a mirror—you never know . . . but eventually I might even start to think you were my mate.

"Now you shouldn't look petrified! Your face has gone quite puce and I thought I saw you shudder. If you feel like shuddering—don't you think it's wrong to let me see? I might still have a little vanity left you know—I was once such a striking and sought-after woman. I must say it's a disappointment to discover that you are so deeply prudish and conventional. As you've pecked me with so many—may I be permitted to ask you a question? Can you tell me one good reason why tonight I should not be allowed to think of you as a mate? You are obviously very frightened of old women—but that is so very childish. I will have to teach you that old age is not really like a germ which you might catch if you get too close to it. If I take you home with me, I will also have to make the whole thing worthwhile for you—I know that. I've always been oddly shrewd though I seem so scattered. I will show you all his 'masterpieces' as you like to call them. Now how could an art-connoisseur like yourself resist such a rare and intense experience? In the morning when you leave me, I may very well allow you to cart away a great stack of them with you in a wheelbarrow. Ah now! I'm afraid that that's the first thing I've said to you which you have found genuinely interesting! . . . Now I've made you jump because you wonder if I'm sane—and if insane, serious. Well, when I look at you with your white teeth, and your chic little summer suit, and your greedy weasel eyes, I feel quite serious. You are so very knowing and so completely ignorant. The shoddiness of your values actually seems to shine out of every pore of your skin like phosphorus. Oh, I certainly think that you deserve to have them. At least you would have the good sense to throw them all immediately on to the market like firewood. You would have none of my procrastinating apathy. You are a journalist after all and more than anyone you ought to know the life span of publicity. You ought to know how long it's possible for his prices to continue their crazy pumped-up pirouette."

"May we please go on with the interview? I soon have another appointment."

"You have another appointment—and you are now obviously starting to regret it. You are such a little opportunist—and you are aware that this might be rather a special opportunity. But now I'm getting tired of teasing you. I'm afraid that I'm too passive to be nearly as predatory as I've been pretending. I'm still glad that I managed to disturb and embarrass you. I feel that I deserved to do that. Today I was forced to sit through a film which made me feel that my whole past was being thrown back at me all curiously curdled and distorted—rather like food that comes back as vomit. And then immediately after that I was asked to answer what to you may seem to be a lot of standard, set-piece questions. But how will you ever know or care what a hive of disturbing feelings those questions may have stirred up in me?"

"I'm very sorry that you have found this interview so painful. I can assure you that I am every bit as anxious to terminate it as you are. There are just one or two questions I would like to ask before

I leave you—naturally you are under no obligation to answer me. You strike me as being a woman with a rather highly developed sense of your own importance. Did you feel that this film distorted the facts when it presented you as quite a minor character while your husband was made to play so very much the star? Did you find it in bad taste that they showed him in so many reels in the company of Marina Casatti?"

"I find your first question too facetious to be worth answering—but Marina . . . I think that seeing Marina again was perhaps the only thing in that vulgar little film that I did like. She was quite important for a while, you know. I think that they had a perfect right to show her. At the time he sometimes claimed that I wouldn't release him. He said to me once that I had the mind of a queen and the soul of a peasant—and that a peasant never likes to let go of a good property. I found that curious because I was always convinced that it was the other way round. I never felt for a moment that he ever wanted to stop clinging on to my passivity. Passivity—even a rather disgruntled and critical passivity—can be quite solid, you know. It can be like a wall, and you can twine yourself on to it like a strand of dusty ivy, and it takes a certain time before you start to loosen all the bricks. But enough of that—let me talk about Marina. I used to hate her so much and now it all seems so long ago. I'm sure that you would find it primitive and peasant-like the way I used to hate her. I remember that I once wrote her name on a large wooden spoon—the kind that you use to stir puddings. I intended to take the spoon up to the local cemetery and to stick it in some newly dug grave. I had heard that you could bring misfortune to someone that way—and I so wanted something quite appalling to happen to Marina. But just as I set off, it started to rain and then my usual inertia set in, and I kept thinking how damp and depressing it was going to be in the cemetery. I thought how embarrassing it would be if I was caught kneeling beside a frothed-up grave by some unctuous little choirboy or church-functionary. I was frightened I might end up on some mortifying police charge for the violation of sacred property. Today, when I saw Marina showing off on the screen, I was glad that I never went near any graveyard with my spoon. She was killed in a car crash, as you may know. You may find it ridiculous, but if I'd done what I wanted to then, I'm certain I would always have felt somehow superstitiously responsible. And sitting there this afternoon in that smoky projection room, all that I wondered was how I could have ever thought for one moment that Marina could get much more out of him than I could. Do you think two people can ever get very different water from the same old polluted well? And what a joyless companion he was at his best—his feeling of failure seemed to be always strapped to his back like a knapsack! It was often also rather like being with some kind of ruthless and canny sleuth. He always seemed to be trying to track down something valuable which he seemed to feel had been stolen from him. He spied on everyone—suspected everyone. Oh, he was so sly! He made everyone feel that he was planning to sneak into their room to ransack their baggage. And then what a morose and unshaven lover—as a performer just about as soft and green as asparagus! But I can see that I am making you very uneasy when I talk like this. I admit that I may be sprouting a few sour grapes because of Marina. Yet seeing her again today I really felt quite sorry that she now only exists as a breasty image on celluloid. You have been really quite patient with me—and we all know you have those nice white teeth—and it may seem rather perverse to you—but tonight I would rather be drinking here with Marina, than interviewing here with you."

"I must be going. Thank you for giving me your valuable time."

"I find it hard to believe that you are really leaving. Journalists are scavengers and they rarely like to leave while there's still a shred of flesh sticking to the carcass. And I would like to know when you are going to send me what you have written about me. I'm convinced that I'm going to like it—that I may feel forced to memorize every word like a poem. One always delights to find oneself described in clichés. It's like being so well wrapped up in thick wads of cotton-wool padding that one becomes invisible. Now what can be more comforting? And then it's so elating to know that even if one's quite badly shaken one can suffer very little real damage . . . But do I see you gathering up all your papers and tucking them away in your ugly brown attaché case? That makes me feel panicky. Oh, please don't leave me! Can I beg you on my knees just to stay and talk a little longer? I would have so liked to ask you to dine with me—but I'm afraid that I've said something to offend you. You see, I know that I should never have sat through that film today. I fear that film can be a little too factual—and its effects can be rather fatal. One should only ever be linked to the past through one's memory. Luckily memory is the most miserable, and unreliable, old muscle. I'm sure that a young man like you must laugh at people of my age because they tend to live too much in the past, but when all the hills in front of you start to seem to be dipping down into the most grey and unmentionable valleys—I can assure you that the very last thing you will want to see is a film which makes you realize that no past exists for you which is in any way very livable to live in. Why on earth do you think that I'm overstaying now in all this sordid plush? Only because all those flashbacks that I've seen today have made me feel so homeless . . . I'm afraid that it has to be rather depressing to be reminded that no one can live very comfortably in a past which they never found remotely pleasant while it was still a present—and which they wasted by always sitting about passively and pointlessly, waiting for some less painful future."

"Yes . . . Yes . . . I think everything valuable has already been covered. A friend of mine has arrived. I would now like to say goodnight."

"How can you be so cruel as to jump up impatiently and leave me here alone? You should tell me where I am—why the deck seems so slippery and keeps sloping away in the storm. And who is she now? May I ask why she suddenly seems to be joining you? I have to tell you that I find her arrival most unwelcome. She looks rather insipid to me with her mousey-pale curls—a little too like some damp, slightly soiled, powder puff. All my life I've known such girls—they balance so badly on their high-heel shoes. All my life I've tried to avoid such girls. And then I find her very rude. How dare she come from nowhere to interrupt us? I wish that she wouldn't stutter and try to apologize. She has stopped the band just when the wallflower thought she was finally going to be able to take to the floor. How can her bogus apologies make amends for that? She is obviously still planning to take you away from me. Well . . . you are a coarse-surfaced and hard thing, just something suitable to strike matches on. But what makes her think that I've quite finished with you? Oh now . . . I see by her face I've frightened her. I'm afraid that was inevitable. Tonight I feel that I might be frightened if I met myself. It would be like meeting some deranged and decapitated ghost that has just discovered it has spent several decades haunting the wrong corridor. But would you please mind taking your hand off my shoulder, young man. I dislike being steadied as though I was a toppling milk bottle. Now I admit that you and your powder-puff girlfriend seem to be suddenly hanging down from the ceiling. You are dangling now in the distance—two very dim chandeliers. But at such moments some unwanted jab of sobriety always seems to come pricking through the novocaine. And one likes to be granted the favor of being allowed to make one's exit unaided."

"Goodnight. Goodnight. If you go through that door on the left I'm sure you will pick up a cab in the street."

"But my hat is tipping over my eye. I must look much more jaunty than I feel. There's still no need for you both to hustle me out. I only long to go back home now. I could ask you to come back and dine with me—but tonight I suddenly feel that I would rather be alone with my monkeys. It's curious, but I always seem to have kept monkeys—I've always been very attached to them—they have amused me more than most things. I've always been fascinated by all their chattering, and their somersaults, and their dirty ways. I love to dress them up in funny suits and give them tea parties with tiny pots, and cups, and cakes. Sometimes I give them paper and strap brushes to their wrists and watch them paint. Once in a while they will do something which is not entirely uninteresting . . . But naturally that's just chance. Most of the time I'm afraid that they just produce a predictable monkey mess. But why should one care about that? It's still rather insane the way I'm devoted to them. I'll often sit up all night with them when they get chills, and I'll hold them wrapped in warm blankets, and I'll slip them little spoonfuls of aspirin in syrup. But then all of a sudden some evening when I'm all alone with them—I start to get the most scary and horrifying feeling that the whole lot of them are dying. I go rushing over to their cages because I keep wondering if anyone has fed them. I am almost certain that they are all starving, and it makes me very angry, and I want to blame someone—but somehow I find that I can't quite remember who it is that I ought to be blaming. And it's strange—but I still don't feed them myself, and I don't give them any water. Instead I draw up my chair, and I sit myself down beside them and I just watch them lying there in their sawdust, all limp, and sad, and panting. And I find that the longer I watch them, the more I suspect that nothing is ever going to save them, and this makes me very agitated. 'What's the matter with you?' I often even shout at them aloud, I feel so frantic—and naturally they never answer me. 'Just tell me what's the matter with you.' I scream at them and I rattle the bars of their cages. And then it's suddenly always quite a shock to realize that the reason why I have such a strong feeling that nothing can ever save them—is that I really care so very little if they are saved or not. For although they've served their purpose, and screeched, and clowned, and distracted me—yet despite all their antics—they've never been quite what I want."

The old woman started slowly shuffling out of the bar with her skirts trailing down limply over her pair of black, button-up boots. Suddenly she turned and saw that the journalist was whispering to his friend.

"Couldn't you wait until I'm out of earshot? Your girlfriend likes me better than you do. But then she has never tried to winkle-pin my character. You find me a sinister old saddle-sore. She thinks that you still ought to see me home—that you've made me dangerously drunk—I look so frail—and she fears it's raining. I'm afraid I have to say that she lacks charisma—but she has a little charity. I should be grateful . . . But I find her sympathy rather like a fur coat offered to one on a scorching day. I've often talked too much about my monkeys—and found my own way home alone."

How You Love Our Lady

Father Callahan must be dead now—"resting"—as he always liked to call it, somewhere in the mud of his own churchyard. Maybe he is even still alive—maybe senile—and living in some cottage with a housekeeper. "O songless bird far sweeter than the rose. And virgin as the Parish Priest. God knows!" They all quoted then. Sometimes they used to quote and counter-quote all through the night. I so loved to listen to them, sitting next to Father Callahan in the wonderful light of my mother's candles. They used to come to my mother's grey Georgian house from Dublin—some of them even came from farther. My mother loved poets, painters, and talkers. She said she could only bear to be surrounded by "free-spirits." She was always speaking about her love for Art and Nature, and sometimes she said that she thought that life should be one long search for the beautiful. My mother never made me go to bed. She said that she detested the tyranny of the clock and that all those who bowed to it were the poor trapped prisoners of the temporal. Often in the mornings when I walked up to my convent through those grey, rock roads bordered by hawthorns, I felt so weightless and really weird from lack of sleep that it seemed to me that there was very little to stop me from floating up to the great white melancholy morning sky, and becoming part of it. And I would feel that I could understand why my mother often started repeating, when she was drinking in the evenings, that she thought that Life and Death were really the same—and both were beautiful.

I never liked my convent. Even Father Callahan could never really persuade me to like those nuns with their long, cold corridors punctuated by tormented, bleeding plaster Christs. Those nuns with their child-skins, their canes, and their crucifixes. I found the other convent girls so brutal, crude, and frightening. They made the new girls hang their breasts over a towel-rail and then pricked them with safety-pins. Any girl who screamed they pricked much harder right on her nipples. I used to be so modest then—I remember that I cried while still only waiting for my turn, finding the mortification of being forced to stand half-naked in front of other girls almost as painful as the pricking. And long before they had drawn a drop of blood from me, I fainted. The Sisters were so cold, so fiercely disapproving, when I came to with ice packs on my head in the sickbay. They asked nothing—but I sensed that they could guess what had happened to me, and that like their own girls, they could feel only contempt for someone so frail—someone so completely lacking in the great qualities: courage, fortitude, self-sacrifice.

I learnt very little in my convent. I saw all my days as lost nights, and dawn only ever seemed to come to me when I was sitting after midnight, talking to Father Callahan in front of the heaped peat fires of my mother's drawing room. I only learnt poetry to please my mother. Now I have forgotten almost all that I once knew. Who would want to listen to it now? My husband George slumped in his zombie stupor in front of the TV in our New York apartment? The elevator man? My colored maid? It is strange, but I still remember certain lines. "A well dark-gleaming and of most translucent wave—images all the woven boughs above. And each depending leaf and every speck of azure sky . . ." My voice must have sounded so pure then. My mother would wipe her eyes when she heard it. She was always so proud of me when she saw me standing there reciting in my pretty white lace dress in the candlelight. In the evening when all her friends were there she would seem to feel a special warmth towards me and it would make her smile with delight if any of them said that I was like her. When we were alone together in the daytime I often felt a constraint, a nagging feeling of inadequacy, as if I was perpetually failing her. Sometimes she made me feel like an egg that has been hand-painted for Easter—an ordinary breakfast egg which shouldn't be fingered too much because all its pretty dye can just come smudging off the hand and then all its drab patches of everyday shell start to show. I knew that I had an underlay of drabness which distressed my mother far more than my occasional displays of insolence and disobedience. Whenever in her opinion I became commonplace she made it very clear that she only longed to get away from me, as if my dullness was like a disease that might contaminate her if she was too closely exposed to it. "There is only one great crime," she would warn me. Her eyes would look almost blind as she spoke, as if they were filmed over with the glaucoma-like glaze of her own intensity. "You can do what you like in this world. But you must always remember, Theresa, that the only great crime is to allow the humdrum to see into your soul . . ." When she was in that kind of mood she nearly always started to talk about elms. She often said that you could get more education from looking at trees and water than you could from waiting your days sitting on a hard bench in some nun-ridden soulless school. And then I would feel puzzled why she thought it necessary to send me to the convent. In any case, elms were an obsession with her and she said they were the great tutors. "Have you ever seen the way that an elm dies, Theresa? An elm doesn't die like other trees, you know. An elm dies from the inside. An elm dies in secret. You should always remember to be careful when you walk underneath elms, for they can be dangerous. Elms are the only trees which give you no warning signs of their own decay. They can just come toppling down with a fearful crash while all their branches still look glorious and intact and all their leaves are still in bud. Once they are on the ground it can be quite frightening to see what has happened inside their trunks. Once they are dead you can see how the rot has eaten into them so hideously that they are completely hollow. People who allow themselves to become trivial and humdrum are like blighted elms. Eventually they are destroyed by being so filled with their own hollowness . . ." The more she would speak about dying elms, the more I would start to feel like one. Every thought that came into my head seemed like a threatening rot, it seemed to be so dull and dim and ordinary. Sometimes I feared that my mother had an X-ray power by which she could detect the banality of my unpromising thoughts and I pined to swallow some magic pill which would prevent me from ever boring her.

"You have misnamed your daughter," my mother's friends would tell her after they had listened to me reciting in the evenings. "The child is no Theresa. She is a Deirdre. Just look at that face! And the girl is ready for her Naisi—but now all our Deirdres are doomed to be guarded by nuns who are far fiercer and more deadly than any jealous old King Concubar!"—"That child is not human," they would keep repeating. "She is one of the Sidhe!" The Sidhe—the enchanted spirit race of ancient Ireland. "God fuck you!" they shouted at my mother, "you are repeating the tragedy of the country. You give birth to a Sidhe—and you allow its lovely spirit to be mutilated in a bleeding convent!" They would lift up their glasses in a toast to me and then tip their wines and whiskies on to my mother's carpet. They smashed their glasses down on the floor and ground them to a sugary powder with their heels. They shouted things like "Long live the Fenian men!" and "Up the IRA!" My mother would laugh and go to play her piano. Father Callahan would take my hand. I would feel his palms which were as cool, smooth, and unused as those of a young child. He always took my hand when they started to blaspheme. When the wine was on them they would hurl blasphemies back and forth across the room like delinquents throwing stones. I was often frightened that some dreadful flaming retribution would strike and smash the whole house. But then when Father Callahan took my hand I felt comforted, thinking that his very presence under our roof must act as some kind of talisman with the power to ward off the scourge of the Divine Anger. "Never be disturbed by blasphemy," he would whisper to me. "Blasphemy is only the lining of the coat of Belief. Blasphemy is only the lining turned inside out."

He must have been a very young man then, Father Callahan. It is hard for me even now to realize it. At the time he seemed like the bleak, beautiful hills that I could see from my mother's window, even older and sadder than Christianity. He drank, Father Callahan. This always rather surprised me. He drank solemnly, treating his wine as though it was a sacrament. And his drinking seemed to increase not only his sadness, but also his sobriety. My mother always served special vintage whiskies and brandies and very good French wines. She said that she could only tolerate the "excellent"—that a true love of quality was a "Life Caring." She collected old blue Waterford glass and had very good plates on her dresser. She wore only beautiful laces and wine-colored velvets. She said that she had to live beside water, that her blood came from the sea, and she claimed as an ancestor some fierce Spanish sailor who had been smashed up on the Galway rocks from the Armada. Outside her house a waterfall crashed through the night. Everyone had to shout in her drawing room. They shouted against the cascade of water that fermented and foamed like angry beer as it hit the rocks. They shouted against the crash of my mother's piano. My mother always played very loud. She knew so many songs. All the new English songs, and the laments of the old Gaels. Her voice could sound as thunderous as any man's, and while she played and sang, her face flushed scarlet, her huge eyes flashed and rolled in her head, her great breasts heaved up and down so violently that they seemed about to break through her wonderful velvet dresses, and her long hair streamed down over her shoulders, ink-black from perspiration. Often as the night went on she seemed enchanted, almost demented by her own music. And frequently by the time that morning started to break on the hills it seemed as though her piano was really playing her—and she was only its exhausted instrument. And many times when she stopped her playing, she would fall like a stone to the ground.

"Your mother is a nymph!" Father Callahan once said to me. "She is surely the very same nymph that sucked Finn down into the waters. It is no wonder that he stayed so long down there that his hair had turned white by the time that he came up again!" I think he knew how much it always pleased her when anyone said exaggerated and high-flown things like that.

I wonder if I ever really properly understood the way that Father Callahan loved my mother, I always felt that his love for her was very different from the love of all the poets and drinkers and talkers who came every night to her drawing room and so often ended up in the "Doss-House" as they called her spare room where rows of mattresses were always laid out on the floor for anyone who felt like staying. I thought then that Father Callahan's love for my mother was mystical—almost abstract—like his love of the blood of the Martyrs—like his worship of the Saints. I felt that there was pain in his love and some deep reconciliation to loss. Whatever Father Callahan really felt for my mother, I was only glad at that time that it seemed to extend to me as my mother's daughter. He spoke only to me in the evenings. Father Callahan never seemed able to interest my mother. She would smile at him sometimes when she was sitting at her piano. But then when she was playing she quite often smiled at anyone who happened to be sitting around drinking in her drawing room. She smiled, but it was as though she did not really see them. She certainly very rarely took the trouble to come over to address one word to him, and I often wondered why she kept on inviting him. She told me once that to dream about priests was very bad—that even if you dreamt about the Devil, it was much, much better. She also said that she hoped that I would never accept any gift from Father Callahan—even if it was something as small as a halfpenny or a handkerchief—for any gift from a priest could bring the most atrocious bad luck. "And that's about all we need," she said.

"What do you mean?" I asked her.

"When you are older," she answered, staring out through the window to the waterfall, "you will start to find out that very many things—can have very many meanings."

"Shall I get you a cup of tea?" I asked her. I always disliked it when she started to speak in riddles. And she seemed so restless that day, unable even to settle down to her piano. I saw the disgust in her eyes and I knew that I had disappointed her. "Yes," she snapped at me, "I suppose that you really might as well do just that!"

"You live too much in the past, Theresa," my husband very often tells me. I wonder if I do. And I wonder if George notices where I really live, just so long as he can still see me sitting in my chair in his expensive West Side apartment. More and more I feel like that crusader that as a child I always hated so—that repulsive little Irish crusader who lay in his open coffin and had his hand shaken by tourists in the vaults of St. Michan's in Dublin. "It is one of the miracles what has preserved him here without embalmment!" the guide was always saying. And surely some guide seeing me sitting with George in our living room could very well say the same about me now. My mother so loved those terrible musty vaults of St. Michan's. She said that they still contained the lovely spirit of Parnell because he had once been laid out in state there. Sometimes she would take me down to visit them as often as three times a week. "Shake the crusader's hand for luck, Theresa!" And I still remember the feel of his hand—so cold—so smooth—so shiny: the feel of a well-soaped saddle. "As you see, the human nail continues growing after death," the guide would keep on pattering. Those dreadful nails! The nails of a society woman—but so much yellower and almost as long as the chicken-bone fingers they were sprouting out of. Sometimes my mother said that she wished my father could have been buried under the church of St. Michan's. "He would have been with us still." And I was guiltily glad that she had never got her wish. I remember that the lights once fused when I was down in those tombs with my mother. We were forced to stand there in the darkness for nearly an hour while the guide, who was always drunk, stumbled around cursing while he tried to find the fuse-box. My mother started screaming. She said that she had felt the crusader brush her spine with his fingernail. All the same, the next week she was saying it was always beautiful to shake the hand of History. And very soon we were both down there again.

"It seems to me that it really was your own lights that fused when you were down in those goddam tombs with your mother!" George sometimes says to me. "It's sick, Theresa! It's really sick the way you live so much in the past!" But often while I potter round his apartment in the daytime, and often in the evenings while I sit watching him as he watches his favorite Late-Late Show while he files his toenails with his nail file, I do not feel that I live in the past. Like that dismal little crusader, I still have a hand which anyone can shake if they feel inclined to—but quite frequently I feel that I do not really live at all.

"You ought to see an analyst, Theresa. You reject everything. It's as if you feel that nothing can ever be so miraculous as all the old times that you spent with your screwy nutcase of a mother and her bunch of provincial Irish bullshit artists. You are utterly out of touch with reality. You really seem to live in some kind of a crazy Celtic twilight . . ." I listen very attentively to all my husband's criticism.

Now I may very well live in some kind of a twilight. But in a Celtic one? That I wonder . . . George often has a curious imprecision when it comes to using words. I watch George sitting with his head in his hands while he tries to think up some advertising slogan for sanitary towels. "Soft—Soft—Thistle-down Soft! Eliminates all fear of those tell-tale bulges!" "It's beautiful George! It really has quite an amazing lyrical freshness!" "I don't need any of your boring patronage, Theresa. Look, you are a woman—you ought to know about sanitary towels. Don't just sit there acting so goddam superior. For Christ's sake just try for once and give me a little bit of help!" I look at him sitting there paralyzed like some great podgy slow-witted schoolboy who has got hopelessly stuck in his lessons. "Have you thought about Baby-bottom Soft, George? Maybe that would be even better than Thistle-down." He considers it. And for one moment we are almost quite close. We suddenly have a bond. We are suddenly a team. But then George shakes his head. "One thing I'll say for you, Theresa. You are certainly never the slightest fucking help."

"Feeling sorry for yourself is your only full-time profession!" that poet of the sanitary towels sometimes shouts at me. "How you love yourself, Theresa—just yourself—and only really ever yourself!" "How you love Our Lady!" my mother said to me one night when I was sitting talking to Father Callahan in her drawing room. She rolled her huge beautiful eyes so scornfully down his long black trailing skirts and then she laughed really maliciously. "I wonder," she said, "just how long you will be able to keep that up!" Father Callahan never seemed to hear her when she spoke like that, although the blood crept out from behind his ears and trickled down towards his nose like some slow advancing army. And soon she was back at her piano and had forgotten him. "O Boyne, once famed for battles, sport, and conflicts. And great heroes of the race of Conn," she would moan, "Art thou grey after all thy blooms? O aged woman of grey-green pools, O wretched Boyne of many tears!" Father Callahan would sit beside me and stare into her fire with his sad bloodshot eyes and speak to me of life, and death, and the nature of humility and evil, and of the Divine Perfections. Quite often he would say that all he prayed for me was that when I was a little older I would still have the strength to remain "white." "White? What is white?" I would ask him, although I knew well enough from the girls of my convent, and I only wanted to hear him explain it. "You will know, my daughter. You will know in your time," he always answered me, pouring himself another brandy. Sometimes he would start to speak so intensely that I really could not follow what he was saying, and frequently his soft voice was completely wiped out by all the clash of glasses, and bottles, and opinions, and the thunderous wail of my mother's singing, but often, while he was speaking to me and I kept drinking her excellent red French wine, Father Callahan's dark clerical clothes started to look brighter to me than all the brilliant silks and velvets of my mother's friends, and I felt that it was of no importance that he was a priest, and that I was a child, for we were like two disembodied spirits who had found such perfect harmony that it was impossible for anything ever to break it—and therefore nothing again could ever make me feel afraid.

Sometimes my mother would suddenly jump up from her piano and start screaming at all her guests. She would tell them that they were all just a gaggle of geese-like fools. She said she felt she would die unless she breathed some fresh air, and could hear the sound of water. And then she would grab Paddy Devlin by the hand—or any other man who was still able to stand—and drag him out through the door and take him down to the waterfall. Father Callahan always became very agitated when she behaved like this, although none of her other guests seemed to take much offence at her insults. Indeed a lot of them were usually sprawling half-asleep on the carpet at the time, or else locked away in some of the lavatories vomiting, and I doubt that they remember all her abuse by morning. But Father Callahan always became very tense and miserable. He never seemed to be able to concentrate on conversation while my mother was out somewhere lost in the darkness. Often she would stay outdoors for what seemed like hours, and the whole time Father Callahan would never stop flicking his eyes towards the door, like a dog that keeps waiting for the return of its master. Once, when my mother had stayed out even longer than usual, Father Callahan suddenly started quoting to me for no particular reason from his favorite Cardinal Newman. "The Catholic Church holds it better for the sun and moon to drop from Heaven, for the earth to fail and for all the many millions on it to die of starvation in extremest agony, as far as temporal affliction goes, than that one soul, I will not say shall be lost, but should commit one single venial sin . . ." "And where is the Charity in that, Father?" I asked him. "There are very many enigmas," he answered me irritably.

Were Father Callahan's enigmas all theological? Even now I feel that there are still so many questions. Even now I still keep asking myself—why did I never guess at that time—why did I never for one moment guess that there was something so elm-blighted, and most certainly enigmatical, behind all my mother's singing, and her quoting, and her over-hectic pagan laughter?

Father Callahan and Doctor Donovan were standing side by side in her drawing room when I got back one day from my convent. The doctor was a very tall man, and seeing the priest standing beside him in his long dark trailing skirts, I remember thinking that Doctor Donovan looked rather like a bridegroom, and Father Callahan like his small black bride. Their faces looked strange—rigid—almost angry—and the sign of them made me feel afraid.

"Daughter, have courage."

"What has happened?"

"Daughter, pray for strength. Remember it is only an antechamber."

"What is only an antechamber, Father?" My heart was pounding. I thought for a moment that he was speaking of my mother's drawing room.

"Life," Father Callahan said slowly. "Life, as you know, is only really just an antechamber to Eternity."

"Has something happened to my mother?" I turned to the doctor. He was so silent. I saw his eyes flick nervously to Father Callahan. Why should he not answer me? He was such an old man. He was such a tall man. He was a doctor. Why could he not answer me without waiting for the priest?

"It's all over with her," Father Callahan said. He looked different to me in the daylight. His face looked suddenly weak and blotchy—rather ordinary and unintelligent, like the faces of so many of the ill-nourished adolescents that always hung around the bar-tents at all the races. "Let us kneel." Father Callahan dropped down on his knees on my mother's drink-stained carpet and the doctor copied him a little awkwardly with his long still thighs. I remained standing. I remember staring at the curtains of the drawing room. I had never noticed before that their scarlet velvet was so shabby. They were drooping down from their poles like limp, faded washing.

"Were you there, Father Callahan?" I asked him.

"I was."

"Did she see you come?"

"She did indeed. The Lord was very merciful. She was conscious for nearly one hour."

"But that is really terrible! She must have known why you had come!"

"She knew, of course."

"But how could you have done that to her, Father Callahan? She must have hated to know. She must have been so absolutely terrified to know!"

"She wanted to know. But in any case she would have had to know. How could she be allowed to go in her sins?"

"But I don't understand how your mind worked, Father Callahan. I know that you never liked to face it—but you know just as well as I that she was never a believer. She despised priests. She despised what she called their doggerel. What use did you think you could be to someone like that? She must have felt a total panic at the very sight of you arriving so horribly final and chilling in your black. Maybe she still had a little hope until she saw you. I wish that you had never let me know the terrible thing that you did to her. Oh, why couldn't you have just kept away from her?"

"I tell you my child that when she saw me, she was glad. My presence in her agony was a consolation. It is to them all."

"But maybe she wouldn't have needed any consolation, Father Callahan, not if you had never made her know only too well why you had come."

"You are speaking quite wildly, my child. It is your grief. You still know absolutely nothing of the facts."

"But I know how much she hated to know anything unpleasant,

Father Callahan. She was someone who cried if other people trod on wild flowers. She was never in the least bit brave. Is that not true, Doctor Donovan? You remember that she was even terrified of injections. She could never bear to know when they were coming. She always stuck her arm out as far as it would go—and she turned her head away—and squeezed her eyes shut tight. The way she would scream and moan—it was really quite horrible to hear it—and always long before the needle had even gone into her!"

"My child, you seem quite demented. You are speaking of things which are quite beside the point."

"You knew her, Father Callahan!" I started crying. "You came to our house every evening. You knew what she was like. You loved her. You know very well that she would have wanted to go like an animal—like a butterfly—knowing nothing. Even if she had no chance—why couldn't you have allowed her to go on still believing that she had some tiny chance? I know that her hopes must have been hopeless. But what right did you have to take those last little hopes away from her? I will never understand how you had the cruelty to do that to her!"

"Don't speak disrespectfully to the Father!" Doctor Donovan suddenly snapped at me from his kneeling position on the carpet.

"She is not railing at me. She is only railing at me as the vessel of something so much higher that it passes her comprehension." Father Callahan looked exhausted and the blotches on his face were becoming so brilliant that they resembled a disease.

"I tell you, my child, that she was serene. When it finally came to her, there was very little struggle. The end is often not at all like you imagine. It is often somewhat of an anticlimax."

"An anticlimax!" I saw him shiver as I screamed at him. "For you it may have well seemed like an anticlimax, Father Callahan. But I hardly think that it could have seemed very much like that to her. She was not a priest you know, Father Callahan. She loved all sorts of things. She loved love—she loved water—she loved poetry—she loved music. She was someone who loved life!"

"She can't have loved life as much as you imagine." Father Callahan bent his head in prayer. "May the Lord have mercy on her."

"What makes you say that?"

"It was horrible . . . But she couldn't be blamed. Something must have entered into her. She wasn't herself. She just turned on herself. She died of her wounds. She grabbed a carving knife. Her real self can't have been with her. It was plain at the end that she never intended it. She was the one that sent for Doctor Donovan. He did all that could be done for her. But she had been too savage . . ."

The Baby Nurse

He was abject in the way he persistently tried to placate her. She always called him "Mr. Richardson" and he hardly recognized his own name when he heard her use it. She always managed to make "Mr. Richardson" sound like something so infinitely shoddy and disappointing—something that only the unfairness of life had forced her to contend with.

"Can I make you a cup of tea, Miss Renny?" he would ask her.

"I could most certainly do with a cup of tea, Mr. Richardson." And she made it so plain that she felt not a grain of gratitude for his tea-making, that she saw it as only one more pathetic inadequate gesture which only served to remind her of the immensity of the debt that he owed her.

Sometimes when they had meals together and he was listening with slavish sympathy to all her complaints, feeling half-suffocated by his own sycophancy as he flattered and cajoled her, suddenly Miss Renny would seem like an innocent. He felt certain that her immense vanity would never permit her to suspect the intensity of the venomous hate he often felt for her. He found he could get some small sour satisfaction just from sensing his own power to deceive her. He felt that she deserved to be deceived by him for he could never forgive her for the way she had originally fooled him. He had been glad when she first arrived. When he had got back from the hospital with his wife he had felt actively relieved when Miss Renny's bulky form had arrived with a suitcase and installed itself in his flat. He could never forgive Miss Renny for having originally tricked him by what he now felt was the sheer fraudulence of all her fat.

Miss Renny was certainly a woman of the most deceptive obesity, for the very plumpness of all the roly-poly flesh that covered her huge frame conveyed a comforting and erroneous first impression that she was cheerful, kindly, and maternal.

A professionally trained baby nurse, Miss Renny carried her overweight with great panache and managed to present it with pride to the world as if she felt it to be her greatest strength. But as the days went by and Stephen Richardson found himself forced to eat more and more meals alone with her, he was very soon to learn that Miss Renny's trust-inspiring corpulence was the most glaring symptom of her main weakness. Miss Renny was extremely greedy. Meats, and cakes, and puddings, excited her. She thought about them. She plotted in order to get herself very large shares of them. It was as if all the calories that Miss Renny loved to consume fired her blood like adrenalin, for despite her amazing bulk she was aggressively energetic and active. As his wife Arabella had seemed to shrink as she lay all day crying in her bed like a quivering little jelly of ineptitude, so Miss Renny had seemed to swell until she filled the whole flat with her combative and competitive competence.

"What's wrong with you? Can I do anything to help?" He kept asking Arabella the same questions until they seemed as monotonous as her refusal to give anything except a choked gulp for an answer.

"Please just leave me alone. I might feel better if I was left alone . . ."

He would see that his wife's spongy, tear-swollen eyes were cursing him for his lack of sympathy and comprehension. He found that he was glad to leave her alone, for she seemed malevolent lying there on her crumpled unmade bed, with an agonized and defensive glare in her eye, looking so oddly ravaged and sluttish. She reminded him of a miser in the way she was stubbornly hoarding some great sack of unshareable hostility.

And all the time Miss Renny had gone flouncing round his flat in a cloud of baby powder and self-congratulation. As if she were inebriated by a sense of her own indispensability, she rollicked around, boiling up her formulas, rinsing out tiny cardigans and bootees. She loudly hummed lullabies as she sterilized with her vast steel sterilizing equipment. Every day she went trundling out on shopping expeditions, puffing, as she pushed the unwieldy pram, and she bought herself more and more cakes and pies and nappy-pins.

"And who is meant to get Mrs. Richardson all her meals? I have my hands full . . ." Miss Renny's eyes would taunt him. They reminded him of two little malicious currants fraudulently nestling under the protective camouflage of the cherubic chubbiness of her rosy-apple cheeks. He sensed that she was only too delighted by the unusual situation which was prevailing in his household and that all her immense energies were directing themselves to finding shrewd ways by which she could best exploit it.

"Don't you worry about my wife's meals, Miss Renny. You just devote yourself to the baby."

His wife refused to have any meals. When he got back in the evenings from his office he would bring her honey and toast, which she would nibble with apathetic and distracted disgust as if it were some dangerous repellent substance which, in typical bad faith, he was forcing on her.

"Why don't you have a strong whisky. If you don't want to eat you might find that a drink would make you feel better."

"I feel as if an ink-fish has squirted black poisons into my brain. Alcohol would only make me feel worse. All you can do is leave me alone."

"Didn't you want to have the child? You should have told me that you didn't want to. Surely you didn't have it just to please me . . ." The infant seemed to be so painfully associated with the despairing state of mind which had followed its birth that at the very mention of its name his wife would immediately go into a choking attack of wild weak sobbing. He would stand by her bed ineptly trying to soothe her until, finding it useless, he would go next door and, in an attempt to curb his exasperation, he would make cocoa for Miss Renny.

He sent for Arabella's doctor, who said that her condition was a common one and that she would snap out of it if she rested.

"It's just the old post-natals!"

The doctor prescribed some pills which had no effect on her behavior. She went on spending her days shut up in her room, and whenever Stephen went in to visit her he found her lying staring at the bleak grey eye of her unturned-on television as if she were watching some invisible horror movie.

"You will be pleased to hear that Miss Renny has got the little Miss off the night-feed, Mr. Richardson! It's all experience . . ." Miss Renny was always talking about her "experience." She made it sound like something that only she, by her superior nature, possessed, something magical that she carried on her portly person like an amulet to ward off the evil influences which would plunge the household into ruin if it were ever removed. Occasionally he felt a sinking faith in the saving powers of Miss Renny's experience, although he always tried to squash these doubts, like a believer who feels imperiled by the needle-jabs of his own thoughts. Sometimes he found himself wondering whether Miss Renny was so over-interested in feeding herself that she was starving the baby. For night and day the infant never seemed to stop screaming. As if the despairing mood of its mother had been instilled at birth into its tiny bones, it filled the whole flat with its wails.

"It's only the wind," Miss Renny would chirp. Sometimes she said it was being naughty.

"If you want to start a family Mr. Richardson—you are going to have to get used to crying."

As weeks went by he started to resent Arabella for her unlifting despondency and saw it less as a disease than a desertion. She seemed to have selfishly sailed away on the tides of her own depression and he felt stunned and bitter that she had left him to cope alone with his dispiriting little household, composed of Miss Renny and the howling bundle which was the baby.

It was the dinners which he felt obliged to eat with Miss Renny in the kitchen which he found the most agonizing experience of the day. Miss Renny had a breast which hardly seemed to be a breast it was so like some great boulder jutting out under her white nurse's uniform. It was as if, with her intensely competitive nature, Miss Renny had felt the need, in all her years of playing a professional maternal role, to grow herself such a monumental breast that she could trust it to dwarf and out-rival all competing breasts. Miss Renny loved to chatter while she ate and, as she talked, she had a habit of thrusting out her great breast, and often she pushed it so close to his mouth that he was sorely tempted to bite it.

"Well I must say that Mrs. Richardson doesn't seem to be all that thrilled by her lovely little baby girl. I don't think she's bothered to take one peep at the poor little mite since she brought it back from the hospital. I've been doing this kind of work for years, Mr. Richardson, but I have to tell you frankly that I've never seen a mother like that . . . My problem was always trying to keep the young mothers away from the babies . . . All day and all night I do nothing except devote myself to your little child, Mr. Richardson. But sometimes I look at that dear little girl when she is sleeping and I find I can't stop myself from thinking that it might have been better for her if she had been stillborn . . ."

"You have to understand that my wife is not at all well, Miss Renny."

"Mrs. Richardson is a very young woman. I'm afraid I can have no patience with that kind of self-pampering laziness. She can hardly hope to get her strength back if she wants to spend her days lying flat on her back and playing the lady of leisure. All my other mothers were up on their feet a few hours after the delivery . . ."

He disliked discussing Arabella with Miss Renny and found he could only steer her away from this topic which deeply intrigued her if he encouraged her to speak of the other families she had worked for. She would then boast interminably of how they had all loved and depended on her.

"I've never known a family where I haven't been able to leave my mark," Miss Renny kept repeating. And he found he always had an instant image of all Miss Renny's families lying in a stricken position with their gashed mouths biting the earth like village victims of some barbaric machine-gun massacre.

He would sit silently nodding encouragement and coughing with monotonous courtesy while Miss Renny chattered. He would note with nausea the pleasure she took in her food, listen to her breathing as it became heavy, almost lustful, as she took off the cover of a dish of stew and sniffed it.

"When I was with Lady Eccleston, Mr. Richardson, I was always treated exactly as if I was part of the family. We often used to sit down sixteen for dinner. Oh, that was nothing for us! Sir Keith was in the government, so we always entertained a lot of cabinet ministers. What a charming bunch of fascinating men they all were too! The baby was Ronald . . . They still send me photos of him. How his mother doted on him! That was a family that made you feel glad to be alive . . ."

Even though his dinners with Miss Renny depressed and bored him to distraction he found himself often deliberately prolonging them. Every night he kept putting off the moment when he would have to go to sleep in Arabella's room. It seemed to him that their bedroom had acquired an unpleasantly sour and stagnant smell as if the malignancy of his wife's mood had permeated its very atmosphere. He disliked lying beside her when she huddled there so inert and rigid on the very edge of the bed that he felt she was bracing herself for some dreaded attack. Sometimes he tried to talk to her but she only answered with a little sniff or a sob. She reminded him of the infant, she seemed so speechless, lying there in the darkness tightly swaddled in her own moroseness. He found it almost impossible to get to sleep feeling his wife's tension to be something eerie and terrifying, like something he had once read about in a ghost story, a headless clammy lady who entered beds at midnight and snuggled between the sheets.

One evening he set up a camp-bed for himself in the little windowless storage room which was beside the kitchen. The only other bedroom in the flat was occupied by Miss Renny and the baby. He found the cold and uncomfortable isolation of the storage room a relief. He could sense that his presence was becoming more and more painful to Arabella, that it pressured her to a point she found intolerable. As if she felt a certain shame at her own distressed behavior, she appeared to be acutely sensitive to his unvoiced resentment at her collapse. If he made any attempt to cheer her it merely seemed to aggravate her guilt which in turn aggravated her gloom. As if she were cowering away from his criticism, the very sight of him now seemed to make her retreat even further into the weird weepy world of her own melancholia.

Miss Renny was displeasingly over-interested in his storage-room move. She offered to help him make up the camp-bed and made him feel there was a symbolic importance to her gesture, for in general she categorically refused to do any housework unless it pertained directly to the baby. She had been insisting lately that he employ a cleaning woman to work full-time in the flat.

"In all my other households I was never expected to be a drudge. I certainly never cooked for myself. I took responsibility for their child and they treated my work with respect. But then all my other families considered that their infant was a gift from God . . ."

Miss Renny managed to insinuate that she assumed that it

was at his wife's insistence that he had been forced to move out from her bed.

"Any woman who cries like that all day," he heard Miss Renny murmuring to the bonneted ear of the infant, "she must be crying for some reason."

On other occasions Miss Renny took a very different view of Arabella's conduct.

"I think you are wonderful the way you put up with it, Mr. Richardson."

"Put up with what, Miss Renny?"

He would stare across the kitchen table and creases of Miss Renny's double chins would look like cruel secondary smiles which were underlining her real smile.

"None of my other husbands would have allowed their wives to get away with murder."

"Get away with murder?" He had acquired a dismal habit of dumbly repeating all her sentences in order to gain time to brace himself for the stab of her coming remarks.

"Murder doesn't have to be committed with a knife, Mr. Richardson. But you seem to be a little too weak to face up to that. I know you like to play the patient understanding husband. That's all very charming and touching. But the whole burden of this miserable household is falling on me. Quite frankly, Mr. Richardson, I don't know how long I will be able to take it . . . I've always been a very cheerful type of person and it takes a lot to get me down. But you feel that the unhappiness in this flat is as thick as porridge and you could eat it with a spoon. I'm afraid it's affecting my health . . . I've always been very sensitive to the atmosphere of the places where I work. I just have to take care of my health . . . I've had to work hard all my life. I've never been able to afford to retire to my bed and throw my responsibilities on to other people like a certain young woman we both know . . ."

He doubled Miss Renny's salary, cravenly submitting to her duplicitous blackmail, for although he dreaded the very sight of her sitting in his kitchen like an over-fed Britannia ruling her invisible waves, he was perversely tortured by an almost primitive terror that she might suddenly leave. When he was in his office in the daytime he was persistently nagged by an anxiety that in his absence Miss Renny might have some unfortunate interchange with Arabella and that he would find when he got back to the flat that she had seized up her suitcase and left. Although he sometimes found himself identifying with the infant and often felt incensed by Arabella's refusal to register the remotest interest in her existence, he also had a terror that he might suddenly find himself forced to handle it. He had such an exaggerated idea of its fragility that he feared that if he was left just one night alone with it, he would somehow manage to snap its frail life-thread by some clumsy masculine ineptitude.

Almost as much as he dreaded finding himself in charge of the infant, he now dreaded being left alone in the flat with his wife. Oppressive as he found the obese and overbearing presence of Miss Renny, at least Miss Renny talked, at least Miss Renny would eat.

"I've always been in love with gorgeous materials," Arabella had once said to him.

"Marvelous silks and satins and furs excite me. Whenever I get the chance to wear them I just can't stop stroking myself. If I see a photograph of myself wearing something fabulous I find myself secretly kissing the photograph."

Now he felt she had self-indulgently wrapped herself up in her new wretchedness in much the same way that she had once loved to wrap herself up in silks, and satins, and furs. He felt chilled by the sight of her perpetually closed door, exasperated by the way she was so concentrated on her own condition that she seemed to have lost all desire to improve it.

"Naturally you are depressed, shut up in this room all day by yourself. For Christ's sake get up, meet people, get out!"

"I don't want to get up, meet people, go out."

He knew she had started to drink by herself and this disturbed and wounded him, for she always irritably refused any drink he offered her. Her refusal to drink with him seemed to express an aggressive refusal to share anything. Miss Renny would show him the depleted sunken whisky bottles.

"I see that a little bird has been sneaking out in the night, Mr. Richardson . . ."

Miss Renny had started drinking rather heavily herself. She now drank the best part of a bottle of vodka every night before dinner, claiming that she needed it medicinally to enable her to breathe in an unhappy household. Sensing the vulnerability of this position, she exploited his reliance on her by ordering herself more and more expensive foods and wines which she charged to his account. If he had once found it unattractive to watch Miss Renny's false teeth snapping up her stew, he found it now far more painful to watch without protest while she went gobbling through great plates of smoked salmon and pâté. All the hocks and clarets that Miss Renny sipped with her supper in no way seemed to mellow her, rather, they seemed to release her animosity. She grumbled incessantly. She complained that the plug of the kitchen kettle was inconvenient—that her bedroom was traffic-noisy—that the water in his taps was so hard that it was chapping her hands. She complained that she felt bored when he left to go to his office in the daytime.

"I've always been a fun-loving person. And whatever you want to say about Mrs. Richardson—you could hardly call her very scintillating company . . ." In the evenings when he dined with her in the kitchen Miss Renny made it more and more obvious that she missed the company of cabinet ministers.

Although Miss Renny loved to complain of her ennui when she was left alone in the flat in the daytime, he suspected that she found many ways to divert herself and that she spent a good deal of her day tormenting Arabella and doing her best to increase his wife's feeling of inadequacy and gloom. Sometimes Miss Renny dropped little hints of her daytime activities.

"I went into Mrs. Richardson's bedroom and I had a little word with her this morning. 'What a selfish young woman you are!' That's what I said to her. 'You have a devoted young husband and you don't care what your disgusting behavior is doing to him. And as for your poor little helpless baby girl . . . I find you inhuman. I'm afraid I just find you positively inhuman.'"

"Yes, yes Miss Renny. Shall we see if there is anything on the television?"

Arabella never once mentioned Miss Renny. But then she spoke less and less. When he visited her she often hardly seemed to be aware that he was in the room.

"Every day Mrs. Richardson looks worse!" Miss Renny would tell him triumphantly every night when he got home. "I suppose Mrs. Richardson must have been quite a good-looking young woman when you married her. I imagine that must have been the reason why you married her. But oh dear, now! Oh poor Mrs. Richardson! Her hair is just hanging down in strings of grease. Her bones are sticking out like a Belsen victim. And then she has this goofy mournful expression as if she can't take anything in. When a woman loses all pride in herself you have to feel sorry for her. They never seem to recover from the havoc it wreaks on their looks."

If Miss Renny spent most of her day teasing and needling his wife, he found he no longer very much cared. He was starting to find Arabella rather monstrous, she appeared to be so totally indifferent to anything except her inner depressive pain-signals. He found her callous that she cared so little what she mangled with her remorseless melancholia.

He had worked for some years in the same publishing house, but never before had his office seemed like such a glittering dome of pleasure. After he had received the hail of Miss Renny's conversation at breakfast, the tinkle of every telephone, the tap of every typewriter, sounded like sublime music. In his office no one said that an ink-fish had squirted black poison into their brain, and the only moments that jarred him were when the typists complimented him on the birth of his baby.

He would lunch in restaurants with friends, but whenever Arabella was mentioned he said she was very well. He found himself reluctant to describe her state of mind as if it might in some way be considered to reflect badly on himself. The dismal closeness of his relationship with Miss Renny he also wanted to hide from the world as if it were some disgraceful sore. He was very careful to avoid asking any of his friends to come to the flat. He had no wish for them to see the way that he spent far more time with Miss Renny than he spent with his wife. He had no wish for them to see the way he sat so passively in the kitchen making no protest at all while Miss Renny ventriloquized for the baby. She would press its bald frail skull against her huge thrusting breast and rock it to and fro while she spoke in a piping squeaky voice, "I went into my Mummy's room today, Daddy. Miss Renny had given me my lovely bath and I was such a nice clean girl, all pretty and rosy. I'm afraid my Mummy's room was all nasty and smelly. Miss Renny says my Mummy has refused to change the sheets of her bed or allow her room to be cleaned ever since I was born. Miss Renny said it worried her to take me into such an unhygienic room and she hoped it wouldn't give me germs. Anyway I was looking as pretty as can be and all powdered. And I really thought my Mummy would be very pleased to see me. But do you know what she did to my nice Miss Renny? She said horrible things and she swore . . . 'Just take it away, you old bitch!' That's what my Mummy said to my kind Miss Renny. 'For Christ's sake take it away!'"

And while Miss Renny was giving it words, he would stare at the infant and find himself unable to take his eyes off its nose. The infant's nose was the only distinctive feature in the amorphous pucker of its wizened little face. As if gazing into a distorting mirror he would see his own nose, a nose which had always seemed to him to be like a house of classical proportions whose elegant façade had been disfigured by the addition of an unsightly wing. So often when he was shaving he had looked at the unnecessary little bulge which lay at the end of his nose and felt tempted to remove it with his razor. And seeing a tiny version of his nose on the baby he felt a pity for it and, as if searching for a concrete object which he could blame as the cause of Arabella's depression, he would feel certain that his wife, ever since the birth of the child, had felt secretly saddened by the sight of its nose. He found it only too easy to imagine that someone like Arabella who was so concerned with the appearance of things might very well feel a despair at the prospect of bringing up this girl who could never be pretty because she had inherited his nose.

"She's the dead spit of her Dad!" Miss Renny loved to warble.

And always he felt a kind of panic and wished he knew of some way to offer restitution to his wife and daughter. He often found himself compulsively thinking about the infant's nose while Miss Renny was telling him about her great dream. She hoped one day to retire and buy herself a cottage of her own by the sea. Such a dream in someone else he might have found quite sympathetic. But hearing about it from Miss Renny, all he felt was disgust, for he saw it as the dream of a burglar. He always had a displeasing image of Miss Renny retiring to her sea cottage with all the spoils that she had thievishly extracted from all the households she had cunningly entered on her baby-nurse cat-ladder.

Sometimes in the middle of the night, lying alone and restless in the storage room, listening to the soft pad of Arabella's feet as she slyly crept out from her room to get herself a bottle of whisky from the kitchen, he would decide to get another nurse to replace Miss Renny. He found that this decision could distract him from the indecision that most plagued him. Should he lock up all the alcohol in the house? Or were her lonely bedroom whiskies the only thing which was now preventing Arabella from becoming suicidal?

By morning his decision to get rid of Miss Renny would fade and become a fantasy. The unexpectedness of his wife's collapse had left him with a feeling of apathetic exhaustion and he felt incapable of making the effort to find a new nurse. In his pessimistic mood, he was certain that he was bound to select some woman who would have all Miss Renny's disagreeable qualities, plus the additional defect of being dangerously incompetent.

Miss Renny sensed the security of her position in his household and became increasingly demanding and aggressive. She had engaged an aged Scottish lady as a full-time cleaner for the flat and she treated this woman who was far older and frailer than herself with a nagging tyranny. Familiarity had made Miss Renny feel that she had the freedom to treat Stephen Richardson as if she were his long-suffering wife. She accused him of taking very little interest in the baby's routines. She complained that he was so withdrawn and silent, and distracted.

"I've always liked the kind of man who has something to say for himself—the kind that can make you laugh." She accused him of being unpopular.

"All my other families were very much in demand. They all had masses of fascinating friends who were always popping in and out for drink and a giggle. In this household you feel so ostracized you might as well be in a leper colony."

When Miss Renny referred to Arabella it was with more and more spite.

"I'm afraid our dear Mrs. Richardson is a complete sham. If she didn't drink so much she wouldn't be any iller than the rest of us—she's the sort of woman who thinks she is so good-looking she deserves to be a duchess and then things don't quite turn out the way she hoped. So what does her ladyship do? She retires to her bed and it's boo hoo hoo!"

Sometimes he found himself weakly trying to defend Arabella and he would try to tell Miss Renny what his wife had been like before she became ill. But as he talked he would start to have the feeling that the amusing clear girl he was describing was just as fictional as Miss Renny's gilded pictures of all her other families. Miss Renny and himself would seem like two tired sailors sitting there spinning their bragging yarns. It was as if they were both trying to drug themselves against their futureless, discouraging present by hallucinating glamorous pasts. With his wife lying there so nearby in a semi-coma of drink and despondency, it seemed futile to try to make her image dance for this spiteful old woman with her skeptical fat-encrusted little eyes.

"My wife is a very talented young actress, Miss Renny."

"Your wife is certainly a talented actress, Mr. Richardson. I've been watching her perform for quite a few months now. I feel like going to the box office and asking for my money back . . ."

Often it seemed to him that Miss Renny might go on living with him forever. He found it only too easy to visualize a fearful future in which he would always go on leaning on Miss Renny and pandering to her caprice, eternally doomed to her stifling domination by the apathy and cowardice which had prevented him from getting rid of her from the start.

And then one day, quite suddenly, he struck out at Miss Renny. As he committed his vengeful act of aggression against her he was surprised by his feeling of the utter inevitability of his action. It was as if, ever since she had first moved into his flat, in some buried way, he had always been planning one day to strike the blow which he knew would jolt her to the very core of her bulky frame which had fattened itself for so long on his food. As he came through the door of this flat at midnight, drunk, and staggering, and deliberately trying to wake up the infant, he had a feeling of exhilaration from the enormity of his act of aggression against Miss Renny. As he held on to the arm of the blonde girl who was with him he found that his fingers were tightening on her sleeve as if he were gripping some sharp sword.

If, by sleeping with another woman in the flat, he was striking at

Arabella, he could see her only as an accidental side-victim. His wife was so depressed already that he felt it would hardly matter all that much to her if she were given extra grounds for her depression.

It was Miss Renny whom he hoped to outrage by his infidelity. He wanted to force her to be an unwilling accomplice in an act that he knew she would consider atrocious. If the crude tastelessness of his sexual behavior appalled her, he wanted her to realize that she was in no position to do anything about it. Miss Renny must be forced to realize, whatever it cost her in terms of anguish, that in his household she was in charge of the infant, but she was not in charge of morals.

He knew Miss Renny quite well enough to know that her man-hate would make her feel a feverish identification with Arabella, that all the blood in her veins would smart as she suffered for his wife in her humiliation.

And he knew with a feeling of joy that Miss Renny was trapped. Just as Miss Renny had managed to trap him into putting up with her obnoxious presence by persistently brainwashing him with the myth of her indispensability, so Miss Renny herself was trapped in his flat for the night. She could leave in the morning, but she had no choice but to remain in the flat for the night, for Miss Renny had nowhere else to go. He was certain that she was too nervously fussy and self-caring to dare to walk out in disgust into the raining streets with her suitcase. He counted on the fact that she was far too parsimonious to go off and find herself a room in a hotel.

He had always sensed that somewhere buried in the center of Miss Renny's confident and overbearing personality, there was a sensitive little pocket of prudery and terror. And before Miss Renny left his flat he wanted to jab this spinsterish and shockable little area of Miss Renny's soul and make her suffer. He did not want her to leave until he had made her feel that she had been bruised and battered. This last night under his roof he hoped she would experience something far more upsetting than she had yet experienced in all her "experience."

The hatred that he felt for Miss Renny as he came swaying into the flat with the blonde girl was quite disproportionate to the harm she had actually done him. He longed to horrify and distress her not so much because he wanted to revenge himself for all the unpleasant hours he had spent under the domination of her greedy, blackmailing personality, as for the fact that he could never forgive her because she had had such a peephole view of the collapse of his marriage. He felt that Miss Renny could never be punished enough because she had penetrated his privacy and watched with her uncaring and prying eyes while the birth of his child turned to something that seemed far less like a birth than some long, drawn out, and painful death. Miss Renny had eaten her cakes and drunk her wine while his relationship with his wife deteriorated until he now felt certain that it was quite beyond repair. For he now found that he no longer wanted Arabella to recover. Having once longed for the return of her old self, it now seemed to him to be something so remote that he had become resigned to its loss and in no way wanted it. He could feel far more regret for his own lack of interest in the return of the old Arabella than he could regret her disappearance. Throughout so many lonely boring dinners with Miss Renny he had been kept afloat by his faith that his unpleasant and severed relationship with his wife was impermanent. As if to a raft, he had clung to his hope that their old flirtatious relationship would be restored unimpaired by her cure. But now he realized he no longer wanted Arabella cured or uncured. He found it impossible to imagine that he could ever revive any physical interest in her again. He wanted to get some doctor to put her in a hospital where he would no longer feel he had any responsibility for her. The prostrated dispirited creature who was lying there in her dirty bed in the flat seemed not only like someone who was dead to him—but like someone who had died before he was born.

"Is your wife away?" The blonde girl asked him as they came into the flat.

"I don't have a wife."

"Well, you certainly didn't manage to keep her very long. I stuck mental pins into that girl when you married her. What a waste of all that green-eyed emotion. But then waste seems to be my middle name!"

He took the blonde girl into the storeroom.

"You must be joking! Are you insane? You have this big flat. Is it some new subtle perversion that you find it exciting to sleep in the broom-cupboard?"

"It has a bed, hasn't it?"

The blonde girl looked at the rickety camp-bed with disgust.

"Did you force your beautiful bride to share this magnificent bed? I don't wonder that she didn't stay very long!"

"Shut up," he said. "Come over here."

"Don't maul me. What's the big hurry? We've got all night. Can't we have a drink first? Why are you being so rough? You didn't used to be rough. Marriage doesn't seem to have suited you. It's made you very peculiar. I've noticed that all evening. What on earth is the matter with you? Are you sex-starved or something?"

He wanted her to undress so that she would be naked when she met Miss Renny. She was starting to irritate him in the same way that in the past she had always irritated him. He found that the parting of her long peroxide hair was too low—annoyingly wrong, so that he wanted to seize her skull and shift it. When he got her to take off her sweater her skin looked too white, unhealthy, as if it were an unpleasant mixture of marble and rubber. He had always found her vulgar, over-compliant and over-available, and he had never liked the way she was both martyred and critical in her over-compliant over-availability.

"It doesn't surprise me that Arabella has left you," she said.

"Why is that?"

"You invented her. Women never like that. Arabella was such a brilliant actress . . . Arabella was so much cleverer and more charming than any other girl . . . I never thought she ever really wanted to marry you. I think she just liked to feel she had the power to make you want to marry her. Arabella was never in love with anything except her own elegant figure. I always felt there was something quite wrong with that girl. She had a peculiar stare in her big green eyes. I always thought she looked a bit psychotic."

"Will you go next door and get us the bottle of Scotch which is on one of the shelves in the kitchen?"

He could hear Miss Renny was stirring. She must have heard voices. She always prowled around in the night and made herself tea and snacks. He had always suspected that Miss Renny deliberately kept herself awake at night for fear of missing some explosive bedroom argument between Arabella and himself. But Miss Renny had been cheated of her arguments. In all her weeks of hopeful listening there had been nothing for her eager ear to pick up except a silence, the futureless silence of two hostile strangers both engrossed in totally different newspapers as they travelled in the same compartment in some train.

The blonde girl went off to get the whisky from the kitchen. As her naked, marble, rubber figure disappeared, his heart was pounding as he listened. Miss Renny was coming down the corridor. He could hear the shuffle of her bedroom slippers. And then he heard nothing.

And then he heard what he had hoped to hear. Two screams. The scream of the blonde girl and the louder scream of Miss Renny.

And then suddenly the blonde girl was back in the storage room. She was very angry, and her bad temper in conjunction with her nudity made her appear a little ludicrous.

"You are a bloody swine! Why didn't you tell me that there was someone else in this flat? Why on earth did you let me go roaming around in the nude? Do you realize that I just ran smack into your grandmother? You should have seen the poor creature's face! If she has a coronary tonight you deserve to be put on trial for murder."

"That wasn't my grandmother. That was my mistress."

"Don't try to be so amusing. I don't find what you did amusing. I find it pointless, and embarrassing for everyone, and really very cruel. But then I shouldn't be surprised by your cruelty. Ever since I've known you the way you have treated me has always been extremely cruel. It was certainly cruel the way you were too cowardly to tell me that you were besotted by the beautiful Arabella. I will never forgive you for that. If you had had the courage to tell me yourself I wouldn't have suffered so much. You think you are being so kind by acting in a cowardly weak way and then you do something which is really quite savage . . ."

"It seems a little late to rake up all that past stuff."

"Oh, so it's all 'past stuff' to you! If it's all 'past stuff' why the hell did you bring me back here to sleep with you tonight?"

"Oddly enough, I needed you tonight. I needed you more tonight than I've ever needed you."

Now that Miss Renny had seen her naked he wished that the blonde girl would leave. He suddenly found her intensity very tiring. She was frenziedly pulling back on all her clothes and she was trying to be as sexually provocative as possible while at the same time she appeared to be enjoying her own display of pique.

"Oh, so you needed me! Well, that's just wonderful! I'm afraid you are going to have to go on needing me. Your glamorous wife has the sense to walk out on you and then you find yourself forced to resort to second best. You never needed me tonight. But I know what you did need. You needed to reassure yourself that I was still infatuated with you. I imagine that your poor little ego must be feeling a little deflated right now and you needed me to pump it up like a bicycle tire. Well, it's a bit late for that, lover boy. I see through you now . . ."

The blonde girl was speaking so loudly that he felt certain that Arabella must be listening to every word. He wondered if she would come out of her room. If she did he decided that he would introduce her to the blonde girl. Both of them seemed so unreal to him that he could feel not the faintest interest in their confrontation. He saw them both as two faded phantoms, and their meeting merely seemed like an eerie abstraction. Maybe they would condole with each other, maybe they would be vituperative, maybe they would be very formal and shake hands.

Miss Renny suddenly seemed to have more substance and reality than either of them. While the spit and spite of the blonde girl's tirade continued, he found that he couldn't stop thinking about Miss Renny. She would leave in the morning. He knew there was no doubt about that. And knowing that she was going, she suddenly seemed to dwindle. In his imagination he found that even her obesity appeared to be oddly diminished. The imminence of her departure seemed to strip Miss Renny of all her omnipotence and she was starting to shrivel away until she became nothing more than an unimportant woman whose profession forced her to live always in the houses of strangers, and whose only future was her own retirement to some lonely drab cottage by the sea.

He was only too certain that he had succeeded in shocking her. She was being so quiet. She was being far too quiet. He suspected that she was now feeling far too frightened even to dare come out of her room. He knew that his behavior this evening would make her feel that the whole flat was dangerously polluted, that all its poisons were even seeping into all the bottles she had so carefully sterilized for the baby. He knew that Miss Renny would never be able to sleep tonight. He could imagine her pacing in panic up and down her room feeling that she was trapped in a cage with rattlesnakes. He was only too certain that all night long her spinster's mind would be tormented by her own obscene imaginings.

And the more he thought about it, the more his successful shocking of Miss Renny seemed unnecessary. It had really solved so little. It had been a symbolic gesture. And now he felt that like so many symbolic gestures it had an in-built and symbolic futility.

The blonde girl was still abusing him. "I don't know whether you realize it—but you are far less attractive than you were two years ago. You used to have a naïve little-boy quality. That's why women liked you. But something unpleasant has happened to you. You seem to have become even more hard and even more weak. I'm not sure that your sort of charm is the kind that ages very well. You may well be the kind of man who ends up lonely. Who is going to want a lot of little Lord Fauntleroy velvet on a man with thinning hair?"

The blonde girl's abuse distressed him very little, for he knew that there had to be an end to it. The blonde girl was not taking care of the infant. He was in no way dependent on her. Eventually the blonde girl would leave. He felt nothing was intolerable if it was possible to visualize some eventual end to it.

Who Needs It?

"Saturdays are crazy! Saturdays kill me!" Angeline said to Mrs. Reilly.

"Saturdays are a problem for everyone." Mrs. Reilly stared mournfully at her own reflection in Angeline's mirror.

"Every week it's always the same story." Angeline carefully formed a kiss-curl on Mrs. Reilly's wrinkled forehead. "Saturdays all the girls come in at once—'Can you touch up my roots, Angeline?'—'Angeline, I'm going out tonight and I look as brassy as the morning sun. Can you give me a bit of a tone down?' You know how it is, Mrs. Reilly. The girls would all rather be seen walking naked down Broadway, than be seen weekends without their hair fixed. I just hate to disappoint a customer—but if you've only got two hands, what are you going to do?"

"Nothing else to do," Mrs. Reilly sighed.

"Saturdays are just so crazy, Mrs. Reilly! Half the week I'm sitting here all alone in the shop with only my own hair dryers for company. So I give myself bleach or sometimes a set of highlights—and then I give myself another bleach and a different set of highlights. My husband says he likes a change. I guess that husbands do like changes really. All the same it's a very good way to ruin your hair messing around with it all day long like that—but if your shop's dead empty what else are you going to do?"

"Nothing else to do," Mrs. Reilly sighed again.

"My husband always knows when business has been lousy when he sees me coming home with a brand new hair color."

"They always know." Mrs. Reilly stared gloomily at Angeline's floor, which was littered with hair clippings, pins, rollers, and cigarette butts, and stained with great patches of old purple dye.

"My husband's never stopped telling me that I've got to do something about Saturdays, Mrs. Reilly. 'Look,' he says 'you want Angeline's Beauty Salon to be a friendly kind of a place—informal—somewhere where the girls can all drop in without an appointment and have themselves a ball—a place where it's a real pleasure to go. Now once you start turning away customers on Saturdays, Angeline—you can really be in trouble. I mean that's no pleasure for them.'"

"No pleasure in that, Angeline." Mrs. Reilly shook her head. "Your husband's quite right."

Angeline handed Mrs. Reilly a hand-mirror. "How do you like the back flipping out like that? I think it's just darling—so much younger. Anyway, Mrs. Reilly, I figured I really better do something about weekends. So now you see that woman over there—that's Mrs.

Klein. I've got her to come in Saturdays to give me a hand with the rinses. She used to work in the beauty business before the war. It's hard nowadays to get people who know the work."

"Nowadays," Mrs. Reilly fidgeted irritably with her own grey curls, "people won't work."

"It's like a favor for Mrs. Klein. She needs the extra, you know how it is." Angeline bent over and whispered in Mrs. Reilly's ear. "She's Jewish you know. She was in one of those camps in Europe. Very tragic."

Mrs. Reilly turned and stared at Mrs. Klein who was down at the other end of the beauty salon rubbing a froth of henna dye into the unsuitably long, mermaid-like hair of an elderly woman with spectacles.

"You'd never know it." Mrs. Reilly gave another of her heavy sighs.

"Well, I just wouldn't like to say that. Mrs. Klein is not as old as she looks, you know. You see the big black circles under her eyes. It's aged her. No question about that. I want you to have spray today, Mrs. Reilly. It's windy outside and it will help to hold your set."

It was getting very hot in Angeline's sleazy beauty salon. Her hair dryers hummed monotonously as they puffed out their dry, burnt air. Women were sitting under them in rows like bored warriors wearing chipped steel helmets. The cheap strip-lighting threw a sickly, green light on to Angeline's dirty basins and her piles of battered *Vogue*s.

Miss Ferguson, an earnest little weasel-faced stenographer, came through the glass door. Angeline bustled towards her, plump, and slovenly, and smiling. "So what's new, Miss Ferguson?" Angeline's tired, pudgy face was a white mask of makeup, her only brilliance was the bleached gold of her heavily teased hair.

"So what style do you want today, honey? Something special. Right? I bet you've got yourself a pretty heavy date tonight!"

"Angeline, you are just terrible!" Miss Ferguson giggled.

"Sit down and I'll shampoo you. You know what my husband says to me, Miss Ferguson?—'You better keep your mouth shut, Angeline. You know too much about all the girls in the neighborhood. You could be one of the biggest blackmailers in New York City!'"

"I just bet you could, Angeline!"

"Look at it this way, honey. You get some married woman and she's quite happy doing her own hair and messing it up for years—then one day she'll come in here and she'll say 'Give me a new color, Angeline—give me something really different.' Well, you can bet your bottom dollar she's not doing it for her husband. Right? Angeline doesn't talk. You can lose customers that way. But she notices. I mean, sometimes you'll get a cute young kid, and she'll come in and tell you that she wants all her hair cut off. I know at once she's got some guy that's giving her trouble. It's crazy! But with the young kids—a guy walks out on them, and the first thing they want to do is to have every hair on their head cut off!"

"Maybe it's psychological," Miss Ferguson said helpfully. "Nowadays it seems like so many things are psychological."

"I don't know what kind of dopey thing it is, honey, but I always try to stop them doing it. I mean what fella's worth going round looking like you've just been doing a stint on a chain gang?"

"Your kind of work must be very individual kind of work. It must be very rewarding." Miss Ferguson's head was tilted backwards in Angeline's basin. "I think that different people's problems are always so rewarding."

"Sometimes they are. Sometimes they are not, Miss Ferguson.

Last week I had a woman walk in here—and she sits herself down and I give her a set and I give her a manicure—and the next moment she's down on the floor, among all the pins and rollers—and she's tossing around and yelling her head off—and she's giving birth! Jesus! What a mess! And my other customers weren't crazy about it at all. She had no right coming in here if she's that far gone. Oh boy! Was I mad with her!"

"But she couldn't have wanted that to happen, Angeline. I mean, she couldn't have—like planned it—could she?"

Angeline shrugged. "I don't know. She was a Puerto Rican—very dark hair—not tinted—real. She wasn't colored—I don't take colored people."

Angeline noticed that Miss Ferguson was looking anxious.

"Look honey, don't get so worried. They don't want to come in here anymore. They wouldn't be seen dead in here now—don't kid yourself. I mean now—Black is Beautiful, right?" Angeline laughed. "They used to try and come in sometimes and then I always said to them: 'Look, I want to be fair to you—I just don't understand your hair.' I didn't want to take their money and give them a lousy job, so I always told them they'd be far better off going to some beauty parlor where they were used to working with their kind of heads. I figured that was fair to them—and fair to myself. Right?"

"I guess that was fair," Miss Ferguson said doubtfully.

"Those kind of heads need special techniques. I mean . . ." Angeline stopped her patter and her beady little puffy eyes flicked anxiously to the other end of her beauty salon. Suddenly there was a stir, and her clients' heads were coming craning out from under their dryers.

"What's all the excitement over there?" Miss Ferguson asked her.

"It's nothing. It's nothing," Angeline said irritably. "It's just Mrs. Klein. I guess that the customers are starting to ask about her tattoo."

"Her tattoo, Angeline?"

"Well, it's not exactly a tattoo. I just don't quite know what you'd call it. I guess you'd say it's more like a brand. She's Jewish and she was in one of those camps in Germany. They did it to her there. She's got those huge, horrible, black numbers stamped the whole way down her arm."

"Oh gee! Isn't that terrible, Angeline? Isn't that a terrible thing?"

"It's terrible alright, you oughta just take a close look at it. Yesterday when she came to answer my 'ad' she was telling me that she can't wear short sleeves even in the summer. She gets all these wiseguys on the subways—and they think they are being cute. 'Are you scared that you might forget your social security number, lady?'—that's what they ask her—all that kind of stupid bull."

"Oh Jesus, Angeline! That's just terrible! But surely they don't have a clue what it is—do they? I mean no one could say that to her—not if they knew her—could they?"

"No I guess they don't know—and I must say I kind of wish that Mrs. Klein hadn't let all my customers know too—if you really want to know something. Just look at them now. Just look at all their faces! I don't know what Mrs. Klein's been telling them what with all the noise and the dryers blowing—but boy—they sure don't look too crazy about it. Oh boy! Has Mrs. Klein upset them! You see old Mrs. Craxton down at the end over there—when she came in here she was just terrific. She was really great—she was laughing—she was having herself a ball. 'I have only one life, Angeline, and I want to live it as a blonde!' That's what she said to me—and she's nearly seventy. Now look at her, Jesus! She looks like she's going to pass out, or have a heart attack or something. And look at Miss Martini and Mrs. Wade. They are sitting there under their dryers and they both look like they are going to their own funerals."

"But you can't blame them, Angeline. I mean a horrible thing like that—it kind of gets you."

"Honey." Angeline frowned and grimly tugged her comb through Miss Ferguson's wet hair. "I am not blaming the customers."

"Have you asked Mrs. Klein about her experiences, Angeline? I mean you see a woman like that—you kind of want to ask her a lot of questions—and you kind of don't want to ask her a lot of questions. Do you know what I mean?"

"No I haven't asked Mrs. Klein any questions, Miss Ferguson—and I'm not planning to ask Mrs. Klein any questions either. Maybe Mrs. Klein likes to tell people things—it certainly seems like she does. But how do I know? I never set eyes on her till yesterday. All I know is that today while she's been down there at the other end of the shop doing the rinses it seems like she's been saying plenty to the customers. I can tell that just to look at them. Oh boy! You sure wouldn't know it was a Saturday. It's like she's hit them all on the head or something!"

"You'd think that there must be things that Mrs. Klein could do about her arm. I mean science is so great now, Angeline. There must be operations she could have—skin grafts—you know."

"Look, I don't know what Mrs. Klein can do about her arm, Miss Ferguson. But one thing I know—I'll be glad to close early this evening. I'm bushed today. I've just about had it. My husband's coming here soon to pick me up for a movie. Herb always wants to make a big night of it Saturdays. I feel more like going home and going right to sleep. I feel like doing that most nights really—but you know how the fellas are—you've got to keep them happy—or I guess you've got to try and have a shot at it. Anyway when you are dry, Miss Ferguson, I'm closing down the shop."

Mrs. Klein was sweeping a rubble of cigarette stubs, pins, and hair clippings off the floor. Angeline was pulling down the blinds. Perspiration poured down the exhausted faces of the two women. The over-heated air was stale with the smell of singed hair, old cigarette smoke, and sickly, perfumed spray.

"Jesus! Well, I guess that's it for today, and it's Sunday tomorrow thank God!"

Angeline collapsed into a chair and stared at the great piles of dye-stained towels, the dirty ashtrays, the tattered magazines, and the innumerable bottles of lacquer, nail-polish, and lotion which lay scattered about without their tops.

"Oh boy!" Angeline looked across her beauty salon into one of the many mirrors and spoke to a reflection of Mrs. Klein. "Leave it! Oh for Christ's sake just leave it, Mrs. Klein! You don't have to bother with all that goddam mess. Now that all the clients have gone there's something I've got to speak to you about. My husband's coming here soon to pick me up for a movie—so I guess I'll have to make it quick."

Mrs. Klein stopped sweeping and turned round. "What do you want to say to me, Angeline?"

"Look," Angeline coughed, "look, I know that you've had a pretty tough time and all that—but gee, Mrs. Klein—I guess I've still gotta say something to you that you won't be too crazy about."

Mrs. Klein's dark smudged eyes stared at Angeline. "So what do you want to say?"

"Gee, Mrs. Klein. I really hate to do this. I know that it may be a kind of a sensitive subject with you—but there's something I've just gotta say to you. If you want to come in to give me a hand here on Saturdays—you've really gotta keep down your sleeves."

Mrs. Klein stood very stiffly with her finger tightly gripping the handle of her broom. "But I only roll up my sleeves when I have to do the rinses, Angeline."

Angeline bustled over to her and slapped her on the back. "Gee I know that, Mrs. Klein. I've been in this business for longer than I'd like to tell you. You don't need to tell Angeline why you roll up your sleeves. You think I don't know what it is to be handling these lousy dyes? But boy! I really hate to have to make a point of it like this. I mean I just love having you working here Saturdays. It's like it's a favor for you, and it's a favor for me. Right? But I have to think of the customers. You see they come to Angeline's because they like a kind of a comfortable atmosphere. Look, why's the place always full weekends? I mean there's pretty heavy competition in this line of business. Jesus! And I'm just not kidding you. But the girls still keep coming in here because they know that Angeline can always make them laugh, Angeline can always make them feel good. Angeline's is a kind of a friendly neighborhood place and they like that. And mostly we get a pretty decent class of person coming in here. It's not often that someone with a headful of fleas comes to Angeline's.

Angeline reached out nervously for one of her hair-rollers. She took a lock of her own dry over-bleached hair and rolled it deftly into a curl and sprayed it with setting-lotion.

"Look, Mrs. Klein, if it was just me it would be different. I have a different point of view. I mean when we are both alone in the shop, you can roll your sleeves up all you like. You know Angeline,

Mrs. Klein. She's been around, she isn't going to turn a hair. She understands that you've had yourself a pretty rough deal and all that. But you know that some of my customers haven't exactly found that life's been all milk and roses either, Mrs. Klein. And they come to Angeline's—to relax—to have a set—to have a touch up—to have themselves a ball. So when the clients come in here I was really wondering if maybe you couldn't wear some tatty old long-sleeved gown that it wouldn't matter if you got the dyes on it. You know—some lousy old garment that who gives a damn if it gets a bit wet."

"No, Angeline," Mrs. Klein shook her head, "no, I certainly don't see myself working with wet sleeves dripping all over the customers' faces."

"Gee, Mrs. Klein, I guess you are right. Maybe that wouldn't be too practical. Oh boy! I guess you are right. I really hate to say all this to you. But it's just the customers. You know what I mean, Mrs. Klein. In this business you have to keep thinking about the customers. You are stuck with them. Right? And you see when you are giving a client a rinse, Mrs. Klein—your arms are so near them. That's the real problem." Angeline was starting to stutter. "I mean—like—your arms are really in their face. Look," she said quickly, "it's not the thing itself. I mean the thing itself doesn't look so bad. I mean it's just a bunch of numbers. But it's the idea. You can understand that. And if the customers aren't comfortable—you can't be comfortable. You know that Mrs. Klein."

"I don't quite understand what you want me to do, Angeline."

"Look, Mrs. Klein. You seem like a very nice woman—a very serious type of person. And it seems like you've gotten yourself a good European education which is more than most of us. So you know what I really think, Mrs. Klein? You are just wasting yourself here. Yes, Mrs. Klein—that's what I think, even if I seem to be speaking against my own shop. You oughta get yourself something with a future like."

"So you don't want me to help out here next Saturday, Angeline?"

"Gee, Mrs. Klein—I'm not saying that, Mrs. Klein. All I'm trying to say is that it would be better for you—not for me—but for you—if you got yourself some kind of weekend work that could really get you places."

"If that's how you feel, Angeline." Mrs. Klein went to get her coat and hat.

"I'd like to settle what I owe you, Mrs. Klein." Angeline rumbled feverishly in her pocket and brought out a few dollars. She started forward to hand them to Mrs. Klein, but lost her nerve and put them down on the side of a basin.

Mrs. Klein looked at the money, hesitated, and then decided to ignore it, and she started walking slowly out of the beauty salon through the rows of Angeline's unoccupied, old, battered hair dryers which stood like desolate science-fiction equipment abandoned somewhere in space.

"I hope that you'll drop by and see us some time, Mrs. Klein. I'll always be glad to give you some highlights or a set. I won't charge you. You know that."

Mrs. Klein seemed not have heard.

"Mrs. Klein! You know that one of my clients was saying today that there are wonderful operations you can have nowadays. Have you ever thought of having an operation—a skin graft, Mrs. Klein?"

"I've had a lot of operations. I'm not having anymore operations, Angeline."

As Mrs. Klein went out through the glass door, a big-shouldered, hearty man with a crew cut and a very heavy jaw pushed past her and came into the shop.

"Hi honey! What's going on? Why are you looking so worried? Was that one of the customers I just saw going out? Has she been giving you trouble? What's her problem? She didn't like her hair? She looked all het up."

"That wasn't one of the customers, Herb. That was the woman that I got to help out Saturdays. I just fired her."

"You just fired her, Angeline!"

Herb shrugged and threw out his huge arms in a gesture of despair. "What the Hell did you do that for, honey? You know you've been losing a helluva lot of customers the way things have been going Saturdays, and you've been just knocking yourself out."

Angeline sat down in front of one of her mirrors and mechanically started to tease her bright bleached fringe.

"Wouldn't you know it!" she said. "Wouldn't you know that Angeline would have all the luck! I mean listen to this, Herb. Just how many people try to get someone to help them out Saturdays in their beauty salon, and they get a woman turning up with big, black, concentration camp numbers stamped the whole way down her arm? I mean can you beat that, Herb? Isn't that just about the end?"

"Is that why you fired her, Angey?" Herb's heavy-jawed face became suddenly very red. "You must be kidding, Angeline! You fired someone just because they have a few numbers on their arms? I just don't get it. Are you out of your mind? How come you did a crazy thing like that?"

"Look, Herb," Angeline said irritably, "just don't start on me now for Christ's sake! I feel like I've really had it today, and I don't need you to put on the Big-Hearted-Joe act, and all that crap. I'm trying to run a beauty parlor—get it? I'm not the Salvation Army. I'm trying to run a beauty parlor—so get that through your thick skull, Herb honey!"

"I don't get it, Angeline."

Herb's face became even redder and he glared at his wife's hair dryers as though they were an enemy. "I just don't understand how your mind works, Angeline. Every Saturday you say you are too tired to enjoy a movie—and too tired to enjoy anything else too—and you know damn well what I'm talking about. And then you get someone to help you out Saturdays—someone who knows the work—and the first thing you do is to go and fire them for some goddam stupid reason which is all up in your own head."

Herb kicked a copy of *Vogue* which was lying on the floor. "I don't know, honey," he muttered. "But boy, you better watch it! Don't come to me next Saturday telling me that you feel like you can't hardly stand up. Sometimes I think that you just try to make yourself exhausted, Angeline, and a guy can get pretty fed up with that kind of crap. To have to live with someone who always feels tired all the time—I mean Jesus! What kind of a life's that for anyone?"

Herb gave the *Vogue* another kick. "I'm just telling you something, Angeline. Just don't count on me too much—and boy I really mean that. A guy who works late most nights of the week wants someone who isn't too tired to enjoy things Saturdays. And one of these days he might just say to Hell with it—and go and find himself someone else—someone who feels like they can stand up!"

Angeline slumped in her chair and held her head with its tall helmet of teased golden hair in her hands. "For Christ's sake, Herb—lay off me, can't you? Why are you always like that, Herb? Why do you always have to hit a person when they are down? Don't get mad at me, Herb. Look, I'll get someone else for Saturdays—I mean I guess I will. You know when you have something happen to you like I did today—it's funny—but you kind of lose your confidence. You start to think that everyone's going to have something the matter, so that you can't possibly keep them. I couldn't keep that woman today. Please, Herb—be fair. You're the one who's always telling me that I've got to make Angeline's into the kind of place where all girls can come in and just die laughing."

Angeline waved her plump little dye-stained hands as she pleaded with her husband. "Look—use your nut, Herb. If you had seen that woman's arm—you wouldn't be so mad at me. Of course I said to her that it didn't look so bad. I mean you have to say that—don't you? But Jesus, Herb! You should have seen the size of her numbers. They were like something you see on the backsides of a bunch of cattle. And it wasn't only her brand either. Her whole arm looked all kind of horrible and shriveled like they'd done something to her muscle. I mean Christ, Herb! You could get a customer and she just wants to relax and have her hair shampooed—and she might take a look at that arm and it would really turn her stomach. And, well, she might just figure like—who really needs it?"

"Okay. Okay. Who needs it? I'm sorry I blew my top. Please just forget it, and for Christ's sake don't let's spend the whole evening talking about it, Angeline." Herb came and sat down next to his wife and put his heavy arm round her shoulder. Angeline tried to push away his arm.

"Look, don't start messing me around, Herb. I don't feel like it right now. I don't feel like it at all. I must have been out of my mind to take that woman. If only I'd never taken her, Herb—I'd never have had to fire her. Oh boy!"

"Well, don't get yourself so excited, Angeline." Herb kissed his wife's cheek. "Maybe she didn't mind too much when you fired her. What were paying her anyway? I know your beauty parlor means everything to you, Angeline. But Jesus honey, it isn't everyone who feels they'll just die if they can't work in your shop."

Angeline's tired face twitched. "Oh Herb," she said impatiently, "that's so like you to say that—just so goddam stupid. Mrs. Klein minded—she minded alright. And you know something funny Herb? Mrs. Klein didn't mean too much to me when she first came in to work here. I only really started to feel something for her when I saw her walking out—all kind of bent, and red in the face, and upset."

Herb shrugged his huge shoulders. "Look, let's face it, Angeline. Maybe you are like that. Maybe you never really start to feel anything for anyone—not till you've got them walking out—just like you say—all kind of bent, and red in the face, and upset."

"Please Herb, I don't need your cute wisecracks. They don't make me laugh."

"I'm not kidding, Angeline. I'm not really kidding at all."

Angeline made an exasperated gesture with her fat little hands. "I don't know why you sound as though that makes it better, Herb. It just makes it quite a bit worse. But I'm not thinking about you right now, Herb. I'm thinking about Mrs. Klein. I sort of keep feeling that I didn't fire her very nicely. I guess she got me rattled. It was the way she kept staring at me with those great black eyes. She kind of made me say things to her that I never should have said."

Herb pushed his tongue into the side of his cheek as though he was sucking a gumdrop. "You sound like you're blaming her, Angeline. I know you love blaming people. I mean I'm just used to you always blaming me honey. But to blame this poor old buzzard Mrs. Klein—isn't that a bit much?"

"I'm not blaming her. Oh Jesus, Herb! Why are you always such a nit? I'm just saying that if she hadn't kept staring like that, I feel that I could have done the whole thing—sort of much better."

Herb gave his wife's back a tolerant clap. "Look, it's not all that easy to fire anyone nicely, Angeline. So forget Mrs. Klein—forget the whole business. It was just one of those things."

"It certainly was, Herb." Angeline shook her head and rolled her eyes up to the ceiling. "You should have seen what happened here today in the shop. Oh boy! Did Mrs. Klein louse up the atmosphere! And I just can't let that happen, Herb. Look—don't kid around—you need the shop—and I need the shop. What are you getting every week Herb? A guy who's nearly fifty and he's working as a soda jerk—what's he ever going to get? I mean Jesus, Herb! We're not getting any younger. Sometimes when I wake up in the night everything really scares me. The shop's all we've got. I've knocked myself out for the shop. I just can't let anything hurt the shop."

"Okay. Okay." Herb again kissed his wife's cheek. "The way things are going—gee—I guess you may be right. You certainly understand the beauty business better than I do, Angey. I guess it's a woman's world and a guy can really get lost in that set-up. So let's just both relax a bit, Angeline. And for Christ's sake let's forget about that woman. Okay—so she didn't work out. Okay—so you fired her. I mean she's gone, hasn't she? So why waste the whole evening beefing about it? You've got what you wanted."

"Oh boy!" Angeline shook her head, "When you say things like that, Herb, sometimes I wonder if you understand anything at all."

"Then forget it. I keep telling you I'm just sick to death of talking about the whole business. Relax. Oh, for Christ's sake relax, Angeline. Look—it's Saturday baby! Let's go out and have a few drinks and try to have ourselves a ball. Gee! You know something? I just love your hair today, Angey. It really looks terrific. One thing about a wife who's a professional—she never lets you get tired of her hair. It always looks great and it's never the same two days running! And boy, it smells pretty good too. It's crazy, Angeline! Your hair always kind of excites me!"

Herb leaned over and whispered in his wife's ear. "You know what I'd like to do, Angey? I'd like to come in your hair. I'd like to come in your hair right now, baby!"

Angeline suddenly started to cry. Her husband quickly stroked her brilliant dry gold hair. "For Christ's sake! What's the matter with you, Angey? I guess you're still upset because I acted so unpleasant when you first told me you'd fired that character. You know I didn't mean what I said about finding myself a new woman for Saturdays. I only said that because I was so mad at you. You know how I really feel about you, Angey. Do you want to feel how hard you've made me right now. Just put your hand on me. Sometimes I get like that just thinking about you. You've got nothing to cry for, Angeline. Most wives start complaining when they've been married as long as you have, Angey. But boy! You sure can't complain about me, Angeline. I still want to screw you just as much as I ever did. All my mother's people are Italians—so I guess I'm kind of hot-blooded. I just wish that your goddam shop didn't make you feel so tired all the time. And Jesus! I wish you'd put your hand on me now, honey. You've got me so hotted up!"

Angeline wiped her eyes with a handkerchief. "Look, Herb—I told you already the shop's all I've got. And today everything's been so lousy here in the shop—that I don't feel like putting my hand anywhere. Can't you get that?"

Angeline blew her nose, and her exhausted little swollen eyes stared aggressively at her husband. "You know something, Herb? You're so hooked on the idea that you're so hot-blooded, and special, and Italian, that you just never seem to take it in that sometimes a person can have something quite different on their mind. Okay—so you've got yourself all hard, Herb. Okay—so you've got yourself all hotted up. But who needs it, Herb? Who needs it?"

Angeline tried to get up from her chair. "Oh Hell now, Herb! Don't start pulling me around for Christ's sake—and get your big face out of my face! Jesus, Herb! Now take it easy. What's the matter with you? You know we can't do it here in the shop. Now just lay off for God's sake—and get your great paws off me—and let me breathe! Don't you understand I don't feel tired—but I don't feel like doing it right now—I don't feel like doing it at all. Right now, Herb—I need you to screw me—just about like I need a hole in the head. I feel so kind of shook up."

Angeline wrenched herself away from her husband and tears which were black with mascara trickled down her tired, pudgy cheeks. "Look—find yourself someone new, Herb. I'm not stopping you. I've never tried to stop you. But go ahead and do it, Herb. Don't just keep talking about it—and don't kid around. I know you think that you're such a big ballsy guy that all the girls are after you—but you've got a face like a Virginia ham, Herb—and your belly is starting to spill all over your belt—and it sure doesn't look like you're going to be the next President yet. So be a bit realistic—and cut out all the crap. It isn't everybody that's going to be crazy for you, Herb. And I want to know—who? I want to know—just exactly who—you are ever going to find? Please don't put on that act with me again, honey. I don't have the patience. And boy—I'm telling you something—you've got to lay off me today, Herb. I feel very bad today. I feel very bad indeed. And I just wish that you could get that through your great big hot-blooded head. It was that woman turning up like that. Wouldn't you know it would have to happen to Angeline? And wouldn't you know she'd end up making me feel like a lousy son of a bitch? Oh boy!"

"Oh to Hell with that woman! To Hell with your shop!" Herb jumped up and started pacing agitatedly up and down the aisle formed by his wife's hair-dryers. "Your shop certainly always comes first with you, Angeline. Jesus Christ Almighty!"

Herb suddenly noticed the money that Mrs. Klein had left. "And what the fuck are those dollar bills doing there on that basin? Oh Jesus! I get it . . . I think I really get it. You get dollars for your tips—and I just get dimes and quarters. I guess that's one more thing for you to throw in my face, Angeline. Jesus Christ Almighty!"

"Cut out the sob-stuff, Herb." Angeline started to tidy her hair. "I just don't feel like telling you about that money. But you know something useful you can do, my big Herb honey! You can fetch me that little pile of dough—and then we're getting the Hell out of here I'm telling you. You know what I need? All that I need right now is a very stiff drink, Herb. Oh boy! Everything just stinks and it seems like some people have all the luck."

Please Baby Don't Cry

The old woman usually stayed in her room. Now that his wife was in the hospital she was frisking round his kitchen in a frilly nylon wrap and her hair was done up in curlers. Lou Alton noticed that his mother-in-law's wizened little face looked animated, rested, almost rosy. She seemed rejuvenated by her daughter's operation.

"Do you think she should have done it, Lou?" she asked him.

"I wouldn't know."

"I guess it must be all over. They were going to do it early."

"I guess so." The old woman was right. It must be all over. The surgeons must have already finished their stitch-work on the sagging skin of those large bitter eyes.

"You know I just can't wait to see her," his mother-in-law said.

"I just bet you can't."

"I don't imagine that she will let me go to visit her in the hospital." The old woman's voice sounded suddenly plaintive. "She's always acted mean with me. It's funny, you know, Lou. Cyd and I have always been very close—but we have never really got on. I guess you may have noticed it."

He had most certainly noticed it. He had been extremely surprised three months ago when his wife suddenly told him that she had arranged for her mother to live with them. "But you have always told me that you couldn't stand her!" "What do you want me to do with her, for Christ's sake?" Cyd had shouted. "Shove her down the garbage-disposal?" He found out later that his mother-in-law had just been fired from her job in one of the Hollywood film studios where she had worked for some years as a telephone operator. She had been caught selling indiscreet items to the fan magazines. She gathered her information by listening in to the private telephone conversations of the Stars.

"She's house-trained," his wife had said to him. "She won't be any bother." The old woman had certainly been very little bother. She very rarely came out of her room. She shuffled out occasionally and made herself a furtive piece of toast in the kitchen. Then she shuffled discreetly back and shut the door.

"What on earth does she do with herself shut up in that room all day?" He often asked Cyd.

"What the Hell do you care? She's not bothering you." He had still been bothered by her silence, by the faint little scuffling sounds that he heard sometimes in the night. His mother-in-law reminded him of some sick old animal crouching alone behind her shut door.

"She would be better off in a dogs' home," he told Cyd. "Why don't you ever speak one word to her? You could ask her to join us sometimes for a drink, or even a meal. It certainly wouldn't kill you."

"You can speak to her if you are so crazy about her," she always answered. "Have all your meals with the old cunt. I'm not stopping you."

The old woman had developed an abscess. She crept silently round the house for a couple of days with her swollen face wrapped up in a tea-cloth. Finally Cyd drove her into Beverly Hills to get her tooth pulled. He had suddenly gone into the old woman's room. It smelled so stale and perfumed. She hadn't opened her windows since she had arrived. He had gone through all her drawers. He had felt like a sleepwalker. He was looking for something. It was important. He had no idea why. He would only know what it was when he found it. Among her musty stays and nightdresses he had found a large pile of papers. He had picked out a page. The handwriting was the thin scratch of a ballpoint. "THE LAST WILL AND TESTAMENT OF ALICE ROSE MARTINI. To my daughter Cyd. Now that I am dead, Cyd, I feel I can say so much to you. I have wanted to say so much for so long but I knew you would not want to listen. I hate leaving you knowing that everything is going so bad for you. I never thought that Lou was right. You used to have so much to offer. As a girl you had looks, you had so much personality. You could have really gone anywhere. You could have made it really big in movies. I don't listen, but I can't help hearing when the house is quiet at night. And then after all these years seeing you still with no kids. I just can't help putting two and two together. He's not really a man. I knew it the moment I first set eyes on him. And you deserve a real man if anyone does. Anyway—everything I have I leave to you. I don't have much as you know. Life was pretty tough on me and your father acted like a louse. I have always had to work all my life. I wanted you to have nice things—Education—all the things I never had. Now when I see the life you lead with Lou I wonder if it was all worth it. Anyway, I leave you the tortoise-shell combs that belonged to Mother. I leave you the brown chair, the one that I brought with me, the one that you now have in your living room. I notice that you behave as if it was yours already. You never even seem to try to stop Lou putting up his feet on it. The cushions are getting really ruined. I haven't said anything. But I can't help minding rather. Anyway, now that it is really yours at last maybe you will take more care with it . . ."

He found many other drafts. "Dear Cyd . . ." The old spider sitting in her room spinning her wills. "He's not really a man." And her daughter most certainly was not really a woman—that was weak—it merely showed she had known where to hit him. He had never mentioned the wills to Cyd. He wondered sometimes what she would think of them. She would certainly not want to let him know. She would shrug of course, smile sarcastically with one eyebrow raised. "So what about them for Christ's sake? Do they really bother you?"

"Can I fix you a nice little breakfast, Lou?" his mother-in-law was now asking him. She had become so bold now that her daughter was in the hospital. She was not making herself any more dry little pieces of toast. She was frying herself eggs, and bacon, and sausages. She was bending over the pan and inhaling the fumes of the fat. She was squeezing herself fresh orange juice, smearing great dollops of jam on her cereal. She was even making herself waffles with a waffle-iron. Did he really need Cyd? Alice Rose Martini must surely be asking herself the same question. Would the two of them really be happier just making a life of it together? The old woman could go on making her wills. He could go on going to the office. Meals would certainly be very much better. Cyd resented even opening a can. Alice Rose Martini really had a far more cheerful disposition than her daughter. At least she seemed to be really enjoying her waffle. She was making designs on it with syrup, golden spirals, great ornate curlicues. Cyd just sat all day on the Swedish sofa, smoking and drinking her martinis. She crossed and uncrossed her long thin legs and stared through the plateglass windows down to the sea.

"You know something, Lou?" The old woman's mouth was crusted golden with waffle syrup. "I didn't sleep one wink last night for worrying. I never liked to say a word to Cyd, but I really don't quite trust her doctor."

"She found him," he said.

"I never liked to say a word to you, Lou. But I just kept hoping that you would make her go to one of the really top-flight Beverly Hills guys. One of the ones that do the big Stars."

"I hardly knew a thing about it. She arranged the whole thing herself. Dot Mansville and the rest of the girls put her up to it. I always thought the whole idea was quite sick, completely crazy. All I wanted was for her to leave me out of it. I figured that it was her operation."

"She would have gone to a decent doctor if you had made her." Behind her rhinestone-encrusted spectacles the old woman's eyes glittered accusingly. "Who's going to pay for it all, for Christ's sake? She would have had to listen to you, Lou, and you know it. You are so goddam scared of her, Lou. That's always been your trouble. If anything goes wrong I swear I'll always blame you. You could have told her that it was your operation."

"I just didn't see it like that," he said. He should have seen it like that. The old buzzard was quite right. In a sense it really was his own operation. Its object, he could only assume, was the removal of himself. Before his wife could free herself from him, she had first felt bound to free herself from all the excess fatty eye-tissue which she felt tied her to him. The concept had a certain primitive grandeur. The sacrifice of the part, for the salvation of the whole.

"I guess you will be going to visit her in the hospital," Alice Rose Martini said to him.

"I guess so." The idea had not even occurred to him. He rang his office. "I won't be in today. My wife has been taken to the hospital."

"One thing I'll say for you, Lou," the old woman said, sitting down in the breakfast alcove with all her waffles and her sausages, "you work hard and you've given her a lovely home."

"I guess it's okay." He looked round the living room. It had a sofa, two steel chairs, and a lamp. It had a pile of magazines on a table. It looked as impersonal, sterile, and neat, as any hospital waiting room. It was certainly okay. It was probably as good a place as any, if you had to wait somewhere for fifteen years to have your operation.

"Why don't you give yourself a break, Lou?" the old woman asked him. "Why don't we both take it easy and maybe go down to the beach?"

"I prefer to stay here in the house," he said. He had never very much liked the beach. He had always been depressed by the flat enervated waters of the Pacific. He had very little desire to sit with his mother-in-law on the grubby sands where the homosexual muscle-boys played their perpetual ball and the bums from Santa Monica lay choking in the sun.

"What will you do with yourself here all day?" the old woman asked him.

"Hang around." He felt suddenly restless and irritable. It seemed to him now that his wife, by her one decisive attempt to defy and reverse her destiny, had totally succeeded in defying and reversing the roles of their relationship. She had finally found, in the inaction of the anesthetized, the needed action which had always eluded her in their marriage. She was now freewheeling on a hospital trolley up the corridors of a future. Now he was on the Swedish sofa, static and disgruntled with nothing to do but wait.

"Cyd's got guts," her mother said to him. "She's certainly got guts, whatever else you like to say about her. I guess she's given you a pretty rough time of it, Lou. It's sometimes hard to know what's really eating her. I guess she's never really known what she wanted. I always hoped that you would make her try to get into movies. When you married her I really hoped that you would help her find herself."

The telephone rang. It was the doctor.

"How did it go?"

"I am afraid I can't possibly tell you that until her eye bandages come off. We will know how it went when we have been able to take a thorough look at the healing." The doctor sounded brisk and bored.

"When will they come off?"

"That, I'm afraid, I can't begin to tell you, Mr. Alton. No case is ever the same. It all really depends on the healing."

"But I don't quite understand how you can tell how the healing is unless you first take the bandages off to see." He knew he sounded ridiculous, medically a moron. But he suddenly felt that the fatuous and persistent inquiries about her bandages were the very last gesture he would ever be prepared to make to his wife.

"When your wife's bandages are ready to come off, Mr. Alton, I will certainly let you know." The doctor was becoming increasingly impatient. He clearly wanted to ring off before his professional secrets could be any further threatened by the idiot curiosity of the amateur.

"When will Mrs. Alton be able to see me?" He hoped that in one incisive, surgical sentence, the doctor would tell him that it would be forever impossible. He had not the slightest desire to see Cyd with her new eyes—eyes that had been both created and bandaged by this most disagreeable brisk voice on the telephone.

"Naturally," the doctor said in the slow and heavily patient tone sometimes employed to children and the feeble-minded, "Mrs. Alton will only be able to see you after her eye-bandages have been taken off." He laughed, a dry little sarcastic puff of a laugh. "You can really hardly expect her to see you, or anyone else, while she has still got them on!"

"Are you pleased with the results of the operation, Doctor?"

"Mr. Alton, I think I have already told you that I am not prepared to give any opinion until I have taken a proper look at the healing."

After the doctor had rung off Lou Alton rang his wife at the hospital.

"Are you okay?"

"Sure I'm okay. I'm fine. I'm really great. I can't speak to you though, I am not meant to take calls today." Her voice sounded muffled and remote, as though she were speaking through a diver's tube from the bottom of the sea. It sounded oddly sensuous, friendly, and pleased. He realized then that she was still half-anesthetized.

"Shall I come to see you tomorrow?"

She grunted, purred. His words had no meaning to her. He repeated them, shouting with the frantic, unreasonable anger with which he sometimes found himself addressing the deaf.

"No, no," she whispered happily. "There's no point in your coming to see me." Her voice trailed away. "I'm absolutely fine . . ."

The next day Lou Alton drove downtown to see his wife in the hospital. A bunch of kids were demonstrating, they had tied up the traffic all the way along the Strip. He found it intolerably hot and aggravating to sit waiting for the cops to disperse them, while his car radio crackled out love tunes and his eyes streamed from the exhaust fumes of the great snakes of stationary cars. For the love of Christ, what did they think they were demonstrating? If they were against the War he was certainly with them. And he would be far more with them if they would only let the traffic move. Maybe they only wanted legalized pot. How the hell could you tell from their placards? "Love!" "Love!" "Politicians take a trip!" How could they expect anyone who was sane to join them for Love? He disliked seeing them smashed with the nightsticks. But why must the silly little pricks paint their faces with blue zodiac signs? Why must they have beads and dirty feet? Cyd had always said he was a fascist. Cyd had said he was so many things. But surely these kids themselves when they were older would not very much care to be forced to sit in the steaming Hell of a traffic snarled to a standstill, nor would they wish to have "Love!" and "Take a Trip" signs waved and cracked against their car windows—not if the only trip they were trying to make was to a downtown Los Angeles hospital—not if they were trying to visit a wife who had just completed her facial operation.

"Are you an expectant?" a nurse was asking him. He was finally in the lobby of the hospital, an ugly orange building that squatted among dusty and distressed-looking palm trees in the suffocating smog-hazed sun. "You don't want Maternity. You want Vanity." He followed the nurse down long bleak antiseptic corridors. "Vanity" seemed to be thriving. It had all the bustle and activity of a prosperous factory. Muzak blared from the ceiling. Women kept passing him; some were being wheeled, some were hobbling. He saw faces patched purple with iodine, tufted with great beards of discolored cotton-wool, faces that were a fence-work of surgical tape. He saw women with plasters covering their entire neck and shoulders. They were White Knights—they were Martians. Their only eyes were the great black holes that had been cut in their plasters.

"What's that?" he asked the nurse. He could hear screaming.

"That's a face-peeling job."

"Why the Christ don't they give her an anesthetic?"

"They did when it was done."

"Then why on earth is she still screaming?"

"You'd be screaming if you had what she's got. They have to burn so deep, you see, and they have to cover such very large areas. The problem is that you can't really keep a patient under all the time it takes for the raw under-skin to toughen. The technique was started in the war you know, they got the idea from working with burnt pilots. We used to give the face-peelings morphine but it led to addiction and complications. We've had them die on us from shock, you know. The hospital isn't responsible. The old fools do it at their own risk. They want to have skin like a baby and so they keep on coming."

His wife was lying completely motionless when he came in to her grim and strongly disinfected ward. He was shocked by the change in her appearance. Her whole body seemed to have shrunk since her operation and her skin had the ashen and papery fragility of someone very old. One of her eyes was still bandaged, which gave her face the unsuitably jaunty air of a pirate. Her other socket was so hideously swollen and disfigured that he found it almost impossible to believe that it still contained an eye at all. The surgeon's knife had cut a neat circle from under the line of her eyelashes to the arch of her eyebrows. The wound still looked fresh and bloody and against its cheerful redness huge casual stitches stood out like the legs of a giant beetle. He stood awkwardly in the middle of her ward. He could think of nothing to say.

"I expect it looks kind of awful. I haven't had the guts to look at it." Her voice was flat and low. She seemed so drained, so dispirited.

"It looks fine." She lay back on her pillows without answering. A shaft of morning sun trickled through the window of her ward and made patterns on her bed.

"I think that they have cut off all my bottom eyelashes." She was whining suddenly with the plaintive petulance of a child. "Can you see if any of them are left?" Her eyelashes had been long and silky. In her present state of physical exhaustion their loss seemed the only thing which could arouse her to any great degree of concern. He looked at the pulp of livid flesh under the eye. He looked at its thick black network of stitches.

"It's rather difficult to see." He saw her whole body twitch with nervous anger as though his inability to see any trace of her eyelashes in some way typified an ineffectuality that she had resented for so long.

"I'm expecting Dot Mansville in a little while." Her voice had regained its old aggressive crackle. "They don't like me to have more than one visitor at a time."

"Do you want me to go, then?"

"No, it's not that. It's just that I don't see much point in your staying here, hanging around."

The next day he again visited her in the hospital. His wife was still bandaged and he sensed a very great hostility emanating from the slit in the swelling which was still all that could be seen of her free eye.

"Dot Mansville and some of the girls came here yesterday," she said provocatively. "They all think I'm going to be much better once it's healed."

"Better for whom? Better for what?" He regretted his words immediately, for although he could tell that he had succeeded in wounding her, his success seemed rather unnecessary, for lying there on her pillows with her purple-jellied eye and her bandages, she looked already so badly wounded as to be almost beyond retrieval. She lay very still. When she finally spoke her voice sounded odd and muffled.

"Please don't try to make me cry, Lou. They say if I cry I'll tear my stitches and get an infection." He watched, chilled, as a bright drop of crystal water squeezed out of the tiny aperture in the mound of discolored and inflamed flesh, and slowly trickled down her blue bruised cheek.

"Please don't cry, Baby. I didn't mean to be mean." Tears immediately started gushing out of her raw pulp of a socket.

"For Christ's sake, stop!" He was shouting. "What had I better do? For Christ's sake stop before you tear your stitches and give yourself an infection! I think I'd better get the nurse!"

"How can the nurse stop me crying? How can anyone ever stop me crying now? If I get an infection, I just get an infection. What the Hell does it matter? Why the fucking Hell should I care what happens to me anymore?" The disastrous appearance of her face was intensified by her weeping. And yet as he watched her choking on her pillows, so disfigured and distressed, she repulsed him no more than she had in all the years that she had been so well-groomed, composed, and caustic, and sitting complaining on his sofa and drinking her martinis with Dot Mansville and "the girls." He saw for a moment in this eye-less, moaning, middle-aged woman some echo of the vulnerability of the nervous girl he had once wanted to protect. He saw also in the fearful distortion of the face he had once loved the squalor of this self-centered and dissatisfied personality who now through vanity had deprived itself even of eyes with which to cry. On an impulse he went over to her bed and kissed the purple festering slit from which her tears were still attempting to roll. He noticed a sweet-sour taste of disinfectant mingled with blood and salt.

"Don't cry, Baby," he said mechanically. "Please, Baby, don't cry." Baby! He thought. How ludicrous. Some baby.

His gesture seemed to please her. She shivered. She clutched at him gratefully. She threw her arms round his neck and clung to him like a child.

"How can you bear to kiss it, Lou?" she said. "I vomit if I even look at it."

"I'm sorry if I upset you," he soothed. Instantly her whole body twitched in a fierce spasm of nervous irritation. He had patronized her, disappointed, infuriated her. She wrenched herself violently away from him. "Oh cut it out for Christ's sake!" she shouted. "I'm sick to death of those lyrics. Why the Hell should you think that anything you do or say can upset me anymore? Don't you see, you fool, that I'm nearly going out of my mind because of the bandage."

"What's wrong with the bandage?"

"Nothing's wrong with the bandage, idiot! But why the fucking Hell haven't they come to take it off?"

"Should they have taken it off?" The idea had never occurred to him. He had taken the bandage's presence for granted as one of the inevitable intricacies of the whole ritualistic operation.

"Of course it should if the other one has!" Her voice rose in a scream. "Only the bastards obviously don't dare show me what's happened underneath!"

"Have you asked the nurses why it hasn't been taken off?"

"I can't ask them anything, you fool! They are all a bunch of lousy Black Power spades. And Christ if you knew how they hate the Vanity patients! They really despise us. They resent us for taking up their time, which they think should be given to the really sick. They have hardly been near me all day. And when they do come they won't say a word. So I have just been lying here hour after hour, never knowing if I have lost the sight of one eye and all my own fault."

"I'll call the doctor immediately. And for Christ's sake stop worrying. Your eye is obviously quite all right." He had no longer any very strong feeling that her eye was obviously quite all right. The bandage looked extremely sinister now that its presence was questioned. He too was now convinced that it was concealing some miserable mistake.

"There's something else!" his wife shouted to him as he was leaving her ward. "You have got to tell that fucking doctor that I will never let him take my stitches out!"

"Honey," he said. "You can't keep your stitches in forever."

"I don't care, you fool!" she was screaming again. "You can tell that doctor that I'd far rather die than ever let him take them out! He has already half-blinded me, hasn't he? Isn't that enough? Do you think I care now if I always keep my stitches in? I've been through as much as I can take! Can you imagine what it would be like to have him poking around with his tweezers in the middle of the wounds? It makes me vomit just to think of it. I just can't have anymore pain, Lou! Can't you understand that? I just can't take anymore! You have got to tell that son a bitch of a doctor that I will never let him take them out!"

"I will do what I can." He walked out into the tiled corridor in which, mingling with Muzak, he could still hear the screams of the woman with the face-peeling job. He stopped a nurse who was hurrying past with a plate of red jelly on a tray.

"My wife seems very upset. Can you give her some sedation?"

"Of course she's upset. They are all upset. Who wouldn't be upset in a dump like this? I'm upset too." She scuttled irritably away.

The doctor sounded cold and impatient when he was finally reached by telephone. "I'm afraid I haven't had time to get round to your wife today. I've been up to my neck in the theatre. I'll try and drop by tomorrow and take her eye stitches out."

"She doesn't want them taken out."

"Well, I'm afraid I really just couldn't care less whether she wants them out or not. If we leave them in much longer we are very likely to find ourselves with a very pretty little infection."

"I don't think you have quite taken in her state of mind, Doctor. She's really blowing her cool. If she has any more pain at the moment I think she might really flip."

"There may be discomfort—but there is really very little pain attached to the taking out of stitches."

"I don't think it's the pain she minds. I think it's more the idea of your touching her wounds."

"Oh well, really, Mr. Alton, I'm afraid that simply can't be helped. Your wife is a grown woman and she will just have to get herself used to the idea pretty quick. Her stitches have quite obviously got to come out and that is that."

"Could you give her a general anesthetic when she has her stitches out?"

He heard the doctor gasp. "A general anesthetic to have stitches out! Oh yes! That would be quite something! And who do you think is going to find the time to administer it to her? You might remember that your wife is not the only woman in the hospital. Has it occurred to you, Mr. Alton, that there might be other patients who might possibly have priority?"

"I will make it worth your while, Doctor. I am quite willing to pay any extra charges."

The doctor capitulated, grudgingly, as though he were humoring an unfortunate. "If it's really worth it to you, Mr. Alton, if you really want to go in for something so needlessly time-consuming and costly, I suppose I will have to go along with you. It still beats me why your wife can't make do with a local."

"Would that mean that she would have to have needles stuck into the surrounds of her eyes?"

"Naturally."

"I insist you give her a general. And there's just one other thing, Doctor." The doctor seemed about to ring off. "Why hasn't her second bandage come off?"

"We were not quite satisfied with the healing."

"Is that quite customary?"

"Under the circumstances, yes. You know, of course, that we ran into complications."

"I didn't know. How could I possibly know? What precisely were the complications?"

"Well, to complete a satisfactory drainage of the tissue under her brows, we had to cut away more fatty surplus than is generally our practice. The removal of the excess under the eye itself went more or less as intended."

"Does that mean that the eye under the bandage has been damaged?"

"No more so than the eye which is at present unbandaged. The sight of both will be completely unaffected if that's what you are getting at. She will, of course, have always just one problem. She will never, of course, quite be able to close her eyes at night."

"Could you possibly be more explicit, Doctor? What exactly do you mean—never quite close her eyes at night."

"Exactly what I said. As you know we had to drag all the skin above her eyes upwards, in order to stitch it to the eyebrow line where her scars would not show. And then as I told you she had quite a really astounding amount of excess fatty tissue. We had no choice. We had to cut it away. Naturally we couldn't do this without seriously restricting the mobility of her eyelids. But there was simply no other way of giving her that really taut and youthful look she wanted. I don't think she should be too bothered by it. In my experience women don't usually care too much about how they look when they are sleeping. Most of them become accustomed to the light after a few months. If they find it a problem they simply wear an eye mask. There is really one thing that I will have to warn your wife—she may of course have a little trouble with formation."

"Formation?"

"Naturally the inability to shut her eyes when she sleeps may result in some sort of matinal formation on the over-exposed eyeball, a congested film of dust, eye-mucous, etc. She will be able to get rid of it, of course, by bathing her eyes very thoroughly every morning with Optrex or boracic. I think that in general both yourself and Mrs. Alton will be very satisfied with the results of the operation. You will certainly find that she has quite an improved appearance."

"Is there nothing you can do to make it possible for her to close her eyes at night, Doctor?"

"Nothing I am afraid, Mr. Alton. When you are dealing with something as delicate as eye tissue, you can't really replace what is cut away."

Lou Alton started walking slowly back to his wife's ward. He turned suddenly and went back to the hospital lobby. He wanted to talk to someone. A nurse. Anyone. Another Vanity patient. He went to a telephone and rang his wife's mother.

"How is she?" He heard the greedy throb of the old woman's excitement. He thought of waffle syrup.

"She's fine."

"How does she look?"

"Oh, she really looks magnificent."

"Oh gee! Isn't that terrific! I bet she looks just gorgeous! I bet she's never looked cuter. I just can't wait to see her."

"She's never looked better. She's probably never had more to offer."

"Well, isn't that quite something? The things they can do nowadays. It's really just fantastic. I guess she should have had it done much sooner."

"Maybe she should have had it done at birth," he said. "These things are so very hard to say."

"Some of them have started quite late, you know," the old woman said.

"Some of what have started late?" His mind was working slowly.

"The Big Names, of course," she said impatiently. "Some of the really top-flight Stars."

"I guess they have. I have never really thought about that."

"I guess that you had better look out now, Lou!" The old woman's voice sounded suddenly waggish. "You have had her to yourself for quite a long time, you know."

"I most certainly have." A stream of images flashed through his brain like the ugly rising past of a drowning man.

"Well, I must say you don't sound too overjoyed, Lou. Maybe you never really wanted her operation to work out too well. Maybe you thought that you were sitting pretty. Maybe you just wanted for things to go on staying that way."

"Maybe." He was wondering what he would tell his wife when he next saw her. He decided that he would tell her that the sight of her bandaged eye was completely unaffected, that she would be totally unconscious during the removal of her stitches. How was he to tell her that her eyes would never again close—that in the nights they would stare forever in the darkness as though they searched even in sleep for the solution that had always eluded them in waking?

Matron

She always liked to boast that never once in her long career had she ever made "exceptions." In her professional capacity she had insisted that everything be done precisely to the rule. Once one started to make "exceptions" Matron was convinced that one invited future chaos, the last thing she saw as desirable while she was running a hospital ward.

Yet she had made a monumental "exception" in the case of Mrs. Appleseed. She admitted it to herself. She thought about it ceaselessly when she went home at night. Her own behavior both startled and appalled her.

When Matron was off-duty she liked to review everything that had occurred while she had been on duty. A perfectionist, Matron demanded the very highest level of conduct in her hospital. She therefore submitted all her daily actions to the most ruthless of mental court-martials. Only if she was viciously self-critical did she feel entitled to behave to others with her renowned severity.

Matron had learnt how to tyrannize the hospital personnel. She had forced them to address her as "Matron" even though the title was anachronistic. "Matron" had a force and a resonance that she saw as hopelessly lacking in the feeble newfangled "Sister" that was currently in usage. She was quite aware that behind her back they called her the "Snorting Dragon" and she was proud of her nickname for she believed that, unless you inspired fear, it was impossible to assert constructive authority.

She was famous for her tantrums. A lot of her ferocity was bluff, for she believed that a capacity for pretence was essential to her calling. The fury Matron liked to display whenever she discovered a sloppiness, or a disobedience, was often hardly felt by her. Perversely, it was all the more frightening for that very reason. Her rages were stemmed from her sense of duty rather than emotion.

In the hours when Matron was off-duty she went back to her functional flatlet in Swiss Cottage and lay down on her bed. She never took off her uniform while she was resting although she was scrupulously clean in her habits and always changed into a fresh uniform twice a day. She removed her elastic belt, and she loosened her collar. She took off her cap and placed it on the little bedside table that held her lamp and a photograph of her adored dead father wearing his military uniform. She liked to place her headdress in front of him every night as if it was an offering.

The idea of wearing a nightgown was ridiculous to Matron. She always lay on top of her bed since she disliked the constricting sensation of lying between sheets. If it was cold in the winter, she covered herself with a blanket. She felt comfortable in her uniform for it gave her the feeling that, like a dozing sentry, she was ever ready to be on call if any emergency demanded it.

Lying flat on her back on her bed, Matron liked to drift into a half sleep while she listened to classical music. She found it pleasant to rest her feet which were always painful and swollen from her ceaseless coverage of the long corridors of the hospital. She knew little about music, but when she turned on her radio, she found it soothing after the clang and the hurly-burly of the ward.

She felt it was lucky that she was a woman who needed little sleep. If she stretched out for only a few hours, she could get up feeling just as refreshed and ready to resume work as if she had spent the whole night sleeping. But in the last few weeks her periods of relaxation had been ruined by a tormenting sense of her own unworthiness. Recently when Matron got to the end of the day she found it hard to believe that yet another night had come and still she seemed to be getting away with it—that the thing she most dreaded had still not happened—that no one had yet accused her and made the unanswerable complaint. It couldn't go on forever like this. She saw her own lapse as much too horrifying. It was also much too public. She knew it was useless to hope that terror of her temper and her olympian air of authority would blind forever all the doctors, the nurses, and the patients, to her disgraceful aberration. They were not paralyzed rabbits, too dazzled by the ferocious blaze of the headlights to see the dark silhouette of the car.

Feeling irritable and anxious lying resting on her bed, her mind whirled like the propellers of a plane as she tried to think up ways to defend her action if anyone should ask for an explanation.

For five long weeks now Matron had allowed Mrs. Appleseed to eat not only breakfast and lunch but also supper sitting beside her husband's bed in the ward. Admittedly Mrs. Appleseed rarely took more than a mouthful when the nurses carried these meals to her on plastic mushroom-colored trays. But for Matron that fact was little consolation. All she could think about was the enormity of the "exception."

It had always been one of her most fiercely held rules that no visitors to the hospital were to be allowed to taste one single crumb of the patient's food. Once she was to allow visitors to start dropping in to have a free meal at the hospital's expense, Matron could only visualize a pattern of exploitative behavior that would expand until the situation became a nightmare. The patients were almost invariably unhungry. Matron saw the visitors of patients as dangerously healthy, all too often young, therefore potentially very hungry indeed. If she was ever once to allow some relative to eat the hospital food that had been left untouched by a patient, then, in Matron's view, there would never be an end to it. Very soon she would have the vaguest of acquaintances dropping in to the hospital to pick up a free lunch or a supper.

To Matron, such a prospect seemed horrific. If she was to allow her ward to be treated as if it was a soup kitchen, she visualized conditions during visiting hours becoming like those in the Underground in the rush hour. All standards of hygiene would instantly drop to danger point. Her nurses would be unable to fulfill their duties for it would become impossible for them to wheel the emergency stretcher-cases through the greedy freeloading throngs.

It was this terrible hallucinatory vision which had made Matron act so harshly to the shaggy-haired young man two months ago. She happened to be making a round of the ward, when she had caught a young man with ill-cut hair eating his mother's custard. His mouth had been full of it when she came storming up behind him and surprised him.

Matron had deliberately raised her voice so that her tone resembled that of a drill-sergeant. She had felt it was immensely important that she should draw as much attention to the incident as possible. She ordered the young man to spit out the custard on a plate. She gave him warning that if he refused to do what she asked, she would make him leave the hospital immediately. She would also give instructions that never again would he be allowed to visit his mother in the ward.

The young man had looked utterly terrified, seeing her looming there above him, blindingly white in her uniform, with blazing blue gimlet eyes. Matron was a very tall woman. She had a particularly massive build and the muscular shoulders of a pugilist. Her victim was weedy and hollow-chested, a deprived-looking young man. Matron had not enjoyed the feeling that she was almost twice the size that he was. Rules from her schooldays still had a strong influence on her, and secretly she had felt quite uncomfortable remembering the old tenet that it was unsporting to attack anyone much smaller than oneself.

She attacked him all the same. She had seen his humiliation as she forced him to cough up his yellow smear of custard while the other visitors and the patients, and various doctors stared at him with the piously horrified, yet perversely pleased, expression of children as they watch another child being smacked.

The young man went scarlet in the face. Matron had hated to see the way she had made him blush. Yet she still felt that it was urgent that he be made into an example. As Matron saw it, the young man was a thief. As a thief he therefore had to be branded.

The young man's mother was under such heavy sedation, she was unaware of her son's public disgrace. Matron had been relieved about that. Any form of emotional upset was rarely in the interests of a patient.

She had noticed that the young man seemed to be extremely attached to his mother, for he came to see her every day and he often left the ward in tears. He was clearly in an over-agitated state and with good reason, for the unfortunate woman's prognosis was extremely poor. Matron tried to take all this into account when she reviewed her treatment of him later that night. When she was alone, she was willing to view his behavior with more leniency. Maybe when he'd taken that custard, it had been a nervous and compulsive gesture. His mother was hardly capable of saying a word to him when he visited her husband whose eyes were invariably closed. Matron kept praying that Mr. Appleseed would open his eyes, for then there would be a hope that all those plastic trays with their varying dishes of stodgy scrambles, their plates of mince and brussels, their bowls of melted ice cream might seem to be intended for him. If Mr. Appleseed would just occasionally open an eye, it might possibly deceive the other patients and their visitors. But even in the most unlikely event that Mr. Appleseed should become quite wide awake, although outsiders might be fooled, it would never fool the nurses and the doctors. All of them knew that Mr. Appleseed's nourishment was now entirely intravenous. All of them knew that it was Matron herself who had given the order that Mrs. Appleseed be given three meals a day on a tray.

Nurse Sullivan had been present when Matron suffered what

she could only describe to herself as her "seizure." Mrs. Appleseed had been sitting for the last three days by her husband's bed. At night she slept in a little guest room in the hospital. There was nothing to trouble Matron about that. It was not irregular. Close relatives of patients who were not expected to last very long were often given permission to sleep in the hospital. Mrs. Appleseed lived somewhere way out over the river on the other side of London. She had stated, in her mousy little way, that she longed to be there to close her husband's eyes. Mr. Appleseed's eyes were shut anyway, but Matron long ago had learnt to accept that bereaved relatives tended to set great sentimental store on the idea of closing their loved one's eyelids. If Mr. Appleseed was to start to fail in the night, London public transportation being what it was, it would be quite impossible for the hospital to notify Mrs. Appleseed and arrange for her to get to the hospital in time. Therefore Matron had given the little old lady permission to sleep in the guest room. Mrs. Appleseed's round cherubic face beamed with astonishment and pleasure. "Oh, thank you, Matron," she had kept repeating like a child.

It was not Mr. Appleseed's free bed, it was her meals, which Matron saw as criminal. When relatives made use of the hospital's sleeping facilitics, she had always insisted they provide their own food. They were made to go out to the local cafeteria—to pick up a sandwich. The way that resident relatives fed themselves was out of Matron's jurisdiction. She did not feel they should try to make it her concern. All she cared about was that they should recognize that exactly the same rules applied to them, as applied to non-resident visitors. Just because they had been granted a bed, they had no right to expect to be treated as the hospital's non-paying guests.

Mrs. Appleseed had sat for three whole days and for the best part of three whole nights beside Mr. Appleseed's bed, before Matron had her moment of insanity. Later when Matron tried to analyze the reasons for her own astonishing collapse of principle, she wondered if she could blame it on Mrs. Appleseed's appearance. Mrs. Appleseed was an old lady with an exceptionally attractive face and manner. Insofar as a woman in her early seventies can be described as lovely, Matron felt that Mrs. Appleseed could be described that way. Her beauty came from a sweetness of expression, the curves of her round cheeks gave an impression of gentleness and generosity. Her eyes were still clear in a way that was rare for a woman of her age, and although she was obviously grief-stricken at the desperate condition of her husband, they expressed no bitterness. When they stared at his dying face they showed nothing but tenderness and a resignation which had dignity and calm.

Although she was an extremely busy woman, Matron always found the time to examine the conduct and appearance of all visitors who came to the ward. She felt it was important to get a personal impression of every single individual who came into her section of the hospital. Sometimes she got such an unfavorable picture that she decided their visits were detrimental to the medical progress of her patients. She then gave obscure scientific reasons to make certain they never recurred.

She had been pleased to notice that Mrs. Appleseed made very little effort to talk to her husband. Matron had seen far too many upset and idiotic women who kept up a relentless patter of inconsequential conversation to patients who were in a state of near-coma. Mrs. Appleseed was obviously sensible. She seemed quite aware that the effort of speaking was exhausting for the ill. On the rare occasion that Mr. Appleseed's lips flickered, she always asked him the same question, but she made it clear that she only spoke to reassure him of her presence and expected no answer.

"How do you feel Harry?" Mrs. Appleseed murmured.

"Poorly," he always whispered. Mrs. Appleseed then leant over and gently stroked his limp and blue-veined hand.

From the start Matron had got a very favorable impression of Mrs. Appleseed's conduct as judged within a hospital context. But innumerable other visitors had behaved with just as much good sense and decorum.

The only feeble excuse the Matron found when she thought about her own behavior, was that at the uniquely discreditable moment when she had first made an "exception" of Mrs. Appleseed, she never could have guessed that Mr. Appleseed was going to live so long. On this point she couldn't blame herself. No one had predicted it. Certainly none of his doctors. Matron had looked at Mr. Appleseed's X-rays the very same morning she had committed her act of irresponsible injustice. Hardly an organ in the poor old man's body was functioning. No one seeing those X-rays could have suspected that Mr. Appleseed was going to turn out to be one of those lingerers, one of those rare and inexplicable cases that defy the dictates of science. No one could have foreseen that he would still be in the hospital five weeks later, that Mrs. Appleseed would have been given more free meals than Matron could bear to count.

Matron had deliberately gone over to talk to Mrs. Appleseed just before she gave her feckless and self-destructive permission. It was her practice to give a little warning to the relatives of patients whom she judged to be dying. Often she discovered that relatives were blindly optimistic as to the chances of the people to whom they were attached. If they were given no warning that death was imminent, Matron had learnt from experience that they reacted to it with much more hysteria and shock.

"This must be a very sad moment for you," Matron said to Mrs. Appleseed. She had judged this to be a tactful opening to an unpleasant and painful conversation. By giving Mrs. Appleseed her sympathy, she was trying to make the old lady grasp that from a medical standpoint she offered her no hope.

"Oh yes . . . It's a tragic moment for me . . . Poor Harry . . . I never believed I would see him in a state like this."

"Have you been married long?" Matron asked.

"Since we were both seventeen," Mrs. Appleseed whispered. "Well, that's not quite true . . . because we courted for two years. Things went slower in those days . . . Actually we didn't get married until we were both nineteen. You must be busy, Matron, I hope I'm not keeping you. I don't know why I'm telling you all this."

"I imagine that you are going to miss him," Matron found herself examining the face of Mr. Appleseed as if hoping to find behind the corpse-like mask of this wheezing, dying old man, the lost features of the boy who had courted Mrs. Appleseed so long ago.

"I'm certainly going to miss him, Matron. Once he goes—I sometimes wonder if I'll see much point in going on. He's such a wonderful man. It's all because of him I've had such a wonderful life." Mrs. Appleseed spoke with sad but dignified simplicity. Just for a moment her voice quavered and then she made an obvious effort to regain her composure.

"One of us had to go first in the end," she said. "We always dreaded the idea of that. We used to talk about it quite a lot. I know Harry secretly hoped that he would be the first. I always secretly hoped that the first to go would be me. And we both knew it was very wrong to hope for that. We both knew it was horribly selfish."

Matron had never been married. She had never had the slightest wish to be married. The aspirations and premises on which married couples based their lives were almost unintelligible to her. However, she could comprehend the unfortunate situation of those who were legally bound and also ill-matched more easily than that of those who considered their marriage a success. Therefore when she was confronted with people who saw their marriages as all-important, she felt so little identification with them, that as if they were creatures from a separate species, they intrigued her. Their weirdness made her find them exotic.

Could it have been something as simple and foolish as her own fascinated yet mistrustful attitude to marriage which had made her treat Mrs. Appleseed in a manner so out of keeping with her most treasured beliefs? When Mrs. Appleseed had been speaking about her long and loving relationship with her husband, had it seemed so confounding that she had seen it as unearthly? Had this given her a brainstorm in which she saw the old lady as a creature higher than mortal and therefore beyond all rules?

Matron never stopped asking herself these kinds of nagging questions while she tried to meet the usual taxing demands that were made on her as she ran the ward. Lately while she was reading the temperature chart of a patient, she found the chart seemed to dissolve into a blaze of different colors. She knew all too well what those terrible colors were. She often now saw them in the night, even when her eyes were closed. They were the colors of all the hospital food that the nurses kept bringing to Mrs. Appleseed as she sat there in the ward. As they flashed inside Matron's brain, these colors acquired all the oily and diverse brilliance of paints squeezed out onto a palette. That glutinous stretch of creamy white was Mrs. Appleseed's vol-au-vent; the great splash of golden brown was her pile of chips; the patch of shocking pink was her blancmange; those cruel little rounds of emerald were her frozen peas; that haunting dab of buttercup yellow was Mrs. Appleseed's margarine.

After that Matron found that all those kaleidoscopic shades would start to fade. She then saw something much worse. She saw only one color and it looked like a vast expanse of blood. And she knew all too well what that great hideous wash of scarlet was. It was the color of the face of the shaggy-haired young man when she had viciously reprimanded him for taking a mouthful of his mother's custard.

Matron realized that she could stop the whole thing now. There was no need to continue to torture herself. She could countermand her own order. Why not tell her nurses to stop providing Mrs. Appleseed with this ceaseless round of illicit food? If this privilege without precedent were to be withdrawn from Mrs. Appleseed, those horrible accusing colors might instantly recede.

It was not too late, and yet she never countermanded her order. To Matron it seemed too late. If she was to cut off Mrs. Appleseed's food at this point, she feared it would be even more disastrous than if she was to go on allowing her to receive it. She would be drawing public attention to her original error, and she was too proud a woman to bear the humiliation. She felt that all her nurses who must already be scandalized by her permission, would be even more shocked and confused if she capriciously now withdrew it. Mrs. Appleseed, because of her sweet nature, had become extremely popular with the staff. If her food was cut off, they might feel Matron was persecuting this poor old lady with her dying husband. Matron saw no way of undoing the harm she had done without doing greater damage to her own prestige. She took no action about Mrs. Appleseed's food and those dreaded colors continued to flash insidiously inside her brain.

At night when she vainly tried to reconstruct her own emotions at that moment when she had first given that disastrous order, all she could remember was that, while Mrs. Appleseed had been talking about her feelings for her husband, Matron had become aware of the color of Mrs. Appleseed's cheeks.

Mrs. Appleseed had fluffy bright white hair and she had very rounded cheeks. As Matron examined these cheeks, she noticed that there was something troublingly wrong with them. The cheeks that went with that kind of snowy hair, surely were meant by nature to be as rosy as the apple in this old woman's name. But they were ashen as if no blood was reaching them at all. They seemed paler than those of her dying husband; they looked whiter than Mrs. Appleseed's curls.

"Have you eaten, Mrs. Appleseed?" Matron had suddenly asked her.

"Oh no. I couldn't eat at a time like this, Matron."

"How long is it since you have eaten, Mrs. Appleseed?" Matron's voice had acquired the drill sergeant's tone that it automatically took on whenever she was trying to extract an answer which was hard to get. Mrs. Appleseed looked bewildered and frightened.

"Oh, I don't know, Matron. Time doesn't mean much to me any more. How long have I been here in the hospital?"

"Mrs. Appleseed," Matron sounded so harsh and accusing, she might have been interrogating a suspect spy, "you know perfectly well how long you have been here. I really don't like it when people lie to me."

"I promise I don't quite know, Matron . . . Everything is so wretched for me at the moment. I can only think about Harry. I feel as if I'm living in a bad dream."

"You have been staying in this hospital for three whole days, and three whole nights, Mrs. Appleseed. You have spent nearly all that time sitting here in the ward beside your husband's bed. Now that's very devoted and admirable. But I'm not concerned with that. I want to know exactly how much you have eaten in the last three days."

Mrs. Appleseed's pale cherubic face looked even more bemused and nervous.

"What have I eaten? Oh, please don't worry about that Matron. Believe me I haven't felt hungry at all."

"I am Matron here . . . I'm afraid in my position I am forced to worry about it. You are not a young woman, Mrs. Appleseed. You have been living in my hospital for three days and three nights. Am I to understand that you are now admitting to me that ever since you first arrived, you've eaten nothing at all? It's just not good enough, Mrs. Appleseed!"

Mrs. Appleseed's gentle blue eyes had stared up at Matron with a look of desperation. Matron's displeasure obviously petrified her. She seemed uncertain what she was expected to do.

Matron was used to bullying. Having worked since she was a girl in so many different hospitals, she had learnt that often only by a little deliberate bullying could you ever get your way. Something stubborn and unpliable in Mrs. Appleseed's otherwise meek demeanor had aroused a reaction that was instinctive in Matron. She had never been able to tolerate it if her wishes were not obeyed immediately. She had always refused to listen to people when they made excuses. If she felt confident of her own rightness on any given issue, even the feeblest opposition made her hackles rise.

"Mrs. Appleseed," Matron now lowered her voice to make it sound grim and serious, "I have allowed you to sleep in my hospital so that you could be near to your husband who is gravely ill. When I extended you this privilege, I never imagined you would abuse it. I treated you like an adult . . . In return I expected adult behavior. I am afraid you have disappointed me, Mrs. Appleseed."

"Oh, I'm deeply grateful for the room, Matron. You mustn't worry if I've got no appetite."

Matron's eyes flashed with a murderous fury which was almost entirely faked.

"Well, I'm afraid you really can't stay on in this hospital unless you eat something! Nobody cares whether you feel hungry or not. Your husband is certainly an extremely ill man, but one never knows . . . It is just possible that he might last for another week. You can't go on sitting here day after day without taking a drop of nourishment. Ever since you have been here, I don't believe that you have even drunk a cup of tea."

"Oh, I always have a glass of water whenever I got to the lavatory, Matron."

"I couldn't be less interested whether you always have a glass of water. You look ashen pale. You have already starved yourself for three whole days. You look really most unwell. I'm going to make one of my nurses take your blood pressure. And I'm going to insist on something else, Mrs. Appleseed. I want you to listen to me carefully for I'm giving you one last warning. If you want to be allowed to continue to visit your husband in this hospital, I'm going to insist that you eat."

She saw Mrs. Appleseed's look of terror. There had been a clash of wills; Matron felt confident that she had won. Her threat had obviously shaken the old lady. She felt it had been well chosen. In this particular stubborn case it was the only one that would have worked.

"But there isn't anything to eat here, Matron." Mrs. Appleseed's voice sounded plaintive. "Even if I didn't feel so choked up inside myself, there isn't anything in this hospital that I could eat."

"Mrs. Appleseed, this is absolute rubbish," Matron said. "Naturally the hospital can't be expected to provide food for visitors. But I'm not asking you to eat in the hospital. I'm insisting that you go out in the street. There are lots of good restaurants round here, there are cafés, there are groceries that sell food."

"Oh, I couldn't possibly leave the hospital, Matron." Mrs. Appleseed's voice was depressed and extremely low. She hardly seemed to be trying to defy Matron. She merely seemed to be stating a fact.

"I have never heard such nonsense, Mrs. Appleseed. I know you are an old lady, but you still seem to be quite active. You managed to walk into this hospital ward and I see no good reason why you can't walk out of it. There are places where you can get something to eat which are right round the corner. No one is asking you to walk any long distances."

"I'm not afraid of the distances, Matron. But I can't possibly leave the hospital. I'd rather die than leave Harry here on his own. After all the happy years we have spent together, I'd feel like a criminal if I was sitting enjoying myself in some café while Harry was lying dying in this hospital. I'd never be able to forgive myself, Matron. Just think how I'd feel if I was out round the corner eating fish and chips, just at the moment that Harry's time was to suddenly come."

Mrs. Appleseed had never once broken down and cried since she arrived at the hospital. Now Matron saw that a tear was trickling down her cheek. Maybe it was the tear, maybe it was the sight of the round cheek that should have been rosy, and instead had an unearthly pallor. Maybe it was Mrs. Appleseed's reference to her happy marriage, maybe it was merely Matron's overriding need to have her wishes instantly obeyed. Matron herself was never to understand why something in her mind seemed to snap.

"You are going to eat, Mrs. Appleseed!" Matron's own voice now sounded alien to her. She felt she could hear its echo as if she was shouting in a tunnel. "If you want to stay beside your husband until the end—you are going to do exactly what I tell you to do. And I am going to insist that you eat proper meals. My nurses are going to serve you food beside your husband's bed, so please don't dare to give me anymore excuses that you wouldn't feel happy leaving him . . . If you don't want to miss your husband's last breath, Mrs. Appleseed, you are going to eat what I tell you to eat. You are going to eat three regular meals a day!"

Nurse Sullivan had received Matron's amazing order without comment. At the time Matron had been obsessed by her determination to make Mrs. Appleseed do what she wanted. She therefore hardly worried about Nurse Sullivan's secret reaction to her inexplicable violation of one of the ward's most rigidly respected regulations. Later when Matron realized the horrifying implications of what she had done, she tried to avoid Nurse Sullivan as much as possible. Every time she saw her walking towards her down a corridor, Matron darted into the nearest lavatory and stayed there until the young woman had passed. Whenever Matron came into the ward and found Nurse Sullivan giving an enema to a patient,

Matron quickly left. She could not bear to meet the ginger-haired nurse's eyes.

Nurse Sullivan had always been Matron's favorite. She considered her much the ablest and most promising of all the young women working in the hospital. Nurse Sullivan was the one that Matron saw as having exactly the right blend of qualities—the only nurse who might eventually make an excellent Matron.

And what must Nurse Sullivan be thinking now? Matron repeatedly asked herself this agonizing question. What must Nurse Sullivan be saying behind her back? Nurse Sullivan must be gossiping about her. Matron liked to feel she was astute when it came to knowing human nature. Not only Nurse Sullivan but all the other nurses must be gossiping about her. And not only the nurses . . . the junior resident doctors too. Even the hospital cleaners and the men who wheeled in the food trolleys. Matron kept hearing laughter in the staff room during the tea breaks. She knew all too well why they were laughing. Everyone in the hospital had lost respect for her.

Matron was an actress. In the public exercise of her duties, she managed to maintain an outward composure. She continued to bark out her orders with all the old ferocity. When her broad-shouldered frame came striding briskly down the hospital corridors, it still carried itself with its usual air of stern and rustling authority. Matron still knew how to wear her spotless uniform in a way that made it seem more accusingly white than anyone else's. She still knew how to carry her starched cap on her iron-grey curls as if it was a crown perched on the head of an imperious queen.

She kept all her old eye for detail. She was still just as eagle-like in detecting the smallest inefficiency. Her tantrums were, if anything, almost more ferocious than they had been in the past.

They could still terrify any culprit. Her outbursts of thunderous accusatory anger were much less acted than they'd been before Mrs. Appleseed's arrival in the hospital. Her fury was even more effective because it was now much more felt. It was as if the violent and explosive rage that permanently seethed somewhere deep down within the confines of Matron's psyche was only too glad to find any excuse to give itself expression. No one seeing the way she continued to run the ward could have guessed that she no longer felt she was the same woman. No one could have suspected that whenever she now gave an order, she secretly felt only gratitude if anyone obeyed it. Something inside Matron was broken.

She was starting to feel tired when she was on duty. Lately when she was doing her rounds of the ward, she was overcome by dizzying waves of fatigue. Never before having experienced such a sensation, she found it alarming. Recently when she looked in the bathroom mirror to see that her cap was perfectly adjusted, she noticed that her face looked nearly as grey as her cropped curls.

To make Matron's situation even more embarrassing, Mr. Appleseed continued to remain alive. Mrs. Appleseed continued to sleep in the hospital and she still spent her days sitting silently beside her husband's bed. Mrs. Appleseed always had some tray of untouched food lying on her knee. She only ever guiltily pretended to eat it when Matron came flouncing into the ward.

Mrs. Appleseed need not have been so frightened to see her. Matron no longer had the slightest intention of going near her. The very sight of Mrs. Appleseed sitting there looking like a ruined shadow of the round-cheeked healthy little old lady who had first arrived at the hospital was sickening to Matron. She only wanted to keep as far away from Mrs. Appleseed as possible.

Matron knew all too well that Mrs. Appleseed was being extremely sly, devious, and disobedient. Matron was perfectly aware that whenever her back was turned, Mrs. Appleseed was being served innumerable hospital meals which she sent away untouched, hoping Matron would never notice. And Matron's trusted nurses were all colluding with Mrs. Appleseed. They were removing the old lady's uneaten food and abetting her in defiance of Matron's orders. There was now the start of a total collapse of discipline and morale in her ward. The situation she most feared was beginning to occur just as she'd always known it would once one ever made "exceptions," permitted the "thin end of the wedge."

She made no effort to chastise her nurses for the rebellious and flagrant way in which they were allowing Mrs. Appleseed to starve herself in public. She never threatened Mrs. Appleseed, made no more attempts to blackmail her. Although in other matters Matron was insistent that the medical disciplines of the ward be rigidly obeyed, in the case of Mrs. Appleseed, she no longer felt in control. If she was to make public battle and force the old lady to eat, it would only spotlight the fact that Mrs. Appleseed should never have been allowed hospital meals in the first place. Whether Mrs. Appleseed was cowed into eating or whether she was allowed to continue her present course of open disobedience, the effect on Matron's authority was equally insidious.

Matron behaved in a way in which she had never before behaved in her entire life. In the case of Mrs. Appleseed's uneaten meals, feeling too battered and conflicted to intervene, she "turned a blind eye." Yes, something inside Matron was broken.

Then to make Matron's position even more insufferable, Mr. Appleseed was starting to make a great stir in the hospital. He was becoming increasingly famous. Matron was all too aware of the interest he was exciting, but, as the existence of both the Appleseeds was, by now, pure anathema to her, she refused to allow herself to get caught up in it.

Mr. Appleseed's doctors were starting to invite other doctors from other hospitals to examine him. Totally strange grey-haired specialists were starting to stream into Matron's ward in order to take a look at Mr. Appleseed, having just been shown his astounding X-rays. They left every bit as excited as Matron had feared they would be. They were unanimous in agreeing they had never seen a case quite like it. It was impossible to understand how the old man could still be alive. They said that if Mr. Appleseed was to live for another week or two, he would be a case for the *Guinness Book of Records*.

Matron grew to loathe the sight of all those over-interested specialists crowding round Mr. Appleseed's bed. Already she found it disturbing enough whenever she was forced to watch the regular doctors from her own hospital approaching Mr. Appleseed's prostrate form. All the time they were examining the old man, she was convinced they were examining the wickedly provided hospital food that flashed its ugly conspicuous colors from the trays which the nurses kept placing on Mrs. Appleseed's knee.

Those highly respected figures, what could they be thinking about Matron's hospital? She had always seen her hospital as an institution that was sacred, since so much of her life had been spent in trying to make it, as nearly as possible, perfect. Now, while the eyes of unknown doctors stared down at Mrs. Appleseed's plates of congealing cod and frozen peas, Matron experienced such a feeling of shame and panic, it was as if the very walls of the building she had loved for so many years were starting to crumble.

Sometimes in the nights, she wondered if she would be able to go on. She despised people who refused to meet the challenge of adverse situations, but sometimes in the night she felt so over-awake, and yet also so exhausted, Matron wondered . . .

Something new and abominable was starting to trouble her. Recently when she examined her own feelings, they filled her with disgust. The more she tried to stifle these repugnant feelings, the more they seemed to rise. How could Matron respect herself as a nurse knowing that in her heart of hearts all she hoped for now was that one of the illest of the patients under her care would hurry up and die.

Hard as Matron tried to fight it, she found that lately she prayed for Mr. Appleseed's decease. Only Mr. Appleseed's death could get her out of her present humiliating position. If that wheezing old man was to die, Mrs. Appleseed and her disgraceful trays of food would vanish from Matron's ward. As time went by, her colleagues and subordinates might eventually forget the horrendous nature of her mistake. The importance of the whole incident might slowly start to fade.

She had always believed in the possibility of redemption in a military rather than a Christian sense. She enjoyed watching old war films about soldiers who were accursed of cowardice in the face of the enemy, and then committed an act of such superhuman heroism that they regained their confiscated stripes and the respect of their fellow soldiers.

Matron's self-esteem was very badly bruised, but she could still imagine herself committing some future act of selfless devotion which would restore the confidence and respect of her staff. But she saw no possible way in which she could regain her inner self-respect while Mr. Appleseed remained alive in her ward.

As the days went by and Mr. Appleseed continued to breathe, Matron began to suffer from a new and secret terror that the old man's incomprehensible longevity which had already gained him such local fame soon might start to spread. She knew there was now a very real danger that he might at any moment become a medical celebrity on some vast new international scale. Doctors and specialists would then start flying over to examine him from the United States, Russia, China, the Third World . . . The idea of this was devastating to Matron. She was certain that all those eminent foreign doctors would arrive with a preconceived and critical attitude towards the wasteful way in which the British Health Service was run. One glance at Mrs. Appleseed's trays of hardly picked-at food would confirm their worse suspicions. At any moment the entire world of medicine was going to become aware of the way she had disgraced the reputation of her hospital. Sometimes in the night she felt deranged, she suffered from such acute anxiety and self-reproach. In these unhinged moments, she was convinced that the shameful situation she had allowed to develop in her ward was never going to come to an end. Mrs. Appleseed would be supplied with free hospital food and sit there, disobediently wasting it forever and ever. Mr. Appleseed, who had surprised medicine already, would survive endlessly to astound further. Matron might find she had an old man in her ward who against all odds, and by all ill-luck, would turn out to be immortal.

Matron felt such guilt about her own secret longing for Mr. Appleseed's demise that she extended more care towards the old fellow than she ever before had lavished on any other dying patient. She gave orders that her two best nurses were to sit by his bedside round the clock. The poor old man now had both his arms attached to feed drips and they had been dragged up high above his head, so he gave the impression that he was hanging like some old white fowl in a poultry-shop.

As a result of his long and inert stay in hospital, he was afflicted with painful bedsores. Matron did her best to see he suffered from them as little as was possible. She gave orders that her nurses were to lift his body and dust his sheets with talcum powder every half an hour.

When Mr. Appleseed finally died and Nurse Sullivan and Nurse Molloy came running down the corridors to summon her, Matron was thankful that in all honesty she could claim that she experienced not the slightest feeling of relief. She listened to the news with detachment. Its importance hardly seemed to register on her. It was as if Matron had the premonition that, for herself, his death had come far too late.

She was standing in the corridor hissing histrionic abuse at a discomforted black trolley-man from Trinidad when Nurse Sullivan and Nurse Molloy came rushing towards her. She had just discovered that this irresponsible man had been distributing food to the patients without first washing his hands. Matron was so enraged that for a moment she found it difficult to shift her attention.

Nurse Sullivan looked extremely agitated and upset. She had become personally fond of Mr. Appleseed in all the weeks she had nursed him and she identified with the distress of his wife. Normally her skin was very white and freckled, but now her face had turned such a strange purple pink, it clashed with her ginger hair.

"Matron, I think you better come at once—Mr. Appleseed is starting to go."

Matron set off with a brisk firm tread and silently followed her two nurses down the swabbed and gleaming passages. Feeling as if she was walking in a dream, she entered Mr. Appleseed's ward. She went over to his bed. She took his pulse. She shook her head. She turned to Mrs. Appleseed who was sitting speechless and immobile on her usual chair. Matron removed the inevitable plastic tray of uneaten food which was on her knee. She gently helped the old lady to get to her feet.

"I think you'd better come with me to the television lounge," Matron said. "You can lie down there on a sofa. We will bring you a cup of tea."

Matron ordered her nurses to draw the curtain round Mr. Appleseed's bed. She put an arm round Mrs. Appleseed's waist, and she helped the stricken, half-fainting old lady to hobble out of the ward.

Once Matron had managed to get Mrs. Appleseed to the television lounge, she tried to make her lie down on one of the shiny leatherette sofas. Mrs. Appleseed refused.

"I think it's better if I keep on my feet. It's really kind of you, Matron, to take such trouble."

"I wish there was more I could do for you, Mrs. Appleseed . . . One feels so helpless . . . There's not much that one can say."

Mrs. Appleseed shook her head hopelessly. She looked deathly ill. Her mild blue eyes had a strange blank stare as if they were incapable of focusing. Matron was alarmed by the way the poor old creature looked. She wished Mrs. Appleseed could manage to break down and cry.

"Would you like to spend the night here in the hospital?" Matron asked her. "I'd feel much happier if you were put under sedation."

"It's very good of you, Matron. I really prefer to go home. This hospital can only have painful associations for me at this moment.

You have been much too kind already. Please don't let me keep you from your duties. I'll find my own way home."

"Is there anyone I can send for?" Matron asked. "I don't like the idea of you going home by yourself in the state you are in. I feel it is vital that you have some friend or relative to look after you. It would be most unwise for you to travel across London on your own."

"I'd like to send for my daughter, Rosemary. Rosemary is working up in Leeds, Matron. She'd be glad to come down to be with me. I managed to stop her from coming to see her Dad in the hospital. I never even told her he was ill. Maybe I was wrong . . . who can tell? I didn't think it would be right for Rosemary to see her father in the ghastly state he's been in all these last weeks. It would have upset her dreadfully. And that was the last thing Harry would have wanted. I don't think it's fair to impose that kind of misery on young people. It's different for old people like me. I think I was right not to let her see him at the end. This way she'll be able to remember Harry only as he was."

Matron asked Mrs. Appleseed for her daughter's telephone number. She said she would arrange for the girl to be sent for immediately. She suggested that Mrs. Appleseed remain in the hospital and rest until Rosemary arrived. She found it distressing to be with this grief-stricken old lady. She was glad to be able to send for her nearest relative. At least that was a constructive action. Although Matron longed to be able to do something to help Mrs. Appleseed, it sickened her that there was nothing anyone could do.

"You stay here in the lounge while I make arrangements. I think that people often prefer to be alone at such moments. Try to relax as much as possible, Mrs. Appleseed. My nurses will bring you a cup of tea."

As Matron went walking down the passages towards the desk, she thought about Mr. Appleseed and she wondered if there were any routines or procedures in his case that possibly could have been overlooked. She had great confidence in Nurse Sullivan and Nurse Molloy. She assumed that they would have already sent for a stretcher so that Mr. Appleseed could be moved as soon as possible from the ward. Presumably they would have started to tidy him up, to brush his hair and put back his false teeth which had been removed in case he might choke.

Although Matron considered Nurse Sullivan and Nurse Molloy to be the most reliable of all her nurses, she had learnt from painful experience that it was never wise to trust anyone to do what they were meant to, unless she was there to supervise them herself. Although she felt little anxiety that her nurses had forgotten to arrange for Mr. Appleseed's stretcher, the more she thought about it, the more she realized she could not have the same one hundred percent certainty that they had replaced his teeth.

Not feeling happy on this point, she decided to check before she made arrangements to send for the old man's daughter. Matron was upset by the painful session she had just had with Mrs. Appleseed, and was already in an irritable state as she went towards the ward. She suffered from a generalized sense of exasperation that so often, with her, culminated in a tantrum. She felt tired. She could not be everywhere, watching over everything and yet the moment she relied on the initiative of others, small but vital procedures always seemed to be neglected. She remembered the complaint of Napoleon, "Where I am not, folly reigns."

As she walked towards the ward, she was seething as if she had already discovered a negligence. If she was to find her nurses had omitted to replace the dentures, there was definitely going to be trouble. They were not students. She saw no excuse for them. It was her regulation that the teeth of newly dead patients be put back in their mouths immediately. They both knew quite well why it was so important. Once you allowed rigor mortis to set in, the jawbones contracted, and it was often impossible to put false teeth back.

When she thought about Mrs. Appleseed sitting there in a state of frozen misery in the hospital television lounge, Matron felt mortified by the idea that her nurses had most likely forgotten about the teeth. Mrs. Appleseed might easily decide she wanted to say a last goodbye to her husband. In a well-run hospital there was no reason at all why the poor old lady should not find him looking as well as possible under the circumstances. The old man's daughter would soon be travelling down from Leeds. For all that Matron knew, the girl might also decide to take one last look at her father. It was for the sake of the relatives she thought it so important that dentures be put back as soon as possible. If she was to discover that her nurses had been careless on this point, Matron knew she was going to be very angry indeed.

As Matron came into the ward, she heard one of the most horrifying sounds she had ever heard in her long nursing career. It was coming from inside the curtains which were drawn around Mr. Appleseed's bed. It was the sound of shrieking, hilarious laughter.

She went rushing across the ward and tore apart the curtains with such a violence that she half-ripped them off their poles. There was Mr. Appleseed looking as if he was carved out of marble lying immobile on his pillows. There were Matron's two best nurses, Nurse Sullivan and Nurse Molloy, rocking around in a fit of loud hysterical giggles beside his bed.

Matron was so shocked that for a moment she just stood there staring at them as if she was paralyzed. Never in her whole life had she witnessed professional conduct quite so disgraceful. That poor old man lying there—that poor old woman sitting in a state of shock in the lounge—while two of Matron's most highly prized nurses rolled around like a couple of idiot schoolgirls beside his corpse.

What could all the other patients in the ward be making of this revolting behavior? Matron could hardly bear to think about it. How could they ever again feel that they were in good hands in a hospital which tolerated such an outrage? And what if Mrs. Appleseed was suddenly to decide to come back to the ward and find Nurse Sullivan and Nurse Molloy doubled up with laughter, choking and hooting, beside her stricken husband's bed. Matron found the whole thing so appalling that she could hardly believe the incident was actually taking place in her beloved hospital.

"Nurse Sullivan, Nurse Molloy, I want you to give me an instant explanation as to what is going on here!" The thunder of her question sounded deafening to herself. Her fury seemed to rebound in menacing ripples from every whitewashed wall.

"I'm really sorry, Matron . . ." Nurse Sullivan was still laughing so hard that she found it impossible to speak. Tears of merriment were streaming down her cheeks. Her amusement set off another violent spasm of laughter from Nurse Molloy. Both nurses then went off into an even louder duet of uproarious hysterics.

"Have you both gone insane?" Matron was now screaming.

"I'm really sorry, Matron . . ." This time it was Nurse Molloy who tried to control her laughter, so as to get enough breath to speak. "It's hard to explain why it seems so funny. But it's Mr. Appleseed's teeth. There seems to be something wrong with them. For twenty minutes now we've been trying to make them stay in his mouth. But every time we get them in, they come slipping out again and there they are lying on his lower lip. It may not sound all that funny, but if you had seen how many times they've fallen out, you might have got a little bit hysterical yourself!"

Nurse Molloy's attempt to give an explanation was fatal for it sent her off into yet another shrill peal of giggles. This had the effect of setting off another outburst of snorting laughter from Nurse Sullivan.

Matron stood and watched them helplessly. She realized neither of her nurses could stop laughing if they tried. Her explosive fury had not had the slightest effect on them. It almost seemed to be making them behave worse. In the degraded state that these two nurses were in at the moment, the very sight of Matron, looking so huge and white and threatening with her murderous eyes, seemed to make them want to laugh even harder.

Meanwhile the whole ward was in a hubbub. Nurses and doctors were rushing in to see what was happening. For weeks Matron had suffered from a paranoid terror that everyone in the hospital was laughing at her behind her back. Now the shriek of the high-pitched titters of her young nurses made her feel that her most dreaded fantasies were turning into reality.

Matron made a plunge towards Nurse Sullivan and she gave her a violent and stinging slap across the face. She then turned round and did the same thing to the astonished Nurse Molloy. Both her nurses still continued to be confused with laughter. But now they seemed to be moaning and half-crying at the same time.

"I hope I have given you something to laugh at." Matron hissed at them. "I'm going to leave you now and give you a chance to pull yourselves together. I am warning you, Nurse Sullivan and Nurse

Molloy, you have not heard the end of this. And unless those teeth are correctly inserted by the time I come back here—I can tell you this—it may well be the end of your nursing careers."

She walked briskly out of the ward. She then slowed down and walked much more slowly towards the lounge for she felt it was her duty to see how the old lady was feeling and do her best to stop Mrs. Appleseed from going to say a last goodbye to her husband at such a uniquely unfortunate moment in the ward.

No one seeing Matron walking down those disinfected corridors which were hung like a second-rate art gallery with splodgy abstract canvases could have guessed that she had decided that this was the last time she would walk through the hospital in an official capacity. She was going to see that Mrs. Appleseed went safely home with a nurse to wait for her daughter, Rosemary. She was going to carry out all the other duties that were incumbent on her as a Matron. Then at the end of the day, she was going to resign.

She knew that this decision was final. As she walked towards Mrs. Appleseed, she felt much more calm than she had felt for many weeks. Knowing she would only be matron for a few more hours, even the obnoxious scene that she had just witnessed hardly ruffled her. All her anger had suddenly vanished and she now saw her situation in proportion. In this new mood of icy objectivity she could admit that she might have exaggerated the disgrace of her decision to issue food that was paid for by the British taxpayer to someone who didn't deserve it.

But even when she conceded that her original view of the importance of the whole business of Mrs. Appleseed's meals might have been distorted, now she had seen what her abandonment of principle had led to, she felt that her original trepidations had been correct.

She was going to resign. No pressure from her colleagues or from the hospital board would ever weaken her decision. All her life she had demanded a perfectionist's standard of conduct both from herself and others. She therefore knew that she could never go on working in a hospital where she had lost the power to exert authority to such a shameful point that when confronted with a situation of disorder, she had found no other resource than to engage herself in a display of vulgar fisticuffs with her own subordinates. Never before in her whole life had she ever once resorted to physical violence while maintaining hospital discipline. When Matron thought about the blows she had given to Nurse Sullivan and Nurse Molloy, she felt so soiled that she was almost suicidal.

She would confess what she had done when the hospital board asked for the reasons for her resignation. She knew she'd find it unbearably humiliating to make this confession. She was still convinced it was the correct thing to do. Her horror of her own recent behavior made her feel that she deserved to suffer. She only hoped that her honesty might in the future turn out to be beneficial to her hospital. Her conduct and the immediate resignation that had followed it, might serve as a warning example to future matrons.

She was going to tell the board everything. She was going to admit to them that she had presented the patients in her ward, many of whom were gravely ill and therefore gravely in need of total quiet, with a scene quite unprecedented in hospital history, such had been the ferocity of its noise and violence.

She would also tell them that after all the years she had tirelessly striven for the very highest level of medical care in her hospital, she had ended up running a ward in which two of its most highly trained nurses were incapable of replacing a patient's dentures.

Starting with her original mistaken food permission, she would describe in graphic detail the way she had allowed morale in her ward to degenerate to a point where its matron inspired so little respect that finally she had been forced to behave like a common pugilist in a public boxing ring. Even if the authorities tried to be lenient with her, she would refuse clemency. To Matron the slaps she had given Nurse Sullivan and Nurse Molloy were unforgivable. It was as if a British officer under enemy fire was to start crazily shooting at his own troops.

When she came back into the television lounge, she found Mrs. Appleseed still sitting on the shiny leatherette sofa. She had the same blank stunned expression. She hardly seemed to notice Matron's presence.

"How are you feeling, Mrs. Appleseed?"

"Poorly."

Matron noticed she used the same word that her dead husband had always used.

"I've been trying to think what would be the best thing to do for you," Matron said. "I've decided that you might feel better if you leave the hospital immediately. As you say, it can only have very upsetting associations for you."

If Mrs. Appleseed was dispatched to her home, it would remove the pressing danger that she might go back into the ward where, for all Matron knew, any kind of abysmal situation of chaos might still be reigning and where this poor old lady might well find Nurse Molloy and Nurse Sullivan still roaring with laughter as they played the fool with her dead husband's teeth.

"One of my nurses is going to take you back to your home in a taxi, Mrs. Appleseed. The fare will be paid for by the hospital." As

Matron knew she would be resigning in a few hours, she had lost her old terror of establishing dangerous precedents.

"You are obviously in a very shocked state," Matron continued. "It is urgent that you go home and lie down. I will contact your daughter, Rosemary, in Leeds and tell her to join you at your house. I will instruct a social worker to stay with you until she arrives."

Mrs. Appleseed nodded vaguely. She hardly seemed to care whether she stayed in the hospital, or left it. She seemed quite willing to do anything Matron wanted.

"Maybe it would be the best thing if I go home right away," she said. "I'll just go back into the ward for a minute, Matron. If you don't mind . . ."

"Why do you want to go back into the ward?" Matron spoke with nervous sharpness. There was nothing that Mrs. Appleseed could have suggested that Matron would have minded more.

"If you go back into the ward, Mrs. Appleseed, you will only get yourself even more upset. I am very much against it indeed."

"But I only want to go back to the ward for just one second, Matron," Mrs. Appleseed said. "I'm not planning to stay there. I know that would make me feel much too distressed."

Matron had the despairing feeling it was going to be just as she had feared. The old lady was going to try to say one last quick good-bye to her husband. Matron was determined to stop her. Even if Mrs. Appleseed became aggrieved, she was not going to care. She was forced to refuse permission for the old lady's sake. Mrs. Appleseed already looked dangerously unwell. There was no way of knowing if Nurse Sullivan and Nurse Molloy had pulled themselves together. If Mrs. Appleseed was to go to the ward and find them still in the disgraceful state in which Matron had last seen them, she refused to take responsibility for the effect it might have on the poor old woman's heart. If Mrs. Appleseed was to insist on her right to see her husband for the last time, she would have to come back and say her goodbye to him tomorrow when Matron would no longer have to feel responsible for what had happened because she would no longer be the matron.

"You are not to go back into the ward, Mrs. Appleseed. You are going to take a taxi to your home. And one of my nurses is going with you." Matron felt so insistent on this point that her voice had regained all its old bullying authority.

"But I have to go back to the ward, Matron."

"Why do you have to go back? I can think of no good reason."

"I have to go back because of my teeth."

"Where did you put your teeth, Mrs. Appleseed?" Matron was staring at the old lady's mouth with an expression of mesmerized horror.

"I left my teeth on the little table beside Harry's bed."

"What on earth made you take them out?" Matron spoke with much more viciousness than she intended. She felt stunned. Why had she not noticed that Mrs. Appleseed's lips were very sunken? She had thought the poor old creature looked peculiar, but attributed it to grief and shock.

"I took my teeth out when I had to eat all those awful meals, Matron. They hurt me when I bite. I always take them out if I have to eat."

Matron told her that she would soon have her teeth back—that at present they were being sterilized. She didn't seem interested at all. Matron was very glad that she didn't have to tell her that her husband's dentures had still not been found.

As Matron went off to fetch the teeth she realized she had to make a public apology to her two young nurses. She would tell them she felt acute remorse for the way she had handled the unprecedented case of the mixed-up dentures. She could hardly congratulate Nurse Molloy and Nurse Sullivan on their recent comportment. However, she would pardon them, on the grounds of their youth and bizarre nature of the situation with which they had been confronted. She would then go on to explain that in all honor she could not find any excuses for her own behavior. She now recognized herself as a figure who was totally unfit to bear the responsibilities of her duties as matron. Tonight, she therefore intended to resign.

As Matron came to this never-to-be-changed decision she had the sensation that her blood was seeping from her body as though she had just slashed her wrists. When she returned to Mrs. Appleseed, the old lady was wrapped in the cocoon of her own misery and she seemed unaware of the agony of Matron's state of mind. She started thanking Matron for all the kindness that Matron had shown her during her stay in the hospital. Her gratitude seemed ironic and tactless to Matron at this moment. But as she was used to acting she tried not to show that the old lady's thanks made her feel only bitterness and pain.

"All my life I'll never forget what you did for me and Harry," Mrs. Appleseed continued.

"I only did my duty," Matron said. "In my line of work I always felt that I was paid to be of use."

Matron's feeling of intense melancholy was increasing by the moment. Yet her stubborn mind was still made up. When she referred to her work, she already referred to it in the past tense.

Mrs. Appleseed suddenly asked her a frantic question.

"Have you ever had the feeling, Matron, that life has dealt you such a terrible blow that you can't see much point in trying to carry on?"

Matron looked at Mrs. Appleseed's desperate greyish-white face.

She wondered how long it would be until Mrs. Appleseed followed her husband. She noticed that the poor old woman's voice was now suddenly choking in her mouth in a way that could only partially be blamed on her present lack of teeth. Matron went over and put her arm round the bereft old lady's shoulders. She could never have behaved with such spontaneity and warmth if she had not known there were only a few more hours in which she would continue to be matron.

Mrs. Appleseed seemed to sense that there was something unusual in Matron's affectionate gesture, that the sympathy she was extending was much more personal and heartfelt than the routine commiseration she extended to all bereaved relatives. After all the long and painful days that she had spent in the hospital, it was the first time that Mrs. Appleseed had broken down, and she suddenly started to cry.

"Cry, cry . . ." Matron whispered. "Have a good cry, Mrs. Appleseed. Don't try to keep it back. It will probably do you good."

As she spoke, she felt that her own empty and ruined future was merging with that of Mrs. Appleseed. She saw it like a grey and polluted river flowing pointlessly into the distance towards an unenticing destination. She visualized Mrs. Appleseed alone in her house once her daughter Rosemary had gone back to work in Leeds. She foresaw all the lonely functionless years that she herself would spend idling miserably in the vacuum of her Swiss Cottage flatlet.

"Cry, cry . . ." she repeated. Then she remembered that she had not yet stopped being a matron. It was therefore still her duty to offer the old lady a support that was in some way rock-like and bracing.

"Even if you feel that you have nothing much to live for, you must try to carry on," Matron said. "You will find that life won't let you do anything else, Mrs. Appleseed. While you are still living—carrying on—that is all that life is about."

Taft's Wife

Mrs. Arthur Ripstone finally told Taft, the social worker, that she would agree to see her son, Anthony, if he was brought to have lunch with her in one of the big West End London hotels. First she suggested the Ritz, then she decided she would prefer Claridge's.

"You understand, Mr. Taft, that if I agree to this meeting I will have to insist on the utmost secrecy."

"Absolutely." Taft already disliked this unknown woman just from hearing the affected rasp of her voice over the telephone. She had an unpleasantly over-ladylike accent that masked some coarser, underlying accent with unmelodious results.

"I must also ask you, Mr. Taft, never again to try to contact me at my home."

"You can trust me, Mrs. Ripstone. I would like to apologize for having written to you at your house. We were extremely anxious to reach you and we could think of no other way." Taft's deep voice was soothing, studiedly avuncular. Through the years he had learnt to cultivate an ultra-comforting manner—so much of his professional life was spent trying to reassure and cajole.

As he went on speaking to Mrs. Ripstone he imagined himself speaking to an obese and arrogant lady in her early fifties. In his mind he endowed her with an ugly high-bridged nose that accentuated the weakness of her chin which receded in crêpe-like wattles into a corpulent rose-pink neck encircled with expensive pearls.

He noticed that when he invented a picture of Mrs. Ripstone, he made her much older than he knew for a fact she was. Only that morning Taft had looked up her age in the orphanage files. Taft deliberately imagined her as old and hideous. Mrs. Ripstone's appearance might come as a shock to her son, but Taft, as the adult who was going to be present at this painful hotel meeting, wanted to be immune to any nasty surprises. He therefore prepared himself for the worst in advance.

"You appreciate, Mr. Taft, that at this moment I am not speaking to you from my own house. I am talking from a call-box in my local village. I only tell you this to stress how violently I feel the need for your discretion in this whole business."

"You can rely on my discretion, Mrs. Ripstone."

"Do I sense something sarcastic in your attitude, Mr. Taft? Maybe you feel I am making an unnecessary fuss about the need for secrecy!" The ladylike voice was suddenly hissing with defensive anger.

Taft realized he would have to be more careful. The telephone was a dangerous instrument. It magnified the tiniest nuance of tone. Mrs. Ripstone had not been deceived by his treacle-sweet courtesy.

Her paranoia obviously had given her more sensitivity than he wished to give her credit for. Unconsciously he must have conveyed to this unknown woman some small particle of the hostility he felt for her. Unless he was more convincingly sympathetic towards her he feared she might do the thing he dreaded—she might refuse to come to the lunch.

"No doubt you see me as some kind of loose woman, Mr. Taft!" Mrs. Ripstone gave a hectic trill of a laugh. "I promise you—nothing could be further from the truth. I am happily married. I have a lovely home down here in Surrey. We have a swimming pool. We have a tennis court. I have two adorable children. They are beautifully brought up . . ."

Taft pressed the telephone receiver so hard against his ear that it hurt him. He rolled his eyes to the ceiling and his face contorted in an expression of agonized embarrassment.

"I have a very good marriage, Mr. Taft . . . My husband is older than me. He is a popular and respected man in the community. He is a very wonderful human being. He is a retired judge . . ."

"Yes . . . yes . . . ." Taft knew this response must sound inadequate but could think of nothing better to say.

"Have you quite understood, Mr. Taft, that my husband is totally unaware of the boy's existence?"

"I rather assumed that, Mrs. Ripstone."

"And I intend for things to stay that way?" The affected voice hissed with such aggression it reminded Taft of the sound of a steaming kettle. "My husband—in his thinking—is an old-fashioned man, Mr. Taft. He is deeply religious. The whole thing would come as a great shock to him. His heart is not strong. The past is the past. I see no reason why it should be allowed to ruin the present."

"I assure you, Mrs. Ripstone, I have not the slightest desire to create any trouble in your private life."

"You sound as if you are blaming me, Mr. Taft! But I not only have to think of my husband—I have to think of my children."

"Of course you do, Mrs. Ripstone."

"As long as you understand that . . . Anyway we will all meet next Sunday, Mr. Taft. I think Claridge's would be as good a place to meet as any. I used to like the Ritz but lately I have found it gloomy. I think the Ritz has rather a dead feeling about it."

"Exactly," Taft said.

"Claridge's is so much gayer. After all we want the meeting to be a pleasant one. Claridge's serves very nice desserts. When I bring my children up to London to visit the dentist they always try to force me to take them to Claridge's. They so adore the desserts."

"Claridge's it shall be," Taft said.

"There's one thing I must warn you, Mr. Taft; you have put a lot of emotional pressure on me in order to make me agree to come to this lunch. I therefore feel you have certain responsibilities towards Anthony."

"Responsibilities, Mrs. Ripstone?"

"Responsibilities, Mr. Taft. I feel it's your duty to warn the boy that he mustn't get ideas. He mustn't be allowed to think these meetings can ever become a habit."

"I don't think Anthony expects very much from this lunch, Mrs. Ripstone." Taft was lying. He wanted to save the boy's pride. He remembered the thrilled, half-tearful expression on Anthony's face when he had been told his lost mother had been traced. Taft knew that Anthony secretly was hoping that once his unknown mother met him she would want to remove him from the Institution and take him to live with her.

"Well, goodbye, Mr. Taft. I am looking forward to seeing you at Claridge's on Sunday. I've a feeling we are going to like each other!" Taft noticed that for the first time all belligerence had vanished from Mrs. Ripstone's voice. It suddenly sounded both coy and flirtatious. Hearing this new note Taft shook the receiver with a violence. It was as if he was trying to shake Mrs. Ripstone off the wire.

"You have a very nice voice, Mr. Taft. I don't know if anyone's ever told you that!" Mrs. Ripstone gave a tinkling seductive laugh. "See you on Sunday, Mr. Taft!"

"Bitch!" Taft said aloud when she had rung off. "Bloody, fucking bitch!" He rarely swore. He went to his desk and started to write out a report on "Battered Wives" in order to try to forget Mrs. Ripstone and the unpromising lunch that he and her abandoned son were soon to have with her.

When Mrs. Ripstone told Taft she liked his deep voice it was by no means the first time a woman had said that to him. The compliment was so familiar that it antagonized rather than flattered him. He reacted with much the same irritability and embarrassment when women told him that he looked like John Wayne.

Taft had always disliked John Wayne as a celluloid hero and he was bored by his films. John Wayne's swaggering and sharp-shooting myth was repugnant to him. Taft identified with losers, and although his strong, broad build and his rugged, craggy face resembled those of the actor he always felt ill at ease and demeaned when anyone told him he looked like the tough cowboy hero.

As a social worker Taft was dedicated and assured. In his dealings with the people he met through his work he was unselfish and straightforward. He became genuinely concerned with the "cases" under his care. He identified with their problems and they found him practical, reliable, and kind.

In his private life, Taft was much less assured and he was often unreliable and devious. He knew he was attractive to women and he had become adept at warding them off. In his sexual relationships he was mistrustful and ungiving. By nature he was a solitary. He had a horror of human intimacy. Any girl who tried to get close to him aroused his terror and dislike, for he saw his emotional self-sufficiency as his strength and he felt she was trying to cripple and ensnare him. Taft was prepared to do his best to meet the varying needs of the "cases" that were assigned to him. But he was in no way prepared to meet the needs and demands of any woman in the bruising hugger-mugger of domesticity. He had chosen to be known only as Taft—he liked the formality. He hated it if anyone called him by his first name for he resented any familiarity.

Taft lived alone in a neat one-room flat near Paddington station. In his kitchen there was one mug, one plate, and one knife and fork. The deliberately sparse utensils in Taft's kitchen made a defiant display of his stand.

At night Taft often went to pubs alone, and he drank quite heavily for he liked to try and blunt the feeling of hopelessness and despair that came over him at the end of the day when his work had exposed him to a seemingly bottomless ocean of human pain, poverty, squalor, and humiliation.

Drinking in pubs Taft was often picked up by women and if he found them attractive he allowed them to seduce him, but he was careful to see that his love affairs had no sequel. As a lover he merely "obliged." He was never the hunter. He was promiscuous not out of excessive lust but out of excessive passivity.

Taft slept with girls on the sofas of other peoples' houses—in other peoples' double beds. In the night he got up and left them to go back to take a bath in his monastic flat. By morning it was as if the sexual experience of the night had been wiped off the slate of his consciousness like an unimportant chalk mark.

Taft had a horror of female scenes and recriminations. The women he slept with were often encouraged and challenged by his elusiveness. Their pride was piqued by the indifference of this handsome, rugged man who treated them with avuncular protectiveness and then became without explanation suddenly so busy and unavailable they could hardly believe he was spitting them out of his life as if they were cherry stones.

Through the years Taft had learnt to devise a technique which helped spare him from the unwelcome consequences, the frantic telephone calls, the tantrums, the insults, and the suicide threats to which he had often been subjected in the past as a result of his fickleness and promiscuity.

Taft had invented a wife. Every time Taft started a new sexual relationship he warned his partner that it could never become serious on his part for he still loved only his wife. Taft's imaginary wife had been killed in a car crash just a few weeks after he had married her. She had helped to disentangle him from so many relationships which he saw as a threat to the astringently lonely existence he had chosen for himself, that in a sense it was true, he did love her.

Taft had told so many different women about his wife that he now talked about this mythical and ill-fated figure with enormous natural dignity. She had become so necessary to Taft as a protection that often she seemed more important and real to him than the girls to whom he described her, and he could therefore often forget he was lying when he claimed he was incapable of recovering from her loss. Shielded from the repercussions of his promiscuity by the excuse of his fabricated bereavement, Taft felt that the dishonesty with which he treated his mistresses was justified because it helped to prevent him squandering emotional energy which he felt was better spent on his "cases."

The Sunday morning following his conversation with Mrs. Ripstone, Taft arrived at St. Michael's to pick up Anthony in order to take him to meet his unknown mother at Claridge's. He then travelled with the boy on the Underground to Oxford Street.

Sitting on the train Taft examined Anthony's face without making it obvious he was doing so. The boy looked so pale and strained and corpse-like it was as if the ordeal of meeting his mother had interfered with the natural flow of blood in his body. One of the nuns at St. Michael's had whispered to Taft that Anthony had hardly eaten or slept in the last week.

Usually Anthony looked so scruffy that his appearance suggested that he got some kind of defiant satisfaction from looking memorably wild and unkempt. Today he had made a self-conscious attempt to look neat. His shaggy over-long hair was slicked down with some kind of cheap hair-oil. It looked flat and unnatural like an oily wig that had been pasted on his head with glue.

Taft saw the boy had put on his best suit—the one he wore for Church on Sundays. It was secondhand, shiny, and ill-fitting. Its trousers were too big for him and they hung in baggy folds round his legs. He was wearing a shirt and tie and this too made Taft feel uneasy. Rarely before had he seen the boy wearing anything except grubby torn T-shirts and ragged jeans. Anthony kept fidgeting with his shirt collars as if he was trying to unfasten a noose which was choking him.

As he surreptitiously examined Anthony, Taft found himself trying to guess what impression the boy would make on his mother. Anthony was surely quite a nice-looking boy. . . But his eyes had a dazed unfocused expression that made people feel uncomfortable. Anthony was tall and well-built for a boy of fourteen, but he moved awkwardly with a deliberate stoop that betrayed his lack of confidence.

"Are you nervous, Anthony?"

"A bit, Mr. Taft."

"You shouldn't be." Taft spoke in his usual deep reassuring tones and he felt a disgust at the hypocrisy of his own comforting paternal manner. Why shouldn't Anthony feel nervous? Taft himself was feeling extremely agitated, though he was much too well-trained and controlled to show it. He felt that his lunch at Claridge's was going to be a catastrophe and he blamed himself for having brought it about.

Looking at Anthony's chalk-white, tormented face, Taft wondered if the whole orphanage policy in regard to the missing mothers was wrong. The staff committee at St. Michael's had decided that if any of the "unwanted" children in the orphanage expressed any wish to get to know their unknown mother, every effort should be made to find her and organize a meeting. The mothers were often hard to trace. They had married—changed their names and their lifestyles. Frequently they had moved to different parts of the country. It had taken Taft a lot of time and dedicated sleuth-work to track down Mrs. Ripstone.

Now having found Mrs. Ripstone living in her Surrey house with her swimming pool and retired judge with his "old-fashioned thinking," Taft wondered if it might not be better for Anthony if she had never been found.

But Taft couldn't be certain. Almost all the "unwanted" children that he had worked with through the years seemed to have a longing to know what their mothers looked like. This longing was tied up with their need to establish some form of identity. Psychically they were all bruised, and they suffered from a painful feeling of confusion as to what they were and how they had come into an existence that condemned them to live in a beggar situation at the mercy of the sparse charity of an institution. Feeling themselves to be outcasts they were plagued by self-blame and hatred and it was hard to convince them they were not intrinsically undesirable.

Taft had tried to stop the term "unwanted" from being used at St. Michael's to describe the abandoned children. He felt the word had a pejorative brutality that was likely to reinforce their belief that there was something essentially wrong with them. Taft would have preferred them to be known simply as orphans. But children like Anthony, technically, were not orphans and the term "unwanted" was still applied to him.

Taft remembered the unpleasantness of Mrs. Ripstone's affected voice on the telephone. Would one meeting with the owner of that distasteful voice help cure Anthony's insecurity; were these meetings between abandoned children and abandoning mothers destructive events—rather than the valuable ones that the staff at St. Michael's believed them to be? Taft felt an immense psychological fatigue. He simply didn't know.

"What do you think she will be like?" Anthony asked him.

"I'm afraid I can't tell you, Anthony. I only talked to her on the telephone."

"Maybe she won't be like you hoped." Taft wondered if he should warn Anthony he had got an unsympathetic impression of his mother. He decided there was no point.

Taft had originally hoped Anthony would choose to meet his

mother alone. But as the idea of lunching with her without a third party to act as a buffer clearly terrified the boy, Taft had felt it would be cruel to refuse to go.

Taft and Anthony went through the swing doors of Claridge's. The lobby was crowded with well-dressed people who were either arriving or leaving with a lot of expensive-looking luggage. Two Arabs with tired and decadent faces were making air-travel reservations at the desk. Taft glanced sideways at Anthony and he saw the boy was shaking.

She seemed to appear from nowhere. Suddenly Mrs. Ripstone was shaking hands.

"You must be Mr. Taft! And you must be Anthony!" She gave them such a welcoming and coquettish smile, Taft suspected it concealed a certain hysteria.

Mrs. Ripstone was in her mid-thirties. She was so overdressed for this lunch that Taft thought she looked as if she had been gift-wrapped. She was wearing a fur stole over a sleek dress that emphasized the curves of a neat little figure. Her face was small and pert and pretty and she had put such brilliant patches of rouge on her cheeks they appeared to be inflamed. Her neck and her wrists were gleaming with flashy jewelry, and on her head there was a provocative little hat with a waving feather.

Mrs. Ripstone was wearing long black spiky false eyelashes which quivered and struggled when she moved her lids, like the legs of an overturned beetle.

"I'm so delighted to meet you, Mr. Taft. Why don't we go into the restaurant? I'm sure we must all be starving. I've reserved us a table."

Mrs. Ripstone led the way into the restaurant. Taft noticed that she minced when she walked and she had very pretty ankles.

"Waita! Waita! I have a table reserved for three!" Frantically she waved a fawn-gloved hand at various indifferent-looking waiters. The more she tried to show that she was at ease and in control in this expensive international hotel, the more she seemed to have the dangerous lack of control of a driverless car that slips its brakes and goes skidding down a hill. None of the waiters seemed to want to find Mrs. Ripstone's reserved table. Her grand manner and her over-stylized gestures of command had no effect on them at all.

After what seemed to Taft like an intolerable amount of commotion, complaint, and handwaving, and she had made everyone in the restaurant stare at her, Mrs. Ripstone was escorted to her table by the head waiter.

"Now what is everyone going to have!" She picked up the enormous and elaborate menu. "They have very nice desserts here," she said turning to Anthony. "Do you like desserts? My children always make pigs of themselves when I bring them up to London and we all have lunch here after the dentist."

Did she plan to say that? Taft wondered. Or in her state of confusion did it just slip out?

"Personally I'm going to start with a very strong martini. I've been rushing round London all day shopping and I'm exhausted. Won't you have a martini, Mr. Taft? Surely the grown-ups are entitled to a few little rewards as the price for growing old!"

Taft agreed that he needed a martini. Looking round the restaurant with its crowded tables of cheerful chattering people who seemed to give off a smell of opulence which mingled with smells of over-rich food, Taft wondered if there could have been any more unsuitable place to have this humanly gruelling lunch.

"I recommend the hors d'oeuvres. Would you like that Anthony? I also recommend the vol-au-vent," Mrs. Ripstone said.

Anthony looked blank. Mrs. Ripstone realized he didn't know what either of these dishes were and she explained in a patronizing way.

"Don't you do any French at your school?" she asked.

Anthony nodded and blushed. Taft had never seen the boy look so stupid. His secondhand suit looked particularly shabby in contrast to the elegant clothes of the other people in the restaurant. Anthony's unhappy, unfocused eyes stared at his mother's face as if he was trying to memorize it.

"Anyway . . . Mr. Taft says you are doing very well at school, Anthony. And I'm very pleased to hear it." Mrs. Ripstone was lying in order to be pleasant. Taft had never told her Anthony was doing well at school. Anthony was a very poor student and he found it hard to concentrate.

Taft said he would like hors d'oeuvres and vol-au-vent. It seemed the easiest. He had rarely felt less hungry. Mrs. Ripstone started to show off again. She ordered herself some turbot and gave a bored-looking waiter elaborate instructions as to how she wanted it prepared.

The woman is under immense strain, Taft thought. The situation must be a difficult one for her. Shallow as she appears to be, she probably feels more guilt towards Anthony than she chooses to show, and her guilt is useless for there is no way she can make reparation to him. After this lunch she will go back to her Surrey home and try and forget him. Anthony is an unwelcome ghost from her past that she would like exorcised. She can hardly feel that his exorcism has been successful while she sees him sitting in Claridge's staring at her with his damaged-looking eyes. Feeling the boy's unvoiced accusation, she can only wrap herself ever more tightly in the cocoon of her own snobbish values in order to defend herself. Taft wondered briefly if he ought to feel sorry for this silly overdressed woman. He longed for the lunch to be over.

Once the hors d'oeuvres arrived Mrs. Ripstone once again turned to Anthony and made another self-conscious attempt to charm him. "You seem very grown-up for your age, Anthony, I didn't expect you to be so tall and handsome!"

Mrs. Ripstone gave her son an awkward and seductive look.

"Have you got a girlfriend yet, Anthony?" She let out a high and suggestive giggle, and she lowered her eyelids so that the black spikes of her eyelashes fluttered.

Anthony blushed and shook his head. He looked desperate.

"I don't believe you!" Mrs. Ripstone gave her son a playful little poke. "I bet all the girls are after you!"

It's horrible, Taft thought. She doesn't know how to relate to the boy. She feels so ill at ease that all she can do is flirt.

"The vol-au-vent is delicious," Taft said. He found it disgusting, but he was hoping to draw the fire of her attention to himself so she would stop tormenting her son with her unnatural badinage.

Mrs. Ripstone turned to Taft with relief. She examined his handsome craggy face with approval. It was as if she had felt too agitated to notice him until that moment.

"I'm so glad you like it, Mr. Taft." Her eyelashes lowered in a girlish flutter. She suddenly seemed tipsy. As this difficult lunch progressed she had been ordering herself more and more martinis.

"It's such a pleasure to meet you, Mr. Taft. You are a lucky boy, Anthony, to have such a charming, intelligent man as Mr. Taft taking an interest in you!"

She ordered Taft and herself two more martinis and said it was time to have dessert. She suggested that Anthony should have the chocolate mousse and Taft should have the lemon soufflé. Both of them nodded feebly, and Taft felt he was behaving as if he was as stunned as the boy.

Mrs. Ripstone said that she couldn't resist an éclair. She ran her hands voluptuously down her body in order to draw attention to the trimness of her pretty little figure.

"I'm going to be naughty for once," she said. "This is rather a special occasion!"

She turned to Taft and said she felt he must have a very interesting life. She then ordered him another martini without asking him if he wanted it. For the first time he looked her directly in the eyes and he noticed that she was examining him in an extremely predatory way through the spiky veil of her lashes.

Anthony sat there unhappily picking at his chocolate mousse. He seemed to have ceased to exist for his mother. She behaved as if she and Taft were alone.

"I had the feeling we were going to get on, Mr. Taft. I liked the sound of your voice on the telephone. It's a funny thing about voices . . . they tell you so much about a person."

The double martinis were throbbing in Taft's brain. He had a feeling of nausea and unreality.

Mrs. Ripstone placed her hand on his in a proprietorial and intimate way. "I hope you are going to keep in contact with me, Mr. Taft." Her voice had become husky with sexual insinuation. He noticed her hat was a little askew. Her eyes looked bright and greedy and they never left his face. He wondered if she was a nymphomaniac.

He felt her hand tightening its grip on his hand. "Now that we have met at last we must really keep in contact. You will be hearing from me," she gave a coy little laugh. "I want to have news of Anthony."

Taft felt the tremor of Mrs. Ripstone's touch sending something rippling through his body like a sharp current of electricity.

"I want to ask you something, Mr. Taft! Has anyone ever told you that you look like John Wayne?"

She was bound to say it. The dreaded compliment hardly irritated him. He couldn't feel it mattered. Neither did he feel it mattered that she had started slyly kicking his ankle under the table—that he was obediently kicking her back.

Pressing Mrs. Ripstone's foot with his foot and looking as confident and rugged as John Wayne, Taft had rarely felt so defeated and depressed. He felt he had failed Anthony at this lunch, but even that hardly seemed to matter, for he could see no way in which anyone could have made this meeting have a more successful emotional outcome for the boy.

Taft could see by the distraught expression in Anthony's eyes that it had been a shock to realize that his mother and himself could only be forever strangers.

The boy had hoped that there would be some kind of automatic human bond between them—but it simply didn't exist. Taft could see that Anthony was disturbed by the act that he could feel so little for this chattering little woman with the over-rouged cheeks—that Mrs. Ripstone obviously felt nothing for him. If they could have felt a mutual antipathy, Taft had the idea it might have been better. It was the absence of any relationship at all between mother and son that made this lunch so tense and embarrassing.

Since his birth Anthony had been "unwanted," whether Taft winced at the harshness of the term or learnt to tolerate it. All his life Anthony would remain "unwanted," and Taft couldn't see there was anything anyone could do about it.

Taft continued to press Mrs. Ripstone's foot under the table, though he felt not the slightest desire for her. It was as if physically he wanted to make some kind of contact with this woman because he hated to see the way that her son found it so emotionally impossible.

Taft saw the boy's future as incurably bleak. When Anthony left the comparatively kindly haven of the orphanage he would be unemployed and homeless. Without friends or relatives, with only social workers to encourage him, he would start to feel desperate in his isolation. Like so many of the "unwanted" children that Taft had worked with in the past he would probably knock about the streets and eventually turn to petty crime. Taft had visited too many children who had been put in St. Michael's and years later, with much the same friendly and cheery manner, he had visited them after they had been put in prison. He found it horrifying that they seemed condemned to spend their lives in some form of institution.

Taft pressed Mrs. Ripstone's foot even harder—there was aggression in his gesture. But she didn't notice. He saw her look of triumph. She was delighted to think she had made a conquest.

She is probably an unhappy and frustrated woman, Taft thought. It's very possible that she leads a dismal life with her retired judge, who may well be too old and doddery to satisfy her. The illegitimate birth of Anthony all too likely was her tragedy. She is profoundly conventional, and she cares only for appearances. Presumably she saw her pregnancy as a catastrophic disgrace and now her whole life seems to be dedicated to regaining the respectable image she feels she lost through it.

Taft suspected that Mrs. Ripstone was only making such an overt sexual play for him because he knew about the event in her past which she most hoped to hide. Knowing he could never be impressed by the act of ultra-pure respectability she put on to deceive the old judge and her Surrey neighbors, she felt she had nothing to lose if she showed him the side of her nature her life now was spent trying to repress.

Mrs. Ripstone raised her glass to Taft and gave him a toast, "Let's drink to the most interesting man I've met in a long time!" She gave him a meaningful smile. Taft wondered if Anthony had noticed how amorously she was behaving.

If Anthony noticed he gave no sign. He just sat there looking depressed. Anthony's general predicament was so unenviable that Taft couldn't believe the boy would feel that things were made much worse for him by the fact that his mother and his social worker had chosen to carry on a pointless little flirtation.

Taft assumed this lunch must have been a harrowing occasion for the boy in the sense that it finally must have smashed any hopes that, late in life, his mother could start to provide him with the affection of which he had always been deprived. But if this lunch, for Anthony, had been a tragic event it had lacked the dignity that Taft felt should be associated with moments of human tragedy. It had been a meal of unleavened triviality—it had been nothing more than a sticky stew of flirtatious chitchat, chocolate mousse, and double martinis.

And now, pressing his foot against Mrs. Ripstone's sandal, Taft knew he was debasing this ignoble lunch even further by his surreptitious show of sexuality. He found this vulgar little woman extremely unattractive. He responded to her advances only out of some kind of apathetic anger that could find no other outlet. He longed for this insufferable meal to be over. By making passes at Mrs. Ripstone he felt he maintained some control over her. He also wanted to have something to do to help kill the time until the bill was paid.

"I have your telephone number, Mr. Taft. I think it's best if I ring you. There might be complications if you were to ring me at my house!" He hated the slyness in her laugh. "I think you can guess why!"

My God! She means it! Taft thought. Because he had been play-acting when he flirted with this woman he had assumed she was doing the same thing. Now he saw she was serious. She intended to see him again. He stared at her with such horror that she noticed.

"Is anything the matter, Mr. Taft?"

"Yes . . . I mean, no . . ." Like someone hallucinating Taft had started to have a horrendous vision of the future. He saw the devious Mrs. Ripstone slipping quietly from her Surrey house while Judge Ripstone was taking a nap. Taft saw himself passively receiving the call she would make him from her local call-box. Her voice would be breathless with intrigue. A secret meeting in London would be arranged, and soon he would be standing on a station platform looking just as stalwart and confident as John Wayne as he stepped forward like a robot, devoid of willpower, to greet Mrs. Ripstone as she alighted, mincing and overdressed, from her train.

After that, Taft saw the lunch. The lunch would be at Claridge's and they would both drink many double martinis before they went up in the hotel lift to the double room that Mrs. Ripstone had taken for the night . . .

"You look so peculiar, Mr. Taft! Is anything the matter?"

Taft was staring at Mrs. Ripstone in such a weird unseeing way that she was frightened. He was having a vision of Mrs. Ripstone and himself grappling in the hotel bed. Their lovemaking was brief and perfunctory. Once it was over Taft saw himself lying naked beside her. He was starting to warn her that she must never expect their relationship to become deep or permanent for he would never be able to love any woman as he still loved his dead wife.

"Are you feeling unwell, Mr. Taft?"

"I'm not feeling too well, Mrs. Ripstone." Taft suddenly felt sickened by the idea that many human choices—choices that were to have disastrous and long-lasting consequences—were made in a haphazard and frivolous fashion. Important decisions could be taken in much the same idle and capricious way that Taft saw the people at neighboring tables order their courses from the menu of Claridge's. First they thought they wanted steak, then on a whim they felt they preferred to have the chicken, then at the last moment they changed again and decided to have fish.

Taft turned his head away from Mrs. Ripstone. He couldn't bear to look to her. He found it too easy to see himself with her in that imaginary hotel bedroom. He was with her as a feeble victim of his own pattern of compliance rather than as a prisoner of passion. He suspected Mrs. Ripstone was much stronger-willed than he was, although his square jaw looked as if it jutted with resolution.

Taft's ugly fantasy of himself in that shared bedroom was so vivid that he found himself carrying it further. As a result of that brief loveless liaison, Mrs. Ripstone would become pregnant. Once again she would conceive in exactly the same unlucky careless way that she had once conceived Anthony . . .

"I'm so sorry you don't feel well, Mr. Taft. Is there anything I can do for you?"

"No. There's nothing you can do, Mrs. Ripstone." Taft said. There was nothing she could do. He felt that was the trouble with this dreary little sex-hungry woman with the feather in her hat. She couldn't even stop him carrying through his distasteful fantasy.

Taft saw the impregnated Mrs. Ripstone confessing everything to her silver-haired husband. The ancient Judge Ripstone would think of his own good name and be extremely anxious to avoid the scandal of a divorce. He would promise to forgive her if she hid abroad for nine months and agreed to place the infant at birth with some adoption service . . .

Taft had withdrawn his foot. Under the table Mrs. Ripstone's sandal groped wildly as she tried to find it. Taft had tucked his legs away so they were out of reach under his chair.

In Taft's hallucination he was no longer lunching with Mrs. Ripstone and Anthony. He was in Claridge's alone and it was fourteen years later. Across the restaurant he could see Mrs. Ripstone but she couldn't see him. She looked much older. Her face was raddled but her curls were still the color of a marigold and the patches of rouge were just as brilliant on her cheeks.

Mrs. Riptstone was lunching with a social worker who was many years younger than Taft. Also sitting at her table there was a teenage boy. He was ashen-pale and he had a psychotic expression. Mrs. Ripstone was ordering him a chocolate mousse . . .

Taft got to his feet in such a masterful way that he felt he must be acting exactly like John Wayne. He had stopped hallucinating. He was back with Mrs. Ripstone in reality.

"Will you excuse me?" he said to her. "I'm afraid I'm really going to have to leave. I'm feeling extremely unwell. I will take Anthony back to St. Michael's and then I'm going home to lie down."

"But this is terrible . . . ," Mrs. Ripstone was stuttering. "I hadn't realized you felt so bad."

"I'm feeling very bad, Mrs. Ripstone." Taft's deep melodious voice had acquired the piously remorseful tone that always crept into it when his indolent sexual compliance ceased and he became ruthlessly determined to terminate a relationship that he found insufferable.

"I'm afraid I'm not myself," Taft said. "I'm suffering from shock. I had a tragedy last week. My wife was killed in a car crash . . ."

Addy

Mrs. Burton was in a taxi on her way to a dinner when she realized with horror that Addy, her old dog, was dying.

For some time she'd noticed that Addy was behaving strangely. It was as if she had become senile. When Mrs. Burton took her out into the street for her evening walk, she now felt obliged to put her on a lead. Addy had once been traffic-trained. Mrs. Burton used to be able to open the front door of her building and wait while the dog sniffled at the lamppost and the railings and then stepped into the gutter to do what Mrs. Burton called "her business." Addy never would have dreamt of defiling the pavement. She did her "business" with such grace and her movements were so feminine and delicate she looked as if she was dropping a discreet curtsey. Having accomplished what was expected of her, she used to come trotting back obediently into the house.

Recently Addy's behavior had become very peculiar whenever she was let out into the street. If any strangers passed her, she started to follow them. It upset Mrs. Burton to see the way she would go limping after their shoes as if she was devoted to them. She had always been a very loving dog, but now when she trailed the heels of strangers her lovingness seemed undiscriminating and deranged.

Mrs. Burton would call her name, but Addy seemed unable to recognize it. Mrs. Burton had to run after the old dog and carry her back to the house otherwise she'd have followed the feet of strangers wherever they happened to take her.

Mrs. Burton no longer trusted Addy's traffic sense. She feared she might suddenly see a stranger on the other side of the street and decide she wanted to follow him. There was a danger she might step into the road without looking to the left or right and go under the wheel of a car.

Three days ago when Mrs. Burton got back from work she noticed Addy did not come bouncing and wagging to the door of her flat to greet her. She barked a welcome, but she remained sitting on her favorite sofa. Addy had very beautiful gold-brown eyes and when Mrs. Burton went over and patted her, she noticed they had an imploring expression. It was as if she wished to apologize for a discourtesy.

Addy's head still looked young and it no longer matched her body. She was a border sheepdog and she still had an aquiline aristocratic head, but with age she had lost her figure and it spread over the sofa like a fat cushion of brown fur.

Mrs. Burton had decided she ought to take the old dog out for a walk. "Come on," she clicked her fingers at Addy whose portly body gave a helpless shudder. She seemed unable to move from the sofa.

Mrs. Burton picked her up and carried her downstairs and took her into the street. When she was put down, Addy's hind-legs collapsed under her. She struggled bravely, but she was unable to take a step. If she wanted to follow strangers, she was no longer able to do so.

Mrs. Burton became alarmed. What could have happened to Addy? She picked her up and carried her to the gutter and supported her and she managed to do her "business." She hated the look in the dog's eyes. It was too like the expression Mrs. Burton's mother used to have when she had to be lifted on to the bedpan. Addy's eyes were yellow with humiliation. Once she'd carried her back up into her flat, Mrs. Burton put her down on her favorite sofa. It was then that Addy had started panting.

Mrs. Burton had wondered if she ought to get the vet. But she couldn't see what he could do for Addy. The dog was really now very ancient and her old age had caught up with her. From now on Addy would have to be treated like a crippled invalid. Mrs. Burton brought her some water which she accepted. She offered her some dog meat which she refused. Mrs. Burton felt it was all right to leave her and she went out to see a play with a woman friend. There seemed to be nothing very wrong with Addy except that she kept on panting.

When Mrs. Burton returned around midnight, Addy was asleep. She looked quite peaceful. Mrs. Burton went to bed, but she suffered from insomnia. She tossed around, restless and anxious. It was as if she was waiting for something unpleasant to happen and yet she wasn't quite certain what it was.

It was around three o'clock in the morning when Mrs. Burton

heard an odd sound from her living room. It was the noise of violent scratching. She got up and went next door to investigate and she saw that Addy was no longer on the sofa. She had somehow managed to get down on to the floor and she had dragged herself into a corner behind an armchair.

Addy was squatting there on her collapsed haunches and with her front paws she was digging the thick wall-to-wall carpet of the living room. She didn't stop when Mrs. Burton found her doing this. Her claws continued to tear at the carpet as if she was a rabbit digging a burrow.

"Addy! What on earth are you doing!" Mrs. Burton found herself speaking very sharply as if she expected an answer. Addy went on with her digging and there was a desperation in the way that her claws ripped the fluffy pile from the carpet. "Stop it!" Mrs. Burton shouted at her. "Stop it at once, Addy! You are ruining the carpet!"

She stopped immediately. She had always been very obedient. Mrs. Burton picked her up and gave her a soft little smack of disapproval. She saw the look of reproach in Addy's eyes. Mrs. Burton was very aware of the softness and the vulnerability of her fat old body as she carried her back to the sofa. Once Mrs. Burton had made Addy comfortable, she kissed her nose to show she had forgiven her. She noticed that it felt very dry. Addy was still panting and suddenly she gave such a loud pant it sounded like an agonized sigh. Mrs. Burton patted her soothingly and left her to go back to bed.

The next day Addy seemed neither better nor worse. Mrs. Burton took her out before she went to work and went through the same routine of lifting the weak old animal while she urinated.

When Mrs. Burton returned in the evening, Addy was still sitting on the sofa. There seemed nothing very much the matter with her except that she still kept on quietly panting. Mrs. Burton was tired and she felt a certain resentment when she had to carry her outside. Once Addy had drunk some water and refused some food, Mrs. Burton put on an evening dress and went off to a dinner party. As she closed the front door behind her and left her on her own, she decided that if the dog still refused to eat in the morning, she would ask the vet to come and look at her.

It was not until she was in the taxi that Mrs. Burton wondered if Addy had been trying to tell her something important. Had she refused to understand the poor animal's message because she didn't want to accept it? Could Addy be dying? Did she want Mrs. Burton to know it? When she was digging the living room carpet, had she been trying to dig her own grave? She had been trained not to cause an inconvenience or mess.

When Addy had followed strangers, had it been an act of despair? She couldn't tell Mrs. Burton that she was dying. Even when she made signals that tried to convey this fact, Mrs. Burton remained deaf to them. Maybe Addy had hoped that strangers could recognize that she was dying and treat her accordingly. Had she followed their heels with this blind devoted hope?

Mrs. Burton knew that she ought to tell the cab driver to turn round and take her straight back to her house. If Addy was dying, it was extremely cruel to let her die all on her own. She had always been so loving and obedient, first to Mrs. Burton's daughter, Devina, and then to Mrs. Burton. One of them should hold the poor old creature in her arms and give her some affection and comfort as she died. Addy was only a dog, but she deserved this human tribute.

Mrs. Burton felt like a criminal, but she did not tell the driver to turn back. Mrs. Fitz-James, the woman who had invited her to dine, had once been a pupil at the same school. They had once been great friends as little girls but the years had passed and their lives had gone in different directions and they had not kept in touch. Recently they'd met at a cocktail party, and Mrs. Burton had been intimidated by the self-assurance with which Mrs. Fitz-James met the world. She had turned into a very striking and elegant woman, but Mrs. Burton disliked the way she had become both snobbish and brittle. Mrs. Fitz-James was married to a wealthy London banker and she boasted about her husband as if she'd won him like a trophy. Mrs. Burton remembered that Mrs. Fitz-James had once won the high-jump on sports day. When she'd been handed a gold cup, she seemed unable to let go of it, but had stood there hugging it to her chest with cheeks that were pink with triumph.

When the two women met again, Mrs. Fitz-James asked Mrs. Burton a few condescending questions and soon made it apparent that she pitied her old school-friend for having made a mess of her life and wasted her opportunities. Her arched eyebrows had risen with sarcastic sympathy when she heard that Mrs. Burton had ended up a divorcee without sufficient alimony. She looked appalled when she heard that Mrs. Burton had been forced to get a job in London in order to support herself.

Hoping to wriggle out of the uncomfortable spotlight of her old friend's condescension, Mrs. Burton reminded her of a silly episode that had taken place when they were both at school. Did Mrs. Fitz-James remember how they had made paper pellets and flicked them at the behind of the geography teacher, Miss Ball? Mrs. Fitz-James remembered and she gave a tinkle of affected pleasure.

Miss Ball was most probably dead by now, but she had once been important to Mrs. Fitz-James and Mrs. Burton, and her voluminous behind was still vivid to them and they were each glad to find another human being who recalled it. It was on the strength of this frail bond that for a moment, they both drew closer to each other, and it was then that Mrs. Fitz-James had asked Mrs. Burton to come and dine.

The moment Mrs. Burton accepted the invitation she regretted it. She suspected it had been issued out of competitiveness rather than affection. Mrs. Fitz-James very probably wanted her less fortunate school-friend to be allowed a tantalizing peep at the desirable life she felt she now led. Exactly as if they were still at school, Mrs. Fitz-James wanted to show off.

Now, as Mrs. Burton rode on in the taxi, she realized that if she had found Mrs. Fitz-James a little more congenial, she would have telephoned her and explained that she could not come to her dinner party. She knew it would be very rude if she cancelled at such short notice. If she defected, even if she explained that her dog was dying, she doubted Mrs. Fitz-James would consider it an adequate excuse. The numbers at the dinner party would be made uneven. Men would have to sit next to men. Her hostess was a woman who obviously cared very much about such matters. If Mrs. Burton suddenly refused the invitation, Mrs. Fitz-James would be extremely annoyed. Women like Mrs. Fitz-James frightened Mrs. Burton. Their self-confidence and elegance and their patronizing attitudes made her feel inadequate and uncouth. Mrs. Burton despised herself for her cowardice, but she knew she was not going to turn back to look after Addy. She tried to persuade herself the dog was not really dying. Addy had become weak and wheezing, but she could probably go on for years in the same condition.

When Mrs. Burton walked into Mrs. Fitz-James's drawing room, her hostess came swaying gracefully to greet her, holding out a beautifully manicured hand that gleamed with valuable rings. Mrs. Fitz-James was looking even more handsome than when her old friend had last seen her, and her honey-colored hair was looped around her ears and held in place by diamond clips. She was wearing a tight-fitting satin gown which showed off her supple and well-exercised figure. The very sight of her made Mrs. Burton feel dumpy, middle-aged, and badly dressed.

Mrs. Fitz-James kissed her and was very gushing and friendly. She made a joke about Miss Ball, the geography teacher. She was trying to put Mrs. Burton at her ease. But they had exhausted that subject and neither found it all that funny. Mrs. Fitz-James then admired Mrs. Burton's evening sandals and asked her where she had been clever enough to find them. Mrs. Burton had owned them for years, but never before had she felt her shoes were quite so shabby, old-fashioned, and down-at-heel.

"I'm really thrilled you could come." Mrs. Burton disliked the way Mrs. Fitz-James was like an actress, word-perfect in her social lines.

A group of guests were standing round the ornate marble mantelpiece in the drawing room. The men looked prosperous and upper-class, and they were wearing dinner-jackets.

Mrs. Fitz-James introduced her to her banker husband. He looked much like all the other men in the room, but his mouth seemed just a little more cruel than theirs, and he had a slightly more supercilious and world-weary eye. When he was told that Mrs. Burton had been at school with his wife, he looked surprised. "How amusing!" he said.

There were also several women in long, glamorous dresses, but Mrs. Burton hardly dared to look at them when she had to shake their hands. She was too frightened that their beauty and stylishness would make her feel even more unattractive and dreary than she'd felt when speaking to Mrs. Fitz-James.

A butler brought Mrs. Burton a glass of champagne. Out of nerves she drank it in one gulp and then wished she'd had the poise and the good sense to sip it.

A scarlet-faced man started to make conversation with her. He had blue, sentimental eyes and snowy-white hair with a fluffy texture as if it had been blow-dried. He told her that he was a racehorse owner and asked if she was interested in horses. She murmured that she liked horses very much, but unfortunately, she had never had much to do with them. He said that racing was a drug, but unlike most drugs it often made you quite a lot of money! Mrs. Burton smiled with fake amusement. She suspected he had made this remark many times before, and, like an old comedian, he believed that well-tried jokes always worked the best.

The butler refilled Mrs. Burton's glass and she took care not to drink her champagne quite so quickly as before. She told the racehorse owner that she worked in a firm which published educational books. "That must be very interesting." His white head nodded knowingly. Mrs. Burton felt the conversation was swaying in the wind like a rope-bridge that connected different terrains.

Mrs. Burton took a third glass of champagne. She wished to God she had never come. She kept thinking of Addy. Mrs. Fitz-James was describing a house she was having built in Sardinia. She complained of the problems she was having getting the plumbing installed and the laziness of the local workmen.

"Have you ever been to Sardinia?" the florid racehorse owner asked her. He was valiant with his good manners. He kept trying to find the perfect topic that would stimulate her.

"No, I've never been to Sardinia."

"I hear it is very beautiful."

"That's what they say."

The butler announced that dinner was ready. The table gleamed with perfectly polished silver and its mahogany shimmered in the candlelight. Mrs. Burton knew from the look of Mrs. Fitz-James's table that the food was going to be delicious. This made her feel unhungry.

Mrs. Fitz-James placed Mrs. Burton between the racehorse owner and another depressed-looking man with grey hair. When the butler filled Mrs. Burton's glass with white wine, she once again gulped it down as if it was water. By now, she was feeling too drunk to care if the other guests at the table looked at her with horror, fearing she was an alcoholic.

"I'm feeling very upset tonight," she suddenly announced to the racehorse owner. She wanted to prevent him from embarking on any meaningless general conversation. He seemed to be a boring and mindless man, but at least he could be her listener. She was angry that she had come to this deadly dinner party and she felt quite unable to find the strength to weave anymore threads of social chitchat. She would speak only about the subject that haunted her.

Her neighbor looked concerned. "I'm very sorry to hear you are upset. What has happened?" She had already noticed he seemed to have a sentimental streak and now his watery blue eyes had become sympathetic and avuncular.

"I'm worried about my old dog. This evening I had the awful feeling that she is dying."

"How old is your dog?" he asked her.

"In human terms she must be about eighty-eight, maybe eighty-nine."

"So she's really a very ancient lady." Her neighbor nodded gravely.

"Yes, I'm afraid that's true. And recently she hasn't seemed at all well."

"It's funny how attached one gets to the old things," he said. "I remember I was very cut up when my old Labrador died."

The butler served Mrs. Burton some creamy white soup which she looked at with a feeling of nausea. The racehorse owner leant towards her as if he was confiding a secret.

"If your dog is very old, I'm afraid she is bound to die quite soon. You will just have to accept it. When she passes on you must look on it philosophically. I'm sure your dog has had a very happy life with you. When she goes—you must comfort yourself with that."

Mrs. Burton looked at her soup and it seemed to have turned a hideous grey. She kept thinking of Addy digging the carpet. Her neighbor kept repeating that she had to be philosophical. He seemed to get a relish from saying that word, just as he was relishing the soup she couldn't eat.

Addy's life had not been as pleasant as the racehorse owner assumed. There had been a few years when she had been well-treated. That was when Devina loved her and they had lived in the country. At that time Devina was always kissing Addy. She played with her all day long and she had exercised her properly and let her run hunting rabbits in the fields.

It was as if Devina's love for Addy had been a childish disease like measles. She had caught a violent dose of it and then when she went off to boarding school, she got rid of it. Devina had once carried snapshots of Addy in her purse. Now she carried love letters from her boyfriend. Devina was glad to see Addy on the occasions that she visited Mrs. Burton. But her gladness was lukewarm. Addy no longer had any real magic for Devina. She would be sad to hear that the old dog had died. Something that had been important to her in her childhood would have perished. But Devina was at university now and all her other interests would soon smother the news of Addy's death.

After Mrs. Burton was divorced, she had moved to London and got a job. She had taken Addy with her, but she had never felt she was her dog. Often she had been quite a nuisance to Mrs. Burton because she needed to be let out and fed. But having known how Devina had once doted on the dog, she had thought it disloyal to get rid of her.

Mrs. Burton had never been a dog-lover and she'd not been prepared to allow her life to be ruled by Addy's needs. When she went off to work, Addy had been left alone in the house all day. Mrs. Burton could never muster any excitement when she was greeted by the dog when she got back home, although she knew that Addy had been moping and pining, and waiting in a frenzy of anticipation for her return. Addy's rapturous delight when she saw her come through the door irritated rather than gratified Mrs. Burton. She disliked all her barking and squirming, and when she jumped up and put her front paws on her skirt, Mrs. Burton had always pushed her down.

Addy's relationship with Devina had been one of mutual passion. After Devina's father left Mrs. Burton, the little girl had needed to stifle her feelings of hurt and betrayal by pouring her love on to an object she saw as perfect because it was not human. Everything about the dog had delighted Devina in that period. She loved the smell inside her ears and she claimed it was like the smell of car seats. She refused to sleep unless Addy was tucked beside her under the bedclothes. Sometimes Devina made her lie on her back with her head propped up on pillows in a position so undog-like, Mrs.

Burton found it almost unkind. But Addy had seemed perfectly happy so she had not protested. Mrs. Burton only made a fuss whenever she found Devina licking her dog's pink tongue because she was terrified her daughter would get some dangerous disease.

Devina used to believe that Addy could understand anything that was said to her, it almost seemed to be true for she instantly obeyed the child's peculiar commands. Devina would give her a lump of sugar and order the dog not to swallow it. Addy then kept it in her mouth gazing up at Devina with an expression of slavish adoration. When the little girl told her to spit it out she immediately obeyed. After that Devina allowed her to eat the sugar lump and she squealed with delight because Addy had been so clever and abstemious. She then overfed her with sweet biscuits to let her know how much the trick had pleased her. She would hug her and pat her until Addy got so overexcited she often seemed like a mad dog jumping around and barking as if she had been driven demented by such intense approval.

In those years, whenever anything upset Devina, her first instinct had been to run to find Addy. She clasped the dog in her arms as if she was a teddy bear and when Devina cried, she liked to bury her face in Addy's thick, reassuring fur.

Sitting at this formal and inane dinner party, Mrs. Burton felt that she suddenly wanted to cry. She battled to prevent herself from doing so because her tears would be hypocritical. Very likely they would be treated with sympathy and that would make her feel all the more corrupt. If she was to cry, her neighbor would explain to the rest of the table that she was distressed because her beloved old dog was dying. It would be disgusting if she allowed all these strangers in expensive clothes to condole with her.

Addy had been used and violated by Devina and Mrs. Burton.

Devina had once needed Addy's love and loyalty as therapy and then she had betrayed her, for she had lost all interest in the dog once her adoration ceased to have any value for her. Addy had been too dumb to comprehend that human beings were fickle. When she was moved to the cold foster-home of Mrs. Burton's ownership, she had always hopelessly tried to re-create the idyllic relationship that she had been falsely taught to accept as her due.

She had guarded Mrs. Burton's flat as she should have been allowed to guard sheep. She seemed only to let herself half-sleep for, if there was any noise outside the door, she always sprang up with the ears pricked in order to bark a warning. Mrs. Burton suddenly remembered that she'd insisted that Addy be spayed. That was one more area where Addy had been cheated.

Although Mrs. Burton had seen that she was kept alive, she now felt convinced her indifference towards the dog had been vicious. Once she'd moved from the country, she had made her lead the life of an urban prisoner. Addy had such a gregarious and friendly nature that Mrs. Burton hated to think of all the hours that the poor animal had spent all alone in the flat.

"Have some croutons," her expansive neighbor said. He was holding out some kind of china terrine. He started spooning some crisp brown squares into her soup. Mrs. Burton was suddenly feeling dizzy, but she looked down at them floating. They became soggy in front of her eyes, but for a while they kept bobbing on the surface and they all seemed like desperate, drowning creatures.

Her soup no longer seemed like soup. As if she was hallucinating, she saw it as a dangerous lake and she felt she ought to dive in and try to save the drowning croutons. But somehow something stopped her and she could only stare at them in panic and watch them as they perished.

"Are you feeling all right?" the racehorse owner asked her. He was not very sensitive, but he had noticed she was looking peculiar.

Mrs. Burton found she couldn't answer him. She couldn't say she felt all right. By now only one of her croutons retained any distinct shape. The rest had sunk into the liquid. It was this last lonely crouton that Mrs. Burton found the most disturbing, for at moments it seemed to be her mother, at other moments it seemed to be Addy.

Before she had died, Mrs. Burton's mother had been very brave and angry sitting in her wheelchair in the home for arthritics. She had watched television most of the day until the arthritis had gone into her lids and crippled their muscles so that she was unable to keep her eyes open. After that she had just sat in her wheelchair, so immobile she'd seemed like a statue.

Mrs. Burton had gone to read to her once a week. But her visits had never been much of a success. Invariably her mother had told her she was reading too fast or complained that she was mumbling. It had never been very long before her mother irritably ordered her to stop reading because she didn't like the book that Mrs. Burton had chosen.

The food in the home for arthritics had been ill-cooked and unappetizing. Mrs. Burton continually sent her mother various delicacies so that the old lady could have some relief from the dreariness of the diet of the institution. When she visited, she brought smoked salmon and jars of taramasalata and pâté. But her mother always left them untouched on the table beside her wheelchair. On one occasion she had screamed at Mrs. Burton like a child. Tears started pouring down her cheeks. She had reminded her that if you couldn't take any exercise, it was impossible to work up any appetite. She had also been very annoyed by some hothouse grapes that Mrs. Burton had once brought her. Her mother had refused to taste one single grape. She complained that the pips would get stuck in her teeth.

Yet Mrs. Burton had always felt guilty that she had not invited her mother to come and live with her. Once her mother had become a total invalid, she still insisted she couldn't bear to be a burden on the family. If this claim had been a lie, Mrs. Burton had taken it literally. She knew she could never have tolerated the presence of that critical old lady who would have sat all day long like some huge accusing statue in her household.

If she'd agreed to nurse her mother, the old woman would have become magnified by Mrs. Burton until she seemed colossal. Her mother's fury at her own paralysis would have paralyzed Mrs. Burton. It would have prevented her from giving any love and attention to Devina, for her confidence would have shriveled like a prune, totally withered by her inability to make any reparation for the cruel disease that had stricken the old lady.

Even when her mother was in perfect health, she had always had an intensely dissatisfied nature. Her mother's bitterness had once been diffused, but her arthritis had brought all its disparate strands together, and it had found a perfect focus. Imprisoned by her pain-ridden and crippled body, she had felt she could give full vent to all her ancient indignation, seeing it as finally justified.

Mrs. Burton knew she could never have allowed her home to be dominated by someone who sat in her wheelchair sometimes expressing her rage by stoical silences, sometimes releasing it in distressing little displays of demonic petulance. Even in her very best periods of bravery, Mrs. Burton's mother would have sat with eyes closed in her daughter's household like some disturbing and vast grey monument that had been erected to commemorate the destruction of every human hope.

At the dinner party, Mrs. Burton picked up her spoon and mashed her last lonely crouton until it became invisible. She was aware that her neighbor was staring at her in horror. She had squashed it with much too much violence. He was obviously shocked by her table manners. He thought, that like an infant, she was playing with her food.

The crouton had completely disappeared, but Mrs. Burton felt freezing cold. Her neighbor found her weird, but he could not guess how restrained she was being. She would have liked to have screamed and jumped up from the table and run out of this loathsome house where ghosts had appeared in her soup and accused her of deserting them at the very moment when they'd most needed her. Mrs. Burton controlled herself and she found her own control a little despicable. She felt deranged by guilts from the past and the present, but she disguised it and her need to do so seemed craven. She thought it shameful she was so frightened to arouse the disapproval of people for whom she had only scorn.

The dinner continued. More and more food was served. The courses seemed endless. Mrs. Burton sat there and quietly endured this dreadful meal, imprisoned by her good manners. She picked at some duck and she dabbed her lips with her napkin in the most ladylike fashion. She did nothing further that could disturb her bovine neighbor. He chatted on to her and she kept nodding and giving him no indication that when she helped herself to a tiny portion of summer pudding she found it an agonizing struggle to force herself to take even the tiniest mouthful. That evening it sickened her to taste anything that was the color of blood.

When Mrs. Fitz-James finally got up from the table after the coffee and the brandy she was followed by all the other women and she started leading them up the stairs to some bathroom where she wanted them "to powder their noses." The men remained in the dining room and they continued drinking port and brandy.

And then Mrs. Burton suddenly rebelled. She felt it would be insufferable to join the little feminine and perfumed cortège of Mrs. Fitz-James. She refused to go up to her hostess's luxurious bedroom and sit around with all these ladies who would make her feel like a used tea-bag while they prinked and gushed and admired each other's dresses, shoes, and hairstyles.

No one noticed Mrs. Burton as she slipped into the hall and got her coat. She opened the front door very quietly and went out into the street. She was glad it was rude to leave without saying goodbye. She was relieved that at last she had done something impolite.

She was fortunate for she saw a taxi and hailed it. On the way back to her flat, she wondered if she had a fever. Once she got back to her building, her legs were shaking as she went upstairs. There was not a sound when she turned her key in the flat door. As she came in, she saw with horror that Addy was not on the sofa. It took Mrs. Burton only a few seconds to find her. Addy had dragged herself into the corner behind the armchair very near where she'd done her digging. She was lying with her face to the wall.

Mrs. Burton went over and picked her up. Addy felt heavy and rigid. Her amber eyes had gone dark. They had the sightless stare of glass eyes. There was no life in Addy's plump body and yet her fur still seemed to continue to have a life of its own. It felt soft and comforting and warm.

Mrs. Burton stood very still in the center of her flat cradling Addy. She noticed how quiet it was. She realized it would always be unpleasantly quiet in the flat now that she would be living completely on her own. She felt much less distraught than she'd felt at the dinner party.

She had allowed Addy to die all alone, but it seemed futile and self-deceiving to torment herself with self-recriminations. If she had missed Mrs. Fitz-James's dinner party and stayed in the flat with Addy, those few hours would have been unable to make reparation for all the days that Addy had spent locked up like a convict condemned to solitary.

Addy was released now. Addy had been too simple. She had seemed to believe that if she behaved as humans taught her, they would start to treat her as an equal, whereas they were only capable of endowing her with certain human characteristics. According to their varying self-indulgent whims they could turn her into a figure which embodied their shifting guilts and fantasies. But Addy had never managed to have any ultimate reality for the people she had been attached to. Once the veneer of their projections was stripped away, they could only see her as a dog.

Mrs. Burton tightened her grip on Addy's motionless body. Through the years Addy had been a witness to so many painful moments in Mrs. Burton's life. She had also been the speechless witness to many moments of happiness. Addy's relationship with Mrs. Burton had lasted much longer than the latter's marriage.

Addy felt like a stuffed toy. Mrs. Burton wished she could feel more regret for her death. All the wriggling life and bark had gone from Addy, but she was no longer threatened by decrepitude and pain and loneliness. Mrs. Burton felt exhausted and frightened of the future. She envied Addy her stillness.

She suddenly wanted to make the dog a little gesture, and she couldn't tell whether her behavior sprang from remorse or affection. As if she was hoping that her animal victim could help comfort her sense of desolation, she bent over and buried her face in the woolly thicket of Addy's brown fur.

Marigold's Christmas

Marigold was kneeling on the floor of the living room. The child was dabbling silver glitter on a fir-cone that she planned to hang on the Christmas tree.

It was only five o'clock but Marigold's mother wished she could have a brandy. As she had never liked brandy, she wondered why she suddenly craved it. She felt she was freezing to death in a snowdrift. This might explain why she kept conjuring up images of kindly St. Bernard dogs and warm golden alcohol in a flask.

There was no reason for Marigold's mother to feel she was freezing: there was a heater in her flat and it wasn't even snowing outside although the London sky looked ugly and ominous and the color of liquid concrete.

Marigold fidgeted. She sensed that the intensity with which her mother was staring at her was unnatural. She was scrutinizing her as if something in her daughter's appearance might give her an answer to the question she kept asking herself. Would it be possible for her to let the child have a happy Christmas?

She learnt nothing from her examination—only details about her daughter which she noted with such detachment she could have been appraising a stranger. She saw fair silky hair with olive under-tones beneath its top layer that thc sun always bleached gold in the summer. Her mother registered this fact without finding that it helped to answer her question.

She also registered that Marigold's eyes were cornflower blue and very round. Her eyebrows were like two arches of tiny pale hairs which gave her a permanently astonished expression. Her daughter's cheeks had more color than usual. She was flushed with excitement because tomorrow would be Christmas.

Marigold started to look a little frightened as her mother con-tinued to stare at her as if she was assessing the value of an object. She held up the fir-cone to show off its silver glitter—trying to get some word of response from her, some sign of approval. She seemed to sense that something was wrong with her mother and hated this silent, distressing scrutiny, which demanded she could neither under-stand nor supply.

Her mother would have liked to have been able to pretend that she admired the decorated fir-cone. But she found she had nothing encouraging to say about it and could only take note of its charac-teristics with the same cold attention that she'd given to the child's arched eyebrows. She kept hoping that by making a very detailed examination she would start to know if she liked the way the cone had been covered by this silvery substance or whether she would have preferred Marigold to have left it as it was. She saw there was hurt and disappointment in the child's face, but she could only record it as a fact just as she'd recorded there was glitter on the fir-cone. If she was pleased to see the pain in her daughter's expression or displeased—she couldn't really tell.

Marigold's mother had never spent Christmas alone before. But she was not going to be alone, she reminded herself, she would be with her five-year-old child.

Yesterday she had forced herself to go out and buy a tree and a string of multi-colored fairy lights. She'd chosen a wretched little plastic brute of a Christmas tree. It had no blue in its pea-green leaves and it lacked all darkness, dignity, and mystery. She could have bought a real tree, but real ones were more expensive and she hoped that Marigold wouldn't know the difference. Once the lights were plugged in, the tree could look quite bright.

Outside the grey sky was getting darker. It was turning into Christmas Eve. Marigold's mother felt a painful sense of apprehension as if something was going to happen. But what could happen? A night would pass and another day would come and she would spend it with Marigold and cook for the child and wash and mend her clothes and tidy up her toys and it would be little different from any other.

She tried to ridicule her sense of panic. Many people would spend Christmas alone tomorrow and presumably they would not die from the experience. It was mindless to pretend that the day was going to bring joy and good cheer to everyone but herself. The Christmas myth was a dangerous one. It encouraged paranoia. She would have ignored it all had it not been for Marigold. If she had been alone she would have shut it out and locked herself up in the flat and not a sprig of holly, not a scrap of Christmas food would have been there to remind her that she was meant to be celebrating the birth of Christ.

As it was she had gone out and got the Christmas tree and the string of fairy lights, but she had refused to buy any colorful paper chains and bells or mistletoe to put above the door. She had half catered for her daughter's need to celebrate while half respecting her own desire to make the festival as cheerless as she could.

That morning, she had trundled off like a somnambulist to the butcher. He'd soon become impatient with her because she had just stood there staring at his rows of turkeys without choosing one. The shop had been crowded and a queue of frantic women jostled behind her. The butcher's face was as red and wet as some of his chunks of meat. He was overworked and he'd become very irritated by this young woman who stared into the rumps of his Christmas fowl with the intense, mystical gaze of the clairvoyant looking into the future in a crystal ball.

"Now, come on, Madame . . . Now, can you please hurry up . . . What is the matter with you? For God's sake, Madame . . . I'm afraid you've got to hurry up or lose your place. I haven't got all day . . ." But Marigold's mother felt that she not only had all day but all evening and all night as well. And then there was all tomorrow and she'd have that too. There would be all those hours to get through and they would all be part of Christmas Day.

She had understood why the butcher was annoyed but found it hard to make up her mind which of those great pallid pimply birds she wanted. She'd known that neither she nor the child would eat a mouthful of turkey and this had made it even more pointless when she dithered there in the shop with an expression of thoughtful perplexity as though her choice was momentous. She'd still felt it was crucial that she buy one of these fat benighted birds. She would be able to baste the frightful creature and that would give her something to do. If she put it in a very slow oven she could minister to it from breakfast onwards. She was certain she would need some kind of occupation tomorrow. If she and Marigold were to eat boiled eggs for lunch and treat the day as an ordinary one, it would only take them a minute to eat their meal. The day would seem so very much longer with its hours unfilled by any preparations for the feast. The child would get no sense she was having a marvelous Christmas.

Marigold's mother had finally chosen a turkey. Her fear of the anger of the puce-faced butcher and the hostility of all the other women shoppers who were queuing behind her forced her to take action. She loathed the way the other customers muttered aggressively and shoved her with their elbows. She had finally chosen the smallest bird in the shop, but it had still looked gigantic. Repulsive and anaemic, she felt it could have fed the Third World.

While she was paying for the turkey she'd only kept longing for the moment when she could throw it out with all the other Christmas rubbish. She was never going to force poor Marigold to start the New Year living day after day on its dull, dry leftovers. The child might not be going to have a very glamorous Christmas, but she would do her best to stop the holiday from becoming a time of torture. She would stuff the bird and serve it tomorrow. Once Marigold had seen it cooked, she'd throw it immediately into the dustbin. She'd be throwing both Christmas and turkey exactly where they deserved to go.

As she was leaving the shop with Marigold she had looked down at the floor and seen something that terrified her. For a moment she'd tried to pretend it was a holly berry, but couldn't fool herself for long. Lying there in the sawdust was a tiny clot of blood. She wondered why the sight of it made her shake. She'd tried to calm herself by remembering that it was not uncommon to see a few spots of blood on a butcher's floor. But she had still grabbed hold of Marigold's hand with such violence that she screamed. Rushing the child out into the street, she'd made her run as if they were running for their lives.

Once she got back to the flat, the spot of blood pursued her. She saw it on the wall, on the carpet. It would appear for a moment and then vanish.

She continued to stare at her daughter as the minutes ticked on towards Christmas Eve. She would have liked to have gone out to a pub, behaved wildly, drunkenly, picked up some strangers and brought them back home with her so she would not be alone at Christmas. She couldn't take Marigold out to pubs or bars and it could be dangerous to leave her alone. There might be a fire. Someone could break in. She felt trapped by the child. Marigold made Christmas Eve seem a prison.

She needn't have spent this Christmas alone. If she'd told any of her friends that Marcus had chosen not to spend Christmas Day with his wife and daughter they would have invited her to come over and celebrate with them. She could have enjoyed herself and drunk a lot of punch and champagne and liqueurs. Marigold could have enjoyed gazing at the lovingly decorated Christmas trees that you found in other people's houses. Her mother could have spent Christmas feeling that she had a proper identity. She could have thought of herself as having a name of her own, Vivyan Holmes. And yet she had chosen to spend Christmas alone, she had chosen to lose her name and feel defined only by her role.

It was only a week ago that Marcus had told her that he would not be able to join them this year. She could never have explained to him how shocked she'd been by this announcement. For the last three years, ever since they had separated, he had always come to the flat to celebrate Christmas with his estranged wife and his daughter. If there had been animosity running somewhere hidden in the arteries and sinews of the situation, it had never seemed to matter. Marigold's mother and Marcus had exchanged presents and the child had been fascinated by the gifts her parents had chosen for each other. She'd always appeared highly relieved that they could muster a little generosity and some pretence of goodwill.

In the past, when Marcus had come over for these Christmas lunches, Marigold's mother had arranged to have a proper Christmas tree. She'd bought brilliant tinsel balls to decorate it, not just one or two dreary fir-cones. She'd tied lots of well-wrapped little gifts and walking-sticks made of striped candy on its long graceful branches, which had gleamed with artificial snow. She'd covered the tree with pretty wax candles, whereas this year she'd only bought cheap plug-in lights. This evening, remembering the trouble she'd taken in the past when Marcus came over for Christmas, she found it peculiar and sad that she'd been able to make the rituals of Christmas pleasant for a man when she now seemed unable to do the same for a child.

Yet in her heart she knew that she'd never really prepared those beautiful stuffed turkeys for the sake of Marcus. Those delicious fruity Christmas puddings with brandy butter had never been made for him. When she'd lit the candles and the tree had looked so pretty, she'd never really tried to make it look beautiful to please him. She'd wanted him to continue to spend Christmas with his family, not because she was eager for his company but only because she needed to believe that Marigold was valuable to him. It had really always been this fantasy that she had been feeding when she made the table look so rich and attractive as she piled it up with winter flowers and tangerines and walnuts.

If she could believe that Marcus loved their daughter it helped her to feel that her broken marriage had a little dignity. She found it intolerable to think of it as a pointless accident which had left her crippled. Her relationship with Marcus had been smashed up several years ago, but if she could feel that despite their differences they still retained a mutual love for their child, the penalties she'd had to suffer would seem much less acute. If they both adored their child, something serious and valuable had been salvaged from a messy meaningless wreckage. The marriage had ruined her career and it had left her poor and lonely and celibate, trapped in the flat with a very young child whom she sometimes felt was eating up her own youth. She needed evidence that the child was precious to Marcus in order to feel more confident that Marigold was precious to her. In the last years she'd spent so much time, day and night, hour by hour, alone with only the child for company, that she sometimes felt this unnatural relentless proximity had paralyzed her understanding of what she felt. When she kept staring at Marigold with pathological intensity, she was hoping to find something in her appearance—something to prove to herself that she cared more about Marigold's Christmas than Marcus did.

Marcus obviously didn't care at all. Just a week ago he'd told Marigold's mother that he would be in Austria for Christmas. He was going skiing.

"Couldn't you wait and go skiing after Christmas?" she had asked. "Marigold will be disappointed."

Marcus had said he was sorry. He couldn't change his plans. Could she buy Marigold a present from him and he'd pay her back when he returned to England. Next Christmas they must all have a terrific family lunch.

She assumed that the Austrian countess had invited him to stay in her chalet. She felt no jealousy that Marcus preferred to spend Christmas in this glamorous woman's company rather than in her own. He had died for her. She could only resurrect him as "Marigold's father."

Her short marriage now seemed as unreal as a dream. She was thankful that just as dreams faded by morning, time had already erased most of it from her memory. The pleasant bits, she was losing them so fast she felt the marriage might never have happened. Marigold now seemed to be the only proof of a mistake that was no less serious for being ill-remembered.

"Marcus and I have a very sophisticated relationship," she told her friends. "We've got an extremely civilized arrangement. Marcus adores the child so he always seems to be dropping round to my flat. I let him see her whenever he wants."

She'd not thought of herself as lying, merely as rearranging and improving on the facts. Out of pride she'd pretended that Marcus was coming to celebrate Christmas Day with his family as usual. Because of this silly proud lie neither Marigold nor herself had been invited to the homes of other families. If their Christmas was to be a happy one, they now had to make it enjoyable all on their own.

Sitting waiting for Christmas Eve to turn into Christmas, as if under a death sentence, she realized that she'd seen the family Christmas lunch attended by Marcus as an event of far too much symbolic importance. She finally recognized that he'd only come to these lunches because of the pressure she put on him. Contrary to the picture she presented to her friends, months and months would go by without Marcus seeing Marigold at all. Only if she badgered him could she make him visit her daughter.

In the past, it had cost him very little to come to the flat for Christmas lunch. He'd only had to eat her good food and put a present for the child under the tree. After the crackers had been pulled he used to put on a paper crown and preside over the table like a king. He'd always left quite soon after the plum pudding, while the whole evening was ahead of him. There had been time for him to start another Christmas which he could celebrate by eating another turkey dinner with his girlfriend of the moment. That had been the Christmas that had seemed happy to him, and the one that he'd counted as real.

"Is it nearly Christmas?" the child asked her. Her mother found the question astonishing. She wondered how the child had managed to whip herself up into a mood of misguided anticipation without any encouragement from her parents. What in Christ's name did the poor little thing imagine that the day was going to bring her?

"No, it's not nearly Christmas," Marigold's mother told the child. "There's a whole night to go . . . You really have to be good this evening. I hope you know that. You've got to go to bed early. You really must try to get to sleep as soon as you can. If Father Christmas arrives and finds you awake he may go back to the North Pole without filling your stockings."

She was thankful that Christmas could present her with any benefits at all. Tonight there was a hope that by using blackmail she could intimidate Marigold into going to bed early. This might be the one night of the year when the child could be forced to go to her room and stay there. Usually she jumped out of bed every few minutes to say that she was thirsty or ill in order to get attention.

Marigold's mother suddenly felt exhausted. She'd have liked to have taken some pills and gone to sleep immediately and missed this long and ghastly Christmas Eve. But tonight she would have to stay up until the overexcited Marigold got to sleep so that she could fill the stocking that the child would hang on the end of her bed.

The idea all at once seemed insufferable to her. Her craving for brandy turned to a craving for champagne. She knew she would never be able to sit up hour after hour waiting to play Father Christmas if she had remained sober. Champagne was festive and extravagant. She badly needed to feel pampered tonight.

She told Marigold she was going off to the supermarket, and assured her that she wouldn't be long. Marigold must be good until she got back. She told the child to put more glitter on more fir-cones.

She felt guilty leaving her alone in the flat, but she couldn't be bothered to look for the child's gloves and scarf and get her dressed to go out. Maybe champagne would help to take away her oppressive feeling of anxiety and fatigue.

The supermarket was crowded with cheerful-looking people who were buying last-minute items for Christmas. As Marigold's mother queued to buy champagne, her sensation of floating apprehension returned. She kept feeling that something awful was happening to Marigold. She could only pray that housebreakers and child rapists had better things to do this evening—that, unlike the child and herself, they were all preparing to have a very happy Christmas.

As she bought the champagne she felt ashamed. She had not bought anything at all exciting to put in the child's stocking. She had got Marigold a tangerine, and a Mars Bar, and a chocolate Santa Claus, and a plastic bag full of nuts.

Marcus had been generous to her this Christmas. Before he'd announced that he would be going to Austria for the holiday, he'd guiltily given her extra money. It was possible that he was hoping that his generosity would soften the blow. But Marigold's mother had not spent any of it on the stocking. For months she'd been saving up her own small salary in order to spend it on toys and books and games, but she had not done so.

As she bought herself the most expensive bottle of champagne she realized that although she had the money, she lacked the will to give her daughter the stocking she was hoping for. When Marigold's mother was a child she had never once received the Christmas stocking she'd always been longing for. Christmas had always brought her disappointment and a sour sense of having been cheated. Her own mother had not believed in providing lavish stockings. She'd always tried to train her children to expect very little, and taught them not to hope that Christmas would bring them much more than any other day.

As one of the salesgirls in the supermarket wrapped up her champagne in holly-covered paper she saw that the store had a section that sold dolls and toys and books, but she knew that she'd never manage to make herself go near it. She examined her behavior with resignation as if she lacked any power to change it. Yet it sickened her to realize that she was unable to give more than she'd been given.

"I'm as pathetic as Marcus," she thought as she left the shop carrying only her own champagne. "We are both equally pathetic and disgusting."

She found it despicable that they were still hoping to grab happy

Christmases for themselves. They were much too old now to make up for the losses of the past, yet they continued childishly to compete with their own daughter—to whom this festival rightfully belonged.

Marigold's mother ran all the way home from the supermarket. She'd been told that it was illegal to leave small children on their own—that fairy lights could short-circuit and set a house on fire. Before going off to buy herself champagne she'd plugged in the lights and draped them over the plastic branches of the tree. They had looked both dim and messy, with none of the magic of candles. There had been something wrong with the stand that held the Christmas tree and the whole thing kept toppling sideways. She'd taken the nasty little tree out of its stand and stood it up on a chest of drawers and propped it against the wall. She ran on in panic.

By the time she got back to the flat she had worked herself up into a shaking state of terror, convinced that Marigold had perished while she'd been shopping irresponsibly. When she discovered Marigold trying to perch her fir-cones on the ill-formed branches of the tree, she felt like crying with relief that she'd found the child alive.

Marigold's mother woke about four in the morning. Her daughter had been too intimidated by her mother's Christmas blackmail to keep jumping out of bed, but had still taken hours to get to sleep. Although Marigold's mother had drunk the whole bottle of champagne she'd felt angry that she had to sit up so late, waiting to play her role as Father Christmas. But she had played it and the child's stocking had been filled.

She'd thought of Marcus in the Austrian chalet with the countess and how unfair it was that Marigold had been taught to believe in a beaming male benefactor.

At first, when Marigold's mother awoke in the early hours of the Christmas morning, she couldn't tell where she was. She woke to great dread and the dread seemed like four black damp walls that enclosed her. She remained in a half-dream believing herself to be in a cell—waiting to learn what her unknown captors wanted from her.

She finally got up from her bed, and she moved stiffly as if her brain was receiving external instructions. As she walked into Marigold's little bedroom she had a sense that she was being ordered by powerful invisible forces to complete a task that was necessary and inevitable. She felt that all the weeks of dread that had preceded Christmas had only been leading up to this moment when she would perform an act of perfect honesty and abandon all her corrupt pretences.

As she took the stocking from the end of Marigold's bed, the child moved restlessly but she didn't wake. She was lying on her back with her head supported by her stick-thin arms.

Marigold's mother thrust her hand into the stocking. She only ever thought of it as a "stocking." In truth, it was one of the child's white kneesocks. As she felt inside it she no longer believed that she was acting on command. She pulled out the tangerine with a snatching childish gesture. Her own fierce animal-like greed frightened her. She could no longer pretend she was acting on external command.

She peeled the little orange fruit and she started to eat it, savoring it very slowly, segment by segment. She felt she'd never tasted anything quite so sweet. She thought of Eve in the Garden of Eden. It was evil to eat this fruit, it was evil to enjoy devouring the forbidden. Yet she still consumed the tangerine with all the pleasure of the addict enjoying the longed-for fix. When she'd finished it she removed the paper from the chocolate Santa Claus. She found the sweetness intoxicating as she bit off his chocolate head.

Once she'd finished eating the Santa Claus she started on the bag of nuts, and as she crunched them between her teeth she felt that she was recapturing something that had always been her rightful property, of which she'd endlessly been deprived.

Only the Mars Bar was left. She licked the toffee that lay at its center very slowly. The only remaining item of her daughter's Christmas stocking was so precious to her that she wanted to make it last.

Once the toffee was finished her whole mood suddenly changed and the sweetness of the Mars Bar seemed the sweetness of sugar-coated poison. The empty stocking lay on the child's patchwork quilt and Marigold's mother looked at it with horror. She wondered if murderers had a similar feeling when they looked down at the unbreathing corpse. As she stared at the limp white kneesock she saw it covered with drops of blood. Panic was making her hallucinate. She knew she'd been prophesying her own crime when all day long she'd seen blood flecks dancing before her eyes—illusory and syncopated.

Now she realized that those crimson spots had found the place from which they could best accuse her. She felt a wave of nausea. The stolen sweets lay thick in her stomach. Marigold would wake quite soon. Children woke early on Christmas Day. The child's first and only thought on waking would be to examine the contents of her stocking. If she was to find it missing or lying on her bed empty she would experience it as a small death.

Her mother wondered whether she was exaggerating the shock and the despair that the child would feel if she was to discover that, after so many weeks of anticipating a miracle, Christmas morning had brought her nothing. Her deserted stocking could always be replenished, but not until the shops opened much later that day. She could tell the child that Father Christmas would be late this year—

that something had happened to his reindeer and his sledge. She could reassure her by insisting he was still on his way—that he'd just been a little delayed at the North Pole.

Having eaten the contents of the child's stocking. Marigold's mother felt it would be unforgivable if she started to feed her a lot of lies. Even if she waited for the shops to open and presented her daughter with a belated but well-filled stocking she realized that Marigold would be receiving it far too late. The Christmas stocking only had a magical value if it was found mysteriously bulging on the end of the bed at the moment of waking. And then how many shops would be open on Christmas day?

"Too late! Too late!" The two words repeated in her head. Marigold's mother felt that she was listening to a 78 record with the needle stuck in its groove. She could still hear the two ominous words repeating and repeating as she ran out of the flat into the cold dark street. Someone had once told her that they were the saddest words in the English language. As she kept running she felt she was not only trying to race against the moment when the child would wake and the words would become true.

She headed to Euston Station. She had a desperate hope that she might be able to find a machine that sold chocolate bars on one of the big platforms. If she could just refill Marigold's stocking with even the dreariest bits of chocolate, at least she would not have the awful moment of waking to find the white kneesock lying empty on her quilt.

Marigold's mother was not very fit. Euston Station seemed to be much farther from her flat than she imagined. She soon stopped, exhausted, and clung to an iron railing. She was panting so hard she felt she might choke to death. Yet she knew she had to keep moving. She wondered if she should have tried to find a chocolate machine in one of the Underground stations. She'd assumed that the machines there would be empty or broken.

Marigold's mother continued to walk down the deserted streets that led to the station. She then suddenly came to a stop in front of a spruce little shop. She found herself gazing through its glass window with a wonder that she'd not felt since she was a very small child. The shop sold chocolates and various Christmas novelties. She looked at Santa Clauses made of every kind of sugar. She gazed at the ones made of stuffed red felt with white cotton beards. She gasped at the sugar plum mice and the fairies in silver gauze skirts who were meant for the top branch of the Christmas tree.

As she stared into the magical Christmas world of the shop window she started to get the same feeling as when she'd got out of bed and eaten the entire contents of her daughter's stocking. It was the same sensation of not being in control of her actions, of being directed by foreign forces. Her thoughts were still very cool and decisive considering she felt they were being manipulated. She realized she needed two objects for her mission and she went off to search for them.

It didn't take her long to find what she wanted. There was some building going on close by. She found a brick and hid it under her coat. She then searched all the dustbins in the street until she found a large discarded paper carrier. It was a little soiled but it would have to do. Armed with these she returned to the shop.

The street was still completely deserted. There didn't seem to be any police about tonight. She wondered if the owners of the attractive little chocolate shop slept above it. She wondered how much noise the window would make when it shattered. She was frightened of using the brick, terrified of violating property. Her parents had given her this fear and she found it painfully difficult to override a terror so deeply instilled. She knew that she could only overcome her horror of smashing that glass if she did it so quickly that she gave herself no time at all to think.

She threw the brick with such force that the pane flew back into the shop almost intact before it crashed and splintered with a noise that sounded loud enough to wake the entire city. She started feverishly snatching boxes of chocolates through the jagged hole in the window. She took every type of Santa Claus, and every type of reindeer. She grabbed an assortment of stuffed animals and jars of candied fruit and she threw them into her carrier. Lights were going on in the houses opposite. She could hear steps on the back stairs of the shop and she realized the owners did live above it and that they were now coming down.

She started running. She ran zigzagging down deserted alleyways. She heard the menacing whine of a police-car siren breaking the stillness of the early hours of Christmas morning. Running with her spoils, she avoided all the thoroughfares and kept to the back streets.

At one point she hid crouching behind a car that was parked in an alleyway and watched a police car cruising past. She assumed they were searching for her. If the police picked her up her daughter would have a horrible Christmas. She assumed that social workers would take Marigold into care and put her in an orphanage or some similar state institution. Perhaps the courts could take away her child indefinitely. She was ignorant of the law.

She was much more frightened for Marigold than herself as she watched the police car drifting past. The two young officers inside were chatting to each other. With luck they were more interested in their plans for Christmas Day than their routine search for a chocolate thief.

Once the car had vanished she felt less haunted and started

lugging the heavy carrier back to the flat, where she found Marigold lying in the same position with her white stick-like arms supporting her head. Even in sleep the arch of her eyebrows made her look astonished. The empty white kneesock was lying limply on her quilt.

She started to take out the stolen items from the carrier and she got more pleasure from the plunder in the paper bag than from any stocking she'd received as a child.

When she had frenziedly grabbed things through the broken window she'd been too stunned by her own behavior to realize how much she was taking. Now she found many surprises and she was childishly thrilled by every new discovery. She found a skipping-rope, a mouth-organ, a box of crackers, a fountain-pen that squirted, a tea set and a toy guitar. She discovered five boxes of chocolates, beautifully wrapped with huge red bows and sprigs of holly.

She felt she'd rarely seen anything quite so attractive as the sugar mice and the chocolate Santas and all the stuffed felt animals that she found in the carrier. A few glass reindeer and other things had been damaged in the hectic collection, but they were unimportant casualties. She filled the white kneesock till it bulged, and hung it in the correct and traditional position at the foot of Marigold's bed. The chocolate boxes and the jars of candied fruit were much too big to fit in the child's narrow stocking, so she put them at the foot of the Christmas tree and perched all the rest of the toys and novelties on its branches.

She then went to make herself some coffee in the kitchen and, as she waited with impatience for Marigold to wake, she felt a mood of euphoria that was fed by a sense of deep relief. By committing a petty crime she'd made reparation for a much more serious emotional one.

She sipped her coffee, waiting for Marigold to wake and Christmas to come at last.

Angelica

For the second evening running, Angelica, the retired actress, had arrived by taxi and come to loiter all alone in the Brompton Cemetery. She was a tall and flamboyant woman and she looked over life-size in her rippling and expensive fur coat. Her golden hair was piled on top of her head and it gleamed like a warrior's helmet. She was very heavily made-up and her skin glowed with the healthy peach tones of a thick and mask-like foundation. Her appearance exuded a confidence she didn't feel.

As Angelica walked through the black iron gates she once again suffered from a feeling of panic and had to struggle with a violent desire to leave. She found it ghastly, this immense London graveyard. She wondered whether there were many places on earth where it would be more depressing to spend a lonely evening than in these sealed-off city acres where the rain was drizzling down on the dead who were all lying there so hugger-mugger under their hideous and diversified stones.

The overcrowding in this cemetery was very shocking to her. She tried to see the congestion as comic. But she found it grim rather than amusing. She was disturbed by the way all the graves and crosses and mausoleums were so closely packed that they looked as if they were all part of one vast greyish white mosaic.

As Angelica set off towards the center of the cemetery she felt she was in a place of remembrance that made the whole concept seem like a fantasy. Most of the inmates in this ill-tended and over-populated cemetery seemed extremely forgotten. They had been squeezed in here and labelled with pious phrases and their dates, but they still seemed so forgotten they might as well never have existed.

Angelica felt that this was a spot which questioned the whole essentialness of existence. This was a place that demanded feelings of melancholy just as it demanded wreaths of flowers. But as she went winding through its maze-like paths and smelt once again the musty stench of desolation that rose from all these urban graves that seemed to stretch out to infinity around her, she was certain she had made the right decision in coming here. For she felt less depressed while she was wandering about amongst all these neglected mounds and these phalanxes of tilting crosses, than she ever felt in Dr. Abelman's office where she went every morning to have treatment for her depression.

She wondered what Dr. Abelman would say if she told him she found visits to Brompton Cemetery much more therapeutic than his treatment. She felt that it was unlikely that he would be very thrilled to hear that she'd come back for the second time to this dismal burial ground. He wouldn't be pleased to be told that one of his patients liked to hang around in this gruesome spot without having even the remotest link with any of the dead. It might be difficult for him to accept that it was very healthy behavior. She didn't think he would be able to boast that it was much of an advertisement for his therapy.

Angelica felt rather gratified by the idea that young Dr. Abelman would disapprove of her presence in the cemetery. She often felt a very deep dislike for him, finding him smug and humorless and dogmatic. However, she concealed these feelings and she was uncharacteristically meek and subdued while she was with him. When she went to his office seeking pills and sympathy for her depression she sometimes thought she must seem like a pathetic old whining beggar holding out her bowl.

"We must try to find out why you react so violently to any rejection," he kept saying to her. "You must try to see your depression is really anger. You are angry that Jason has left you. We must examine the way that your relationship with that young man was destroyed by your insecurity and jealousy."

Dr. Abelman believed there was a point in speaking to her with a certain brutality. He thought she could have a happy and productive future if she would only allow him to change her. He felt that once she gained some insight into the patterns of her past behavior she could learn by her mistakes. But Angelica, who felt so fierce and defeated and futureless, only found herself more and more depressed every moment that she listened to him. She had little faith in the effectiveness of his therapy, and often the naïvety of his suggestions seemed so exasperating it made her want to scream.

"I would like you to have a much fuller social life than you do at present," he kept telling her. "You would feel better if you went out much more and attended the opera and the theatre. You should try to mix with people of your own age. Your attachment to this young man was clearly a very neurotic one. You should try to strike up some new acquaintances with whom you can have an interesting and lively exchange of ideas, establish mature and valuable relationships."

Dr. Abelman longed for her to have "lively exchanges of ideas," and Angelica always felt bemused whenever he mentioned this strange ambition. She wondered where he had got it from. Such exchanges seemed so pathetic and futile as an aspiration. Angelica always found it useless to try and make Dr. Abelman understand how much she had disliked the parties she had gone to lately, for she'd seemed to spend them sitting with a whisky on some sofa and staring with disgust at the ears of the other guests.

She'd wonder why they were not ashamed to go on laughing and chattering to each other in such a confident and mindless fashion when all the time they had these absurd rubbery appendages clamped to the sides of their heads.

She dreaded it whenever any of them came over and tried to speak to her, for she felt she couldn't bear to talk to them unless they first removed their odious ears. The young men seemed quite as insensitive as the old ones, expecting her to enjoy making conversation while they made no effort to prevent her from seeing the repulsive hanging skinflaps of their lobes. The women also repelled her, for though they had various elaborate hairstyles, she could still see the sickening bulge of their ears showing through their curls. Sometimes she found the women were almost worse than the men, for she felt there was something deceitful in the way they seemed to be trying to hide the pink deformities that sprouted out like fungi from both sides of their faces by draping them with coils of silky hair.

When Angelica went out to parties, it was the enormous variety in design of the ears of the people that she met that she found so revolting, much more revolting than if they'd all had one uniform brand. She loathed the way that some of their ears were multicolored with inner-rims and outer-rims of different shapes and shades that ranged from violet to raspberry—from off-white to bluish-black.

"Is anything the matter, Angelica?" It was never very long before someone asked her this question.

"No. This evening I'm afraid I suddenly don't feel very well at all."

Angelica would have just caught sight of the ears of a couple of homosexuals, noticing that the older one had ears which were a pale tomato cream and inlaid with a jeweled cluster of navy-blue spots. The younger one had yellow wax ears which were flecked like a bird's egg, with tiny freckles of coffee brown.

"You really do look quite pale and ill, Angelica. Perhaps you would like us to get you a taxi to take you home."

"It's been such a lovely party, but I think I must be coming down with some little virus. It would be very kind if you could get me a taxi."

She would have just caught sight of a distinguished white-haired politician and noticed with a feeling of nausea and despair that he had the most terrible orange plastic hearing-aid stuck deep in the disgusting hole of his raw-meat-colored ear.

"Ears obviously must have some special significance for you," Dr. Abelman kept suggesting with his customary owlish solemnity.

"Oh no. I don't think ears mean very much to me at all." Angelica was invariably very stubborn on this point, as she kept trying not to examine Dr. Abelman's baroque-looking ears with their curlicue arches and their dark inner courtyards of hair-tufted skin.

She could have easily explained why the ears of every person that she had met in the last few months filled her with revulsion. But she had never felt there was any point in trying to explain anything she saw as important to Dr. Abelman. He was far too unimaginative and his literal mind had such very great difficulty in following any fanciful flights. As Angelica found him deeply unsympathetic and difficult to speak to, she often wondered if it was not rather pointless paying so much to come every morning to talk to him.

She could have explained to almost anyone in the world except this bespectacled young doctor that ever since Jason had left her, although she hated being alone, she disliked people coming to her house almost as much as she disliked going to other people's houses to be entertained. She now loathed being with friends almost as much as she loathed being with crowds of strangers. She only became obsessed by the ugliness and absurdity of the ears of other human beings because it made them all seem so very flawed. But their true flaw, only symbolized by their ears, was that they were all quite incapable of distracting her.

Recently she had found that both men and women were equally incapable of pleasing and amusing her. Even when they were generous, sympathetic, and flattering they still aroused her anger. They seemed to prattle incessantly. When they invited her to restaurants and parties she accepted gratefully and her smile was false and gracious, but her eyes were fixed with fury and horror on their ears.

The whole time that she listened to them flirting and gossiping, and speaking of their careers, their money difficulties, their love affairs, she found that their distressingly visible ears made them all seem so unattractive that they seemed indistinguishable.

She tried to pay attention while they discussed current political events, the books they had read, the films they had seen, the taxes they were being forced to pay. When they talked they bored her so much that she found it hard to believe that it was not their deliberate intention to do so.

Lately her feeling of generalized free-floating boredom had become so sharp that she often felt that it was drilling through her like an instrument of torture. She was often frightened by the way that her interests had become so shrunken that they seemed to be incapable of focusing on anything except her own menacing moods. All her energies were now devoted to trying to placate them.

In recent weeks, whenever Angelica left her house and went out to attend any social occasion, it was only in the hope of improving her own moods. She felt obliged to treat them as if they were sickly and demanding invalids who might conceivably benefit from a little fresh air.

But once she found herself surrounded by people who were laughing and drinking and joking she was invariably disappointed. She only wished that she had stayed at home drinking whisky alone in her bed.

Her moods tended to deteriorate and become fouler and more petulant in the very pleasant circumstances where she had hoped they might improve. Sitting, unhungry, at dinner parties she would stare at all the expensive foods that seemed to flow on and off her plate in great tidal waves of courses. She viewed her fellow guests with a paranoid rage and horror. She felt certain that she had only been invited because she was generally considered to be pitiable. Whenever anyone tried to speak to her she suspected that they were only making an effort to be kind to her because they realized she was lonely and humiliated. She found their kindness as distasteful as all the rich sauces that smothered the fish and the meat that her hostess kept trying to feed to her. Neither friendliness nor hospitality could cheer her. All the while she was receiving it Angelica never stopped feeling that now that Jason had grown tired of her she only wished that she was dead.

But she didn't feel that for one single moment when she was drifting around all by herself in Brompton Cemetery. Once she was surrounded by the deceased nothing in their situation seemed at all enviable. All her self-dramatizing sentiments seemed contemptible and she realized they were completely bogus. When Angelica was all alone in the huge and creepy burial ground, the dead called her bluff.

Lately whenever she had telephoned her daughter, Susan, she had laid great emphasis on her despairing state of mind. "I have reached a point of unhappiness, darling, when I wonder if I can really go on."

However, she had just discovered that when she was alone with all these hordes of unweeded people in Brompton Cemetery their mass indifference to her wretchedness was more cheering than her daughter's automatic solicitude. Their indifference was so total that it became contagious and while she was with them she felt temporarily forced to share it.

And there was another reason why Angelica's depression lifted the moment she came into the cemetery. As she walked through its somber gates all her self-pity instantly vanished. She recognized it to be such an unsuitable emotion that it seemed to go immediately underground, like the bones of all the inmates.

"Lately I feel that I am becoming more and more like those stiff and pointless female figures that you sometimes see in bad, nineteenth-century oil paintings," Angelica had told Susan very recently. "Day after day as I sit here, I feel so unreal that I start to think that some unknown artist has only put me here in order to balance the strip of sunlight on my Wilton carpet, to make some kind of subtle color contrast with the blackness of my own stupid piano. I begin to think that, like those wretched painted women, every fold in the beautiful material of my dress is now far more interesting than the wrinkles on my face. It's very demoralizing to be forced to realize that you have got to a point in life when even your clothes and your furniture have far more interest and function than you do. You start to hope that the unknown artist will suddenly decide that the composition would be just as good without you—that he will soon take some tuft of cotton-wool soaked in turpentine and just wipe you out."

Angelica had seen the nervous concern on her daughter's face. As she burdened Susan with her dissatisfactions she had got an ignoble pleasure from her knowledge that she could always ruin the unlucky girl's peace of mind. Susan's vulnerability in relation to her mother aroused Angelica's sadism. She was ruthless in the way she liked to make her daughter worry about her. She found Susan kind and reliable, but she also found her distressingly ordinary. Angelica always wished she could like her only child more than she did. Susan's lack of worldliness and ambition appalled her. The sight of her daughter's healthy and humdrum face always startled her. She saw it as sad and disturbing. She felt baffled as to how she had ever produced it. She found it indistinguishable from the robust, pleasant faces of all the hundreds of young married women who were to be seen pushing their baby-strollers and lugging their string bags of groceries through all the supermarkets of every sleepy country town in England.

Angelica saw Susan's life as so dismally lacking in drama that she often managed to convince herself that she was doing her daughter a favor by force-feeding her with her own surplus. Lately she had started to telephone Susan incessantly. Angelica would drink whisky alone in her bed at night and then with her mind boiling with alcohol she would wake up her daughter and accuse her of neglect. "Now that you have a husband and children you only long to forget about me. You would like to see me six feet underground, so that you can inherit my jewelry!"

Angelica knew all too well that she had given Susan an almost pathological dislike of jewelry. Her daughter's clothes had a deliberate down-to-earth dinginess, and Susan only seemed to feel comfortable wearing brown sweaters and worn corduroy trousers. All forms of display and adornment were abhorrent to her. She was devoted to her husband, Michael, who taught English in a private school for boys in Sussex. Susan, herself, ran a successful little kindergarten for pre-school children in her local village. When she spoke about Angelica she usually spoke with a shrugging and maternal tolerance. "After dealing with Mother, coping with a lot of kids seems like child's play!"

After her behavior towards her daughter had been particularly outrageous and taxing, Angelica often started to suffer from remorse. Susan would then suddenly receive a gift package containing several hundreds of pounds worth of jewelry.

"Yet another irritating parcel of Mother's guilt-encrusted pearls and rubies!" Susan would complain to Michael. "If Angelica would only realize what a bore it is for me to have to spend my whole morning queuing in the post office in order to get her tiresome jewelry back to her."

Susan very much disliked going up to the city. She saw its pace and petrol fumes as equally threatening and polluting. In the last few months she had felt obliged to make a trip to London once a week, in order to visit Angelica.

"Why do you allow your huge monster of a mother to bully you?" Michael couldn't bear to see the way that Susan could be emotionally manipulated by Angelica. "She doesn't need to be visited as if she was some kind of terminal invalid. She is far better off than most people. She really lives in rather splendid style on all the loot she has collected from your poor dim wretch of a father. I very much suspect she only ever regarded him as an investment and his death was no doubt quite a bonus for her. You shouldn't allow yourself to be browbeaten by all her hysterical histrionics. I know that she wants us to weep because she has just lost her lover. But I don't see why we all have to accept Angelica's view and treat this very trivial fact as if it was some world-shaking tragedy. Your mother is still quite a formidable and handsome woman and no doubt she will soon find some new and unfortunate fellow. I just wish that I could get it through your head that Angelica is quite all right."

"I don't think that Mother is all right." Susan could be very stubborn, as she stood by the stove in her kitchen and fried fish fingers for the children's tea. "You ought to see the way that she sits there day after day in her throne of a chair in that vast, looming drawing room with all its ormolu and crystal. I can't stand all those old tapestries and gilded mirrors reflecting other gilded mirrors that she so loves. Mother has always done up all her houses to look like very grand Venetian brothels. And now she is getting older, and now that she is alone there is something quite sad about that. Every time I've visited her recently she's been wearing some outrageous and splendid new hairstyle and she is dyeing her curls brighter and brighter and her clothes are getting more and more extravagant and magnificent. And the look in her eyes really makes me feel frightened for her. Mother can be very selfish, but she is also quite self-aware and sensitive. Self-obsessed people can suffer just as much as unselfish ones. Mother knows that she is all dressed up with nowhere to go."

"Your mother will survive us all. She has an ego like a bulldozer."

"I wish I could agree with you. I only pray that her doctor will be of some use to her. I think she is far more vulnerable than you like to imagine. But then I know you have never very much liked her."

"I like her perfectly well," Michael would keep insisting. "I have nothing against Angelica except I find her quite exhausting. I can see that in some ways the old flamingo is really rather a marvelous eccentric personality. But I'll never forgive her for the way she takes advantage of you . . ."

In the cemetery Angelica moved just in order to keep moving. She felt she was walking with the easy indolence of the very rich when they go shopping. She stopped here. She stopped there. She read some of the epitaphs rather critically. She could have been deliberating whether or not to buy herself a plot.

This evening the whole place appeared to be deserted. The foul weather had apparently discouraged all other visitors. The rain was eating up the light so fast it seemed as if it was already nighttime.

On the left side of the graveyard far away in the distance, she saw a shadowy silhouette moving and her heart started pounding. It was that old man—that horrible old fellow that she hated. Yesterday evening he had started following her. Everywhere she went he had pursued her, hobbling painfully on his arthritic spindly legs. He had kept a discreet distance, but all the time she had been aware that he was keeping a very strict eye on her. He seemed to be employed as some kind of gardener or caretaker in the cemetery. Before he had decided to supervise all her movements he'd seemed to spend his time pottering around with a broom and sometimes he swept a few leaves off a grave.

She hated the old man because he seemed to find her presence in the cemetery very suspicious. Something in her appearance had made him fear that she was deranged and he also seemed to have detected that her derangement had not been caused by a grief that he could respect. When he followed her she was disturbed by the idea that he felt obliged to do so because he was trying to protect his tombs. He obviously thought that he could expect any kind of obscene and ghoulish behavior from a stagey-looking woman in a fur coat who loved to wander without good reason in a city graveyard in the rain.

Angelica decided to keep very far away from him. She must never let him know that she had come back here. If he started following her this evening she thought she might very well become hysterical and start screaming at him, "Get on with your sweeping, you old fucker!" If he hoped to keep his graves free of leaves he had set himself a task that left little time for idling. She felt it would be most unwise of him to provoke her this evening. He would never guess how important it was for her to be allowed to spend some time in this cemetery undisturbed by his hostile spying. If he made her feel persecuted she feared she might become dangerous. She knew she was unwell. She did not feel she was in control. This morning lying in the bath she had felt so demented and raw that she had started to feel sorry for objects. She had cried for her toothpaste tube because it had lost its top. She had cried for her bath mat for she had suddenly noticed its sad worn fringe. She had recognized that this was a very bad sign and it had made her think she had better return to the cemetery.

It was when Dr. Abelman had suggested she join a bridge club that Angelica had first suddenly had the idea she wanted to visit Brompton Cemetery. His belief that joining any such organization could help relieve her depression seemed so fatuous that she secretly decided she only wanted to do the opposite of anything that he advised.

Dr. Abelman made her feel there was no point in trying to fight her depression, that she might as well try to increase her feeling of gloom by putting herself in the most undesirable situation she could think of. It was then she had thought of the Brompton Cemetery. She had sometimes passed it when she was driving out of London, and she had detested the look of its weird still world where the dead had been scattered, thick as grass seed.

While Dr. Abelman went on enthusing about his frightful bridge club, she wondered what would happen if she was to go to that eerie cemetery and sit for a while on some gravestone. Maybe it would be like taking a bath in freezing water in order to feel better once it was over. In the cemetery she would certainly not have any of the "lively exchanges of ideas" that her insensitive doctor was so keen on, and that seemed something in its favor.

After she left Dr. Abelman she had gone home and telephoned Susan. "I don't think I could possibly feel worse," she told her. "I really think something will snap if I go on feeling like this."

Susan had immediately offered to come up to London and spend the night with her. Angelica said that she couldn't see there would be much use in that. She didn't feel it would help her. She heard a little gasp. She knew she had hurt Susan's feelings. The tone in which she had refused her daughter's offer had been most unpleasant and rejecting. But Angelica felt too savage and discontented to bother to apologize for her ingratitude. She rang off and then she wondered whether she'd told her daughter the truth. Was it really impossible for her to feel any worse? It was then she'd decided she would go off to the Brompton Cemetery and test the truth of her own hectic statement. On her way there in a taxi she had started to feel so frightened she felt she might be playing Russian roulette with her own sanity. She had hated every second she had spent in the graveyard. But when she'd left yesterday evening her relief at getting out had made her feel almost euphoric. Although this feeling had not lasted she was still glad to have experienced it. She knew that no game of bridge was capable of lifting her out of her black moods for even a second.

So she had come back once more to this oppressive place hoping that her fear of being alone with the dead would again drive out all other painful feelings. And already this seemed to be working for she felt lightheaded. She had the sensation that she had split in two and part of herself was walking at her own elbow like an over-solicitous nurse endlessly taking the temperature of her own mood. "You do feel much less wretched since you have been here?" "Surely it's so abysmal here it can only make you feel better." "Surely you are minding much less about Jason now?"

"Oh yes. Oh yes." Angelica was surprised that she could answer her own over-pampering self so quickly.

"Oh yes . . ." She already felt very much better. Her terror of the inhabitants of this immense burial ground always acted on her nervous system like an anesthetic. It numbed all her usual feelings of anxiety and distress. All she could feel was the sickly sweetish sensation of pure fear. The dead continued to terrify her. "But can it be the dead that I'm frightened of," she thought, "surely it really has to be death." But she still found it seemed to be the dead themselves who petrified her. She couldn't believe she would ever learn to get accustomed to them. She felt she'd forever feel menaced by all the paraphernalia of their grisly crosses, their mausoleums, and their elaborate statuary.

"God saw her footsteps falter and he gave his loved one sleep." Angelica stopped at a grave and she read this epitaph several times. "Mary Wilkinson 1780–1820." She could identify very easily with this woman. Angelica thought she knew very well how she must have felt as she faltered. At this moment Mary Wilkinson seemed very much more real to her than Jason. But Angelica was glad to find that she didn't envy this lady and she was glad she was able to walk on and leave her sleeping under her unpleasantly rain-stained stone.

"I am afraid that Jason was a real disaster," Susan had said to Angelica a few weeks ago. "I can't bear to see the way he has managed to upset you. And he was such a worthless little creature. I suppose he was quite pretty. But he was never nearly good enough for you. And I'm sure you knew it, Mother. I have to say that I found him an extremely embarrassing figure at all your parties. He dressed up for them much too much. And it used to annoy me to see the way he adored to rush round pouring out drinks for your guests and smiling his awful little 'action-man' smile. He never seemed to know how he wanted to be treated. Was he meant to be the son of the house? Or was he the waiter?"

Angelica had looked at her daughter with a certain surprise. Susan was usually so charitable in her attitudes towards other people that it startled her mother to hear her being critical and acerbic. Susan was generally very good-natured and long-suffering when Angelica behaved in an infantile and self-dramatizing fashion. She therefore tended to see her as rather blinkered and easily fooled. For this reason it was quite a shock for her to realize that her daughter was quite capable of being sharp and observant and harsh.

Angelica would have liked to pretend that Susan was jealous of her relationship with Jason, but she knew that would be extremely far-fetched. She had to recognize that Jason, with his gold hair and his periwinkle blue eyes and his effete and weak little face, would not have much attraction for her daughter, Jason's idle and exploitative nature could also only arouse Susan's scorn.

Dr. Abelman had accused Angelica of bringing out the weakness in Jason's character. "Your attitude towards this young man was very castrating. You did nothing to help him build up his sense of masculinity. Naturally he resented you for this. You treated him like a pretty trinket. You took no interest in his work."

Angelica had acted with the hypocritical meekness and compliance that she always chose to show Dr. Abelman and she made no protest. However, she had found his accusation quite absurd. When he assessed various situations and made his inevitable errors she never bothered to correct him. She rather enjoyed knowing she was partly to blame for his idiocy because she had fed him false information. She liked sitting there feeling wily as she stared at him with dumbly admiring eyes while he puffed himself up and delivered his silly pronouncements. She could see that he thought he was being very wise and god-like.

Angelica had secretly wondered how this dreary young doctor dared to accuse her of taking too little interest in Jason's work when from an objective point of view such work had to be considered remarkably uninteresting. When she had first met Jason, he had been running a small boutique which sold kaftans, Eastern straw table mats, and various kinds of candles, tapers, and oriental beadwork. Everything in Jason's shop had been would-be exotic, tawdry, and of a very specialized appeal. When he had moved into her house and became her lover, she had urged him to close it. Once his boutique could no longer be regarded as a desperate bid for financial security, she had found it ridiculous for him to spend his days sitting in a stuffy little incense-smelling interior waiting for nonexistent customers. Jason had seemed only too relieved when she had encouraged him to get rid of his hopeless little shop. He had given her no hint he found it in any way emasculating.

"Jason seemed to have such a shallow, vain, and greedy personality," Susan had said to her mother. "When he used to look at you he always seemed to be looking into your necklace rather than your eyes."

Angelica had made a weary dismissive gesture with her hand. "Oh yes," she said, "Jason would have certainly loved to find a reflection of himself in my jewelry. You have a very clever point there. But it doesn't help me when you caricature him. I do the same all day long. It never makes me feel any better. I sit here in my house and I tar and feather him with various unpleasant qualities. Sometimes I make him so mean and trite and disgusting that I really overdo it. I then quite defeat my purpose. I endow him with so many nasty traits that I start to feel quite sorry for him. I see him as a poor lost little soul cursed by his own horrible character. That makes him seem very sad indeed. When I start to pity him it's always rather fatal for me. I only wish for one thing then. I only wish to God that he would come back!"

"I don't think that Jason will ever come back." Susan had said this to her mother in her most gentle solicitous tones. "And if you want my frank opinion, I don't think that Jason is the real reason why you now feel so demoralized and blue. You are still a very beautiful and talented woman, Mother. You are someone who once had a brilliant career. I feel convinced that your real trouble is that you have far too much talent and energy to be satisfied leading the lazy life you now lead. It is just not enough for you to sit about in an expensive Chelsea house planning social dinner parties. You were never meant to be a woman who goes to dressmakers and hairdressers. You were not born to spend most of your time lolling around in bed with your Pekinese while you gossip on the telephone to other rich and idle ladies. You are simply not fulfilling yourself, Mother. I am certain that is the real reason why you feel so frantic and depressed. I am convinced your doctor would agree with me. I don't believe you will ever be happy until you start working again. The theatre is so exciting nowadays. I never can understand why you don't go back to the stage."

Angelica had been lying on her huge eighteenth-century four-poster bed during this conversation. She had propped herself up on a mountainous pile of feather pillows and brocaded bolsters. Her head had started to ache while her daughter talked. Susan could sometimes make her feel quite ill, she could be so tactless and bossy.

"Can I just beg something of you, Susan? Can I just implore you on my knees that you never suggest that I take up acting again? If there is any solution for me, the stage is certainly never going to be it. You know how to run nursery schools for toddlers, Susan. I would never presume to give you any advice on that subject. I never want you to dare to speak to me about things which you know nothing about. I can assure you that a stage career is not something which can ever be capriciously resumed once it has been disastrously broken. My career came to an end a very long time ago—I gave up the stage when I first started you."

Angelica had seen the stunned and miserable expression in Susan's eyes. She noticed she had managed to make her daughter blush. She was terrified that Susan was about to suggest she find herself work in television. She therefore didn't care how much she had wounded her. Angelica only wanted her to cut short her visit and leave. If only the girl would have the good sense to get out of her house immediately. If only she would go off and catch a train and get into some smokey compartment and go chugging back to that dull little schoolteacher man she had married—start preparing supper for those mousy little thumb-sucking grandchildren.

Angelica could never bear it when Susan brought up her acting. Whenever this happened she could only loathe her daughter for not realizing that the whole subject was so disturbing to her that she found it torture to have it mentioned. And because Susan seemed unable to grasp this, Angelica often turned on her with a terrible spite and fury and did her best to punish her. In certain moods Angelica only wanted to make her suffer from a sense of shivering inadequacy. She felt that Susan deserved to be made to feel that her whole existence was worthless because her birth had never been any compensation to her mother for the loss of her stage career.

As Angelica circled round the Brompton Cemetery, she wondered why she kept picking out all the stones and the crosses which had been erected by daughters who mourned their mothers. It offended her to see the way that the modern ones had put up marble monuments which had the slimy texture of plastic. Some of them had even put a nasty little patch of green glass in front of their mother's tombs, so that it lay there like a tiny emerald lawn. It also distressed Angelica to see the way that a lot of the older Victorian mothers were starting to lose their names under the mossy patina of urban dirt which was forming on their stones.

Occasionally, Angelica noticed, there would be a daughter who shared a grave with her mother. She tried to imagine herself sharing with Susan. She found that she always had the same immediate reaction. That would only lead to trouble. She discovered that her imagination was pitifully feeble. She could only ever envisage Susan and herself continuing to retain in death the very same opposing attitudes and qualities that had always grated and clashed in life. Angelica had an image of her own role which filled her with apprehension. She saw herself eternally criticizing, exploiting, and condescending to Susan. "I must now be truly insane," Angelica thought. "I feel it would be fatal for me to try to share a grave with Susan just as I feel it would be a disaster for both of us if we were to try to share a flat."

The rain was getting worse. When Angelica stroked her coat it reminded her of the fur of a dog that has just emerged from a pond. She knew she must be frozen to the bone but somehow she couldn't feel it.

"Aren't you frightened you will get pneumonia?" the self that seemed to walk at her elbow asked her. But that self seemed tiresome and over-fussy. She could answer it that she felt fine—that it was a long time since she had felt quite so buoyant and well. As she walked through this jungle of graves a new bounce seemed to have come back into her step and she had the feeling that once again she was suddenly walking like a girl.

She realized there was a very good reason why she felt this unlikely surge of well-being as she walked in this detestable cemetery. She had stopped waiting and that had improved her state of mind far more than Dr. Abelman would ever be able to comprehend.

Recently she'd felt that it was waiting that was depleting her physically—that it was this pernicious waiting that was destroying her equilibrium and making her so angry, unbalanced, and melancholy.

She had always found waiting intolerable and recently she had felt she could die of it as she restlessly wandered backwards and forwards from her bedroom, to her bathroom, to the drawing room, and all the time she had not been able to stop waiting—waiting for Jason to telephone her, waiting for him to write, waiting for him to explain why he'd left without even leaving her a note, waiting for him to tell her that he now realized that he'd made a very great mistake when he left, waiting for the sound of the doorbell that would announce his surprise return.

But in the cemetery she no longer felt she was waiting for anything. Waiting seemed much too futile here. She could imagine that all around her the dead were lying there in the mud and waiting to be alive again . . .

Angelica deliberately started heading for the very heart of the graveyard where the people who were buried there somehow managed to seem even more dead than the ones who were buried on the sides. She found that if she concentrated she could still just hear the sound of traffic as it rumbled down the Old Brompton Road. But she could only do so by an intense effort of concentration. It was as if the dead had a silence that was so powerful that it could drown out all the ugly and trivial noises of the living.

Angelica started walking much faster as if she had a purpose. She suddenly knew where she was going now. She knew exactly where to find him. Although she had visited him for the first time yesterday evening, she remembered his position very well and she could find her way to Major Arthur Coleman just as easily as if she was one of his sorrowing relations.

As she went hurrying towards him she had the feeling that he was the real reason why she had left the comfort and warmth of her house to make this horrible cold visit to this cemetery.

Once she reached the Major she read again his dates: "Born 1895—killed 1917." It was getting wetter and darker by the moment but she could just make out his fading inscription. "Life claimed him so he never knew Death." She found this a little puzzling and for a moment she wondered if there had been an error and the wrong words had been put on his tomb. Maybe someone intended it to read, "Death claimed him so he never knew Life." However she had to dismiss this idea very quickly. To make sense of such an epitaph Major Arthur Coleman would have had to have died stillborn.

She wondered if he had any descendants who still visited him as he lay lost in this wilderness of grass-bound graves. She felt certain that he had never been married. She found it intolerable to think that he might have ever been married. If anyone now came near him she would only allow it to be a figure that was very remote from him—maybe some grand-niece. But even that was not an appealing idea to Angelica. Dr. Abelman had often maintained she had been over-possessive of Jason. But now she found she felt much more over-possessive of Major Arthur Coleman. She wanted to be the only person in the world who knew of his existence—more precisely of his nonexistence.

He must have been rich, Angelica decided. Or at any rate the young Major's family had been rich enough to buy him an individual stone. She was glad that he had not been jammed into the reserved military acres within this cemetery where 1917 as a year of death seemed just as commonplace as all the identical cheap white crosses that had been issued by the army in much the same way that they provided uniforms.

"I think you can only like men if they are rich," Jason had once said to her accusingly.

Standing in front of this soldier's grave it seemed a very odd charge to have to answer. But Angelica still wondered if it could be true. Certainly when she tried to give life to the dead young Major she immediately made him financially secure. She would also have to say that Susan's father, Henry, had certainly been very rich. But then if she was to be honest she would have to confess that she had never really liked her late husband. So nothing was to be proved by thinking about him.

She decided that Jason's complaint was only half-true. However, she felt it was interesting to examine why he had made it. She had often found Jason very irritating because he was so spoilt and indolent. He was such a self-applauding young figure that he found it impossible to understand why he often angered her. His mind was very simplistic and he had decided she resented him for not having enough money.

Jason was much too egocentric to be interested in understanding other people's reactions. He had never bothered to observe Angelica very closely. He had never realized that she was like a woman who had been in a car crash many years ago—that she was a person who continued to suffer every day from the results of ancient injuries. He had never quite understood that he was living with someone who had all the rage and malevolence of the cripple. Marriage, motherhood, and innumerable love affairs had all disappointed and enraged Angelica. She always found them to be very dull and wretched substitutes for her lost stage career.

It was as if her acting career had been the only heavy vehicle which was capable of carrying the crushing weight of her enormous vanity. She had sometimes had the feeling that her vanity was like a ponderous force that existed almost independent of herself. Far more involved with it than she had ever been with her daughter, Susan, it had always plagued her like a nagging, demanding child which she never learnt to come to terms with.

Her vanity was incurably restless; it had a desperate need to feel that it was moving. It was insatiably greedy and it longed to feed on the approval of larger and larger audiences.

When her career had crashed, Angelica had never forgiven herself for being the one who was responsible for the accident which had left her vanity permanently confined to a wheelchair. For many years her whole life had been spent trying to conceal and forget what she felt to be both her crime and her catastrophe. At the age of twenty-nine she had been forced to give up her brilliant stage career, because without obvious reason she had suddenly lost her nerve.

A very similar thing had happened to Angelica's uncle. A rather humorless, fierce man, her uncle had once had a distinguished military career in India. When he had returned to England he had bought himself a house in Sussex and as a child Angelica had often stayed with him. He was an expert horseman and he was the local master of foxhounds. One Saturday he had arrived at the meet as usual. It was a cold day, and the horses snorted dragon-like breath into the frosty air. The horses had whinnied, and reared, and bucked as they became impatient to get started. Everyone wondered why the hunt never seemed to move off. They wondered why the hounds remained in a huddle, fidgeting and burrowing like worms and baying loudly as the red-coated huntsmen cracked their whips in a frantic effort to control them. Young men and women wearing bowlers, and older ladies in black silk top hats, seated on side-saddles, were forced to jag the mouths of their horses as they became more and more uncontrollable, lashing out with their hooves and biting. They soon started to become angry at the inexplicable delay. Still no one realized what had happened. A groom went over to help the Master. He assumed he must be having some kind of trouble with his stirrup or his girth. It took the groom, just as it took the rest of the hunt, quite a while to understand what was happening. It took everyone present a long while to believe what they could only find unbelievable. The reason why the hunt never moved off was that the Master had quite suddenly lost the courage to mount.

The poor man had just gone on standing there by the side of his sixteen-hand bay mare. Under his black velvet cap his skin was so pale he looked almost unearthly. As his mare sweated with impatient energy, his forehead also became dotted with perspiration, and his whole face looked measled with shame and anguish. Everyone waited. Everyone went on waiting. Then finally the huntsmen lost their patience. They cracked their whips and the whole hunt moved off and left him.

The following day the hunt committee had a meeting. They decided not to take action for a while. They all assumed that the Master would resign. But he was stubborn. To everyone's dismay he turned up at several subsequent meets and always the same thing happened. He would just stand by his mare and perspire with the same horrible humiliated expression on his face. He once managed to put a foot into his stirrup, but he still never mounted. He just went on hopping foolishly about on the leg which was still unable to leave the ground.

Angelica had often wondered whether her own paralyzing loss of nerve had been inherited, whether it ran in her family like a disease that runs in the blood. Or had the dismal example of her uncle made her psychologically prone to the same complaint by undermining her faith that confidence was something to be counted on?

After the hunt had tactfully asked Angelica's uncle to resign he was never the same again. He became so withdrawn and silent that the whole household became frightened of him. He would take long walks, but otherwise he spent most of the day shut away in his study. No one quite knew what he did in there. Angelica's aunt blamed the hunt for their lack of patience. She cursed them for their ingratitude. She said that they had killed her husband's self-respect, that she doubted he would live very long. She had been right, for he had contracted Parkinson's disease. Angelica had always wondered if it was a ghastly fear of his own inexplicable terror of horses which made his hand shake so much when she watched the way he had to be fed like a baby with a spoon.

Had the sight of her shaking uncle given her a fear of losing courage, which had finally frightened her into the very state of nervous cowardice that she dreaded? Angelica could never decide, although the question still went monotonously round and round in her head like a goldfish in a bowl. She always felt that if she could find the reason for her loss of nerve she might magically recover it. Out of pride she would admit it to no one, but she had still never lost hope that she might one day be able to act again. When she was alone at night, she would turn on the television in order to watch the performances of the older actresses. She was always mercilessly critical towards them, feeling that they bungled their roles. But her envy of their national notoriety and the pleasure that they seemed to be taking in their profession would make her feel hot, as if she was running a fever. Angelica would quickly switch off the television, and feel that she had switched off the whole magical world of illusion that she had once loved. Her room seemed immediately dark, even if all the lights were blazing. She would feel that she was like an autumn leaf that had been pressed inside the dark pages of a heavy book. Parchment-crisp, and with every vein still showing, she kept her outline, but her preservation was to no purpose. Recently she had kept asking herself if Jason had left her because she was too old. She wondered if he would have minded her being old if she had not given him the feeling that she was something far more oppressive than old—that she was a woman who for a very long time had been dead? Angelica often felt that she was dead in the very same way that she was certain that Jason would also feel himself to be dead once he reached her age. Jason was as vain as she was. He was young and beautiful and for the moment his vanity was still able to feed on the world's response to his boyishness and his beauty. But he was a young man without direction. He was without any specific talents, interests, or accomplishments. Angelica often took some vengeful pleasure in prophesying that Jason would feel he was prematurely perishing with his own vanity, once it slowly started to starve to death from the lack of nourishment it was likely to find in middle-age.

Angelica had been playing the lead in a successful drawing-room comedy when her nerve had suddenly left her. One morning she had woken up in a state of white panic. She could remember the name of the theatre where she was expected to appear that evening. She could remember the exact time that the performance started. But, in the night, it was as if certain cells in her brain had been inexplicably damaged, for she found that try as she would, she could not remember the name of the play.

Angelica had found that she could still remember the real-life name of the actor who played opposite her—remember the oily smell of his coarse hair and the feel of his short-fingered hands when for a few weeks he had been her lover. But these memories were so useless they only increased her state of terror, for they in no way helped her to remember any of the lines that she had heard him speaking night after night. If she could just recall some of this actor's lines she kept hoping she might be reminded what the whole play was about. It might help her to know if it was classical or modern. Was it a comedy or was it a tragedy? If she could just remember something about the play, she might suddenly have some memory of the role she had been cast to play in it. She might know if she was meant to be an empress, a suburban housewife, or a whore.

Angelica kept having the agonizing feeling that she was just about to remember—just about to remember. But then it was as if amnesia had rushed into her brain like water. She had lain in bed and she had cried. She had started shaking so violently that she wondered if she was developing Parkinson's disease like her uncle.

She found that whenever she closed her eyes, she immediately began to see a stage. It was a stage that had no scenery. It had no props to remind her what role she was expected to perform against the blank of its dull, brown backdrop. For a moment she would start to think that she was standing on that stage and while she stood there her brain started filling up with water. Her mind felt it was about to burst; something was filling it up with so much water. She could just make out that down below her there was an audience which was crouching in rows in the dark. The audience was hissing and booing because it knew that there was something wrong with her. It could see that her head had become enormous, that it was swollen with liquid as if she was a victim of hydrocephalus. The audience seemed like a giant mass of evil as it kept screaming and jeering at her. She knew that it was soon going to pelt her with eggs and ice-cream cones. She could feel how much it resented her so for not knowing what part she ought to be playing.

Angelica had managed to get out of bed. She had staggered round her bedroom like a drunkard, trying to find the script of the play. Once she found it and read the title she felt that all the water was suddenly draining out of her brain. She remembered everything. She rang for her maid and told her that she wanted to run through her lines. Her maid gave her a strange look. She had sensed that something in Angelica's manner was very peculiar and it frightened her. When the girl ran through the lines of the play with her and fed her all her cues, Angelica was astonished to find that she was word-perfect. But once she was left alone she immediately telephoned her manager and told him she felt deathly ill and would be unable to appear on stage that evening. It was arranged that her understudy should take over her role. The next day, claiming that her doctors insisted she see specialists, Angelica flew off to Switzerland, where she booked herself in alone at a hotel. She had remained there in hiding for many weeks, feeling unable to get out of bed. Whenever she tried to walk she felt dizzy. She kept having the sensation that she was perched on the parapet of a high turret with a compulsion to jump that struggled against her terror of the hurtling fall.

When she recovered enough to return to England she stubbornly maintained that her illness was physical. She would drop mysterious hints about her rare and dangerous medical condition. She insisted that her doctors had ordered her to have complete rest for many months. She would admit to no one that she had developed a horror of facing an audience. Some kind of shame made her refuse to admit to the world that ever since her brief seizure of forgetfulness, she lived in perpetual fear that she might once again have the feeling that certain sections of her memory were being swamped as her brain filled up with water. She had no way of telling at what moment this terrifying thing might happen to her. In the theatre they called it "corpsing." The very idea of facing any audience had now become enough to make her start shaking. When she thought of trying to resume her career she could only imagine herself as standing there on the stage with a waterlogged brain, while her disconcerted fellow actors stared at her in disbelief and horror as some offstage prompter was forced to hiss out her entire part.

Very soon after her return to England she startled her friends by her sudden marriage to Henry. Her marriage was a calculated act to salvage what was left of her pride. She became pregnant with Susan and she was able to tell the world that she was unable to take any parts until after the child was born. Henry had admired her for many years. She had always found him a chinless and unexciting young man, and it had bored rather than pleased her that he was mindlessly, uncritically, bedazzled by her. She had never expected nor wanted the marriage to last, but always hoping for the miracle return of her nerve she had felt that she was playing for time. At that moment Henry's enormous wealth had been very valuable to her, for she had been able to use it to camouflage her humiliating failure. It had enabled her to buy outrageously expensive and memorable clothes. She suddenly owned several houses. She had land, valuable possessions, and jewelry. Henry's money had enabled her to live in grand style and it gave her a stage where she could be admired and envied. She entertained lavishly, treating money with contempt, as if she were recklessly scattering it like confetti. She was able to tell the world that the idea of acting now bored her. "If you are not doing it in order to earn a living—why spend your nights laughing and crying in public in order to get clapped by a lot of vulgar people?"

She became a professional society beauty, and a professional popular hostess. Outwardly she was untiringly flirtatious and ebullient, but inwardly she felt humiliated and stunted, for she felt she had restricted herself to two simple roles when she should have been playing many challenging and world-famous parts.

"It's a bore having you hanging around in London," she had told Henry. "You would be far better off improving your out-houses and pottering about your woods with a gun. I think you would be much happier if you spent more time playing the big squire on your estates."

She was always sneering at him. Whenever he spoke to her she had snubbed him. His vulnerability made her vindictive. She had seen him as having less function than a servant. When he entered a room with his nondescript face, his loose mouth, and his baffled, unhappy eyes she wanted to leave it. She told him that he had no humor, and he went off and bought a book of collected jokes, which he tried to read aloud to her in order to disprove her accusation. She became increasingly irritated by his suffering and inarticulate sexual desire for her. Day and night she sensed that he was hoping that she would allow him to sleep with her, although he had long ago lost the courage to try to approach her for he knew that it would make her far too angry. She saw Henry like a gnat, exerting a perpetual pin-prick pressure. She decided that he must be made to live in his house in Somerset. He was puppet-like in the way he made no protest at the plans she made for him. When he moved to the country she sent Susan to live with him there, accompanied by a nurse. Angelica occasionally went down to Somerset to visit them. She considered that the marriage was over, but had no wish for a divorce. She went on living in his house in Chelsea. She had many lovers and kept changing them with great rapidity. She found it impossible to find any man who could keep her interest for very long. Her life lacked challenge, and the act of acquiring a new lover could stimulate her for a little while, but once he had been acquired her interest palled.

But now when she was standing in front of the grave of Major Arthur Coleman she could imagine a relationship with him which would have been very different. "Life claimed him so he never knew Death." When she stared at his buoyant, unusual epitaph she felt an anger at the tragedy and the waste of his death. She felt quite certain that she could have loved him, this doomed, young soldier, bon viveur. Although he was too claimed by life to ever know death, did he ever have any premonitions how soon it was coming to him?

Born a few years after he had been killed—Angelica saw a cruelty in the mistiming. When she stared at his grave she felt she was starting to see his face hazily emerging from the blank bit of grey stone that lay under his epitaph. He looked very old-fashioned, beautifully glamorized and ethereal with his hair slicked down and his huge eyes dark-shadowed as if he was posing in his uniform for a period photograph.

When Angelica compared Jason to the Major she felt he lacked all panache. He had very little mystery and he was devoid of poignancy. He seemed so inferior to her image of the young and dashing officer that she suddenly found it almost impossible to understand how she had ever allowed herself to become so unhappily obsessed by him. Arthur Coleman made Jason seem cheap and modern and unappealing. He had none of the gallantry and the romance of the fallen soldier. Arthur Coleman reduced Jason and made him seem ordinary. He turned him into a dreary little creature who belonged with the unexciting crowds of youngish people with fume-stained and impoverished faces who swarmed the dirty London streets wearing shoddy and self-conscious clothing.

Angelica found that, curiously enough, it was Jason whom she felt she had invented as she stood like a grief-stricken fiancée looking down at the tomb of the lost Arthur. She saw this First World War casualty and herself as well matched. They'd both been fatally crippled by wounds acquired in another era. If Arthur Coleman were to suddenly rise up from the ground Angelica had no feeling that it would frighten her. She believed she would embrace him. She saw this soldier as having served his purpose just as he had served his country. He had done what Dr. Abelman had so singularly failed to do. He had killed her self-destructive obsession with Jason.

She could see the ease with which she had been able to conjure up an attractive and lovable Major. She had only needed to keep her eyes fixed on his death date. She saw that she could make herself feel a real sense of loss and sorrow when she thought of all the dances she would never be able to have with this phantom. She saw how she could nearly make herself cry when she thought of all the wine and the kisses and the jokes she would never be able to share with him.

And when she recognized how much passion she would have liked to have poured out on Major Coleman it made her have complete distrust for her old feelings for Jason.

Angelica knew that she could go home now. Jason had lost all his power to make her wish to hide from the world behind the prison-like arched railings of this cemetery. All her interest in him had died so suddenly that he now seemed far more dead than the Major. If she was to return to her house and find that he had decided to come back to her, that he was there, wearing fancy patched jeans and sprawling on the sofa of her drawing room, she felt she might easily start to scream as if she had seen some ghastly resurrected apparition. It was the everyday Jason that she dreaded she might find drinking her whisky with a shifty, disarming, little-boy smile.

When she thought about him as she was standing in the Brompton Cemetery, she found her images all came from her surroundings. It seemed to her that when he had left her with such aggressive abruptness, her memory had buried the unsatisfactory, everyday Jason and replaced him with a glorified statue. But now the original figure of her young lover was rising up again and smashing the romantic statue she had erected in his honor. She remembered the grey and annoying soles of his bare feet as he sat around all day on the carpet of her drawing room, with his blond John-the-Baptist hair dripping down over the pop records that he liked to play so repetitively on her stereo.

"What have you arranged for us to do today?" He always used to keep asking. "What have you arranged?" Most of the time he seemed to be bored as a lonely child on a dull Sunday afternoon.

"I have arranged for us to commit double suicide," she would snap at him. She was always infuriated by this question for it made her realize she felt far too tired to have the energy to spend her days amusing him.

Angelica felt quite free to leave now. She had come creeping into this cemetery, a woman with jangling nerves, who felt imprisoned by a sense of bitterness and defeat. But now she believed she could leave with the confidence and freedom of someone who had made an important decision. She would go home. She would go back to all the ordinary routines of her life, and she would secretly go on loving the Major.

Everything was shadowy and misted in the rainy twilight of this cemetery, and her own thoughts seemed to be the only things which were bright and clear. If she wanted to go on loving an elusive phantom, she now saw it as lunacy not to go on loving the Major. The rasping reality of his presence would never be able to tarnish his golden, gallant image. Arthur Coleman would never be able to give her any chafing memories. She could be quite certain that her vanity would be safe just as long as she saw that her affections remained cautiously focused on his invisible soldier's body. The Major would most certainly never tell her that he only really liked sleeping with people who were as beautiful as himself.

Even in this graveyard Angelica could still hear Jason whispering these words so gently. He had been lying beside her in her large billowy bed. He had sounded very affectionate as if he was sleepily and sweetly musing aloud. She had not answered, stretched out beside him. She had felt lifeless and stiff as a chloroformed patient being wheeled from the operating table. She had never expected that Jason's narcissism would turn on her and stab her. It had always amused her to flatter him. She had loved to keep praising his physical beauty. She had assumed that he would always be pleased by the way she was prepared to share his obsessional pride in his own beauty, for she could believe that she herself still had beauty—while she still had him.

Now that Angelica could see that all her romantic feelings for Jason might just as well be transferred to the Major, she felt she was able to step back and stare at her old relationship in much the same detached and critical way that she liked to stare at the names which were engraved on the various gravestones in this cemetery. She could admit that she had underrated Jason when she assumed that he would find her attitude towards him so flattering as to be forever satisfactory. She could understand that he might well have felt threatened by something covetous and greedy in the way she had loved to keep kissing and praising his body. Had he started to see her as an aged thief who was trying to appropriate for herself the only valuable asset he believed himself to possess?

Jason had always had indolent, amateurish, theatrical ambitions. He believed that with his good looks he could very easily become a popular television idol. He had hoped naïvely that she would help him make contacts with producers and directors. He had never been able to understand why she had so little interest in helping him to "get spotted." Jason had always seen her as an actress from such a hopelessly bygone era that it never occurred to him that she herself nursed unrealistic ambitions, had secret fantasies in which she recovered her nerve and made a sensational theatrical "comeback."

When she had made no effort to help him make useful film contacts Jason had started to distrust her and he had slowly grown to loathe her. Just as she had seen little future for herself in promoting a theatrical career which was not her own, so Jason had seen little point in continuing to be the lover of an older woman, who threw jealous dramatic tantrums, and only wanted to use his beauty like a raft to keep her own vanity afloat as it passed through the choppy seas of middle age.

Angelica suddenly had the feeling she was acting. Thoughts kept rushing through her brain, and it was as if she was acting them, rather than thinking them. She had the curious sensation that she was performing for the Major, that he was her captive and unresponsive audience. She knew her role was not particularly engaging, but that didn't seem to have much significance. All that now seemed important was that she should realize, once and for all, that this must be her last act.

When Jason had left her he had taken away any sense that she was still attractive and that her life still had potential. She could see now that it was the theft of this feeling rather than the loss of this shiftless and bored young man which had brought about her collapse. When she had wanted him back it was as if she was hoping that he would bring her back this valuable feeling, as a conscience-stricken thief might return a stolen purse. This feeling would not have been so vital to her if she had not needed it to prop up the rickety fabric of her fantasy that she would one day make a successful theatrical comeback. When she left the Brompton Cemetery Angelica was now convinced that it was this deadly pipe dream that must be left behind with the Major.

Angelica decided that she would telephone Susan when she got back home and she'd tell her the truth about her stage career. She would try to unpick all the boastful, defensive lies that she had told her daughter throughout the years and admit that it was cowardice rather than marriage and motherhood that had brought her career to such an abrupt full-stop. She'd explain how she'd developed such a terror that she might "corpse" on stage that she had to decide she could no longer act. She would tell Susan that she now wondered whether her seizure of stage panic had been as neurotic and unmotivated as her vanity had always liked to imagine. Was there not always the possibility that her fear of making an appearance had been perfectly valid and she had used stage fright as a cover-up for her own incompetence? Maybe she had been frightened to test whether the success of her youthful stage appearances were due to her beauty rather than to any real gifts as an actress. By retiring so young had she not evaded all trial of her talent and allowed herself the luxury of a lifetime spent mourning the tragic waste of abilities which very probably existed only in the fancies of her own mind?

Angelica wondered why she had such a need to confess all this to Susan. She had never told Dr. Abelman that she'd ever had an acting career at all. She couldn't bear him to know about its ignominious ending. She was frightened that if he knew he would have many views on the subject and they would be simplistic and censorious and she felt it would be insufferable to have to listen to them.

As his approach to all problems was very heavy-footed he would probably make some irritatingly useless suggestion. He might well urge her to join some amateur theatrical group—the kind of untalented group that tours all the prisons in England putting on embarrassing productions of Shakespeare for the hapless inmates.

But with Susan she was finally going to be honest, so that something beneficial would be gained from her eccentric visits to the cemetery. She was certain that her daughter would treat this attack on herself as just one more histrionic declaration. "We all get moods like these, Mother," Susan would very likely say with her usual patient, schoolteacher briskness. "Remember, they always pass. You should try to take more care of yourself—maybe cut down on the whisky—see that you get more rest." Angelica knew that Susan would never be able to believe that she was speaking seriously. Since her earliest childhood Susan had been brought up to accept without question her mother's version of her own life, and by now she would find it more painful than Angelica had if she was suddenly forced to revise it.

She re-read the Major's epitaph as if it was a courteous way of saying goodbye to him and started slowly walking back towards the entrance of the cemetery. She noticed that two figures were coming in. In the distance she could just make out that they were a man and a woman, and the man seemed to be pushing something that looked like a wheelbarrow.

For a moment Angelica felt an unreasonable surge of resentment and antagonism, as if the Brompton Cemetery had become her own private terrain and the new couple were trespassers. Then her attitude changed and she decided that she would like to speak to them. Normally it never occurred to her to wish to speak to strangers. But after the lonely one-sided dialogue that she had been carrying on with the Major, the idea that this couple could listen and respond made them seem very attractive.

She felt certain that they would be quite glad to talk to her. They too must be suffering from a feeling of chill and panic as they walked through the chaos of graves in the rain. In these stark unusual surroundings she believed she would be able to speak to this couple in a more honest and intimate way than she had ever been able to speak to her husband, her daughter, her lovers, or any of her friends.

She saw they were heading for a clump of evergreens that lay upon the far left side and Angelica started to follow them. There was something very purposeful in the brisk way they were walking without speaking. They seemed to know their way through all the complicated, twisting paths, and she felt they had visited the Brompton Cemetery many times before.

The couple suddenly stopped, and as Angelica came nearer to them she saw that it was a pram that the man had been pushing and that it was loaded with potted geraniums. The woman was kneeling down in the wet grass beside a mound without a stone. She had a trowel in her hand and was ripping out all the dead flowers that had been planted on this newly dug patch of earth. She kept tossing them over her shoulder with a frenetic violence. She then very gently replaced them with the geraniums which she took from her battered and paint-chipped pram.

Angelica stood at a distance and hesitated before approaching her. She felt suddenly intimidated by the way the woman seemed to be totally absorbed in trying to plant the geraniums so closely together that they spread over the mound in a solid quilt of red. The man was standing a few yards away from the woman and his back was turned to her. He looked as if he was keeping guard. Angelica saw that he was about thirty-five, that he was not good-looking. He was wearing a shabby raincoat. The expression on his face was both embarrassed and grim. Something about the way he was just standing there with his arms crossed made Angelica feel that he must have stood and waited while the woman planted her flowers many times before. After hesitating, Angelica decided that she would walk past the woman and she would smile at her. She hoped she would realize that this was not a meaningless social gesture. It was with the woman that Angelica now felt that she would like to establish an intimate relationship. The man she found a little unprepossessing. She felt there was something rather gloomy in the way he just stood there like a sailor on deck staring out over the sea-like grey wash of tombstones.

Angelica suddenly had the feeling that the woman would not find her deranged if she tried to explain how she had cured her depression by using the grey stone of the Major as if it was a sounding board.

She suddenly longed to tell someone that she felt happier than she had felt for years. She felt futureless, but that very feeling now gave her a perverse sense of freedom. When she left and went out of the gates into the Old Brompton Road, she would know she was not going anywhere in particular. Coming out of the colorless enclosures of the cemetery she would be glad just to blink like a blinded mole, unaccustomed to the vulgar flash of advertisements and lights in all the shops. The usual crowds with their plastic raincoats and umbrellas would be jostling along the pavements if she was to walk down the Earls Court Road. Having no direction, she would be glad to let them push her along wherever they were going.

If some odor of the cemetery was still clinging to her damp fur coat no one would notice it in this street, where seedy Oriental restaurants expelled a steam of cheap sour fat smells from all their cellars. She would attract very little attention as she was sucked along in the current of the evening rush hour, one more woman with bitter, exhausted eyes, whose beauty was now something that was clumsily stencilled on the corrugated surface of her face with makeup aids. If she did not stand out in the crowd, it would not trouble her. She would be much too glad to feel that she could still be part of it. She would be happy just because she was no longer in the Brompton Cemetery with its haphazard stones that insisted on nothing except losses from the past—happy just to forget the way that the cemetery seemed to offer her nothing except its own dismal future. While she was with the crowd that breathed, and hurried, and sweated, she would feel exuberant like a schoolgirl on holiday. She would find it intoxicating to escape from the cemetery's sombre insistence that there was nothing but the past and the future, and she would skim along the wet pavements as part of the crowd that she would love for making her feel she could still be part of the present.

Angelica was certain that the kneeling woman would understand her new mood. If the woman responded to her smile, she decided that she would invite the couple to come back home with her. She felt a great sympathy and liking for the woman. It was very possible that she was also trying to come to terms with a festering sense of general failure. Maybe she was trying to speak to herself through the medium of that geranium-dotted mound, just as she had tried to speak to herself by making use of the grave of the Major.

Angelica started walking down the path that led past the spot where the woman was kneeling. When she got close to her she smiled. The woman looked up from her planting. Her distraught eyes stared at Angelica. They seemed not to see her at all.

Angelica walked quickly on. She felt that something was pressing inside her chest, interfering with her breathing. The woman's snub was registering on her very slowly. She could remember every detail of the woman's face. She could still see the way the rain had turned her hair into a dark paste that smeared her forehead. She remembered the shine on the knobs of the woman's angular protruding cheekbones, her over-long upper lip, the anguished expression in her cavernous, exhausted eyes. Angelica was used to attracting a lot of attention wherever she went with her still handsome face, her exaggerated halo of bright golden curls, her makeup which was applied as thickly as grease-paint, her general air of hectic and arrogant authority. It shocked her to realize that the woman had chosen to notice nothing about her at all.

Angelica suddenly wished that she could run. She cursed her weak ankles. She longed to run out of the iron gates and into the streets. The strange woman had ruined the Brompton Cemetery.

Angelica knew that she could never again come back. She realized that she would have many lonely evenings in the future. She would have moods of panic and black depression and she'd drink whisky until she felt that the alcohol was burning a passage through the center of her brain. She'd often get extremely drunk, and extremely maudlin and poor Susan would have to listen to the scream of her melodramatic ravings. But however dark her moods might become she knew she would never come back to the cemetery.

Angelica was convinced that the woman had refused to acknowledge her smile because she saw her very presence in this cemetery as an obscenity. Her unseeing stare had made Angelica feel like a criminal. She felt accused by the sorrow in the eyes of that woman, just as yesterday she'd felt accused by the antagonistic looks of the decrepit old caretaker.

She was certain that the woman with the gaunt cheekbones had not come to soak for a while in the melancholy atmosphere of this graveyard, hoping that when she left she would feel more grateful for life than when she had arrived. She had not come here to hover neurotically round the grave of an unknown soldier hoping she could derive some tiny sense of her own vitality by devoting herself to the grey slab that symbolized his deadness. When that woman had come through the black iron gates of the cemetery with her pram-load of geraniums she had not come trundling in with a load of selfish depressive anxieties that she was asking these weed-strewn inmates to dispel.

Angelica shivered. The kneeling woman had made her feel trite and despicable. It suddenly occurred to her that even if Jason was buried here in this cemetery it would not be right for her to come to visit him. If he had a place here she might be able to view him with less resentment and bitterness. It was possible she then might be able to endow him with a few of the heroic qualities she had found so pleasant to ascribe to the Major.

But even if she was to come to Jason's grave and was to stand beside it with her head bowed while she strewed it with some of the feelings of sadness and regret that she'd been able to whip up for the long-dead officer, she realized that her emotions would still have no validity since she would always be acting them rather than feeling them.

Angelica saw herself as a creature so pathetically in need of an audience that even if she was to come as a mourner to this vast metropolitan graveyard, there would always be a part of herself that stood back so that it could play the role of the applauding audience to the sensitivity of her own feelings.

She knew that she would most certainly never return. The woman with the geraniums had made her feel too ashamed. She knew that woman had not come here to play-act. She had not come here to stalk about among the graves as if she was striding the boards. Angelica could see by the sorrow on that stricken woman's face that she had lost someone she loved.

Angelica had created a great storm about her losses, but

confronted by this grieving couple she recognized them to be very trivial losses indeed. If she could be made to feel more self-disgust within the cemetery than she often felt in the world outside its railings, she knew that nothing could induce her to make another visit.

As Angelica walked out into the Old Brompton Road, the lights of the passing cars seemed unkind and over-bright and searching. They in no way seemed pleasant to her just because their glare was strange after the greyness of the cemetery. There were people with umbrellas walking the pavements. They were breathing, smiling, talking, but that in no way made them seem attractive. She had hoped that after the loneliness of the time she had spent amongst the tombstones, it would be elating to feel she could belong with them. But she looked at them all with disgust, seeing only faults in their complexions, their bodies and their clothing. She was once again all too aware of their ears and she found the idea of trying to belong with them intensely unappealing.

As she went out of the gates she felt like an outcast. She suddenly loathed the woman with the geraniums for driving her back into the world. She detested her for making her feel there was something repulsive in coming to visit the Major.

She started wandering slowly up towards the Earls Court Road. She noticed that the wet pavements outside all the houses and restaurants were littered with the most repulsive conglomeration of aggressively uncollected rubbish. There must be a strike. And even if the strike was to one day end, Angelica was certain that it must be far too late, for the rubbish had been allowed to pile so high she could hardly believe that it was now possible for anyone ever to collect it.

She realized that she had not got rid of the dark cruel vision that came from her paranoia. She had not found calm or acceptance from visiting the peaceful non-striving world of the buried. She was tortured by the feeling that she had put on some kind of ghastly performance within the cemetery and it had made her a laughing stock. She had presented some part of her life and it had provided a very shaming spectacle.

Now Angelica felt the consuming fury of the disgraced performer—a murderous loathing of the audience who had failed to appreciate the display she had put on for them. But she also recognized that it was insane when she tried to blame the dead for their lack of enthusiasm for the shoddy little show she had just enacted in their midst. All her anger had to be transferred therefore to the living, for she suspected she would have no more success if she was to perform in front of a live audience than she'd had with the vast deaf multitudes of the deceased.

When she reached the Earls Court Road, Angelica stood on a corner, and with a wicked and baleful eye she watched the crowds as they went streaming by her. So many Arabs and Indians and Africans passed her she could hardly believe she was in London. She disliked the look of all of them, finding them alien, but not in the least exotic. She saw them as having very dark ears under their turbans and their romantic flowing headdresses.

Her attitude to the English people who hurried past was equally ungenerous. She assessed them with the same coldness that she'd always assessed the people she had allowed to stream like strangers through her life.

She saw various unexciting-looking young matrons and they seemed very like Susan. They were pushing small children in prams and strollers. Most of the kids that these young women had produced seemed truly awful to Angelica. Her attention deliberately focused on the ones who were either bawling or whining. She saw them as sticky and smelly and unrewarding, and she couldn't believe their mothers really liked them.

It quite pleased her to see that many of these young women looked tired and harassed, for she could feel no pity for them. In her opinion, they had been idiotic and lazy and they'd settled for a life of the most horrible domestic routine and drudgery in order to give birth to more mindless and ugly human specimens who would lead much the same lives that they had.

When she examined the young men who were going by her, she soon picked out the ones who could remind her of Jason. Some of them seemed to be even vainer than he was, and they took more care with their appearance. She noticed one or two who were much more beautiful than he had ever been. They were taller and better built and their faces were stronger and more intelligent. She would have liked to have pointed them out to Jason and she cared very little if this desire was spiteful and unworthy.

It gave her a malignant pleasure to imagine a discerning and powerful film director who was looking for a glamorous male to cast as the juvenile lead in an important movie. If languid little Jason was to try for the part, she was certain he would never be able to compete with the handsome figures she could discover in the streets. But although she was relieved that it was so easy to find young men who were much more attractive than he was, she was glad she didn't envy any of the girls who were walking arm-in-arm with them. For surveying the crowds like a street prostitute on the lookout for clients, Angelica's vision was so bitter she could only see every man that passed as the bearer of a couple of sickening ears.

For a moment she stared downwards at the rainwater that was trickling sluggishly in the gutter. She noticed that it had a thick top scum of oil from all the vehicles which were jamming, and hooting, and blowing hot foul air from their exhausts as they headed down to the river. She wondered if these oily rainbow colors had a modern beauty. If they did, she knew she was never going to learn to like it. The gutter water was heading for a drain, and she saw the Earl's Court crowds as hurrying towards a very drain-like future.

Angelica tried to imagine what would happen if she was suddenly to start to sing a song as she stood there on the corner? What would happen if she was to start to do a little dance? She assumed that all the young men would laugh and nudge their girls as they pointed out a poor buffoon of a woman who was making an exhibition of herself on a busy street.

If she began to sing and dance she imagined that one or two old ladies with respectable hats and handbags would frown and purse their lips as they went limping along the pavements on painful swollen legs. They might think of reporting her to a policeman, but if they decided she looked quite harmless, they would not bother to waste their time and they would shuffle off and leave her. A certain amount of unshaven men with eyes that looked like bleeding pools of alcohol would be bound to stumble past her as they went from pub to pub, as if they could never abandon their quest for the perfect drinking bar. They would stare at her with a glazed incuriosity, seeing a noisy woman whirling in her fur coat in the rain, and they'd go staggering on. As they drifted past her in their habitual state of topsy-turvy unreality she would never be able to startle them, although they might well mistake her for an escaped circus dancing bear.

Angelica could hardly believe that all the homosexuals who were hanging around waiting for assignments would be all that impressed by her performance either. The stern and sadistic boys dressed in black leather, the ones with the fierce compressed lips who wore studs and swastika armbands in much the same way that she wore jewelry, they would simply all ignore her. The boys who looked just as flamboyant and feminine as she did might feel more threatened by her extrovert display, and they would quickly cross to the other side of the street.

But she wondered what would happen if all these crowds were suddenly to stop and gather round her? What would happen if they all decided to postpone all their important engagements and chose just to stand around enraptured listening to her song and applauding her while she danced? If they reacted with no embarrassment seeing a crazed woman performing her sad and drunken antics on a rainy urban corner—if, on the contrary, by some inexplicable miracle, they adored her performance—if they encouraged more and more people to gather round her—if they all roared encouragement as they begged her to continue, Angelica wondered if she would still see all these people as quite so sordid, dull, and doomed.

But she knew that she was never going to dare to perform for the crowds. She knew she must never forget the only valuable lesson she had learnt in the cemetery. She must forever abandon the destructive fantasy that she was ever going to act in public again.

As she went on looking at the driven, ugly faces of the people who were streaming past her, she felt a savage resentment as she remembered the lady with the geraniums. Angelica suddenly longed to be back alone with the dead, back alone with her heroic imaginary Major. But she started waving for a taxi that would take her back to the comforts of her home.

The Shopping Spree

Mrs. Williamson floated aimlessly round the "Better Dresses" Department, like a great barge which had accidentally slipped its moorings. "Charge up anything you want at any of the stores where he has an account," the lawyer had told her. His eyes had gleamed with voracious pleasure. "We always advise our clients to do that in cases where the husband may contest alimony and much valuable time be wasted. Not that I feel that in this particular case you are going to have much trouble! He has really put himself in a position where you can take him!" The lawyer had laughed, a sound terrible, legal; the wind whistling through archives, licenses, and stamped documents. Mrs. Williamson had sat silently on her chair.

Since that interview, she had lived on in the house where she had spent her ten-year marriage. "At this point," the lawyer had said emphatically and repeatedly, "you must on no account leave it; to do so could only jeopardize your chances of possessing it." Mrs. Williamson had wondered where he thought she could possibly go to. He had seemed to see seductive alternatives of which she was entirely unaware.

But she had stayed on in the house. Her wounded vanity had ached in the nights like a perpetual toothache, and in the mornings she was already afraid because the evening would come so soon.

Today, Mrs. Williamson felt no urge to buy, or acquire. This shopping expedition was merely one of the many meaningless activities with which she filled her time since Eric had left. "Keep yourself busy," her friends had all advised. "That will stop you brooding."

The women shoppers seethed round her, jostling and bargain-seeking. Mrs. Williamson was grateful because their bustle and purposefulness were in a way catching, and almost camouflaged her own futile and directionless presence. She moved heavily across the floor, to where some crumpled garments were hanging on a rack. She tried to look at them with interest. They appeared so very lifeless, undesirable, and discarded. Dreary caricatures of her own being. They depressed her. She preferred the scarlet notice on top, "Drastic Reductions As Advertised!" At least that message had a certain warm vitality, the reassurance of promises well kept. She reread it several times. "May I help you?" said a soft voice at her elbow. Mrs. Williamson spun round. She saw a plump and elderly little woman in saleslady black. She saw compassionate eyes behind thick spectacles.

"Yes!" Mrs. Williamson wanted to shout out loud. "HELP me, kindly maternal little lady! Help me! YOU must, must help me!" She was instantly ashamed of her impulse. Regressive infantile behavior. "Forty-year-old women can't go round screaming for help to mother figures," she thought bitterly. "No thank you," she said in deliberately crushing tones, "I prefer to look by myself." "If you want help, ask for Miss Estelle," said the other with dauntless persistence. "Here's my card," she pushed it with insinuating pressure into Mrs. Williamson's hand.

Mrs. Williamson had now become haughty and strong. She ignored the card and firmly picked a dress from the rack and studied it with falsely keen attention. Beige net; the bow on the back seemed both unnecessary and vulgar. "An ugly and ill-conceived garment," she thought wearily, pushing it back on the rack with disgust. Two young women, wearing peddle-pushers, their glossy hair tied in ponytails, seized the same dress with immediate excitement. "Isn't this just darling!" one of them held it against her body with lascivious longing. Mrs. Williamson lost confidence in her own taste. She remembered that she had never really been able to understand Cézanne, although she had always pretended to Eric that she did.

"Have you found anything you like?" It was Miss Estelle who had been hovering, a faithful carrion crow at her back. "No," thought Mrs. Williamson abjectly. It occurred to her suddenly that she had never been able to find anything that she really liked. Eric had called her a "damper" and a "cold-water thrower." She wondered if she had really liked Eric when she had had him, although his unexpected and humiliating departure had certainly left her wounded and writhing in a vacuum. "No," she said flatly, "I have not found anything that I like."

The dark cavernous nostrils of Miss Estelle flared with the excitement of the hound that has finally caught blood-scent. "I have other things," she said. Her voice was husky and thick with enticement.

The voice of the Circe. A voice ancient as Lilith's. "I have many other things which I can just guarantee you will find enchanting." Mrs. Williamson was now lost. Her Achilles' heel was pierced by this triumphantly felicitous phraseology. Enchantment! Who, and what else in her life guaranteed the magical, the rapturous? She weakly followed Miss Estelle to her Aladdin's cave of a changing-cubicle.

Miss Estelle gently and helpfully took off Mrs. Williamson's scarf and hat and hung them briskly on a peg. Mrs. Williamson was at once delighted by this authoritative and solicitous gesture. She realized that Miss Estelle in her great compassion had instantly divined that she had not enough free will to make even this commonplace action herself. She was immeasurably soothed and reassured by this perceptive and immediate understanding of her condition. She began to love the soft brown eyes shining through the thick lenses with eagerness to enchant and serve.

"What size are you, please?" Mrs. Williamson was disappointed. The question seemed gross, crass, almost impertinent, coming from a woman of Miss Estelle's obviously delicate sensibilities. "Rather large, I'm afraid," said Mrs. Williamson apologetically, smiling a confidential and slightly ingratiating smile. Miss Estelle was unsmiling. Did she find this answer tiresome, stupidly evasive? "Perhaps if you were to remove your clothes, I might get a better idea." Did she scorn prevarication? Was it merely the impatience of the physician, eager to complete the thorough examination, so as to get on with the diagnosis of the disease? Or, a more fearful thought, was she exasperated?

Mrs. Williamson became suddenly frantic. She remembered that Eric had always told her that she never knew when she was going too far. She stripped with nervous haste, throwing her overcoat clumsily onto the ground. Miss Estelle stooped down and picked it up. She folded it over a chair with uncomplaining patience. Mrs. Williamson felt instantly more secure. She unzipped her dress and stepped out of it with the pride of an Empress, kicking it arrogantly away from under her feet. Once more Miss Estelle stooped, gently picked up the dress, and quietly hung it on a hanger. Mrs. Williamson guiltily scanned her face, still searching for the dreaded sign of exasperation. She remembered that Eric had often told her that if one gave her an inch, she would take a mile. But the eyes behind the horn-rims were still benevolent. Mrs. Williamson felt unexpected elation. She tore off her nylon slip and tossed it, too, recklessly down onto the pin-strewn floor. "Eric would certainly have called that taking a mile," she thought wildly.

Miss Estelle hesitated for a second, then, for the third time she stooped, she picked up the still body-warm slip and, without the least sign of protest, she folded it softly and placed it to safety. Mrs. Williamson felt dizzy with pleasure. She loved the way that Miss Estelle had handled her garments as if they were worthy of boundless love and respect. After all, they had clung snug and damply secret to her person, and Miss Estelle was right to be considerate and treat them as a very close part of a human being.

Eric's treatment of her clothes when he found them on the floor had been very different. Mrs. Williamson suddenly wondered if Eric wasn't really a very boorish and insensitive man, and was quite surprised at herself for having been so upset by his departure.

Now Mrs. Williamson stood half-naked in front of the changing-room mirror, cruelly and totally exposed by harsh neon-lighting. She saw her own wrinkled scraggy neck, the heavy breasts sagging ponderously in the shoddy brassiere, the unsightly bulges of the diaphragm and stomach. Her eye caught the blue mottled and fatty flesh of thighs swelling obscenely out of transparent panties. She was truly sad that Miss Estelle had to see these things.

In the last five years, she had certainly never allowed Eric to peruse and study her nakedness in this way. She had been clever about always undressing behind dressing gowns and bath towels. Now here she found herself, flagrantly exposing the more unpleasing and unsavory aspects of her body to a total stranger. Was Miss Estelle indeed a stranger? Why was the idea so insufferable? That so-gentle voice. The compassion of those eyes. It was as if she had always known them, feeling and comprehending their importance. Could it be that she had known them in some previous reincarnation? Mrs. Williamson was vague about reincarnation. Her friend Mrs. Ducas Rawlings Junior often spoke about it. She believed in it absolutely. Something about coming back as a dog or a cat. No, that wouldn't explain this uncanny sense of familiarity with Miss Estelle. All the same, Mrs. Williamson wished that she had listened with more attention when Mrs. Ducas Rawlings Junior had tried to explain the whole thing.

Then Mrs. Williamson became aware of the silence of Miss Estelle. There was something cosmic and brooding about this silence, something which brought out ancient forebodings and presentiments of the ill-defined but blackly thundering disaster.

Mrs. Williamson shivered, standing in her semi-nudity in the fitting-cubicle. Miss Estelle's eyes were silently searching her body, seeing and weighing up imperfections. Mrs. Williamson was in torment. She was filled with sudden hatred of her own flesh. Greyly rotting poisonous tissue! Would that she could tear it off herself, scrape it away, rip it away with her nails, chastise it finally for its as yet unpunished criminality of failure. Would those brown eyes never stop staring? How long could reason endure this damnable uncertainty? Sword of Damocles drop with your cruel dismembering thrust of disapproval!

"Do you ever wear a foundation garment, Honey?" asked Miss Estelle gently. "It's quite amazing the difference they make. Maybe you would like to stop by at our lingerie department on your way out. They've got some quite lovely things."

Mrs. Williamson was unbelieving. She looked straight into the brown eyes, seeing through and dismissing the horn-rims. Had Christ looked like that at the woman taken in adultery? She in no way resented the indirect but strongly implied criticism of her underwear. Lingerie could apparently be improved so easily. But criticism and scorn of things beyond remedy; derision and disapproval of things which could not be changed by the quick visit to the department store: yes, there lay the true assassination of the human spirit.

Mrs. Williamson looked once more into the thick lenses of Miss Estelle and knew that she would never know fear again. Miss Estelle not only would, but should, strike, abuse, condemn the superficialities, but just as surely would she leave the soft vulnerability of the soul intact. Mrs. Williamson started moving round the fitting-cubicle with a brazen abandonment. All shame at her nudity's ugliness had departed. Mrs. Williamson was both bold and free.

"I think you ought to be able to take a fourteen," said Miss Estelle. She was lying. Mrs. Williamson recognized it immediately. She realized also with a lightning intuition that Miss Estelle, with her great past experience of shapes and sizes, could only make such a mistake quite deliberately.

Mrs. Williamson felt that she was swelling, pregnant with her gratitude for the generosity and sympathy that had motivated this wild distortion of the truth. She hoped that Miss Estelle could not remark how badly she was swelling and be forced against all her boundless goodwill to suggest a larger size.

Suddenly Mrs. Williamson felt an insane desire to dance. She had never been able to dance. On the one single occasion when Eric had taken her onto the dance floor, he had said it was like having to trundle round with a bloody great sack of potatoes. Now she knew that Eric had been wrong about this as he had been wrong about so many things. "None so blind as those who won't see," thought Mrs. Williamson wildly. Yes, she could dance, she knew it. She could dance for Miss Estelle. Her dancing would have fire, spirit, light! Yes, she could dance for Miss Estelle. She could dance all the dances of Aphrodite and Astarte. The dance that was danced before Urania. The dance of Salome before Herod, and the imperishable dances of Terpsichord, Dionysus, and Persephone! She felt suddenly outrageously constricted by the narrow confines of the changing-cubicle. She felt tearing and overwhelming longing to shatter those hideously partitioned yellow-cream walls. O for the pure whiteness of Space! Yes, if she only had space, she could truly dance for Miss Estelle. She could dance for an Eternity, through the billions of light years, on and on, never tiring. Not only could she dance for, but she could dance with, Miss Estelle!

The thought shocked her. She was appalled, terrified by the monstrous daring of this new conception. No, she would not be afraid. Yes, she could dance with Miss Estelle! They could both step out of life and dance into Infinity, whirling, whirling, through immortality. Just the two of them on and on, never tiring! Mrs. Williamson felt giddy with ecstasy, drunken with fantasies. She took a small but savage dance step across the fitting-room floor, and her heavy breasts rattled dully against her diaphragm. Miss Estelle disappeared. Mrs. Williamson was semi-nude, cold, and alone in the changing-cubicle.

Miss Estelle came back in a few minutes with a huge load of black dresses on hangers. "Perhaps you would like to start trying these fourteens," she suggested in her usual coaxing and gentle tones. Mrs. Williamson instinctively recognized that Miss Estelle was urging a time-wasting course of action. Her time was, however, not valuable. If Miss Estelle was willing and eager to pursue this already foredoomed project, she had no objection whatsoever.

"Which one would you like to start with?" said the voice, low, silky, seductive. Mrs. Williamson looked at the black dresses rather blankly. They appeared to her to be identical. She knew, however, that this was only the fault of her own wretched lack of discrimination. She chose one at random. Miss Estelle was apparently quite delighted by the flare of her selection. She smiled with obvious pleasure at the choice. It was the first smile that she had given.

"I knew that you would just go crazy over that one," she said. She was purring now, purring, a gratified milk-fed cat. She, Mrs. Williamson, had caused that pleasure purr!

"It has that gorgeous flared back-panel," continued Miss Estelle rapturously. "I can see that you are going to look just beautiful in it." She was sighing now, sighing with esoteric fervor. Mrs. Williamson looked at herself for a moment, anxiously in the mirror, dreading the unpalatable image which greeted her habitually from the glass. But there was no need for her to fear. She could see herself now. She could see herself as she truly was. Had she been blind all these years? Was she seeing herself through the eyes of Miss Estelle? It didn't matter. Not now, when she could see her radiance reflecting, twinkling at her.

Yes, she could see now that she had that ephemeral and intangible thing called Beauty.

Mrs. Williamson realized all at once that Miss Estelle was an Artist. Her life was dedicated to the service and the adornment of the beautiful. She, Mrs. Williamson, decided she would play Mycena to Miss Estelle's artistry. She decided she would buy many things, in fact she would buy up the entire Store, if necessary. It was her Duty now to intensify and heighten her own natural and new found loveliness. She would bedeck, she would bejewel. She would acquire costly apparel. She would have satins, silks, soft furs, and gold. She would have velvets, laces, brilliants, tulles. She would find true satisfaction in her knowledge of Miss Estelle's heartfelt approval of the fitness of her action.

Eric would never see the wonder of the things that she would buy, but ah would he have to pay for them. He would pay the piper, and Miss Estelle would call the tune. There was poetic justice!

Mrs. Williamson struggled enthusiastically into the little black dress. Miss Estelle moved up helpfully behind her. Suddenly Mrs. Williamson felt a searing burning sensation as Miss Estelle ripped the zipper through a roll of flesh on her back. Mrs. Williamson made no protest. So this was the Pleasure Pain that everyone was always talking about. She had never known what they meant until now. This was fusion, euphoria, ecstasy; this was the cataclysm of the Senses. Rip on, rip on, soft hands! Miss Estelle became suddenly aware of what she had done. She rubbed the reddened back with hysterical distress. She muttered tender and repetitious apologies. She appeared to be almost tearful. Mrs. Williamson watched her from the cosmic heights of her contentment. She felt completely removed now, abstracted by delight. She could hardly even enjoy the sensations tingling down her back as the gentle, helpful hands attempted to iron out her pain. She did, however, feel an unexpected and unwelcome resurgence of sorrow mingled with some extreme resentment, when Miss Estelle left her to find larger dresses.

The little saleslady reappeared triumphantly, waving a white and gold spangled chiffon object, banner-like, above her head. "You're going to just love this," she said, "it's got real style!" Mrs. Williamson looked dubious; this was the very first thing that Miss Estelle had said with which she was tempted to disagree. Despite her newfound sense of the potentiality of her personality, this dress still seemed to her to be far more suitable for a movie vamp of silent screen days. Her only concern however was in sparing Miss Estelle from all hurt and discouragement. "When would I even wear it?" she asked, courteous, but hesitant. "Why for your dressy outdoor dining!" protested Miss Estelle excitedly.

All at once Mrs. Williamson shrank, shriveled as a deflated child's balloon. Every trace of ecstasy and elation vanished. She remembered that it was extremely unlikely that anyone would ever ask her to dine again, let alone dressily and outdoors.

Far more mortifying, however, was the cruel realization that Miss Estelle was capable of referring quite casually to the possibility of her spending nights of glamour with indeterminate others. Miss Estelle had showed not the least trace of emotion, she had indicated not the least trace of jealousy! If it had been the other way round . . . If she, Mrs. Williamson, had had to entertain, even in the wildest fantasy, the notion of Miss Estelle dining with others, dressily and outdoors! No, she would not think of it, she could not think of it! Madness lay that way.

"I don't go out much in the evening," she said heavily, she was still hoping that Miss Estelle would redeem herself by showing at least some small personal sign of gratification and relief on receiving this piece of information.

Miss Estelle was preoccupied with unraveling the tangled stole of the chiffon gown and did not reply. Then desperation came to Mrs. Williamson, mantling, enveloping. Should she tell Miss Estelle more? God, was this the moment? Dared she run the risk of incurring Miss Estelle's boredom? Surely what she could tell must arouse pity, not ennui. But could she ever tell? Could she even tell Miss Estelle about the horror of those lonely nights spent turning the television on and off? Could she ever express to anyone what it felt like to be forty and discarded by Eric?

Miss Estelle of the compassionate eyes would have to understand that she could no longer participate in this farce of the buying of clothes that no one would ever see or admire. After all that had passed between them, Mrs. Williamson knew that her relationship with Miss Estelle went far deeper than the ordinary one of client and saleslady. O Miss Estelle! O Stella! O star-like Being! What sudden cement-like block has sealed off your sensibilities?

Mrs. Williamson's heart was bleeding under her nylon brassiere. Miss Estelle must stop! She must instantly stop all this ludicrous pretense of the trying on of clothes and tell how she spends her evening when she leaves the store. Good Christ, how does she spend her evenings? This is insanity! Such terrible thoughts are winging through the brain.

Miss Estelle was speaking now. What was she saying? Something about seeing what she had in stock. Mrs. Williamson stood stunned in semi-nudity in the changing-room.

Miss Estelle all at once had acquired will-o'-the-wisp inapproachability. She was flitting now. Flitting feverishly back and forth from the fitting-cubicle to some mysterious back region, from where she produced an interminable number of gowns and outfits. She showed Mrs. Williamson ones which she assured her would be "just perfect" for barbecue-type evenings, television informals, theatre galas, European trips, film premieres, and all-season cocktails.

Mrs. Williamson tried on every single one. She was a robot now. She had passed to the stage of pain which is beyond feeling. Miss Estelle told her that she looked "darling" and "divine" in all. Two hours passed before Mrs. Williamson recovered her capacity for feeling sensation of even the most commonplace nature. Slowly, with the unpleasant tingling of the wearing off of anesthesia, she became aware of both heat and extreme fatigue. Far worse, though, than either of these mere physical discomforts was the slow but shocking realization that she no longer derived any active pleasure from Miss Estelle's company. The truth was she simply preferred remaining in the store rather than going back to her empty house.

Miss Estelle was speaking again. She was telling her that she had the figure for special-type clothes whereas so many of her clients didn't. Then it was that Mrs. Williamson felt once again a volcanic stirring of feeling. Then it was that the agony of Mrs. Williamson began erupting in a molten lava of violence. She was outraged. She was not only outraged, she was staggered by this casual mention of other clients to whom Miss Estelle was obviously promiscuously and indiscriminately compassionate and comforting.

It was at this very moment that Mrs. Williamson realized finally that Miss Estelle had failed her, not only as a saleswoman—she had not provided enchantment—but also as a human being.

Mrs. Williamson stood uncomfortably encased in a pink taffeta crinoline. She was silent. Her silence was deadly. She asked the price of it suddenly. Her question came swift as the rapier thrust. As she was planning to charge any purchase that she might make to Eric's account, price was of no interest to her whatsoever.

Miss Estelle looked taken aback, as though startled by the unmistakably malicious and spiteful tone of Mrs. Williamson's query. She seemed momentarily flustered. Then she giggled the low, conspiratorial giggle of the female exploiting the male. "It's a little highly priced," she admitted, lowering her voice tactfully. "But when he sees how gorgeous and sexy you look in it, you'll find he won't complain too much."

Mrs. Williamson started ripping the dress over her head with paranoiac fury. She struggled, suffocated, and stifled in the layers and rolls of pink material. Miss Estelle eased and helped her, gentle and understanding as ever. Mrs. Williamson emerged ashen-pale, sweating, and disheveled. Her mouth was trembling. "I don't like it!" she shouted. "And I don't like any of the others either!" "Honey," said Miss Estelle with sympathetic reproach, "I have got many more to show you, you haven't seen our Spring lightweights." "I don't like any of them either!" screamed Mrs. Williamson. She was staggered by her own violence. "What?" cried Miss Estelle, genuinely shocked. "None of them?" "None!" thundered Mrs. Williamson. "None," repeated Miss Estelle, a plaintive echo. She seemed to find it quite impossible to believe that her last few hours had been entirely wasted.

Mrs. Williamson put on her old clothes. She felt immense vindictive delight in having so successfully distressed Miss Estelle. She noticed with malicious pleasure that the soft eyes had become less gentle and compassionate behind the thick lenses. She walked out of the fitting room, vengeful and powerful, and took the elevator to the lingerie department.

The Eyes of Leonora

The eyes of the dying can become cold as the lens of any camera. They take mechanical pictures of those who surround them. They focus on their doctors and their nurses. They shift their glassy stare to the grim and rigid faces of their distressed friends and relatives as if they have some need to photograph only their uselessness—to capture some last image of their inadequacy which they can blame, retain, and carry to eternity.

When I went to visit Leonora in her hospital, her open eyes looked frightening underneath her head bandage. I went to see her with her husband, Richard, and her six-year-old twins.

Originally I'd been worried that the four of us might prove too much for Leonora to cope with—that she might find our visit exhausting. She had been taken out of intensive care only in the last two days. Richard had begged me to accompany him. He dreaded taking Amy and Isobel to see their injured mother. He still felt he ought to take them to see her because he thought the sight of them might bring her comfort.

"How are you feeling, darling?" Richard said as we entered Leonora's sterile little private room.

He had brought her a huge bunch of roses and he waved them with a nervously hearty gesture.

Leonora didn't answer. Her brown eyes looked at the beautiful flowers. They seemed to film every petal and in particular every thorn. But there was no gratitude in their glassy stare, certainly no pleasure. Leonora just lay there inert on her pillows. She didn't even give one little grunt.

Richard looked hurt and frightened by her lack of response.

"I'll get a nurse to find me a vase," he said. He seemed to be talking to himself to break the silence. He went out into the hospital corridor. He obviously wanted to feel active. Leonora's eyes followed him as he left and they took a slow-motion picture of his exit. And because they only seemed to record the pointlessness of his search for a vase they made his quest seem exceedingly futile.

What use were roses to Leonora? I wondered if she was in severe pain. As she didn't seem to want to speak, it was impossible to tell. She had one arm in a plaster and the other was attached to several drips. Her fractured ribs had been strapped up in yellow elastic tapes. One of her legs was uncomfortably raised in traction. How could a bunch of flowers seem very useful to her? And yet I wished she would make some little movement or sound to show she registered the love and concern with which Richard had selected the roses for her.

A nurse had found Richard a vase and when he returned he filled it with water from the basin. From under her bandage his wife's eyes watched him as he started arranging the roses with all the care of a florist trying to display every flower and fern to its best advantage.

Richard had been taking tranquilizers ever since he had been told the news of Leonora's car accident. His medication didn't seem to be working. As he placed rose after rose in the vase I saw that his hands were shaking like those of an alcoholic.

Leonora must have seen the way that her husband's hands were trembling but it didn't appear to concern her, and she showed no sign she was glad that Richard was putting her flowers in water to prevent them from wilting.

Amy and Isobel were sitting on two hard narrow chairs beside their mother's bed, their thin pinched faces looked bloodless from the shock of their mother's accident, and their round blue eyes were ringed with pale mauve circles of anxiety. The two little girls resembled each other but they had different coloring. They were not identical twins. But now in the hospital the similarity of the expression of fear and horror with which they both stared at the bandage on Leonora's head made them look identical. I felt that they would carry the memory of that bandage for the rest of their lives, that they would see it in bad dreams and wake up screaming.

Amy was clutching a bag of grapes and Isobel was holding a bag of oranges. As Leonora lay there completely immobile and registered not one iota of pleasure at their presence, both her children looked stunned and humiliated. They just sat on their chairs gripping their gifts with such awkwardness and force that their knuckles became gleaming white. The twins had obviously hoped that their fruit would restore their mother. Now that she was making it so clear that she didn't want the contents of their paper bags they didn't know what to do with them.

Richard kept compulsively arranging and rearranging Leonora's roses. He had found an occupation that he could pretend was so engrossing that he could ignore his wife's unresponsiveness, and disregard her cold, inhuman stare.

I felt I must try and break the silence for the sake of the twins.

"Have you seen the lovely fruit that Amy and Isobel have brought you?"

My voice sounded over-loud and inappropriate. I took the bags of oranges and grapes from the grip of the twins and held them up to Leonora. I was hoping she would give some little nod to show that she appreciated that her children had done their best to please her.

Leonora's eyes looked at me directly and I felt that they were taking a quick snapshot of my idiocy. She was obviously far too badly injured to eat one single grape.

When she refused to give even a twitch or some tiny cough to show that she was pleased that the twins had come to the hospital with their useless brown bags of fruit, I suddenly wanted to scream so that the noise would blast and smother her silence.

I wished to God that Leonora would close her eyes. If she would only shut them we would all be able to accept that she was asleep or in some kind of coma. If she would only close her lids we would have to stop waiting for her to give us a sign that our visit was of some value to her. But while her eyes stared out from under the bandage we all felt that she could have made some little movement or sound if she had wanted to. And I could see from the wounded expression on the faces of Richard and the twins that they were shocked by the way she seemed to find their presence so meaningless—

that they felt that she was cruel that she refused to pretend that she found it otherwise.

I got up from my chair and went out into the corridor to find a nurse who could give me a bowl to hold the fruit that the twins had brought their mother. I was glad to escape for a moment from that sterile little claustrophobic room where pain seemed to mingle with strong smells of disinfectant.

When I returned with the bowl I found Richard still fiddling neurotically with the roses. He kept arranging them and rearranging them. The twins were so immobile they looked as if they had been frozen. I put the oranges in the bowl and draped the grapes over them with all the care and artistry of a painter preparing a perfect model for a still life.

Leonora watched my efforts and her eyes recorded them with such coldness that I had no illusion that she found my fruit arrangement very valuable.

As she stared at the grapes and the oranges, I felt frightened. She made me realize that she was much more seriously injured than any of us chose to register.

All the warmth, spontaneity, and the affection that we'd all once loved in Leonora already seemed to have died. Now only her eyes were still functioning with their cold and camera-like action. They could still record images in a reflex fashion although their photography was now just as useless to Leonora as it was to her family. For her brain now appeared to be totally concentrated on the difficulty of dying and it had ceased to sort out any of the exterior information that her eyes relayed to it. Richard and her daughters now meant no more to Leonora than if they had been three oranges—three unwanted grapes.

"I think we should go now and let Mummy get some sleep," I could see no reason to prolong this painful visit. Richard nodded in agreement and the twins got up like somnambulists and followed me to the door. I wondered if they all felt as guilty as I did. Did they have the same unworthy longing to be three thousand miles away from Leonora? Did they also only want to flee from this hot and hellish room where one was always within range of those glassy reproachful eyes which seemed to take police mug-shots as documentation while they accused one of one's uselessness?

"We'll all come back and see you tomorrow," I said. My words seemed to echo like the mocking cry of a cuckoo as they hit the white walls of the hospital room.

We were not going to see Leonora tomorrow. That night she suffered a severe internal hemorrhage and she was rushed into intensive care. She died in the early hours of the morning.

None of us accepted that we were seeing her for the last time as we stood in the doorway of her hospital room and Richard and I waved to her and the twins blew her goodbye kisses.

At first her eyes automatically recorded us all as if they were carrying out some group photography. But then suddenly they seemed to recognize that we were all about to desert her and this appeared to stimulate her brain. From under her bandage her eyes suddenly seemed to come to life as if they were trying to communicate rather than record. Her head twitched and her mouth opened as if she was making a painful effort to speak to us. We waited and we waited but no words came out. Finally we gave up hoping that she would speak and we all waved again and her children blew her more kisses and we left.

When we heard the news the following day we all tried to

interpret what Leonora had been saying to us with that last imploring look.

Richard felt that she had been trying to apologize for not having said a word to us—to explain that she felt far too weak and annihilated to convey how much our visit meant to her. When the twins heard their father's explanation they seemed very relieved by it and they felt certain it was the correct one.

I never told Richard that I was not totally convinced by this interpretation of Leonora's last unspoken message, but then I never told him about my dream.

I had been a friend of Leonora's ever since she was a girl and after she died I kept remembering many things she had done and said when she was young.

When Leonora was eighteen and very beautiful and popular, I remembered her telling me that she couldn't enjoy the fun of being young because the idea that she was going to die eventually spoiled it.

I think it may have been this particular memory that sparked off my nightmare. I was standing in the doorway of her hospital room. Richard and the twins were standing beside me. Leonora was lying in bed with a bandage round her head. All that part of the dream was realistic. Leonora didn't say a word but her dark eyes kept staring at us and they grew bigger and bigger until they looked like huge black lakes of fear.

And suddenly I could hear her speaking although her lips never moved. But I could hear her talking voice-over as if I was watching her in a movie.

And although I knew that it was Leonora speaking, it wasn't the way that she'd ever spoken in real life. Her words were too weird and unnatural. But the conventions of the dream-state are elastic, and they allow for much perversity.

"Go away!" said the voice that I recognized to be that of Leonora. "Just go away!" Her command was hysterically repeated. "Can't you take away your flustered unhappy faces? For God's sake go away with all your grapes and your oranges and your roses. Do you have no pity? Why won't you show some little grain of mercy? Can't you see I'm much too petrified to talk to you?"

Her eyes grew even larger and larger as if exasperated by our criminal lack of comprehension. They resembled two vast and angry craters that oozed volcanic matter. A trickle of blood started seeping through her bandage. Her words still never came from her lips. They appeared to reverberate, hideously magnified by some invisible microphone that was secreted in the hospital walls that surrounded her.

"Why do you keep on standing there?" The voice of Leonora asked us. It now sounded so over-amplified it had acquired a high-pitched screaming volume which made it intolerable to listen to.

"Can't you see that I've gone into an arena where no human help can reach me? Can't you see that I've left the plane and my parachute hasn't opened? I'm not frightened that my injuries will kill me. I'm only terrified that I may die of fright."

The Answering Machine

In the last few months she had started to leave messages for herself on her answering machine. When she left her flat and went out to ring her own number from her local pub, the Red Oak, she found it comforting to hear a voice saying that she was out and asking anyone who wished to contact her to leave their name and number so that she could return their call when she got home.

If it had not been her own voice telling her that she was out she would not have believed that it was true. She so rarely went out. But her taped voice sounded very convincing, very matter of fact. It seemed inconceivable that it would lie.

Sometimes she telephoned her own number many times. The other customers who came to drink in the Red Oak often grew quite impatient with her because she monopolized the only telephone in the pub and they wanted to make urgent calls themselves. "Will you be very long?" she would be asked.

"I just need to make one more call." Apologetically, but with defiance, she then inserted yet another coin, and she listened to the message she needed to hear repeated yet again.

When she telephoned her own number from the Red Oak she first listened to herself asking anyone who called to leave a message after the beep and then she would leave one. She wanted to have something to look forward to when she returned to her flat.

The hours that she spent there alone could often seem so long that she got a feeling of suffocation as if some well-meaning but inept euthanasiac had put a plastic bag over her head which made it difficult to breathe without it killing her.

At the beginning the messages she left for herself were invariably formal and solicitous. "It's me . . . I am sorry to have missed you. I have been thinking about you a lot and I am dying to hear all your news. I hope you are well and everything is going all right. I've tried to reach you a lot of times this week but you always seem to be out. I'll keep on calling until I find you in . . ."

Once she got back to her flat she liked to hear this in the silence.

Since Trevor had died so suddenly six months ago she found it hard to care if she was well. Now that he was no longer there to look after her she lacked the energy to do it on her own. But it reassured her to hear her own voice insisting that she still cared very much.

She also found it reassuring to hear that she was still trying to reach herself. Lately she often had the frightening sensation that her brain had become exasperated with dealing with the oppressive monotony of her unhappy feelings—that it had developed a horror of trying to keep in touch with them.

She had started to feel that her brain was now only prepared to operate like the engine of a car. It still performed mechanical functions and propelled the vehicle of her body from A to B. It got her to the lavatory and it got her across the room to the kitchen where it gave motor energy to her arms so that she could put her kettle on the stove.

But it didn't seem to care what she experienced while it continued to mobilize her so that she never needed to be stationary. It had become an engine that had all the fuel to keep the wheels of its vehicle turning. If those wheels felt that they were burning as they rotated on the tarmac—if they screeched like an animal in agony as they rounded every corner, that was not an engine's concern.

When she played back her messages on her answering machine after she returned home from visiting the Red Oak, they helped to take away her fear that she had become such a burden to her own brain that it had given up trying to dictate to her behavior and now it would allow her to carry out any kind of dangerous and irrational acts without interference.

The voice that she listened to on the tape could seem like the voice of her own brain. It maintained that it was still trying to reach her—that it had only failed because she always seemed to be out. When she was sitting drinking a tepid beer in the Red Oak she often felt so displaced, deranged, and lonely that she could understand why her brain no longer always managed to reach her. She was certainly not an easy person to contact. Half the time she couldn't manage to feel that she existed anywhere. That must mean that she was often "out."

She didn't need the help of her brain to realize how much the owner of the Red Oak loathed her. Mick Kilkenny was a large and unkempt Irishman. He had bulbous toad-like eyes with whites which were marked like a map with small red rivers of alcohol. He always glared at her from the moment that she came through the door of his pub.

Although he was such a large broad-shouldered man and she was small and frail, she could sense that he was very frightened of her. All the time that he was serving drinks to his other customers he continued to keep a wary eye on her. It was as if he saw her as a female terrorist and feared that she might suddenly produce a bomb from her handbag.

She sometimes wondered if it was some expression in her eyes that made him feel so threatened by her, something that made him realize that he had a female customer drinking in his pub who was not always in contact with her own brain.

Her outward behavior while she remained in the Red Oak was impeccable. She always ordered herself a beer, but that was merely to stop him complaining that she only came to his pub to make telephone calls. She had never once got drunk. She never sang tuneless, overloud songs or became quarrelsome and got into fights like many others who came to drink in his sleazy establishment. Yet when she went up to Mick Kilkenny's bar to order her beer and she handed him the money he always looked at it with disgust and fury as if she had offered him a handful of excrement. He made it obvious that he had to repress a violent urge to hurl it down on the ground.

But he was still forced to accept it. She had never once given him any ground for refusing to serve her. She always dressed up with great care before she went off to telephone in the Red Oak.

She put on a hat, she put on clean gloves, and her best shoes. She could have been preparing herself to attend some formal church service. She was never going to allow him to accuse her of looking like a tramp. Yet the very respectability of her appearance seemed to alarm him rather more than if she had come in staggering, looking wild, dirty, and dishevelled.

Mick Kilkenny was almost permanently semi-inebriated for he spent his days helping himself to very large portions of his own whisky. But his high-flying state of half-intoxication did not seem to blunt his sensitivity to the inner states of those whom he encountered. As he spent his life teetering on the brink of irrationality he was all too quick to detect the weakness of those who were hovering over a similar abyss.

She was never quite sure what she had done to incur his loathing but she knew she could never deceive him for a second. He had sensed from the beginning that her presence in his pub was abnormal. He had never been deceived by her outward display of mouse-like respectability. Many of his other customers became so violent once they had over-drunk at his bar that they threw broken bottles and they had punch-ups, and blood started to splash over his dirty tables which were already sticky with beer. But she could tell that the owner of the Red Oak was not very troubled by this kind of delinquent behavior even when it started to get so out of control that he was forced to call the police. All that he hated was the sight of the most quiet and inoffensive of his customers making a series of discreet and whispered telephone calls, as she stood by a wall that was decorated by obscene graffiti in the dingy and ill-lit corner of his pub.

She could feel the man's scarlet toad eyes glaring at her while she picked up the messages that she had left on her own machine.

She sensed how much he longed to interrupt her conversations although he could only see her lips moving as she left messages for herself. As he was too far away behind his bar to hear what she was saying she wondered why he resented her conversations so much. How could he tell that the telephone calls she kept making were not very usual calls?

She had always been a timid character. She would never have dared to brave the cruel and discomforting rays of Mick Kilkenny's hostility if she had not started to act only on the compulsions of her feelings, ignoring any signals of good sense that came from her brain.

She could have made her calls from so many other public telephones in her neighborhood but she felt compelled to go on making them from the one in the Red Oak. She didn't care that it was situated really unpleasantly close to the toilets and whenever the door swung open, a stench of stale urine came floating out mingled with odors of a more foul and obnoxious nature.

As she felt a generalized sense of impotence she was glad to have found one small way to assert a tiny bit of power and she was not going to relinquish it easily. She recognized that she had the power to irritate Mick Kilkenny. And she knew the British law and she assumed that he knew it too. It was illegal to refuse to serve food and drink to individuals on the grounds of race and sex. A public telephone was there for the use of the public. Anyone who had the correct coins was entitled to use it. She didn't see herself as a very useful member of the public but while she was still alive she was a member all the same. As such she had her rights and she was never going to allow a big slob of an Irishman to violate them. When she made a trip to the Red Oak and ignored the malevolent glare of its proprietor it was the only moment of her day when she felt she was very brave.

Her answering machine originally had belonged to Trevor. When he was still alive she used to be out all day for she'd still held her job. She had always suffered from mild arthritis but after his death it had suddenly become acute and she had been forced to stop working because her fingers became so stiff and inflamed that she found it too painful to use a typewriter. Her doctor said that it might have been the shock of her husband's death which had brought on this crippling condition which affected both her hands and feet.

Her job had not been very well paid but she had kept it for fifteen years and never once thought of leaving it. She'd done all the secretarial work for Mr. Hitchens. He was a florist with a shop which was situated in Central London. Her responsibilities had been varied and they seemed humanly important. She had seen to it that the wreath arrived on time for the funeral, and the bouquet of orange-blossoms was delivered to the bride.

She'd liked the idea that she was always dealing with the sale of flowers and plants for that made her work seem less arid than if she'd worked for a firm which dealt in domestic appliances or helicopter parts. Her little office had been at the rear of the shop and if she left the door ajar she was overwhelmed by the smell of the orchids and roses and lilacs which were on display in the front of the premises. The different beautiful scents that came floating back to her had been so powerful that she often felt intoxicated and she could forget she was in the city and believe that she was working in some magical fragrant garden in the countryside.

When she'd handed in her resignation to Mr. Hitchens, and he'd accepted it, she'd experienced such a moment of panic that she feared she was going to fall in a faint on the floor. She'd realized at that moment that from now on she was condemned. She would never again be "out." She was doomed to be "in" forever. And the place where she would always be "in" was the place where she most hated to be. For although she recognized in the abstract that she was very fortunate that Trevor had left her the flat because it was warm and pretty and comfortable and many people would envy it, she felt it had walls like those of a prison. Every minute that she spent there she suffered as though she were a criminal who had been placed in "solitary."

From the moment she'd been told that Trevor had died, everything about her flat had become obnoxious to her because he still seemed to inhabit it without ever making an appearance. Every second that she was in her flat, memories of Trevor came out like rats from the floorboards and they gnawed at her continually. They crept round her bedroom in the night and they gave her insomnia.

In the first weeks after Trevor's death she had thought of selling the flat and moving to some new place where there would be more hope that she could escape from the sharp teeth of her memories. But her inertia was too powerful. She couldn't feel any real desire to make a new home for herself. Where would she find the energy to buy new equipment for its kitchen? If she were to move and bring her old furniture and pots and pans with her she knew she would be transporting objects which all had painful associations. She would never really feel that she had moved.

When she had told her employer, Mr. Hitchens, that she could no longer continue to do his secretarial work, she had hoped for a moment that he would suggest that she start working in the front of his glass-plated shop and sell flowers and plants to the people who came in from the street. But Mr. Hitchens had not suggested anything of this kind and she soon realized that this hope had been pitifully unrealistic.

He only ever chose very young and pretty girls to sell his flowers. He liked them to have bloom and beauty like his wares. He wanted them to attract customers to his shop and increase his sales. He would never think of employing a middle-aged saleswoman with clumsy, half-crippled hands. Every bunch of flowers that he sold had to be wrapped quickly and skillfully. He obviously thought that she would fumble with the tissue paper with her stiff and unwieldy fingers. The task would take her an inordinately long time and at the end her wrappings would look highly unsatisfactory and lumpy in their lack of expertise.

If she was no longer fit to sell flowers how would she ever find a way to get out of her flat in the daytime? She had started to have dreams in which she was dangling over a cliff and only holding on to land and safety with arthritic fingers that had no strength to support her weight. In those dreams she felt that the grip of her hands was loosening. She was slipping. She was slipping . . . Before she let go, she always woke up screaming.

The day Trevor had died, she had got back a little late from work. She had been supervising the floral decorations of a church in the suburbs where a wedding was going to take place the following morning.

She had hardly got through the door of the flat when the telephone had rung and it was the police ringing to inform her of his death. She'd felt her hand stiffening as she held the telephone to her ear and later she suspected that the arthritis which was soon to plague her had become acute at that very moment.

In her dizzy state of shock she had glanced down at her answering machine and registered that someone had left a message. She had assumed that it had to be Trevor. She often found a message from him when she got home from work in the evenings. As a gynecologist, his hours were very irregular. He had many emergency calls from his patients. A protracted labor with complications could keep him at the hospital all night.

If he failed to reach her at work he always left a message on the answering machine so that she would have some approximate idea of when she could expect him home. He didn't like her to stay up if he knew that he was going to get back very late. But she had never managed to sleep very well until she heard his key rattling in the door. She had only managed to catnap. She always had a meal prepared for him whatever time he got back and she usually insisted on getting up to heat and serve it to him.

Trevor had always been on call for his patients and throughout her long marriage she had always been on call for him.

After his death she found herself without a role, without usefulness, and every lonely and idle hour that she spent in the flat seemed like a torturer who had arrived with the sole intent of testing her endurance.

Trevor had been on his way to visit a pregnant cancer patient when he had suffered his fatal heart attack. His car had crashed into a lamppost. No one except himself had been injured. As a doctor, he must have been aware for a long time that he had a serious heart condition. He had never told her but she didn't resent this. He'd always tried to shield her from anything that would cause her anxiety and upset.

"But he was a doctor," she'd kept saying to the police when they telephoned to inform her of his death. Her brain had allowed her to repeat this sentence but she had known that it was already withdrawing all responsibility for the things which it would permit her to do and say in the future. She was aware that it was ashamed of the way that she kept producing an irrelevant fact in a fatuous attempt to prove that the police had to be mistaken.

It was during that traumatic telephone conversation that she had first started to register the advice of her brain and then to promptly disregard it if her feelings found it unacceptable. "You think that doctors are there to save lives," her brain had told her. "But whatever made you think that doctors never die?"

She had not picked up Trevor's message until the funeral was over and she had answered all her letters of condolence. She just let it stay there, a frightening little red light on the answering machine. She couldn't bear to play it.

Then one day she wondered what she was waiting for. She had to pick up Trevor's message eventually. She couldn't wipe it off the machine without hearing what he had to say to her. Yet she knew that the sound of his voice was going to be profoundly painful. She realized that the passing of time was not going to make this message from the dead less disturbing.

She poured herself a large drink before she pressed the button on the machine. She felt like a patient getting ready for a dangerous operation. And then she docked the machine with a shaking arthritic finger and Trevor was once again speaking in the flat. And for a moment he seemed to be alive again.

"It's me, darling . . . I won't be late tonight. I've just got to make one house call on a patient but that shouldn't take too long. I ought to be back by nine thirty. Don't do any cooking because I thought it might be fun to go out. Miss you . . . See you soon . . ."

She had sat there very still once his voice had stopped. Trevor's message seemed so ordinary. It lacked any drama. It didn't seem as if it came from the dead. But it had upset her in a different way than she had expected. It had made her feel very angry with him. She found his message intolerable. He was not going to be back around nine thirty and she found him cruel and dishonest to pretend that he was. In an impulsive mood of anger she had slammed down her hand on the machine and she had wiped out the tape. As she heard the click as the device whirled she felt like a murderess. Now she knew that Trevor was really dead. She was never going to hear his voice again. In a frenzy she had started to get dressed. She didn't know where she would go but she knew she had to get out. She was certainly not going to stay alone in her dreaded flat with only that vicious little black machine for company. She suddenly loathed that inhuman dark plastic box which could bring back the dead and then eradicate them. For by now she already regretted having wiped out Trevor's message. If she had kept it she could have played it back and back and felt that something of Trevor was still alive.

As she was leaving her flat she'd found herself thinking that she ought to leave a message on the machine to say that she was going out and telling anyone that called when she would return. She knew that it was most unlikely that she would get any calls that evening, but her mind was operating in a reflex fashion that sprung from long and ingrained habit. In the days when she used to leave the flat to go off to work she always first checked to see that her keys were in her handbag and after that she left a message on the machine. "Neither Doctor Clifton nor I are here to take your call at the moment. But if you leave your name and number . . ."

In the old days she had seen these two procedures as an intrinsic part of going out. But now it was different and yet after some hesitation she went through her old acquired routine and dictated a message. All the time that she was speaking she had felt the disapproval of her own brain. It kept asking her unwelcome questions. Why are you doing this? Who do you think is going to care that you are going out? When will you stop hoping that Trevor may try to reach you?

She had left the flat, and hobbled out into the street on painful arthritic feet. As she had no particular destination she had decided to go and have a drink in the Red Oak. She usually avoided going to pubs because she found them noisy and smoky. But her feet were hurting quite badly and she didn't want to walk very far. The Red Oak had seemed as good a place to go as any.

She had ordered a beer and Mick Kilkenny had given her his first look of dislike and distrust. She could tell he thought that there was something very wrong with her and she wondered what it was. She'd sat down at a small table and listened to a jukebox which was playing screeching songs about love. That evening the pub had been filled with men who worked on a local building site. They were all bantering and drinking beer and they were wearing overalls which were stained and filthy from their work. Their faces were still coated white with construction dust and she thought that for some of the young blond men it was like a flattering makeup. It made their eyes look startlingly blue.

She envied all these men for the way that they seemed so happy to be in the Red Oak. They had finished their work and now they could joke and relax in a gang. There was a young girl with a wild spiky hairstyle using the public telephone and she envied the way that she was giggling and flirting into the phone. The girl was obviously making plans to meet someone whom she wanted to meet.

The jukebox went on throbbing its monotonous ugly songs and

the singers all screamed that they wanted someone, that they needed someone, or that they were crying for someone. And she wondered if the Red Oak was really preferable to her flat. It didn't have the chilling silence. But it had a rowdy camaraderie which she found detestable for she knew that it was something she would never learn to share.

Having nothing to do except sip her beer she noticed small things and she saw that the public telephone had become free. And she had realized, only very slowly, how much she needed to make a call. She got up and walked to the telephone and it had taken her an unnecessarily long time to fumble in her purse and find the appropriate coin. But suddenly she could hear herself ringing into her own flat. And for a moment she felt an irrational excitement waiting to hear Trevor answer. She hoped that he was going to tell her that he was back in the flat, and he was waiting for her there. That would be very different from the message that said that he was soon going to be back.

But then she heard a mechanical click and there was only her own voice on the answering machine. For a moment she'd felt such an electric shock of disappointment that she'd wanted to ring off. But her own voice on the machine had sounded so pitiful and despairing, that when it had asked her to leave a message after the beep she found herself leaving one just as if she were leaving one for a friend. "Sorry to have missed you. I'm dying to hear all your news. Hope everything is going well. I'll keep on calling until I reach you."

And later after the pub dosed and she got back to the flat she was glad to see that she had a message on her machine, glad that it showed a glowing red number one rather than the blood-red zero that she dreaded now that she had wiped Trevor's voice out of existence forever.

When she played back her own message in the silence she had

felt comforted by its friendliness. Her brain tried to remind her that she was only listening to herself, but it couldn't make her feel that this was really true. The voice she heard seemed transformed by its distance and the mechanical medium through which it reached her. It sounded a little like herself but not the self she was familiar with because it came from outside. It was the voice of a woman who seemed to lead a very different life from her own. She could hear loud music playing in the background behind the voice and there were sounds of uproarious laughter. The woman seemed to be speaking from a party where everyone was a little drunk and enjoying themselves immensely.

It had been so long since she heard the sound of a human voice in the flat that she was very glad to hear one. Ever since Trevor's death, and her feet made it increasingly painful for her to walk, she had found less and less reason to go out. She had very few household needs as she existed on tea and milk and cereal. Occasionally she ate some toast and a couple of tomatoes. A grocery store on her street delivered any food that she required with all her other scanty household necessities such as cleaning fluids and light bulbs and aspirin for her arthritis. She had no reason to go shopping. The boy who delivered her groceries was from Pakistan and he spoke very bad English. After he had carried her provisions up to her flat he always pointed at the receipt which he wanted her to sign and then said, "Thank you very much," after she had signed it. She always said, "Thank you very much," trying to make her gratitude sound meaningful and personal, and that was the extent of their conversation. The boy then vanished. Until he arrived with another load of groceries no other voice was to be heard in her flat.

Once she discovered that a friendly message on her machine

could help relieve feelings of despair and isolation she started to leave more and more messages for herself.

Her eccentric little trips to the Red Oak served several purposes. They gave her a reason to leave her flat, and they gave her a medium through which she could express various unhappy feelings and fears which she could tell no one else. The messages she left for herself soon stopped being formal ones. They became long and rambling and confessional. The self that spoke from the Red Oak could say childish incoherent things to the self that would listen to its ramblings in the flat without any fear of ridicule. It knew that it had a sympathetic ear.

"It's me . . . I've got to talk to you. Everything is getting worse by the minute. I miss Dad and Mum. I know that's silly when they have been dead for so long, but I have been missing them all day. I miss them almost more than I miss Trevor. Well, that's not really true . . . But I can't live with all this missing . . . I will telephone you later because I don't know what to do."

"It's me . . . I have been alone all day in the flat and now I'm alone in this awful smelly pub and I feel I've gone from the frying pan into the fire. And I've been having horrible upsetting thoughts. I've been thinking that I haven't got any real friends. When Trevor was alive he was so popular and easy to get along with, that we seemed to have lots of friends. But now that Trevor's gone I see that they were never really my friends at all. They wrote to me after his funeral but now they have dropped me completely. That must be my fault. It means they never liked me. I can't have made enough effort with them. That was arrogant and now I'm punished for my arrogance. When Trevor was still around I didn't feel I needed friends. Trevor was my real friend . . . Well, you know that

Trevor was everything to me. I'll try and talk to you later. I haven't got anyone else to speak to."

"It's me . . . I'm afraid I'm not very well. My hands and feet are getting more and more painful. If they get much worse I'll have to go into a wheelchair and then I'll have to be put in a home. I really couldn't bear that . . . You know how active I used to be. I was always rushing around. And I couldn't live in an old persons' home. I think it would be even more lonely than the flat. I know that I won't like the other people in the home. Just because they are all cripples in wheelchairs, that won't make me like them. I will really have to do something . . . You know what I mean . . . And I'll have to do it soon before I lose all use of my hands. By the way, I haven't dared to tell my doctor how bad my hands and feet are. He would say that I'm already not fit to live alone. Aspirin doesn't work anymore and I'm in agony most of the time. But I'm never going to let him put me in a home. There is a line of people behind me. They seem to be getting quite angry because they want to use the telephone and I've been talking too long. I will try and ring you again once the phone gets free."

When she played back her messages once she returned to the flat, she found she listened to them with detachment but great interest and sympathy as if they were bringing her news of her own state of mind which she was unable to comprehend until she heard it spoken aloud.

It was on a Friday evening that she fell down in the Red Oak. She was holding the telephone when she fell. She was dead by the time she reached the hospital. Later the autopsy established that she had taken a massive dose of sleeping pills and combined them with whisky.

Mick Kilkenny was very angry when the police came to question him about her death and informed him of its cause. He told them that he had never liked the look of her. He'd always known there was something peculiar about her. He'd felt she was a woman who was going to cause trouble. She had a funny unfocused look in her eyes as if she wasn't quite right in the head.

"If she wanted to take her own life why couldn't she fucking do it at home?" he asked. "I think she had a bloody cheek coming here to die in my pub. The people who come in here—they come to drink and enjoy themselves. They don't want dead women dropping all over the floor."

He told the police she hadn't been much of a drinker—that she was usually a one-beer type. He hadn't noticed that she was throwing back whiskies the night she had died. The pub had been very full and his assistant barman must have been the one who served her.

"Do you know something?" he asked the police. "She was never off the telephone. And I always thought there was something suspicious about all those calls that she used to make. I mean, why did she have to make so much use of a public telephone? She was a well-dressed woman. Why didn't she have a telephone of her own?"

Mick Kilkenny said that he'd always suspected that she was mixed up in some kind of criminal activities. She had always looked very sly and guilty when she was making her calls. She kept looking around her to see if anyone was listening.

The police never discovered any evidence that she had been involved in any illicit activities. They had difficulty finding out where she lived but after making extensive inquiries in the neighborhood, two young officers broke down the lock of the door of her flat. They noticed that there was a message on her answering machine and they played it back hoping that the caller would have left a number which might help them track down her next of kin.

They heard a woman's voice which sounded weak and choked. Behind it was the sound of loud music and laughter. "It's me . . . I've done it . . . Maybe I have been very stupid but I don't think so . . . I put all my eggs in one basket and now I can't go on because all my wretched shells are broken . . . I'm just waiting for something to happen and I desperately need to go on talking until it does . . . I really have to talk to someone. It's frightening, the waiting, and I couldn't bear to wait for it all alone in the flat. Once something happens you will never get this message but if you were to get it, I know that you of all people would understand that what I've done is the best for both of us. At least I thought it was the best when I did it. And now it's rather late to start having doubts . . . Oh my God! Something is finally happening! I'm all dizzy now with heart pounding and I feel bubbles in my ears. There's something sharp like an awful knife cutting slices into my chest and my stomach. All you can do is pray for me—please pray it won't take too long . . . I only want it all to be over. You know that's the only thing I've wanted for ages."

The voice on the tape paused. There was a silence and then it said one more sentence. "If there had been children it might have been different."

After that the police officers could only hear music and a jumble of voices.

"I wonder who she was leaving the message for?" the younger policeman said.

His companion shrugged. "It sounds as if she were leaving it for a man. Maybe some fellow lives with her here in this flat. I found some men's clothes in the cupboards and there's a razor and a toothbrush laid out in the bathroom."

"She says that she doesn't expect him to get her message," the younger police officer said.

"Maybe the bloke has just walked out on her. Maybe that's what made her do it."

"If there is a bloke and he does come back to this flat he's not going to like it when he gets this message," the younger officer said. "It's quite a bloody nasty message. It really shakes you up to listen to it."

"I think we should wipe it off," the older policeman said. "Foul play has been ruled out. I don't see the point of keeping it. All it can do is make some poor bastard feel horrible." He pressed a button and the message was eradicated. The two policemen went down to the flat below to ask the occupants if they knew anything about their neighbor.

The flat below was inhabited by a young married couple with a half-clad sticky-looking baby which cried continually throughout the inquiries. The couple looked frightened of the police as if they thought they were being investigated for murder. The wife said that they didn't know anything about the woman who had lived above them, they had only just moved into the building. They had passed her on the stairs quite often. She seemed to go out a lot. They hadn't any idea where she went. They didn't think she had a man living with her but they could be wrong. They had never spoken a word to her. "She seemed a very quiet sort of person," the young wife said. "She struck us as the self-sufficient, decent type. She seemed to be a woman who kept herself, very much to herself."

FACT

Never Breathe a Word

We only ever knew him as McAfee. The harness room had no electricity, and only a crack of a window, and when it rained he often spent the whole day in its darkness. He would crouch there on a low stool, polishing up a stirrup, rubbing yellow soap into a saddle, and he always seemed more like an animal than a man, and he made the harness room seem like his lair. My sister and I liked him rather as we liked hunting, and halters, and snaffles—only because he was to do with the horse.

Every morning he would arrive on his bicycle to take us out riding, and we would go out jogging along behind his huge bay mare, two plump little girls in cork-lined velvet riding-caps, on two plump little barrel-bellied ponies. McAfee spoke very little on these rides, and when he did it was difficult to understand him. He had a rasping Ulster accent and he had lost every tooth in his mouth, and although he owned a brilliant pair of over-white and over-even dentures, he refused to wear them except for "special occasions"—when he took us to horse shows or out hunting.

He chain-smoked as he rode, holding his cigarette between his dark, lumpy gums, and when he went over a jump he never lost it. "You're alright!" he always shouted automatically whenever we fell trying to follow him over stone walls and ditches. Perdita once broke her collarbone and never dared mention it to anyone when she got home. "You just never breathe a word," McAfee told her. "I don't like people who are over-fussy."

He had once been a professional jockey and one of his own shoulders had been broken so often in racing falls that it had become deformed. His right arm was far shorter than his left, and it dangled down uselessly from a hump. Yet when he was riding, he made the peculiar way that he sat so crookedly in a short-stirruped jockey's crouch, holding both his reins in his left hand, seem correct, like some superior technique. It was only when he dismounted that it was always shocking to see that he was not much taller than we were. The moment that he got down from his mare he looked as though half of his body had suddenly been amputated, and one saw that he had the over-large head and torso and the diminished child's legs of a dwarf. He waddled from top-heaviness when he walked. The way he always kept his bandy little spindle-legs in their riding breeches and boots so very far apart made them look as though they were perpetually gripping the flanks of some invisible horse.

At that time Perdita and I loved horses with a single-minded and sentimental passion. We would talk for hours about their different characters, be worried that we had hurt their feelings. We loved the smell of their sweat, the spikiness of their eyelashes, the velvet feel of their noses. McAfee always made it very plain that he found our attitude extremely silly and irritating. To him a horse was as functional as a tractor, and he wanted it correctly used in order to get the most out of it. "Jag her mouth!" he would shout at us if our ponies reared. We were always too scared and he was always cantankerous and scornful. "You should have jagged her mouth, and brought her down over herself, and then jumped yourself clear. You should have learnt her . . ."

"Couldn't you break a horse's spine doing that?"

"If you're so feared to take a risk, Caroline—you'll have all your money, but you'll never do a thing with a horse."

McAfee had ten children, and his house was five miles from ours, and sometimes when we passed it on our rides, they would all come out into the chicken-yard to wave. Occasionally Mrs. McAfee came out, a thin, exhausted-looking woman with mole-grey marks under her eyes. She was usually holding some half-naked and bawling baby. McAfee's children would gape at us with respect and curiosity because of our ponies, and Perdita and I would gape back with respect and curiosity because the McAfees were so many—and because they looked so muddy and so poor.

The way that McAfee sometimes spoke of his old racing days made us realize that he felt that there was a sadness and a disgrace to the fact that he had ended up his life as a children's groom. He only ever seemed happy when he was telling us some of his old racing tricks—showing us how he used to press up his foot under another passing jockey's stirrup so that he would lose his balance and fall. "And nothing could ever be proved!" McAfee's grin would show all his empty gums.

One day we were going down a lane and McAfee suddenly reined back his mare in order to ride alongside my pony.

"How would you like to be the best wee rider in the whole of Ireland?"

I thought he was taunting me. I found it very dispiriting, but I knew only too well that McAfee thought that I would always be a hopeless rider—that I had bad hands—no natural seat—very little control—and I rarely used my knees. Often when we went out hunting McAfee had told me that he was ashamed that all the other grooms should see him with me. "With all of them looking at you, Caroline—I would have really hoped that you wouldn't have made such an exhibition . . . It breaks my heart that you couldn't have done better than that."

But now McAfee was whispering as though it was a secret. "I would like to see you the best rider in the whole of Ireland."

I shrugged as though the idea bored me. I wished he would change the subject. It seemed pointless and painful to talk pipe dreams.

"How do you think that all the really big people in the horse world do it?" I couldn't understand why McAfee kept on whispering.

"How do you think that they manage to be always up there with the hounds at all the hunts—to go round all the shows carrying off all the cups? Why do you think that the walls of their stables are red with rosettes? Take a big woman like Lady Mary Berry—how do you think she does it?"

I thought of Lady Mary Berry. I had seen her at all the horse shows, fat-faced and formidable, in her bowler and her impeccably shined boots, coolly taking perfect double-banks—the crowds all clapping . . .

"How does she do it?"

McAfee leaned down over the side of his mare's neck and whispered to me through his gums: "Pills."

"Pills?"

"All the big winners—they all do it the same way. There's only one reason why they manage to carry off all the competitions at the Balmoral—and the Dublin—and all the important shows over in England. They all take the pills."

"How can pills make you a good rider?" I felt slow-witted, but I just couldn't understand.

McAfee seemed to be rather flustered as though he hadn't expected the question. He thought for a while, and then he suddenly said, "Hands!" And I wondered why he seemed so pleased with his answer.

"Without good hands—you'll never be a rider!" McAfee's mare reared and whinnied as he cracked down his bone-handled crop on her haunches to emphasize his point. "It's been that way since the beginning of time. You've got to have the feel of a horse's mouth. No one's ever made a name for themselves in the horse world unless they've taken the pills for their hands."

"Do you take the pills?" If McAfee took the pills, I was wondering why he wasn't more internationally famous as a horseman.

"I always used to take them in my time. I couldn't have raced without them. I haven't taken them lately . . ." His voice sounded suddenly depressed. "Now I don't have much occasion."

When we got back to the stables McAfee helped me dismount from my pony. "You think it over, Caroline. It's a terrible thing to see you riding the way you do. You never breathe a word to a soul and I'll be seeing what I can do for you."

All that night I felt vaguely disturbed and tempted by the idea of McAfee's pills.

A week later we were going through a bridle path in some woods and McAfee suddenly said, "I've got them!"

"Got what?"

"I've got hold of some of those pills."

"Where did you get them?"

"I went round to the stables at Mount Stewart and bought a bottle from Lady Mary Berry's groom." He gave one of his crafty gummy grins.

"Can I see them?"

"I wouldn't dare to give them to you in the daylight. At first Lady Mary's groom didn't even want to sell them to me. They are very hard to get. They are as precious as gold. He made me pay the earth for them. He says that everyone in Ulster is after them. Once people know that you've got them—they always manage to steal them away from you. I promised him that I wouldn't hand them over to you in a place where anyone might see."

"But who on earth could see here?" We were so far from anyone, with about two miles of dense trees and scrubby undergrowth separating us from the nearest house.

McAfee rolled his eyes and his manure-clogged fingernail pointed in a paranoid way at the trunks of various beeches and oaks. "How do you ever know who might be watching you?"

He looked suspiciously at the plump little form of my sister with her pigtails and her black velvet cap as she jogged along on her lazy pony, slushing through the winter leaves. "How do you ever know who you can trust?"

We came to a clearing encircled by dripping laurel bushes. "You better meet me right here in this spot tonight, Caroline. You know how to get here. But you've got to wait until it's dark. Daylight's not safe. And don't let people see you setting off. They might guess where you're going and follow you. Once it gets dark I'll be waiting for you here—and then I'll give you the pills."

Once it got dark I had not the very faintest desire to have the pills. I didn't even believe that they would work on me, though I imagined that McAfee of all people should know what he was talking about if it was to do with riding. In any case even if the pills were as good as he claimed I only wanted to stay in the nursery and toast bread on a fork on its wood fire—to read comics in the warmth and the light in my dressing gown—listen to a serial on the radio. The idea of bicycling off alone in the dark to that dank, dismal clearing in the woods terrified me. I decided that I wouldn't go.

But then I kept on thinking of poor McAfee waiting, and waiting. I was frightened that he might wait for me there all night in the wet and the cold and by morning he would be so furious that I would never dare to go riding with him again. I only wished to God that I had never let him think that I wanted to take his pills. I couldn't even remember that I had ever actually told him that I was interested in taking them—but somehow he had just assumed it because he knew that I secretly wanted to be the best rider in Ireland. I couldn't stop thinking how hurt and disappointed he would be if I just let him wait out there in the woods and never turned up. He cared so much about making me a really good rider. He had taken so much trouble to get hold of the pills for me, and they had cost him so much money.

I went out to the shed and got out my bicycle. There was no moon that night and it was drizzling. I felt a terror and a desperation as I peddled off, wobbling along in the muddy ruts of wheel tracks. At that time I had a horror of the dark and could only ever sleep if my bedroom was a blaze of nightlights. I didn't dare look to the right or the left. On either side of me the darkness seemed like an evil, inky soup, floating with every ghastly kind of supernatural spook and spectre. I tried to concentrate on the weak, swaying light thrown by my bicycle lamp. When I got up to the woods, I found it even worse. My tires made the crackle of footsteps as they ground the rotting beech-nuts. Every branch seemed like the grabbing arm of some insane old woman strangler.

Finally I got to the clearing and I saw that there was no one there, and suddenly I detested McAfee. He had made all this peculiar fuss about meeting me up here in the woods—and then he hadn't even bothered to come. He had made me make this loathsome, lonely ride in the dark for nothing.

And then suddenly something rustled in one of the laurel bushes, and somehow I knew it was McAfee. But why was he crouching in the middle of a soaking bush? He had known I was coming—so why was he hiding?

Out he came from the laurel leaves with an odd little hop like a rabbit. Seeing the shadow form of his stunted legs and his hump, I thought of Rumplestiltskin. When he turned on a torch I saw that he was not wearing the old tweed cap that he always wore in the daytime. He was wearing his best shiny bowler, the one he only ever wore when he went out hunting. And I didn't know why it chilled me so much to see that he was suddenly wearing his false teeth.

He just stood there staring at me. I felt that he was frightened of something and couldn't understand what he could be so frightened of. I had never seen him show any fear before, he had always seemed like a man without a nerve in his body when he was riding. And all the light from his torch seemed to be reflected in his teeth . . . They looked dazzling as though they were painted with phosphorus—they were the only glowing thing in this hideous winter wood.

"Have you brought the pills?" I didn't want the pills. I just wanted him to say something—anything—to stop silently standing there on his bandy little booted legs, looking so foolish in his bowler.

He seemed to be unable to speak. He made some odd, fish-like sucking movements with his mouth, and it was as though he was so unused to wearing his teeth that he was gagged by them.

I started to get back on to my bicycle. I wanted to get away from him. It seemed to me that McAfee had gone mad staring at me in this peculiar, wary way as though he didn't dare take his eyes off me for fear I might suddenly attack him.

"You mustn't go!" His voice came through his dentures with a whistle. He fumbled in the pocket of his jacket and then handed me a grubby little glass bottle full of pills.

"Swallow them down, Caroline—they'll do you a lot of good. You'll be sorry forever if you don't take them."

I looked suspiciously at the bottle. I didn't like the look of these scruffy little white pills.

"What are they?"

I saw that there had once been some writing on the label of the bottle, but it was now unreadable because someone had scratched it off with the point of a knife.

"No one quite knows what they are. But it doesn't matter—they do wonders for everyone. You be a good wee girl. You just swallow them down."

"Why has the writing on the label been scratched off?"

McAfee suddenly flinched back, rolling his eyes as though I had struck him in the face. "I didn't do it."

"Who did it?"

"The bottle was like that when they gave it to me."

"I don't want to take them unless I know what they are."

"That's right. I think that you are quite right." He almost seemed relieved, as though someone else had tried to make me take the pills and he had always been very much against it.

"You should never ever take pills, Caroline—not if you don't know what they are."

I wondered if he would mind if I went home now, for he no longer seemed to feel that I should take them, and I no longer felt I had to worry about hurting his feelings. But he still seemed to be waiting for something, and I still hated the way that he looked so cowed as he kept on staring at me, for it frightened me to feel that I could frighten an adult.

"Maybe I should take back the pills where I got them, and I'll get them to put on a nice, clean, new label." Now he only seemed to be chattering for the sake of it—saying anything that he hoped would please me.

"When I take back the bottle, Caroline—I'll complain to them about the label."

"That's the best thing to do."

All at once his manner changed, and he no longer seemed frightened, and the whites of his eyes seemed to turn mauve he looked so angry. "If I take all the trouble to get you new pills—you've got to take them—and there's going to be no nonsense. People don't like you mucking around with them."

Something in his new expression made me panic, for I saw that he had the same ruthlessly concentrated look on his face that I had seen so often whenever he put a horse at a jump, cracking it across its rump with his bone-handled crop, jabbing blood from its flanks with his spurs. A suspicion which had been burrowing like a blind, black mole through my brain ever since he had first showed me his pills, suddenly surfaced and turned from suspicion to certainty. McAfee was a poisoner . . . It all made sense to me now. If his pills were really pills to make you ride well—why had he insisted that I take them at night in this far-off wood? Why couldn't he have given them to me in the stables? I understood now why he had seemed so terrified that someone might see him giving them to me—why he had acted in such an odd, shifty way, rolling his eyes, and whispering, whenever he even mentioned them. I was now quite certain that the word "Poison" had once been written on the label, and he had scratched it off because he knew that I wouldn't take his pills if I read it.

I had only a confused idea why McAfee so wanted to poison me. But I was quite accustomed to finding many adult impulses inexplicable. And at that time the murderous plots of books and films were so interwoven in my mind with the threatening and violent images of various inner fears and fantasies, that I felt no particular need to find a good reason for McAfee's murderous intentions towards me. I found it explanation enough to assume that he must have always secretly hated me—all those years that he had been forced to take me riding through those endless Ulster lanes and gorse fields. I wondered why I had never realized how serious he had always been when he had kept on telling me that he detested bad riders. For, finally, tonight he had tried to make me take poison, and I was quite certain that if I had been stupid enough to take his pills—by now I would have already been dead, and buried by him under some oak in this wood.

I made a dash, and I jumped on to my bicycle. McAfee appeared to be taken by surprise and quite unable to understand why I was suddenly crying.

"Caroline . . . Caroline . . . What have I done?" he kept repeating.

He made a gesture as though he was going to grab my back wheel, but then seemed to decide against it. I started peddling, and peddling, and I had the nightmarish feeling that my wheels were just churning, churning in the same mud rut. But when I turned to see if he was chasing me, I saw that he was standing quite still, looking very tiny, and dispirited, in the clearing. At my last sight of him, he was slowly loping on his stunted legs, like some lame animal down the bridle path.

"Caroline . . . Caroline . . . ," he shouted after me. "Please . . . please . . . Never breathe a word!"

The only person that I ever told about my meeting with McAfee was Perdita. She agreed immediately that he was obviously a poisoner. We both felt that it would be very unsafe to tell this to anyone—for you could never tell what a man like that might do to you. We decided that we would never go riding with him again, and we would never go near the stables.

For many months McAfee went on sitting all day alone in the harness room. He went on pointlessly polishing the bits of our unused bridles, soft-soaping our girths, rubbing yellow wax into our saddles. Our ponies grew fatter and fatter, from lack of exercise. McAfee went on curry-combing them, making them bran-mashes, plaiting up their manes with little red ribbons. Since Perdita and I seemed to have lost all interest in riding, it was decided after about a year that McAfee was a waste of money, and when he was fired our ponies were put out to grass.

When I see Perdita now we still often talk about McAfee, and our conversation always only turns into questions and finally becomes frustrating, and tiresome, like trying to do a crossword if you know that you will never see the answers. Always she asks me the same things. How did McAfee think that he could get away with it . . . ? What were his pills, and how and where did he get hold of them . . . ? How much did Mrs. McAfee ever know . . . ? How many other children were given similar pills by McAfee . . . ? If I had taken them what would . . . ? "Please . . . Please . . . ," I always answer. "I don't even want to talk about it. Please . . . Please . . . Could you just stop breathing a word!"

Betty

In Ulster during the war I was looked after by a nursemaid called Betty. She was plump, and flirtatious, and rather backward, and she told me that her mother was always praying for her because she didn't think that Betty had a hope of marrying, because no woman ever got married if they "held themselves so cheap." But Betty was always hopeful, and she squeezed some elderberries and she rubbed the juice on her freckles, and she went and had her ginger hair permed to a gollywog frizz in Bangor, and every day, clip clop, in her utility high-heeled shoes, she would take me walking past the hideous grey maze of Nissen huts of the American camp which squatted at the end of our drive.

"Say hello to the soldiers, Caroline. Ask them for some chewing gum. It doesn't look funny for a child to do that." And in the end Betty always got talking to the GIs and I remember one of them saying to her that he found there was so little to do with his leave in Ulster, that he would rather be sent to the front and lose a leg, than be stuck away in "this god-forsaken fucking back of nowhere."

"Don't you ever use such wicked language in front of a child! Can't you see she's listening? She listens to everything. She's very sly. She's never as deaf as she pretends to be. And I don't appreciate it very much myself. I don't think that's a nice thing to say to a girl about her country." But I knew that Betty was only pretending to be angry, and that secretly she felt very much the same as him. She had told me that she prayed to God every night that the war would make it possible for her to end up as a GI bride.

"War's a terrible thing—but sometimes you have to be rather glad of it. At least it can give you a few opportunities. Kids and housework. Kids and more housework. That's all that any Ulsterman can offer you."

Betty was always talking about the GI rations. "You just take what one of those military fellows gets for lunch—and you give it to an Ulster family. They'd all be able to live on it until the baby was old enough to grow grey whiskers and pass on to a better world."

Betty also never stopped talking to me about American salads. "You just couldn't believe the salads that they have over there in the States. I've seen them in the magazines. They are all beautiful colors like the rainbow—they just make your mouth water. You could live all your life in Northern Ireland but you'd never get anything as colorful as that."

"When I grow up I'm going to marry an American," I told Betty.

"It's not up to you," she said, "it's up to God. And you better just pray that he'll be a bit good to you. You are not a bad wee girl when you are not in one of your sulks. And I must say that I wouldn't want to see you waste yourself on anything you'll ever find around here."

The war never made what Betty wanted happen. Only one GI ever proposed to her. He gave her a tin of spam and two packets of American cigarettes as a present and he took her into Bangor and they played the pin-machines in the Fun Arcade. It was sunny that day and they walked along the seafront and then they sat on a bench. He told Betty that she looked as if she had trapped the sunshine in her hair, and she said that the way he talked made all the local fellows seem like speechless bullocks, and that you would never find an Ulsterman who used a shaving lotion with that special delicious American smell. When they said goodbye he told her that he wanted to arrange for her to join him in Denver, Colorado after the war was over.

The next time he took her out it was all a failure. When they went into Bangor, he tried to buy himself a soft drink, but there was nowhere open because it was a Sunday. He then suddenly got in a terrible temper, and somehow he blamed Betty, and he started using insulting language about her country and said that he hadn't been able to find a place where you could go dancing for three months.

After that they went down on to the beach, for there was nothing else to do. All the Bangor streets were so dismal and grey and deserted that she felt that they might have both found it gayer to have taken a walk round a cemetery. The sky was very overcast that day and he never once said that she had trapped any sunshine in her hair. A lot of seagulls kept circling around overhead and he only spoke to complain that their screeching was getting on his nerves.

Once they got down on the beach, the sand was all pebbles and very uncomfortable, the seaweed had a strong sour smell of town sewage, and Betty said that the wind was coming in so hard from the channel that you thought that the Isle of Man would suddenly land in your lap. He got in an even fouler temper because they couldn't find any shelter and she felt that he was even blaming her for the wind.

While they were trailing around miserably by the sea edge, to make things worse he suddenly got a pebble in his shoe, and she said that no child could have made more fuss about it, that he behaved as if he felt that his whole foot would have to be amputated. Betty tried to make a few jokes to cheer him up but he never laughed once, and when they finally sat down he used his army greatcoat selfishly to cushion himself, never caring that the discomfort was far worse for Betty, for she was only wearing a thin little silky frock.

He kept staring sulkily out to sea and then he started muttering that he had "just about had this fucking war." And secretly Betty couldn't feel that he was really in the war, not when he was sitting there on the beach, on a Sunday, in Bangor.

He never stopped chain-smoking American cigarettes and he never offered her a single one. And then for no particular reason his mood changed and he started getting very fresh. But she said that it wasn't at all in a nice way—it had "no respect." Finally, somehow, there was some kind of a scuffle and something fell out of his pocket and she saw that it was a snapshot of his wife and kids. "Imagine going all the way to Denver, Colorado, and finding that!"

Betty didn't mind too much because she knew that a whole new regiment of GIs was due to arrive from the States the following Saturday. "There's plenty more where he comes from," she said.

Piggy

The damp, stone, Victorian passages smelt of football boots and antiseptic. The dining room always had a lingering smell of bad stew. "Madame Souri a un jardin," droned on the French master, while outside the school the seagulls screeched as they circled through the mist that hung over Belfast Lough. Lessons were dreary, but they always seemed better than the breaks, when McDougal would get the boys to gang up on the new boys.

McDougal dominated Stoneyport Preparatory School partly by his character but mostly by his size. At eleven he was almost as tall as a full-grown man. He also had a thyroid condition which gave him additional power, as it made him freakishly overweight. He was a gingery-haired near-albino, with a snout-like nose which had given him the nickname of Piggy. He had powdery white eyelashes, and his tiny eyes were pale, and weak, and twitching. He had eyes which always seemed to be excited by some new and unpleasant plan.

McDougal could always get all the other boys to carry out his wishes, and the way they obeyed him was abject, and lacked any affection. No one in the school liked Piggy McDougal, but they all respected and feared him, because he had hatreds which were formed, while theirs were still diffused and shifting. McDougal's hatreds were so unswerving, and dependable, and had such a simplicity, that like an efficient transport service introduced by force on a country verging on chaos, they were welcomed by all the boys who felt themselves imperilled by their own state of confused preadolescent anarchy.

McDougal hated two things, new boys and Catholics. If he could have found a new boy who was also a Catholic . . . But that was impossible at Stoneyport Preparatory School for no Catholic had ever been admitted there. The headmaster had no wish for the school to be burnt down. In Ulster things got around very fast—people felt very strongly—you couldn't be too careful.

McDougal was therefore cheated of a chance to confront his supreme archenemy. But every term brought him a new little troupe of new boys. He had also discovered that there was a derelict cottage just outside the school grounds in which there lived a whole family of Catholics.

Even now I still wonder how McDougal found out that the cottage was full of Catholics. Did his obsession make him more than usually sensitive to all the suspicions and rumors which were always trickling along the Ulster grapevine? Or did McDougal simply make a mistake? Was that family never really Catholic at all? Did

McDougal suspect this when he organized us on half-holidays, and fired us all on so that the whole school would go out to stone them? Did he think that this family looked so dilapidated and depressed—that this family looked so hunted when the stones came showering down on them from behind the hedges—that they looked so exactly like Catholics they deserved whatever they had coming to them?

"Blackwood," McDougal said to me one day, "I don't like girls being allowed in this school. It makes the whole place look feeble." I was only allowed to go to Stoneyport Preparatory School for Boys as a favor because it was wartime, and with gasoline rationing it was the only private school which was anywhere near our house. I was a day-girl while all the boys were boarders. I arrived every morning in a pony and trap.

Ever since my first day at Stoneyport I had been plagued by the terrible fear that McDougal would eventually turn on me. I knew only too well how much he disliked anything which he felt was odd. He detested Derry Green because he had a birthmark. He disliked all the boys who wore spectacles, and gold bands on their teeth. He always tormented the ones who wore plain grey socks instead of the proper Stoneyport uniform kind, which were grey with a thin rim of blue round their tops. McDougal's obsessive hatred of new boys was mainly caused by the fact that their fluster, their general look of lostness, and their homesick "blubbing," made him find them all extremely odd.

McDougal would stand on the cricket field, and his thyroid-condition thighs always looked inappropriate, they were so much too massive for his shorts. McDougal nearly always seemed to be accompanied by Johnson, and McAlister, Barcley Jr., and McBane. He dwarfed them by his height and his bulk, but they were active and they were wiry. The four of them often appeared to be like the gundogs which snarl around a gamekeeper's boot. McDougal could invariably assemble them the very second that he needed them. It was as if he owned some kind of dog whistle to which they were sensitive though its timbre was too high for the average human ear.

"Get that sneak!" McDougal would shout. They were so well trained, they would get the new boy down on his back in a second. They dragged him to a grassy patch behind a great dump of gorse bushes where no master would be able to hear any screams. Johnson and McAlister would twist his wrists and pinion them behind his head. Barcley Jr. and McBane would sit on his feet. "Now he's going to start blubbing. The bloody, feeble, little blubber!" Then a crowd would form as it does with a street accident.

"Someone hold his nose!" McDougal would shout. Some boy always volunteered. McDougal would step forward like a general taking a salute. He would open the flies of his shorts with the ritualistic slowness of a churchman divesting himself of his robes. His penis always looked very pink and swollen as he held it like a pistol and took his careful aim. "Hold his nose tight. Make him open his mouth. Bloody little fool! The bloody little blubber!"

The new boy would be writhing frantically on the grass, scarlet, and scratched, and choking. The golden jet of McDougal's urine would sometimes miss his mouth, splash on to his hair, or his spectacles, trickle down over his tear-stained cheeks. "Keep him still damn you!"

Sometimes McDougal's aim was very good. "Keep on holding his nose. I want him to swallow it!" When he had finished McDougal always smiled with a fatuous conceit. "I think he swallowed quite a bit. Who else wants a turn?" The members of the crowd would file up, boy after boy, and they would all open up their flies. There would be the same struggling, and choking, and screams, the same near misses, the same good aims. Finally, McDougal would tire of watching performances which he clearly felt were very feeble copies of his own. "Let him go. He must have drunk enough pee to make him stink like a lavatory." "Is it poisonous to drink so much?" I once heard a nervous weasel-like boy ask McDougal. He shrugged irritably as he answered. "Who the Hell cares?"

When McDougal told me that he didn't like girls being allowed in the school, I knew that exactly what I had always feared—that my oddness would make me one of his special targets—was just about to happen. Previously I had always managed to keep in with McDougal. At that time I felt that the most vital thing in my whole life was keeping in with McDougal. Far more slyly craven than any of the boys, I had always treated him with a consistent and repulsive sycophancy. I would laugh at all his jokes, which were invariably cruel, but rarely funny. I gave him my sweet-ration coupons, and stole cigarettes from home and brought them to him. "Blackwood's not bad for a girl," he would sometimes say, looking at me with tiny, white-lashed eyes.

My abject slavishness was not the only reason why McDougal had never set his hound-dogs on to me. McDougal had once told me that he had never seen a girl without any clothes on. He then kept dropping more and more threatening hints. And finally he asked me if I would agree to undress in front of him. Far too intimidated to risk getting myself into his special bad favor, I agreed. McDougal then decided the undressing should be done in some rhododendron bushes which were safely far from the school. As we set off together, I found, inevitably, that he had ordered Johnson, McAlister, Barcley Jr., and McBane, to come tagging along too.

All four of them were desperately shy and awkward. As they walked beside me up to the bushes, they were as downcast as mutes escorting a coffin. They stood in a semicircle in a hollow walled by rhododendrons. There was a respectful hush as I undressed and the whole occasion seemed more and more like a burial.

No one seemed to get the slightest excitement or pleasure from my striptease. I felt mortified and humiliated, and the boys appeared to feel mortified and humiliated too. The very leaves of the surrounding rhododendrons seemed to be drooping, as if they too were distressed by a feeling of anticlimax, squalor, and shame.

In Ulster at that time it was quite common to view nakedness as something to be feared, like murder, and Johnson and McAlister, Barcley Jr. and McBane, looked really frightened. They might as well have been standing outside the Headmaster's study waiting to be caned. And to my surprise, for I had such an exaggerated inner picture of his omnipotence, it was McDougal who was obviously the most petrified of all. Standing there in the hollow, he lost all his confidence, he lost all his authority. We all had an in-built Presbyterian prudery, but McDougal seemed to feel more pressured by it than any of us. The nervous blink of his white eyelashes became far worse than usual. His mouth was slack and trembly. He kept fidgeting with his hands.

"I've never seen a girl before." He whispered this with a kind of horror, and he sounded almost tearful. "I didn't know it would be like this."

By increasing everyone else's embarrassment, McDougal appeared to be increasing his own. He seemed to know he was doing this and yet was unable to stop himself. "I'm an only child," he suddenly mumbled, as if he felt this explained something very important. He was prolonging an occasion which was becoming more and more painful by the minute, for he seemed unable to decide how long he ought to go on looking. The presence of the other boys pinioned him. In front of them he was ashamed not to get his money's worth. He didn't dare do what he so clearly wanted to, put a stop to the whole thing and get away.

"Have you had the curse yet?" McDougal's porcine face, usually so florid, was ashen, and his forehead was streaked with nervous mottles. Instinctively I sensed that I must not tell him that I had never had it. I could tell by the superstitious terror that I saw in his tiny eyes, that the curse was anathema to him, that anyone who had had it could use it as a weapon to terrorize him. When I refused to answer, my silence seemed to chill him, for I noticed that his teeth were chattering like those of a winter swimmer. All at once, heady with the realization that for once the roles were reversed, that McDougal's fear of me was now far greater than my longstanding fear of him, I put on all my clothes without caring whether he wanted me to keep them off, and I started walking back to the school, knowing he wouldn't dare to make a move to force me back into the bushes. I sensed with an immense and spiteful pleasure that he had temporarily lost all control of the other boys—that they felt he had failed them in a situation when they had looked to him for leadership—that they had noticed that his behavior throughout the undressing had been exactly what he had taught them to despise. McDougal had been "feeble." His whole comportment had been odd. And most disillusioning of all, throughout the whole dismal occasion McDougal had looked as if he was just about to "blub."

All the rest of that term McDougal appeared to retain his peculiar fear of me. He stopped asking me to steal him sweets and cigarettes. He never made the boys gang up on me. He never spoke a single word to me. He hardly seemed to see me. During lessons he took great care never to choose a desk which was anywhere near the one where I sat. And all the time I knew that McDougal was very aware of me, that he was deliberately avoiding me as if he felt that I had the evil eye.

I was only too glad to have this inglorious power over him, only too relieved to have temporary immunity from his attacks, but I never lost the nagging feeling that there was little hope that this happy state of things would last.

When one day McDougal suddenly told me that he didn't like girls being allowed in the school, his face had such a look of loathing that I realized that all those quiet months his resentment and his belligerence had only been storing up for this moment.

"If you don't want to have your life made Hell for you in this school, Blackwood—you are going to have to make yourself useful." McDougal then told me that he wanted to arrange a raid after school—that he wanted to have another bash at the Catholic fuckers who lived in the cottage near the village of Ballycraig. He said he wanted me to collect his ammunition and be his ammunition-bearer. "If you don't want to get a stone in your mouth, Blackwood—you better see that I don't have a moment when I don't have something in my hand."

After school McDougal started his raid. Johnson and McAlister, Barcley Jr. and McBane, walked in front with him like generals. I followed immediately behind them dragging a load of stones in a pillow slip, and the rest of the school came after me in a straggling file.

As we marched we all had a feeling of excitement and release. It was a Wednesday, and a half-holiday. Usually everyone dreaded the dullness of half-holidays when they would lounge around, homesick, write letters to their parents asking them for stamps, or just lie on their stomachs in the school fields and restlessly suck the juice out of the stalks of pieces of grass.

But on the way up to the cottage, the jail-sentenced mood that half-holidays usually brought to Stoneyport pupils seemed to have suddenly blown away like thistle seed. "They can't expel all of us," someone said as we passed out of bounds. "They must have noticed we've all gone. I bet they know what we are doing, and I bet they don't really mind." Our usual fear and hatred of all the masters had suddenly vanished. We felt that we had their unspoken approval—that their power was behind us. We had lost all memory of the torture of all our daily gangings-up, splittings-up, suckings-up.

For one moment on our march we all felt that we were rather a marvelous little unit. Everyone was elated, even the new boys, feeling that we would all stand by each other, feeling that the cottage was malignly advancing on us, rather than the reverse, feeling that in view of the threatening provocation from the cottage we were all extremely brave.

The cottage lay in an isolated position about half a mile from the village of Ballycraig. It was a dirt-streaked, whitewashed little building, and it was roofed with a moth-eaten thatch over which tarpaulins had been roped in its weakest patches to keep out the rain.

McDougal ordered all the boys to surround it, to station themselves behind the safe cover of trees and hedges, to see that none of the occupants managed to escape. Then, bulky and thyroid, he walked out into the open, and he started the attack. He bombarded the cottage with stones which I handed him from my pillow slip. His aim was very bad and it took a long time before any of them hit the tiny dark windows. But eventually this happened and an old woman came out into the garden in which there grew a few rows of bluish cabbages, amongst which pecked a small coterie of underfed hens.

At first she just stood there looking puzzled. She had untidy white hair, and was wearing a drooping long black skirt and an apron. Her arms were red and chapped, she had a collapsed mouth, and her skin was a crisscross of deep wrinkles.

"Fire!" McDougal shouted, and all the boys hurled their stones at her. The chickens all squawked, a sheepdog started to bark, and she gave a scream and ran back into the cottage. There was a sound of commotion inside it, and shadowy faces came peering through the tiny windows.

Her husband finally came out. He was wearing an old tweed cap and overalls, and he was as white-haired and tissued with wrinkles as she was. "Fire!" shouted McDougal, and the old man retreated back into the cottage.

McDougal was just about to order his troops to advance on the cottage when suddenly out came five of the old woman's grandsons. They were all teenagers and the oldest must have been about nineteen. They wore open shirts, and heavy farming boots, and one of them was carrying a pitchfork. As though they had one voice between them, they all started cursing, and they picked up any stick or stone that was to be found on the ground and started hurling them at their hidden enemies who were crouching behind the hedges.

Seeing the size of the grandsons, hearing the ferocious cursing of the grandsons, seeing that the grandsons were starting to throw pieces of iron farming-equipment, and big rocks and heavy logs, the Stoneyporters instantly lost their solidarity. Like a flock of migrating birds they all left their strategic positions and ran back up a hill to where they could watch the rest of the battle from the safety of some dense trees. Far more frightened of the grandsons than I was of McDougal, I dumped down the pillow slip of stones beside him, and followed the deserters.

Abandoned by everyone, even by Johnson, McAlister, Barcley Jr., and McBane, McDougal stood alone in the open in front of the cottage. He seemed to lack the initiative even to take cover. He just went on ineptly standing there. His behavior was much the same as it had been during the undressing. It was as if his own cowardice were giving him courage by making him too frightened to move.

McDougal kept on picking stones out of the pillow slip, and he went on throwing them in a weak and mechanical way at the cottage. His gestures no longer appeared to be aggressive, they were clearly so mindless and unplanned.

Usually McDougal looked massive and formidable, but now it was as if his very bulk, like his bravado, had suddenly diminished. A pink-faced, flabby David, for once he had a certain pathos standing there alone confronting the five grandson Goliaths.

If the grandsons had realized that all their hidden Stoneyport enemies had long ago done their rat-scuttle from behind the hedges, they might have killed McDougal. Not grasping this, they were still cautious, and instead of advancing on him they stayed in crafty positions keeping behind the cover of some chicken sheds.

They had found an ammunition treasure trove of horseshoes, and as they kept hurling them at McDougal it was only the iron-weight of these objects which prevented a lot of them from striking him. But eventually one of the youths did a super-throw, and McDougal gave a howl, and suddenly he was hopping on one leg and clutching at his other knee. The pain in his leg apparently returned some sense of self-preservation to him, and he retreated, limping behind a hedge, and the grandsons booed and cheered.

It was all over. And then suddenly a six-year-old girl, wearing a grimy little crumpled frock and carrying a school satchel, came down the lane which led to the cottage. Unaware that there had just been a battle at her home, she was whistling and skipping as she came. Her jauntiness, in his state of humiliation and defeat, obviously enraged McDougal. He picked up one last stone and threw it from behind his hedge with what remained of his strength, and it hit her smash in the face.

She fell down in the lane and her face was spurting blood and there was a thundering rumble of anger from the grandsons and they all came rushing out from behind the chicken sheds waving pitchforks, spades, and scythes. McDougal and all the rest of us who had been watching from the hill were seized by a collective panic and we all started running back towards the school. It was as if we were trying to run away, not only from the pitchforks of the grandsons, but also from the guilt of the hideous thing we now felt we all had done.

"Do you think they will ring up the police?" I heard McBane ask McDougal once we were back at the school and sitting around on desks in an empty classroom.

"Those kind of people don't have telephones," McDougal said. On the surface he was calm but the nervous blink of his eyelashes showed his agitation. "Do you think she was blinded?" McBane asked him. I expected McDougal to give some kind of shrugging, contemptuous answer. But McDougal didn't say anything.

His silence apparently infuriated McBane and it was the only time I ever saw him turn on McDougal. "You bloody fool!" he said. "We are all in for trouble. And it was you who got us into it."

"What are you making the big fuss about?" McDougal's tone was plaintive. "Nothing's going to happen. I bet you that nothing is going to happen." McDougal was right, for nothing ever did happen, but McBane refused to believe him.

"There's going to be bloody ructions," McBane kept on grumbling.

"Those kind of people don't go to the police," McDougal said. "Those kind of people don't know how to. I just bet you that nothing ever happens."

"You bloody fool!" McBane said. He jabbed the point of a compass into a desk as if he was trying to run it through the bulky body of McDougal.

Memories of Ulster

And for all that I found there I might as well be
Where the Mountains of Mourne sweep down to the sea.

Many people from Ulster have always felt that the man who wrote that song was a liar. "If the fellow once managed to get himself out of Northern Ireland," a woman from Belfast once said to me, "it's a bit hard to believe he's all that sincere when he pretends he was always fretting to get back. But the tune's all right, and the sentiment is all right. And in Ulster, of course," she added, "the tune and the sentiment have always been the thing."

That was long ago. But I still feel surprised whenever I hear Ulster mentioned in the news. It always used to seem like the archetypal place where nothing would, or could, ever happen. For as long as I can remember, boredom has seemed to be hanging over Northern Ireland like the grey mists that linger over her loughs. Boredom has seemed to be sweating out of the blackened Victorian buildings of Belfast, running down every tramline of her dismal streets. Now, when Northern Ireland is mentioned, the word "internment" rattles through every sentence like the shots of a repeating rifle. And yet for years and years so many Ulster people, both Catholic and Protestant, have felt that they were "interned" in Ulster—interned by the gloom of her industrialized provinciality, by her backwaterishness, her bigotry, and her tedium.

In 1940, war was seen as a solution. "All the American troops will liven things up a bit round here." But the last war never broke the back of Ulster's boredom. Everyone kept predicting—almost with pleasure—that the Belfast docks would be a prime German target, that Hitler would almost certainly launch his invasion via Northern Ireland. All the signposts were swivelled round in the Ulster lanes to trick his troops, and force tanks which had hoped to roll towards Ballynahinch into ending up in Ballygalley. However effective all these crafty precautions would have been in the event of a full-scale Axis landing, they turned out to be needless. There were very few raids, and one of these by error bombed what Protestant Northerners called "collaborationist" Dublin. This was said to be an act of God.

The American troops livened things up very little in Ulster. They hadn't much to do except hand out chewing gum to the kids. They slouched miserably through their "duration"—and then they were gone. The few bonneted black faces which appeared in Ulster prams were the only memorable trace that they left of their unenjoyable stay.

And day after day—post-war, just as they had pre-war—in the grey squares of the Ulster villages groups of men in tweed caps, most of them toothless and out of work, went on standing around in huddles. They would rub their hands and mutter, and sometimes have a smoke, like people on a platform waiting endlessly for some cancelled train. And day after day—post-war, just as they had pre-war—in the wealthy suburbs of Belfast the wives of industrialists went on reading the Bible, drinking their sherry, and eating scones. In those days all their houses were meant to contain that most curious of rooms known as "the parlor." The parlor was always musty and unused. There every stick of silver, every horse-show trophy and spoon, every candelabra and christening-cup that the family had ever acquired was always laid out day and night, as though in defiant display of the rewards of Protestant virtue. Far too valuable to be used, and very heavily insured, there used to be a desolation to all this silver, which was polished daily by the maid and seemed to be perpetually waiting on its mahogany table as if in preparation for some longed-for, but never-arriving occasion. And very much the same effect used to be created, in the rooms which were in use for entertaining, by all the plaster Peter Scott geese, which were nailed so that they appeared to be flying past the photograph of the Royal Family in a freedom arc up the side of the wall. Sometimes one had the feeling that these status-symbol geese themselves secretly knew that their flight was an illusion: that they were just as static as their owners, that they would never fly out of these stifling, expensive interiors, where the light could hardly penetrate all the Gothic-cathedral stained glass of the windows.

Then there were the Ulster Sundays. Post-war, there were still the Ulster Sundays: the war changed them not at all. On Sundays all the towns were still closed down, so that they seemed like the ghost towns of Colorado, and the Day of Rest went on being so well observed that the serving of a cup of tea was still damned as a violation. When anyone died, people still went on saying that they feared it was a "judgment": that the dead one must have gone out driving, or drunk a Guinness, or read some novel on a Sunday.

And the war never changed the sermons which were preached on those Ulster Sundays, and the families still trailed off to listen to them. They would go all dressed up with hats and gloves and coins for the collection, taking their bored and dressed-up children. One particular sermon I heard in Ulster has always stayed with me. It was delivered on a Christmas Day, and the minister preached it from a pulpit decorated with holly. He said that on this special day he would like to start by quoting "the most beautiful words in the English language." His choice was curious: "The womb of a virgin hath he not abhorred." In his own terms, it was a daring choice. And some puritanical hesitation seemed to panic him, forcing him into a slip. He paused dramatically before delivering his words, and then boomed them out in ringing church-chant tones: "The worm of a virgin hath he not abhorred." I looked round his congregation. Surely they would have some reaction to this most unusual Christmas Day text. But all the scrubbed faces seemed to be in their usual trance. Glazed eyes just went on staring despondently at dusty hassocks, at the bleakness of the altar, stripped of all ornamentation to make a contrast with the idolatrous churches of the Papacy. Not one single person reacted to the minister's beautiful words—for not one person had heard them. His congregation had been interned by his sermons for far too long for his words to have any more power to penetrate the defensive depths of their devout deafness.

"Do you come from Northern Ireland?" I remember Foxy Falk barking the question at me years ago at an Oxford dinner. I was used to contemptuous responses from English people whenever I answered this question. "The South of Ireland is very nice," was all they would usually say. Or else, making one feel like some kind of mongrel impostor: "Oh, then you are not even proper Irish at all." But I felt that the question, when asked by Foxy Falk, was going to lead to something a little different. A collector of Ming vases, Cézannes, and Persian carpets, he was a man who said that he believed in "the rule of the elite and the artist." He was tyrannical, reading Keats's letters aloud to people who had little desire to hear them, forbidding anyone in his household to use the telephone because he felt that it had ruined the art of conversation—and thereby creating daily difficulties as to grocery orders, etc. He would intimidate by his spluttering rages, which made one fear that the boil of his anger would crack his arteries. He was famous for the fact that he had once been Pavlova's lover.

"Do you come from Ulster?" I saw that the charge behind his question had already turned his whole face to a tomato-colored balloon. Then his fist came smashing down on to the table so that the knives went shivering against the glasses. "All I can say is that the place where you come from ought to be blown up! It ought to be blown sky-high, and wiped from the face of this earth!" If he felt like that . . . I found myself staring blankly at his poor old turkey wattles, which were wobbling with agitation as they dripped down over his high Edwardian collar.

Then he calmed a little and explained that Pavlova at the height of her fame had danced in Belfast, and that the theatre had been totally empty except for two people. He claimed that she had never felt so insulted and distressed in her whole life—that Belfast was the only place in the world which had ever given her such a criminal reception.

Maybe because of the bombastic way the whole subject had been approached, and because I felt I was being personally blamed for the disastrous unsuccess of her visit, all I could feel was a sudden impatience with both Pavlova and her lover. Why were they so astounded by what to me seemed to be so very unastounding? What could have made them think that her dance could ever set the grimy dockyards of Belfast dancing? When had that most austere of cities ever pretended for one moment that its prime interest was the dance?

I thought of the Ulster Protestants. Surely they had enough problems without having to be "wiped from the face of this earth" for being a poor audience. A fear of Catholics bred into them from childhood until it became instinctive like a terror of spiders. Their lifelong drill of eccentric Ulster commandments. "Never drink from the same glass that a Catholic has drunk from. Any such glass should be broken immediately." And then their feeling of always being beleaguered, with the enemy pressing its full weight against the feeble ribbon of the border. Their suspicion that the enemy's prohibition on birth control was a crafty long-term plan to out-breed them. Finally, their way of seeing the enemy—it's a very common way of seeing enemies—as dirty, lazy and cruel, plotting and promiscuous, and with one extra unforgivable vice—prone to dancing on a Sunday.

What happened? Everyone asks this as they look at the rubbled streets of Belfast and Londonderry on the television. The question never seems to be well answered, and only leads to more questions. If there had been no Catholics, would the Ulster Protestants have found it necessary to invent them? Certainly for years and years they provided the only spark of thrill and threat which could blast the monotony of the Ulster everyday. Month after month I remember listening to the same repeating rumors that the Catholics were marching up from Dublin—"mustering" on the border—and infiltrating industry. Did all those interminable Ulster sermons seem less tedious when it was envisaged that iron-handed Papists might very soon try to put a stop to them? Did the polluted belch of Northern industry seem less hideous if it was felt that greedy Papal fingers were tentacling out to grasp the factories?

Can there be a boredom so powerful that it finally acts like an explosive? Marx said that the cottage must never be too near the castle. If England was the castle, was the provincial cottage of Ulster just a little bit too near?

"Wouldn't you think that people might be less bigoted in this day and age?" English people keep on asking me that. "You certainly would think so," I answer. And immediately I find myself doing a double take. "Why would you think that they might be?" I wonder. "What reasons are there for thinking so?"

Every day the Ulster victims are flashed on the British television screens. They stutter out their tragedies in accents so unintelligible to the English that they might as well be speaking Swahili, and then they are cut off in mid-sentence for lack of television time.

When the Reverend Ian Paisley makes an occasional BBC appearance he seems awkward, oafish and provincial. He seems to lose all his rhetorical teeth when he is speaking to an English audience. He needs the roll and rattle of the Orange kettledrums to accompany his impassioned and oracular calls to duty. He needs to have his fanatical congregation, and King Billy of the Boyne, and The Lord, behind him. To see him on the BBC, who could believe that he could be idolized in

Ulster? Who would ever think that he was an innovator—that back home in his Northern Irish church he has invented something quite as new as the "paper collection"? For Ian Paisley has said that the Lord wants no more coins . . . During his services, when the collection plate is passed round the congregation, the pounds pile up on it like great mounds of crumpled Kleenexes. But then when the plate is handed in to him, Dr. Paisley refuses to bless it. He just looks at it in sad silence and he shakes his enormous head. "The Lord," he says, "is not going to be very pleased with this." And the plate is sent back to the congregation for another round.

And while the Reverend's collection plate is circulating, the IRA seem less and less heroic as they blow the legs and arms off typists, and plant their gelignite wires across the routes of the school buses. And yet Ulster's rate of mental disease keeps on dropping as the troubles persist. Doctors claim they have never known it so low. All the while the Ulster Defense Association, dressed up like Ku Klux Klansmen, like Knights Templar from Outer Space, are drilling, and recruiting from the Orange Lodges of Scotland. They too set up their "no go" areas and their kangaroo courts. Last week I spoke to a Protestant who lives in County Down. "You don't like to go out at night," she said. "You feel that you might run into some roaming regiment of UDA with all their guns, and their goggles, and fishnet stockings over their mouths. And you feel that they might not like the look of you. They might set up a kangaroo court, and you'd be tried in their pouch." War games . . . And on both sides how many really want them to end one can sometimes despondently wonder. Has the whole province become intoxicated with its new-found power to seize the international headlines from its ancient overshadowing and world-important sister, England? Does it now feel some perverse and destructive terror of sinking back into a humdrum and peaceful obscurity in which the individual Ulsterman will no longer feel the superiority and glory of springing from a world-famed trouble-spot?

"Why not move all the Protestants out?" English liberals keep suggesting. "Why not move all the Catholics out?" Another common, and less liberal, suggestion. Both suggestions make it all sound so easy, like moving pinned flags on a staff map. Families, farms, occupations, the tie to the place of birth—all these things are made to seem like trifling, selfish quirks, which should be sacrificed for the greater good of the community. But who is going to decide which community most deserves this greater good? Then you are back again with an "Ulster problem."

"Why can't they all just get on with one another?" The English can seem very smug at the moment . . . If the IRA started hurling high explosives into the shopping centers of Maidstone or Colchester, how long would it take before Catholic families living in the areas began to feel afraid of reprisals?

Burns Unit

"At least you are lucky to live so near the best burns hospital in the world . . . The new techniques are staggering. East Grinstead is still farther ahead than the United States and Russia. McIndoe got his start in the war. His hospital was near the aerodromes. He got all the burnt war pilots . . ."

As a visitor it was the afternoons which always seemed the worst inside the sealed-off, germ-free, center section of the Queen Victoria Burns Unit. There was an eerie timelessness to their hush and their languor. The burnt would be there so very still inside their isolated and tropically heated glass cubicles like dogs napping in some invisible sun. In the afternoons all the corridors were deserted and desolate, their silence only sometimes broken by the sound of some nurse's sterile blue plastic galoshes, which would make a squish as if she was plowing through winter leaves. One kept expecting these hospital passages to smell of antiseptic, but instead they smelt unpleasantly of nothing. The air had a curious heavy lifelessness. Sometimes one felt its very sterility could choke one, and realized that one missed the presence of germs.

They were far too still, those afternoons with all the patients lying there under their afternoon sedation, with their burns drying out in the artificial heat like washing in a boiler room. One started to feel submerged as if one were on a submarine missing anything that could call to mind life on land. One kept hoping that it would soon be a mealtime so that at least one would hear the commonplace clank of the huge steel sterilizing container from which the patients were distributed their surgical-gauze-like hospital food. One missed the purposeful bustle of all the white-masked specialists and surgeons who only visited and did the grafts and operations in the mornings. One missed anything which could break the germ-free Unit's oppressive afternoon atmosphere of motionless and patient waiting—anything which could stop one feeling that the main activity in this Unit was waiting—waiting to be better—waiting to be dead.

At the main desk in the afternoons, the on-duty head nurse would be sitting slumped over her evening newspaper. Behind her there stood the great huddle of silent television sets which relayed the pictures of all the patients who were on the danger list. The cameras above their beds photographed them from odd and aerial angles, and their images as they appeared on the screens looked weird and fragmented. Where was the familiar crackling chatter of news commentators? Where were all the usual panel games and the breezy flashing faces of pop singers? One felt disoriented and disturbed seeing only so many never-changing, soundless images of burn-blotched stomachs and strapped-apart thighs in close-up. There was something grisly about the way the cameras kept such stubborn focus on so many disembodied genitals all pierced with the essential badge of the burnt, the catheter.

"You will get used to it all," they said. But I never did. When my daughter was on television I never got used to seeing her there. One day she appeared simultaneously on three different sets. None of the three hers quite seemed to be her. All the same I often found myself leaving the real her who was lying unconscious in her cubicle, in order to go out into the corridor to look at them. Hour after hour there was often nothing to do inside the germ-free Unit and I kept staring at these screens as if, by association, I expected them to act as some kind of distraction. And sometimes I found that if I stared at them long enough I could start to have the insane illusion that if someone was to unplug all these television sets, her illness would disappear with her image.

"You will get used to it all . . ." But I never got used to the way that all the patients in this hospital were laid out on display like exhibits, that they could all be viewed from an outer "polluted" corridor which was arranged like the reptile house at the zoo. As you passed glass window after glass window, each room seemed like a glass cage showing a different tropically heated and brilliantly lit specimen. Were they all beyond caring that they were so exposed to the morbid curiosity of the most casual of passersby? Stripped by necessity of even a sheet to cover their nakedness, was there some good scientific reason why they should be so totally stripped of privacy? There they all lay like Francis Bacon figures framed in their dehumanized postures with black charred legs strapped apart and their genitals pierced by their catheters. There were women whose breasts were blown up like balloons in two giant vermilion blisters. There were infants in cots, tiny pieces of purple zebra flesh, their only clothing the bandages that covered a recent graft wound. There were faceless men lying there with pipes which were feeding something vital into something scarlet which must have once been a nose. Sometimes one of the glass display rooms would suddenly be empty and one would see only the narrow surgical bed with its brilliant orange rubber anti-sticking burn pad. And as in a reptile cage which at first sight seems to contain nothing, one would start to feel that some living creature must still really be lurking on that flaming pad, that it was invisible only because it was so well camouflaged by its natural surroundings.

On certain days as one walked down the outer corridor one would see a brightly lit tableau of doctors and nurses keeping a tense round-the-clock vigil about a bed. Hour after hour they would hardly move. Their arms were lifted as they supported their huge bottles of blood, saline, and plasma, and they looked as if they were holding them up on high, like chalices. All day and all night they fingered the tubes of the drips as if they were rosaries. Was it possible that they could save that pulpy object? Did one hope that that pulpy black object in its coma could be saved? Did they all know it was beyond salvation and yet still feel bound to give it the respect of some kind of public and scientific last rites? Was it out of respect for it, or for their own techniques, that they refused to pull down the blinds?

No visitors were ever allowed inside the sealed-off center germ-free section of the Burns Unit. This rule was observed with severity, but it was relaxed for the mothers of child-patients. Inside the

Unit the mothers were the most feared and despised minority. They were regarded rather in the way that some British people regard Uganda Asians, as a race of interloping undesirables who had somehow managed to insinuate their way into the country by craftily acquiring a bogus passport. Although the mothers wore the identical regulation white gowns and caps and masks and galoshes as the hospital workers, never for a moment were they made to feel that anyone was fooled by their external trappings. As a Belfast Protestant claims he can spot a Belfast Catholic walking in any crowded thoroughfare, so a mother could instantly be spotted among all the other white-clad figures who thronged the hospital corridors. Once detected, the mothers always aroused a frisson of fear, and hostility, for they were all known to be Typhoid Marys. They were carriers of foreign bodies that were deeply threatening and unwelcome to the Unit. Into this impersonal and functional sealed-off world of science they brought their total uselessness; they brought personal panic, anguish, and hysteria, and most dreaded of all they brought squeamishness and germs. With their undesirable qualities oozing from every pore, the mothers would go flitting around the unpolluted passages with their deranged eyes peering over their masks as they tried to get some kind of a prognosis from hospital personnel passing by, who very much resented being waylaid and pestered because they were all passing with some vital purpose.

"Will they be able to save his sight, Sister?"

"Will she have to have very many more grafts?"

"That, I'm afraid, you will have to ask the doctor . . ."

"I'm very sorry but I really can't give you an answer. I suggest you ask the doctor."

And everyone knew that it was impossible to ask the doctor

for, whoever he was, he was unavailable. If ever you found a doctor he always turned out to be an under-doctor and he would suggest you refer your questions to some higher and absent doctor. One day as I was walking down the corridors of the Unit I was certain that I had found the doctor. He was very old with bushy eyebrows which looked even whiter than his surgeon's cap. He walked with a stoop, but there was immense pride and authority in his slow plod. His intelligent exhausted eyes looked worn out and black-ringed from sleepless vigils. He was frowning and preoccupied and his handsome craggy face appeared to have been prematurely aged by the grinding responsibility of his daily life-and-death decisions. McIndoe must have once walked the wards of the Burns Unit with the same confident dignity. Now that McIndoe was dead, this distinguished old surgeon must surely be the man of supreme authority and genius in this hospital. I stopped him and asked how my daughter was progressing. Over his surgical mask his exhausted old eyes stared at me astounded. I realized that he didn't speak English. Later I saw him walking with the same proud and dignified plod carrying a mop and a pail. Finally it became clear that he was the man who was employed to clean the nurses' lavatories.

"You will get used to it all . . ."

But I never got used to the way that once the mothers had been swabbed and dressed up like medical extras in a television hospital comedy they lost all individual identity. Once they were admitted into the sterile section it was as if they shared a single code number and were all referred to very simply as "the mother." Inside the suffocating highly heated cubicle the child whose body was the color of blackened bacon would be screaming for water with the terrible delirious thirst of the newly burnt.

"Tell the mother to tell the little girl that she can't possibly have any water. She's having all that she's allowed through the drip in her hand."

"Get me some water! Get me some water!" And then, as if she had remembered being told that you only get what you want if you ask politely, the child would start whispering.

"Please may I have just one little sip of water. Please. Please. Just one little tiny sip . . ."

"Tell the mother to tell the little girl that she can have one teaspoon of water in two hours time. And tell the mother to tell the little girl that it's no use her making such a racket. She's got to wait two hours." And then a little later . . .

"Tell the mother that all she's doing is upsetting the child. Could you tell the mother it would be really much better if she were to leave . . ."

And then, out of the stifling cubicle, and into the corridor, where all the other screams which were coming from all the other glass cubicles were relayed on an amplifying system. Why did they have to turn the amplifiers up so loud? Was there some good medical reason which would justify it? All the screams seemed to be only too audible without this kind of magnification. You could feel you might go berserk in these corridors where such a hideous chorus of pain-screams were piped like music. And yet it was obvious that apart from the visitor-mothers no one in this closed medical community was in the least disturbed by it. How long would one have to stay inside the Burns Unit to become immune to this chilling broadcast of howls? Would one ever learn to ignore it as one learns barely to hear canned music?

"McIndoe had the magic touch," someone told me.

"McIndoe could go in to see a woman who would never again be able to speak except through a plastic tube in her cheek and when he left her she felt like a queen . . ."

McIndoe's legend was so alive inside the Burns Unit that it was with a feeling of grief and almost grievance that you realized that, when you sat with his plaster bust in the waiting room, that was the closest you could ever get to meeting him. Every day there were so many hours of waiting while, over-lifesize, and up on his pedestal, McIndoe never stopped smiling. He looked so strong and capable in his surgeon's cap. There was something comforting and all-knowing in his smile. If there were no other visitors in the waiting room one sometimes felt tempted to start asking him questions. He at least was pinioned there in his plaster. In the Unit that he had created he seemed the only medical figure who was unable to shake you off and hurry away. McIndoe must surely know the prognosis for every single patient that was lying there so raw and naked in those germ-free box-rooms. They must all be doing very well. He seemed so obviously delighted with their progress. The prognosis for all of them had to be excellent, even for that new man who had just been brought in from a chemical explosion. For why else would McIndoe be smiling?

And then staring up at him one could sometimes imagine that something less consoling was creeping into his smile, some touch of Olympian and scientific ruthlessness, some touch of the greed of the genius.

"McIndoe got all the burnt war pilots . . ." For a moment one could start to see him like a farmer praying for rain. Then a deluge of charred guinea pigs showering down on the Tudor motels of East Grinstead from the sky . . . Convoys of ambulances sirening through the blackout. The germ-free units mushrooming with saline plants, plasma-drips, body suspension belts, "blue rooms" with the sterilizing "blue light." And McIndoe smiling, seeing supply meet demand.

On the day that my daughter was to be discharged from the Burns Unit I sat for the last time in the visitors' waiting room with McIndoe. As I looked at the face of this perennially smiling plastic surgeon I could imagine that yet another element was creeping into his plaster expression, a certain dread, a nervousness, an edgy fear that I might try to express my gratitude. Long-dead, and perched high, and preserved as the hospital's idol, McIndoe still seemed alive enough to fear that, in all the weeks I had spent in his Unit, I had grasped almost nothing of his values. All that he seemed to be praying was that I would not disappoint him by showing that I had still failed to understand that he would be bound to feel the same contempt for gratitude that he felt for all the other gratuitous emotions which were in no way allied to effective action. To him any graft was more valuable than any amount of gratitude. He saw sympathy as a very wretched substitute for skill. He saw precision and plasma as incomparably superior to compassion.

As I left the waiting room I looked back at McIndoe, and his statue face now suddenly seemed to be amused at the idea that visitors to his Unit could ever expect to find their visits enjoyable. Clearly he was only too aware they would be bound to feel that there was something inhuman in the machine-like, skilled routines, in the apparent immunity to suffering, of his team of white-coated workers in this sterile medical compound. But this could concern him very little because he knew so well how the burnt became different. They learnt that even the coldest and most impersonal curative action was less inhuman than sentimental and empathizing inaction.

McIndoe had seen the way they would refuse to be discharged from the Burns Unit when there was no longer any medical reason for them to stay on there, for what they feared was not the callous impersonality of this aquarium-like scientific depot. Their terror was the outside world where they knew they would be treated with something which would be inconceivable within the Unit, the twin cruelties of pity and horror.

Women's Theatre

As though a Women's Institute fête had been expecting a visit from the Queen and had only been informed after it opened that she was confined to her bed with a heavy cold, a feeling of letdown hung over the Women's Lib rally. Where would the spark come from now? All the goods laid out on the stalls looked suddenly secondhand and shoddy; the band was still playing but now it seemed amateurish and out of tune.

"Where's Kate Millett?"

"Which one's Millett?"

"That can't be her. That's a man, you fool!"

It was smoky, claustrophobic, and hot, sitting on the hard benches in the Open Space Theatre.

"What does Millett look like anyway?"

"A sort of dumpy Mary McCarthy. But they say she's not coming . . . They say that on Friday she saw the play."

We too had just seen the play. "*Holocaust Theatre* is the real end of a nightmare," Jane Arden, its author, had claimed in a program note. But did the audience agree with her, who had sat in a circle for what seemed like so many hours? Surely Jane Arden, with the rhapsodic rhetoric to which we had all now become accustomed, would be the first to say that endness was only really fractured beginningness and all part of the nuclear feminine-masculine principles which it would take a thousand years to sort out.

The meeting was starting in earnest. In the same center of the same stage where there had just been eight extremist women writhing naked while they moaned and masturbated, and complained that they were oxen and had "holes inside," there were now four more women—but they were moderates. Edna O'Brien, Anne Sharpley of the *Daily Mail*, Jill Tweedie of the *Guardian*, and their chairwoman, Mrs. George Orwell. Unlike the previous female cast they were all sitting on chairs instead of potties. If they had holes inside, one sensed immediately that they would be the very last to mention them. They had serious-looking pencils and papers and a table. They spoke the language of the *Observer* and the *New Statesman* rather than the Underground. Clearly, if they were to have their way, there would be no more talk of "milky breasts and the music that sings from these contained vessels." They wanted orderly and constructive discussion of the need for nursery schools and equal opportunity and pay for women. They wanted the meeting conducted as it might have been if Kate Millett had been present—if only she had not seen the play!

But their Mrs. George Orwell was a Kerensky and was to prove totally unable to control the harsh forces of chaos and revolution which were to unseat her from below. She opened the discussion by suggesting that the audience was gathered there to discuss the various socioeconomic problems confronting women in 1971. Instantly a hippy, a man hippy, with a Vanessa Redgrave white-bandaged head and a white bunny rabbit embroidered on his arm, appeared very much like a conjuror's bunny and seated himself at the conference table. It was assumed by some of the audience that he was a proper member of the Women's Liberation panel, that he had been invited to join them in the interests of democratic liberality. But this was not the case. He was doing some kind of an aggressive sit-in, something perilously near to a grope-in. He was only there because he wanted to be allowed to do his thing. Mrs. Orwell, gallant and foolhardy, tried to ignore him just as she seemed to feel she could afford to ignore the restless, menacing mood which was already stirring in the little basement theatre stuffed thick with women. She went on talking pleasantly. The women watched her, and waited. Their faces were implacable and their eyes had the ruthless glitter of the tricoteuses.

There they all sat, the solid phalanxes of card-carrying members of Women's Liberation and the more virile rows of ladies from Gay Liberation. There were many old-timers—pioneers of the Movement with cropped hoary heads and far more muscle than any stevedore. They had the very same physiques as the burly women who were once employed as bouncers in the lesbian tourist nightclubs of Berlin and Paris in the Twenties. What interest could they possibly have in Mrs. Orwell's cheery talk of nursery schools? They had fought alone on their barricades throughout the old dark days of the sexual Depression. Surely, to them, Holocaust Theatre must seem like apricot purée for babies. What man would have ever cared or dared to challenge one of them alone on a dark night? What man would dare to challenge their daughters, the new little Gay Lib girls? They were as hard and springy as wire-wool with their hair quiffed up like messenger boys and heavily oiled with men's hair-lotion. They seemed to be all boots and studded leather, sitting there with their thuggish little deliberately delinquent faces in deliberately defiant couples.

On the back benches behind the two main parties were ranged the great blocks of unaffiliated sympathizers who were wearing anything from kaftans to hot pants. Many looked a little bovine, neither over-zealous nor over-intelligent. Lumpen Lib. The cast of *Holocaust Theatre* were mingled with them and still wore the strait-jackets and lunatic-asylum apparel—symbols for male oppression—that they had worn for the play. There also seemed to be a lot of women from America, and here and there, like rare chaff, a sprinkling of men. Mrs. Orwell smiled engagingly at her motley audience and told them that she didn't believe in all this stuff about female oppression—that she had never known a case of a couple who were in love where one of them had ever tried to dominate the other. From the back a man muttered that he had never known a case where one of them didn't. But he kept his voice down, there in the catacombs of Women's Lib.

"The real thing now," Mrs. Orwell went on firmly, "is how are we meant to bring up our children? Must little boys still be brought up as manly little boys, and little girls like pretty little girls?" Was Mrs. Orwell deliberately tempting her fate? She was acting as chairwoman to an occasion which was surely intended to promote the opening of the world's first real "Women's Theatre." And yet, as though it was an unmentionable bad smell, she had still not made a single reference to the play.

A member of her panel agreed with Mrs. Orwell and said that the point of a meeting like this should be a heightened consciousness of what it meant to be female. And this remark seemed to do it. Suddenly from the back benches there was a horrible, haunting howl, as though one of the women there had gone into labor. It was the authoress. It was Jane Arden, who had written *A New Communion for Freaks, Prophets and Witches* and had invented *Holocaust Theatre.*

She was standing up with her blazing eyes and her tousled gypsy's hair and she was waving the fist of the rising worker. "Your panel is all shit! What are all you women doing sitting there at that table? What is this—a bloody boardroom? Get off your chairs and come and meet us! We are all oppressed! We want the whole bloody society torn up by its roots! We are on the edge of a new dimension! Don't you see the holocaust is here? I have a black man sitting here next to me. And he is oppressed." A little shiver of unease went through the liberal wing of Lib. Did he like being called a black man by Jane Arden? The whole meeting turned and stared at him. She had made him look so nervous. But for all anyone knew, he might well be a "fascist male" black man.

"Shit! Shit!" she chanted. The clock seemed to have been turned back an hour and we were listening again to the monotonous complaining choruses of her play: "Desolation! Scrubbing! Oxen! Fracture! Shit!" "Everything you have all been saying is just bloody bourgeois shit!" she screamed at the panel. No one really seemed to have said very much so far. No one was ever going to be allowed to say anything very much for the rest of the meeting. Mrs. Orwell agreed that Jane Arden was right when she said that this was a holocaust. "Hear! Hear!" called the audience each time Jane Arden yelled "Shit!"

"Now that's quite enough, thank you," Mrs. Orwell said and she tapped grimly for order on her table. Edna O'Brien was just able to murmur that she thought that there were no men, and no women, and no children, that there was just "to be." And then the hippy jumped up with his bandaged head, looking like Victorian pictures of the risen Christ, and embarked on a filibuster. "The whole structure of society is rotten. The whole structure stinks. The whole structure is sterile and rotten and it stinks." On and on his hippy bromides rolled. Was there someone who could stop him? Edna O'Brien tried by leaning over and patting him on the back as if he was a begging dog who was clawing her leg. Mrs. Orwell tried to interrupt him and make one last shot to get back to babysitting and equal pay. He turned on her with the snarl of a dog. "You shut up!" he said. "Oh man, you better just shut up!"

The cannon rumble of "Shit! Shit!" was starting again. Then two granite-tough butch figures from Gay Lib leapt up from their seats and linked arms, and, purposeful as two traffic wardens who have spotted a badly parked car, they started walking towards the hippy. He might soon wish he had never spoken a word at a Women's Lib meeting, never made a single mention of the fabric of society. He now looked as vulnerable as the fragile rotten structure he had talked so much about. They came up to him and spat in his face and hissed: "You prick! Oh you bloody prick!" He went scurrying away and sat cross-legged on the floor and for the rest of the evening seemed to be sulking and meditating.

Later Jane Arden was to complain that Mrs. Orwell and her panel of "liberal democrats" wrecked the "ripple." But after the rout of the hippy they seemed to lose all power to control it. From every part of the hall women were jumping up and starting to scream all at once. No speaker seemed to agree on any single point with any other speaker. No speaker ever allowed any other speaker to finish. A woman seemed to be saying that every time she washed her husband's underpants she kept thinking that no one had ever washed hers. Another was shouting that she was here tonight because she was a victim of male domination. From the stuffy standing ranks at the back of the hall more and more women were trying uselessly to get a hearing. The French Women's Liberationists are asking that a wreath be placed under the Arc de Triomphe in honor of the wife of the unknown soldier. Was someone now trying to ask for an English equivalent? Were members of Gay Lib trying to make their usual demand that lesbians get the legal right to sue for alienation of affection? How could you tell when someone was yelling so much louder that they wanted the destruction of the nuclear family, someone else that they wanted a redefinition of the female role?

A pretty working-class mother tried to say that she had three kids hanging onto her skirts and her problem was how she could ever get out of the house. Jane Arden had said all the women at this meeting were on the edge of a new dimension and in this moment of liberated lunacy who could dare to bring up something quite as boring as their babysitting problems? A man got up and asked if he could read a statement. "It is not always an unadulterated joy to be in possession of a cock." He was loudly hissed and booed. Someone was screaming that men should be forbidden to speak. "Make them learn what it's like to have to listen to women!" A man said he had had a mother and two wives and he couldn't remember doing anything else all his life. He then walked out. The "black man" tried to express sympathy and solidarity with the women. He said he had found that the breasts of one of the actresses who had stripped naked in the play were exactly the right size. Was he aware of the full enormity of his faux pas? Had he simply misunderstood the whole point of the play? Had he not grasped that when that actress exposed her breasts it was meant to be the tragic high point of the whole evening—that her poor naked nipples had symbolized woman's degradation, misery, and exploitation throughout the millennia? He seemed hurt and puzzled by the storm of booing. Did he feel so aggrieved because he knew he was the only person who had made any attempt to say that they liked the play?

From the start only a hissing and rather hysterical hatred of men had ever really unified this disgruntled audience. Quite suddenly this hatred directed itself full force onto Mrs. Orwell and her bland panel: "You with your bloody bourgeois jobs and your husbands and all your au pairs!" Two avenging furies from Women's Gay Lib marched towards them goose-stepping like Prussian soldiers. Their great boots struck sparks from the floor. They picked up the panel's heavy trestle table as though it was a piece of tissue paper and lifted it high in the air as if they were performing some complicated modern ballet. Were they going to smash it down on the heads of the flustered panel? There was certainly a feeling now that only a little ritual bloodletting could provide them in their frustrations with any real catharsis. But they only carried it rather tamely to the other side of the stage. "You bloody pricks!" Their disgust with the panel extended to the entire audience. Even their great army boots seemed quite revolted as they clumped out down the aisle.

There is almost nothing that looks quite so embarrassingly naked as a debating panel which has been suddenly stripped of its table. Even the actresses of *Holocaust Theatre* in the most poignant moments of the play, when they bared their breasts to show their female abasement, never looked nearly as nude and degraded as Mrs. Orwell and her committee. Their very nylonned knees, spotlit, seemed indecently exposed. They sat stunned, and as though trapped in invisible stocks.

A woman came running down the aisle waving her arms for silence. She was the manageress of the Open Space Theatre. She seemed to be very deeply distressed. She said that she had made considerable sacrifices to put on this Woman's play, to allow her theatre to be used for this discussion, and the disgraceful behavior of the women who had attended had made her deeply regret what she had done.

Now that the panel, the symbol of order, was deposed, some of the women went on shouting "shit" and "prick" and expressing various unintelligible grievances, but the fun had gone out of it. The rally broke up and there was only the horrible flatness and frustration that often falls after the Demo, when even the most militant start to realize that the pigs are still in power and really very little has changed.

The next day I talked to Jane Arden at her house in London. Before she invented the *Holocaust Theatre*, her most famous play was *Vagina Rex*. She sat facing me on the floor wearing a kaftan. She looked rather beautiful, and she spoke with intensity, at great speed, using the druggy rhetoric of the Underground. The word she seemed to use most frequently was "impacted"—a word I had previously associated only with wisdom teeth. She kept applying it to society, to emotions, to the female role and the nuclear family, and I kept on visualizing all these things, with far too many roots sunk deep in someone's gum.

She too had found the rally disgraceful: it had just been a "bank of fragmented language." I would have expected that in some way she would have found such a "bank" to be rather nicely "unimpacted." But it appeared that she had felt outraged that her *Holocaust Theatre* had not been made "central to the discussion." She was bitter about Mrs. Orwell and the way in which she had chaired the meeting: "that woman" and her bunch of "liberal democrats" had ruined all the "vibes."

I asked her what she would have done if she had chaired such a meeting. Her head tossed—she found the question stupid: "I would have allowed the vibrations to enact. I would have tried to seal off the abscesses. I would have had a show of hands. A show of hands always means vibrations. It always means: 'It's me.' 'It's me' is what revolution in the real sense is really about. I would have asked: 'How many of you here are fragmented? How many of you here fear death? How many of you here feel impacted? How many of you wake up and want to scream in the night?' Women are changed once they see *Holocaust Theatre*. Once you have cracked their boxed-in, fractured processes of thinking they can never be the same again. I hate Germaine Greer because she retreats from her humiliation. The real poets of oppression have to be grafted onto their oppression. I am much more identified with exploitation."

She saw me looking round her large and luxurious house, which stands on the Little Venice Canal, only a few doors from Lady Diana Cooper's. "I know I don't look very exploited outside, but I still feel it inside. I'm not separate from my work of art. Every nerve center in *Holocaust* is me." She said that American women and members of Gay Lib seemed especially "open" to *Holocaust*, and that Kate Millett herself had been very "responsive" and had deplored the lack of a similar theatre in the USA. She became messianic: "I woke up one morning and suddenly I knew that I had to stop masturbating in my fantasies—that I'd go mad if I didn't reach out to women. All my judgments have always been formed by my vibrations and I knew it was the moment to start the ripple. I got onto the telephone and gathered a great group of women together. I asked them if they were prepared to be totally committed to me and my idea. I warned them that if they followed me, everything else they cared for in their lives would have to go."

"How many stepped forward?"

"Only the eight who are now playing at the Open Space. Women are so horribly timorous. It's their conditioning."

"Did any of the women who stepped forward have children?"

"Some of them had kids, certainly." She went on. "The Church has failed women—I can give them a way to work out their rituals. I've always been someone who would stand on her head to make things richer."

Portrait of the Beatnik

Almost every day in some newspaper or magazine, the American Housewife makes her new complaint. A Beatnik philosopher has told her that she lives in "the Age of the White Rhinoceros," and another has told her that it is "the Age of Fried Shoes." "Where," she asked, "is all this Beatnik Movement leading us?" Her question is gratuitous. There has never been a Movement, merely a mirage, merely a masquerade.

The Beatnik is simply a bourgeois fantasy that has become incarnated and incarcerated, in a coffeehouse and a "pad"; he is merely the Bohemian in every American businessman that has got out. He is a luxury product, the revolutionary who offers no threat, the nonconformist whose nonconformity is commercial. He shocks and scandalizes without creating anxiety; he is the rebel not without cause, but the rebel without repercussion.

Supposedly revolutionary, the "Beatnik Movement" is unique in that it enjoys the recognition, the support, and succor of the very society whose dictates it pretends to flout. It has all the trappings of the subversive, the meeting in the darkened cellar, the conspiratorial whisper behind the candle in the chianti bottle, the nihilistic mutter, without the mildest element of subversion. No one in the future, when filling in an official form, will ever be made to swear that they have never been a Beatnik.

The American workingman is unconcerned with the Beat Generation and its quest for "the primitive Beginnings." The Beatnik scandalizes and interests only the middle-class public from which he springs. As opposed to the Bum (who might well be said to be more truly Beat) he is quite popular. He presents no obvious social incitement or question. He is "cool" and polite. Whereas the Bum rolls in the streets of downtown Los Angeles, drunk and cursing, the Beatnik sits peacefully in his coffeehouse, nonconforming over cappuccino, a safely licensed anarchist. Everyone knows where to find him: he is always in his Beatnik Joint or in his "pad." Everyone knows who he is because of his beard, and *Life* magazine can photograph him whenever it wishes.

Unlike the delinquent (with whom he is often confused), the Beatnik only ever troubles the Police over the technical issue of whether or not, if he reads his own poem to Jazz in a coffeehouse, it constitutes "entertainment" and therefore invokes the need for an entertainment license.

The Beatnik in his bold rebellion against American Bourgeois Values, is about as dangerous as the three revolutionaries in

Orwell's *1984*. Like them, he has been put by the State safely in front of a chess set in the Chestnut Tree Café, and there he is allowed to sit being revolutionary.

The Beat Generation has declared that it will take no part in the "middle-class rat race"; it has protested "a sacred dedication to poverty"; it has denounced all Western civilization as "square shuck" (phoney).

A popular misconception is that the term "Beatnik" signifies one who is beat in the sense of "downbeat," or "licked"—whereas to the Beat Generation it signifies "the beatific one."

The ego-ideal of the Beatnik is the "cool hipster"—the man who sits detached with his own flask in his own hip pocket, the man who is "way out," the man who doesn't "wig" (care), the man who finds beatitude in noncommitment.

The "square" is often not "hip" to the fact that despite similarities of dress, the Beatnik is by no means his existentialist predecessor. An obscure Beat philosopher finally clarified this point when he said, "The existentialist cat dug like that the positive answer of nothingness, in the face of nothingness, is positivism—we dig that the positive answer of nothingness, to nothingness, is nothingness—Man, isn't that farther out?"

The Beatnik rejects articulateness, speech involving a conversational commitment constituting lack of "coolness." Paradoxically, therefore, the Beat Generation can only speak in order to say that it will not speak, and Jack Kerouac and Allen Ginsberg who are generally known as the Beat spokesmen, are by very definition, as well as by their success and achievements, nonhipsters.

Ideally, a truly "cool cat" should be completely self-contained and therefore completely silent. The average Beatnik compromises, however, by speaking in language cut to the maximum. His talk, an abbreviated version of already abbreviated Jazz talk, amounts to complete code. A "T.O.," for example, is a much used Beat word for a rich society woman who questions prostitutes, with half-thrilled envy, about the physical mechanics of their trade. An amateur hipster might be trapped into thinking that a "T.O." was an initiate, for it derives from "To be turned out," meaning initiated, deriving from "To be turned on," referring to "On pot," which stems in turn from "On the pod" of marijuana. The expression is now, however, only used to describe not the initiate but the would-be but too-afraid initiate. It is often claimed by the Beatniks that many women living in Park Avenue penthouses, and many wives of successful movie stars living in Beverly Hills mansions, are secret "T.O.'s" in regard to Beat.

No professor of semantics could be more severe about misuse of vernacular than the hipster. The charlatan can be spotted instantly, and denounced as a "square." He often, for example, makes incorrect use of the term "to ball" which (in the Forties) meant to make love. Now, however, the expression "I balled the cat" could only mean to the truly Beat, that you were grateful to someone, so grateful in fact that you would only have liked to have balled them in the old-fashioned sense.

Beatific talk is the very soul of brevity, if not wit. It is deliberately functional, for the hipster rejects euphemism. He "sets a scene" when he tells, "wigs" when he's worried, "gigs" when he works, "bugs" when he's annoyed, "wails" when he functions, "floats" when he's drunk, "grazes" when he's content, "bends" when he's tired, "scenes" when he arrives, "splits" when he goes.

The Beatnik, in his rejection of the popular American concept that Success equates with Manhood, stresses a non-virility often mistaken for homosexuality. He is essentially asexual. Once again the ideal of the "cool" precluding the personal commitment demanded by sexual activity. He has, however, no particular objection to sexual intercourse as long as it is conducted quickly, clinically, and above all wordlessly. The Beat "cat" approaches the Beat "chick" with the ritualistic "pad me"—his "pad" being his home where he keeps his foam-rubber mattress. The "chick" can either reply "dig" (a sign of cool acquiescence), or otherwise she can merely snap "drop!" (a much-used abbreviation of "drop dead"). In reverse, the "chick's" approach to the male is equally formalized; she must say "I'm frigid," to which he can either reply "I'll make you wail" (function) or, otherwise, "don't bug."

Despite his rejection of marriage as middle-class "shuck" (phoney), the Beatnik's Wedding is an important event in any Beat community. He marries in the Ocean, only at midnight. He and his Beat Bride-to-be stand naked in the waves while the rites are performed by a Beatific friend who reads a self-composed hymeneal ritual poem, which is then followed by a lunar incantation. The Bridegroom then silently hands the "chick" a ring of flowers which she must throw into the waves in order to symbolize that her hipster is giving himself to "The real mama, the Ocean, the mama of the whole race of Man," while she is herself uniting with "The Old Man of the Sea."

Non-Beatnik grandmothers and aunts are invited to attend these services, and often leave in tears before the wedding breakfast, which naturally takes place in a "pad" and is as formal as the Sea Wedding. The newlyweds sit in a semicircle composed of silently contemplative friends, "light up on muggles" (smoke marijuana), and continue their search for "the inner luminous experience."

Beat philosophy is misty, mystical, and eclectic. Claiming to embrace Zen, the Beatnik philosopher paradoxically rejects discipline; he therefore replaces the Zen Ideal of a total commitment to the moment by a Beat ideal of a striving towards a state of totally noncommited contemplation. As a result he often merely arrives at a condition very similar to the one in which the American Housewife watches her television.

He prefers Jung to Freud, the concept of the collective, as opposed to the personal, subconscious being "cooler" in the sense that it predisposes less commitment to self. Other influences on his thought have been St. Francis of Assisi, Nietzsche, Ouspenski, and St. John of the Cross. He admires Joyce for his obscurity.

Within the confines that he has set himself, the Beatnik adheres to his conventions of nonconventionality with the enthusiasm of the Rotarian Club member for his rules. Every hipster wears the strict uniform of classical Bohemianism. He is heavily bearded. He has an open sandal, a chunky raw-wool sweater, and a little leather cap with a button on it. All his clothes must be bought secondhand. A similar Beat regulation is that his "pad" or mattress must be acquired only from the Salvation Army. Beds are considered "square" so it must therefore be put straight on the floor of his "pad" which is also his home, and ideally should be a battered shack. He must also hand-paint his floorboards with enigmatic and abstract ("way-out") designs, for one of his slogans is "In the meaningless lies the meaning."

The true Beatnik should never "hustle" (do any paid work). He must sleep all day and only emerge by night. In the corner of every Beat "pad" there must necessarily be a gigantic stack of unwashed dishes.

As a deliberate reaction against the Hollywood emphasis on the breast and the flashing lipsticked smile, the appearance of his female

Beatnik is characterized by a studied and aggressive asexuality. Pale-lipped and unsmiling she sits in a high-necked shapeless tunic made of woven wool. Her legs must always be crossed and heavily encased in black woolly stockings. Her cheeks are whitened with thick, white makeup base, her hair hangs dank and darkly jagged. She is to be seen nightly alone, staring over an unplayed chess game with a mystic and heavily mascara'd eye.

In order to ensure the correct attire of visitors, many a Beatnik coffeehouse has an adjoining dress shop: a Beatnik boutique. There, on sale, are elaborately designed thirty-dollar Beat Generation tunics made of raw Mexican wool, sackcloth shirts, primitive leather water-pouches, and Beat jewelry made of iron.

I spoke with an ex-Beatnik turned Beat dress designer. She sat in her workshop and sewed the thong on a rawhide sandal. She spoke of her Beat past with the apologetic nostalgia sometimes found in retired members of the Communist Party. "Jesus, I dug Beatific—Man, the swinginest [it's the best]—like dug splittin' [I felt obliged to leave it]—I dug giggin' for bread to wail [I was obliged to work for the money to go on functioning] . . ."

Her friend, another renegade Beatnik, who was sitting in the corner painting papier-mâché model figurines of Beatniks (later to be sold in a boutique) was less enthusiastic about the Movement. "Beatific's a bug," she said.

The Beat coffeehouses are characterized by their extreme gloom, and by their cathedral silences. They attract not only the hipster but also the wandering psychotic who gets mistaken for Beat because he is "way out." They also shelter two unfortunate byproducts of Beat. First, the Bogus Beatnik: the Hollywood agent and the successful car salesman, who, having worked by day go corruptly Beat by night.

Secondly, the hypocritical hipster, who, unaware of the deeper philosophical significance of the Movement, has taken out "Beat" as he might take out an insurance policy, merely to protect himself against any future censor from a success-worshipping society. Failure is impossible to anyone who is Beat, for they have rejected aspiration.

The entertainment at the Beat coffeehouse consists of "Prose and Poetry readings" and folk-singing, the latter being part of the quest for the "primitive beginnings." No alcohol is served, for the Beatnik rejects "lushing" (drinking) as part of bourgeois "shuck."

Short, silent, homemade Beat movies are also shown. As there would appear to be only a limited number of these films, the more popular and "farther out" ones are shown up to four or five times on the same night. An old man looms upon the screen, huge and fearful. The camera remains lengthily upon the vast cigar which he holds between his teeth. An adolescent appears, white-faced and knuckle-clenching, his eyes roll, his face contorts. The Jazz background music mounts to a crescendo. The boy "splits a gut" (laughs), he lifts his hand, and with a sudden frenzied violence, strikes the cigar from the old man's mouth. The camera follows the cigar which rolls in the dust. The old man shivers. He rocks, holding his head in agony. He staggers to a lavatory. He vomits. The camera remains upon the lavatory pan until it slowly dissolves into a vagina. The audience slowly turn their heads to see if everyone else is "hip." A voice always says, "Dig that crazy sequence!"

Between the runnings of films, Beatific poem-reading takes place to the accompaniment of Bongo drums.

The take-off

on one

and

a half

push up
not all
at once
just cool
hip.

The unsuspecting tourist suffering from the "square" illusion that it is possible to drop in at a coffeehouse for only a few minutes, then becomes "hip" to his error. Once "Beat readings" are in progress only someone with the courage or the insensitivity that would enable him to leave the front pew of an Anglican church while the parson is delivering his Easter sermon can even conceive of making an exit under the condemnatory scrutiny of the Beatific congregation's culturally pious eye.

The tourist often finds towards dawn (for there is an important Beat tenet: "Night sleep is for Squares") that after a whole evening on cappuccino and "Modigliani's" (described on Beat menus as "Murals of ham and gherkin on rye"), he is slowly becoming "cooler and cooler," and "further and further out."

The "entertainment" often ends with a famous Beat musician, Lord Buckley, giving a nasal rendering of the story of Jesus of Nazareth walking on the waters. And der Naz said, "Walk cool, Baby, walk cool . . ."

Ever since the publication of *On the Road*, which focused upon the Beatnik a furor of public interest and attention, Jack Kerouac's right to the title of "Father of the Beat Generation" has been jealously contested. Kenneth Rexroth, an elderly and obscure San Franciscan poet, made the first violent attempt to secure the title for himself when he protested angrily to the Press that he had been living all his life "the kind of life that Kerouac just writes about."

Another far more powerful figure then emerged in the form of a lesser-known (and therefore "cooler") poet named Lawrence Lipton. A man approaching sixty, he denounced Kerouac for being in his "thirties, and therefore unfitted to represent the Beat Generation who were essentially a product of the 1950s." He was appointed "Grand Lama" in Venice West, a slum area of Los Angeles, where there are many suitably Beat and dilapidated shacks, and he is now hoping to establish it as the new Beat World Capital.

I spoke with the "Grand Lama," he reclined on his "pad" Pasha-like and smoked a cigar. "Our pad," he said, "has the same symbolical importance to us, as did the couch of the Bohemians of the "Thirties. Beat, you will understand, my dear young woman, is far more than a religion. Beat, my dear young lady, is a way of Life."

He closed his eyes.

"Here, down in Venice West," he continued, "we have a new kind of Beat, the real Beat, the Beat Generation of the future. I have called them by their true title, The Holy Barbarians, and the report that I have just finished making about them will be called by that very name. I have already received extensive inquiries about it, not only from the Book-of-the-Month Club, but also from several television programs, the M.G.M. Studios, and many anthropologists from U.C.L.A. I tell you all this, you will understand, merely so that you will really grasp how big this whole thing is. Already my poems are being scribbled on the lavatory walls of New York, already our Movement is spreading to Japan, Italy, France, Germany, and Great Britain. The Holy Barbarians, you will see, my dear young woman, will very soon be of worldwide interest!"

We had a long silence.

"I," he continued, speaking with a slow and portentous solemnity, "am the Mentor of the Holy Barbarians. They call me The Shaman of the Tribe. I interpret their way of life to the public. I have probably made more tape recordings of Beatnik conversations than any other living man." He languidly waved his hand at a mountainous stack of tape spools lying on his floor. "There," he said, "you have one hundred hours' worth of authentic Beat conversations, private philosophic conversations, you understand, taking place in simple pads, amongst young and simple people, but ones who are asking, more profoundly, more honestly than any previous generation, who they are, and where they are going . . ."

Once again he closed his eyes. "We, the Holy Barbarians, finding nothing in the West, have turned towards the East. We reject your Audens and your Spenders and all their affiliations. Our poets' Search goes inwards for The Luminous Experience. We reject and scorn your Angry Young Men with their social preoccupations. We seek much further for the non-political Answer." "The Lama" suddenly looked at me with a suspicious, visionary eye. "That does not in the least mean to say," he added quickly, "that we do not utterly reject the Russian way of life. We in fact even have an expression amongst our hipsters, There's no Square like a red Square."

Once again we had a silence. "We, the Holy Barbarians, have totally rejected racial barriers," he went on. "We call a negro a 'nigger' and a 'spade,' for he knows we say the words with Love. You might really describe us in fact as a Community of individuals seeking only for The Beatific Vision, The Experience of Holiness, The Orgiastic Fulfillment, in Self. Our hipsters would say that we seek only to flip our wings.

"I'm afraid," he said, suddenly smiling with scornful patronage, "that that will have very little meaning to you.

"We," he continued, making heavy use of the Papal we, "might well be compared to the Early Christians. We are the Outlaws from the Social Lie. We are the Persecuted People, the Apocalyptic People, the Nocturnal People. The people of the night," he added, for fear I had not understood.

As I was leaving, "The Lama" stood in the doorway of his shack. "We have many, many Artists down here in Venice West," he said, "all of them living in dedicated poverty. Some of them are among the most creative talents in America. I should very much like you to have a look at them. I will telephone you as soon as I have arranged to have you shown round their pads." Suddenly I became cool, visionary. I saw that "The Lama" had already, mystically, ruthlessly, appointed my future Duties. He had ordained how my life from then on was to be spent. Like a Florence Nightingale, or a conscientious Inspector of an Insane Asylum, making daily rounds of condemned Artists in padded cells.

Printed in the United States
by Baker & Taylor Publisher Services